MORTAL GAMES

MORTAL
GAMES

Pierre Salinger
and
Leonard Gross

Doubleday
NEW YORK
1988

All characters in this book are fictional.
Any resemblance to actual persons,
living or dead, is entirely coincidental.

Library of Congress Cataloging-in-Publication Data

Salinger, Pierre.
  Mortal games.

  I. Gross, Leonard.   II. Title.
PS3569.A4595M67   1988   813'.54   87-20199
ISBN 0-385-23672-7

1

André Kohl drove his Fiat into the Place Vendôme, stopped in front of the Hotel Ritz and experienced the sudden, overpowering feeling that Act Two of his life was ending.

Much later, he would recall that this was the moment in which he first thought of his life as a three-act play, a confirmation of his increasing suspicions that he had been performing all these years in a carefully scripted drama as a means of walling out all of life's caprices. For the moment, however, he was too preoccupied with the immediate implications of his insight to consider its more subtle meanings.

Just three weeks earlier, after fifteen years of a storybook life in Europe, he had abruptly determined to chuck it and return to the United States. It was the second radical decision he'd made in the space of a week, the first having been to quit his job, without question the best job in the media, arguably the best job in the world. As epic and life-changing as both decisions had been, none had ever seemed easier to make. The period since had been one of relative detachment, akin, he was sure, to what one must feel in the weeks following surgery, when psychological as well as chemical euphoria obscure the finality of the act, and the knowledge that, however positive the outcome, you are no longer the person you were. Objectively, however, André had known that a moment would come when all such opiates would wear off and he would feel himself being cut away from his past. The logical moment would have been during a twilight as he looked from the window of his apartment on the Quai d'Orléans at the barges on the Seine and the flying buttresses of Notre Dame, or one early morning in Varengeville-sur-Mer as he stepped onto the veranda of his Normandy home to inhale the fragrance of his apple orchard. Yet in neither place had he experienced the sense of dispossession that now suddenly engulfed him. Why here, why now?

As André emerged from his car, the Ritz doorman came toward him, wearing his trademark blue uniform and billed cap. André didn't know his name, but the man's round and ruddy face, as often as not punctuated with a whistle in his mouth, was as familiar to him as the harmonious, wall-to-wall buildings that enclosed one of the world's most famous squares. At least once and often twice or three times a week since 1968, André had driven up to the Ritz, en route to a lunch or dinner with a news source, or for a drink at one of the three bars; and nine times out of ten this very doorman had walked briskly to his car to take it from him and dispatch it to a special parking place, at the curb, if one remained, or else on the broad sidewalk in front of the hotel. It was a privilege accorded André, whose sudden need for the car to return in haste to the office because of a breaking story had been demonstrated enough times to make a vivid impression on the doorman. And always a special smile accompanied the effort, not because a good tip would result, but because it was for the doorman a small but important part of the ritual that defined and enriched his life.

Now, as the smiling doorman took his car from him and left him momentarily alone in front of the hotel, André understood his sudden sense of loss. This small exchange between humans was part of his ritual, as well, an infinitesimal part to be sure, yet an integral part, one of a multitude of pieces that, like each line of dialogue in a play, had been slowly and carefully fitted together into a cohesive story: his. Within days, the curtain would fall for the second time on this private drama, with but one rise and fall of the curtain remaining. It was bittersweet knowledge, bitter because at his age endings of almost any kind were acknowledged with remorse, sweet because he knew that Act Three, the one in which the protagonist is at last united with the woman of his dreams, could not begin until Act Two had ended, and he wanted this final act to begin more than anything he had ever wanted in his fifty-six years of life.

It was twilight of the twenty-first day of June, 1983, the longest day in the year. The sun had passed below the rooftops, but its fading rays still lit the sky, reflecting a faint pinkish glow onto the sandstone facade of the buildings that surrounded the square. The Place Vendôme is not a square, of course, but an octagon with long sides to the east and west, smaller sides to the north and south and four short lines at each of the corners angled at forty-five degrees. It is these four angled lines that make the Place so graceful and distinctive. In this vulnerable moment André permitted himself the indulgence of metaphor, seeing in the design a symbol of all that was fine about Europe: beautiful, to be sure, but also considered and ordered. Only now that he would be leaving did he realize how much he would miss it.

He turned toward the hotel, his unprepossessing build a perfect match for the sense of deference he projected, a quality that never failed to surprise new acquaintances familiar with his gruff television image. His black hair, accented by strands of gray, was a good bit shorter than it had been when he was on the tube. Long hair had supposedly made him look distinguished, but it had also made him look older. Two months ago it hadn't concerned him that he looked his age; since then—since the advent of Meredith Houghton—age had been very much on his mind. For years, he'd turned a deaf ear to arguments that exercise could turn back the physiological clock; four weeks ago, after concluding the most tumultuous assignment of his career, he had begun to take increasingly long and vigorous walks. To his grudging satisfaction, the payoff had been almost instantaneous. An hour earlier, as he was shaving, he'd decided that he looked better, meaning younger, than he had in several years. Perhaps he was imagining it, but he had the distinct impression that the lines dug into his craggy face by years of deadline pressure had softened considerably in the month since he'd quit his job. His natural look was that of a brooding man, to the point that friends would admonish him to "lighten up." That was not the easiest thing to do when one was preoccupied day in and day out with a world whose events seemed like the symptoms of a terminal illness, but that inventory of his face an hour before had disclosed an expression that could almost be described as pleasant.

Now, however, the brooding countenance had returned. He was not looking forward to the hours ahead. Jacob Jones, his diminutive expatriate friend with the extraordinary gift for commerce as well as the ability to disarm those who ran it, had called ten days ago to invite him to a small dinner party at the Ritz, to be attended, he said, by "a few important people you'll enjoy." Nothing more—typical of Jones, who never let something sound simple and straightforward if it could be presented as complex and mysterious. "Black tie," he'd admonished, and so, to his mild annoyance, André's newly resilient body was clothed in a tuxedo, the one piece of male clothing he found truly ridiculous. Left to himself, he would almost never wear anything other than a sweater and slacks. What bothered him far more than the formal attire, however, was the prospect of having to feign interest in the "important" conversation that would surely dominate the evening. As the chief European correspondent of the United States Broadcasting Corporation, he would have been eager to listen in the prospect of gaining valuable information; as André Kohl, private citizen, he had suddenly lost all appetite for significance.

André fingered his black bow tie, making certain that it completely covered the top button of his dress shirt, and then walked the thirty feet from the curb to the entrance of the Ritz, a semicircular enclosure into which horse-drawn carriages had been driven less than ninety years before. Normally, half a dozen chauffeurs hung about the entrance, their long cars parked along the curb or on the sidewalk. Tonight, André noted, there was a platoon of chauffeurs, and cars to match. One of those cars belonged to the mayor of Paris. There were several government cars, as well, and two motorcycles and motorcycle policemen for each car, a sure sign that a number of ministers of the French Government were attending a function inside. Were these the "important people" to whom Jacob Jones had referred?

At 9 P.M. exactly—the hour specified by Jacob Jones—André went through the revolving door of the Ritz, its motion facilitated by a young uniformed page. Jacob had made quite a thing about arriving exactly at 9 P.M., which had puzzled André for two reasons, first because it was a bit late for this sort of dinner party even by Paris standards, and second because in the more than twenty years they had known one another André had never been late for an appointment with the entrepreneur. Normally, he was the first to arrive at parties, or for lunch or dinner dates, for the same reason that he arrived at airports at least an hour before his flight times. Controlling time was important to him, his way of assuring himself that, despite the precipitous nature of a life dictated by events over which he had no control, he still did control something. Ironically, arriving on time for this dinner—his last with Jacob Jones for a while—had been something of a challenge because of a call at eight-fifteen from Mike Paul, USBC's boss of network news. Why Mike had called had never been made clear; he'd seemingly wanted just to chat even though André would be seeing him a week later in New York. Each time André had tried to end the conversation, Mike—normally the soul of brevity in his telephone conversations, particularly transatlantic calls—had kept it going. Finally and apologetically, André had said, "Mike, I've got to go."

Just inside the entrance of the hotel stood Josef Bisevac, the tall and husky security guard, a Slav with a soldier's bearing who for years had genially but carefully screened all who walked through this door, turning back those who didn't belong. Josef offered his hand. *"Bon soir,* Monsieur Kohl," he said.

André's hand felt lost and overmatched in Josef's big, powerful grip. "What are you doing here so late?" André said.

Josef smiled. *" 'Tout* Paris' is here tonight."

"What's going on?"

Josef regarded him quizzically for a moment, then smiled. "Monsieur is joking."

"No, I'm not."

Once more Josef stared quizzically at him. Then, seeing that André really wasn't joking, he gestured down the long and opulent hallway leading to the Salle Vendôme.

André looked past Josef down the hallway. "Oh, my God," he said.

A dozen violinists and violists stood in two lines of six each on either side of the entrance to the banquet hall, forming a corridor of strings. At the end of the corridor stood Jacob Jones, all five feet four inches of him, grinning in his lopsided way, and massed behind him were at least two hundred men and women, all of the men in tuxedos, and all of the women in long gowns—and all of them, quite obviously, there to greet André. Suddenly, André understood why Mike Paul had called from New York: to keep him from arriving early and spoiling their mutual friend's surprise.

For a moment longer André stood where he was, unable to move. Then he began to walk slowly toward the Salle Vendôme. As if on cue, the ensemble began to play the Spring concerto from Vivaldi's *The Four Seasons,* and moments later André was walking, dumbfounded, through the corridor of strings toward his beaming host. Jacob Jones was clapping, and behind him, so were all the guests.

A smiling Josef watched the tableau from his post at the front door. Happy guests always made him smile; it made him feel good to be part of something that lifted people's spirits. He felt especially good that something so nice was happening to Monsieur Kohl, who, no matter how rushed, always stopped to shake hands and exchange a few words.

The musicians were following André into the Salle Vendôme now, still playing Vivaldi, their music mingling with the guests' applause. Suddenly, Josef's smile vanished, replaced by an anxious frown. Just behind the musicians walked two men in formal attire whom he recognized instantly even from a distance. On their arrival the previous day, he had wondered about them only because he'd never seen them before. Yet they certainly appeared to fit the profile of guests of the Ritz Hotel. Their hair was nicely trimmed. They were wearing dark, conservatively cut suits, white shirts and muted ties. Both were in their mid-thirties, Josef judged, a time when men who are going places begin to arrive. Adding to the aura of success was the expensive leather attaché case each man carried in his left hand. So Josef was not surprised when one of the men asked, in broken but understandable English, for the registration desk.

But now he *was* surprised, because all of the guests at the party were people Monsieur Kohl knew personally, and these two men did not appear to be like people he would know. If asked why he thought so, Josef would not have been able to explain it; all he knew was that he had never seen men like these with Monsieur Kohl. And why, if they had been invited to the party, were they entering the Salle Vendôme obscured by the musicians, and after all the other guests were inside?

"Watch the door," Josef said to the young page. "Any problems, ask the concierge." He walked quickly to the reception desk to find the *chef de réception,* David Campbell.

"This dinner," Jacob Jones was saying, "was organized to make André Kohl regret his imminent departure so much that he'll change his mind and remain." The guests laughed, and applauded, as much in appreciation for the dinner they had just finished as for their host's remark. It had begun in the adjoining garden, with champagne and Russian caviar passed by waiters wearing white gloves. Then the guests, seated under massive crystal chandeliers and surrounded by mirrored and tapestried walls, had consumed a dinner that, even by Ritz standards, was extravagant. Cold poached sturgeon, with a hollandaise sauce; *canette de Barbarie aux pêches;* then salad, then cheeses, and finally individual Grand Marnier soufflés. And all of these with wines so special that the waiters pouring them bent down to whisper their identity to the guests. As a gesture of the hotel, the sommelier, Georges Lepré, had brought two bottles of 1966 Château Pétrus Pomerol, valued at 9,300 francs each, to André's table. At seven francs to the dollar, that translated to $220 a glass.

"It is a tribute to André," Jacob Jones was saying, "that if a bomb were to explode here tonight, France would be politically, economically and culturally leaderless." Jones was exaggerating, but not a great deal. The current ministers of finance, foreign trade, foreign affairs and defense were there, as were the men who would most likely take their place after the imminent special election called in the aftermath of President-elect Camille Laurent's stunning renunciation a month earlier. In the midst of these government officials was the young, newly elected mayor of Paris, his dazzling wife at his side. The presidents of two of France's three television networks were there; so were André Fontaine of *Le*

Monde, Robert Hersant of *Le Figaro* and Serge July of *Libération.* From film came Roman Polanski, Bertrand Tavernier and Isabelle Adjani. At least half a dozen financiers were present, including Baron Edmond de Rothschild. "And a fitting tribute it is," Jones went on, "because almost since his arrival in Paris in 1968, André has not only interpreted the French to his vast American audience, he has worked to define and interpret America to the French. More than anyone, he has been the conduit between the two cultures, and if that conduit is more firmly in place than ever, and less obstructed than it has ever been, we owe these conditions in part, at least, to our guest of honor."

André wanted so much to believe that. He'd given up so much to come. Mike Paul had told him at the time that he was crazy; by now he would probably have been the anchorman. No matter; he'd had to leave. It was 1968; his country seemed to be self-destructing. He needed to distance himself from it in an attempt to understand its calamitous course. Almost twenty years had passed; would he understand the country he was returning to, so different from the one he had left?

Jacob Jones chuckled. "I do not feel I am exaggerating when I suggest to you that since his arrival in France, André's heart has been as full as his stomach."

At the back of the Salle Vendôme, Josef listened to the guests' appreciative laughter with foreboding. His own English wasn't good enough to understand the joke Monsieur Jones had just made. Neither, he was certain, was that of the two men from whom he hadn't taken his eyes since entering the salle. He'd checked them out with David Campbell, and everything on their records seemed in order. They were Jordanians, officers of a bank. But they hadn't laughed just now along with the other guests, and they hadn't laughed at Monsieur Jones's opening remark, either, nor had they applauded.

At functions as large as this one, there were always tables at the edges that didn't quite fill up, principally because some invited guests had been unable to attend, but also because Franco Gentileschi, the maître d'hôtel, ordered at least one extra table to be set to handle last-minute invitations. It was at just such a table that the two men had taken seats. Two chairs on either side separated them from the only other couple at the table, and they had not tried once to make conversation. Of all the guests in the room, they were the furthest from the table of the host and guest of honor. Their backs were to the east wall.

Josef was sure now that they didn't belong. He didn't dare leave the room to get help; whatever happened, he would have to go it alone. Ever so slowly, he began to edge his way toward the two men.

"In the United States, we have a saying. We like to 'quit winners,' " Jacob Jones went on. "Perhaps it was this desire that caused André to decide that he would resign his position as the chief European correspondent of the United States Broadcasting Corporation in the wake of the biggest story of his life.

"We've all been following the story since André broke it last month: A ring of ex-Nazis running a paramilitary organization in Latin America. A secret network within the American CIA that not only knew of the organization but helped to set it up."

Jacob Jones paused a moment. Then, perhaps to be certain that no one missed the point, he added, "I do not wish to dampen this happy occasion with reflections on such matters. I mention them only to remind you of the diligence and stature of the guest of honor."

André listened with increasing discomfort to his host's escalating praise. It wasn't the flattery that bothered him so much as the distortion it represented. Everything Jacob Jones was saying was true, yet not true because it was not complete.

In a few moments he would be called upon to give his valedictory, and it, too, would be only a fragment of the truth. He would tell them, truthfully, how much living with them had taught him that he would never have learned in the United States: the equilibrating sense of history that not just the French but all Europeans exhibited; the great satisfactions they experienced from little pleasures, and how much richer that made life. Time passed more slowly in Europe because Europeans savored time and knew how to prolong it.

For all such lessons he was grateful, he would tell them, but if he were to speak the truth he should also say that the French were the most impenetrable people he knew, private, mannered and, apart from their families, incapable of intimacies beyond those socially required. Is it a coincidence, he ought to ask in the service of truth, that the English-speaking peoples use a French word, *façade,* to describe a false or superficial appearance?

He could say none of this, of course, and besides he knew it was not entirely fair. The French had no exclusive on pretense. The proof was in this room. They were all here tonight not because Jacob Jones felt obliged to honor André but because the guests he could command in André's behalf were people he wanted to know. Jacob Jones—deal-maker *extraordinaire,* with contacts at the highest levels of governments, the man American and European corporations went through if they wanted to do business with the Russians—had never performed an uncalculated act in his life. His saving grace was his candor. "The best friendships," he had once told André, "are those in which there is an equal profit to both partners." Friendships? Profit?

Did he have an equal capacity for candor? If he were to be truly honest, he should tell the guests that quitting winners had only the merest fraction to do with his resignation. Yes, it had always been in his mind to "quit winners," but not at the age of fifty-six, at the height of his powers, in the immediate aftermath of that "biggest story of his life." He'd quit because he'd suddenly discovered that there was an unbearable separation between reality as it truly exists and the reality he'd been reporting for these many years. He had functioned all of his professional life on the assumption that he was privy to great events; he had learned in the course of this last assignment that his knowledge was limited to 10 per cent, if that, of what was really going on. Which explained why he was sitting at a sumptuous banquet in his honor in the best hotel in the world and tasting not the exquisite food and wine he'd just ingested but his own bile instead.

André could no more share that intolerable revelation with his audience of friends than he could share the untold portion of the story he'd uncovered—a story that would be made public only if he were injured or killed or disappeared at any time prior to his natural death. That was the bargain he had struck with Camille Laurent in exchange for the President-elect's resignation.

All André wanted now was to carry his secrets with him to New York, where he would marry Meredith Houghton and create a world small enough so that everything in it could be genuine.

Jacob Jones was finishing his extensive introduction. "When our guest of honor has finished his remarks, he has promised to play for us, one final time, the 'Moonlight Sonata,' which, whether we asked for it or not, has closed so many Paris parties." As the guests laughed once more, Jones grinned at André, that crooked trademark grin. Then he looked back at the audience. "Ladies and gentlemen, please greet André Kohl in a manner he will never forget."

They rose as one to applaud and cheer. When, moments later, André stood, the volume rose. He walked slowly to the rostrum, and waited for the ovation to end. He did not trust what he was seeing or hearing. Perhaps it was genuine; it was equally possible that the guests were performing, doing the expected.

Finally, the applause came to an end, and the guests resumed their seats. André took a moment to gaze across the candlelit room, now silent with expectation. In that moment, he saw two men rise from a table at the back, and an instant later a third man crash into them and knock them to the floor. There was a burst of fire from what sounded like a machine pistol, and then, instantly, the sound of panic. As one, the guests bolted from their seats. Most crawled under their tables; the bolder and more frightened rushed for the doors.

Bare seconds had passed, seconds in which years of conditioning compelled André to watch rather than take cover. Automatically, he tried to remember where he could find the closest phone so that he could call the bureau and get a camera crew to the scene. An instant later, he realized that there would be no story for him to cover; he was no longer the chief European correspondent of USBC. He could not help but wonder, nonetheless, which of the celebrated guests had been the object of the terrorists' attack.

He never saw the two men who grabbed him, one on either side. "We're friends," one of them whispered to him in French, but he was suddenly too alarmed to believe that. He felt himself being half-carried to the west wall of the Salle Vendôme and through a mirrored door that he hadn't known was there. Then they were half-pushing, half-carrying him down a flight of steps, and moments later they were in the hotel's newly modernized kitchen, filled with gleaming copper pots.

"Help me," André cried. Three cooks stepped in their way. The men drew guns. The cooks fell back. When André tried to resist, he felt a gun in his back. "Don't be crazy. *We're* here to help you," the man behind him whispered. Still, André didn't believe him. He was certain he was being kidnapped. One of the men went ahead of André, darting through a maze of narrow corridors, while the other remained behind him, prodding him on. "Faster," he kept saying. André's heart raced; his head pounded; he fought for his breath. They ran through the corridors for the length of a city block, the two men pointing their weapons at anyone who stood in their way, pushing others aside. Then they came to another stairway, which they prodded André to climb. At a door, they stopped. One of the men pushed the door open a crack and peered through it. "Let's go," he said, and a second later, André found himself at the Vendôme entrance of the hotel, being rushed through the human pandemonium and past the astounded concierges. Then into the street, and into a car, which sped away even before his door was closed. The momentum slammed him against the back seat of the car, and only then did he realize that a man was sitting at the other end of the seat.

"Hello, André," the man said.

André peered into the darkness. The light from a street lamp glistened on the barrel of a pistol, and then shone briefly on the man's lean, expressionless face just as he turned to look behind them.

"Sexton!" André said. "What the hell's going on?"

2

The car, a Citröen, shot out of the Place Vendôme and down the rue Castiglione to the rue de Rivoli, where it turned right at such speed that André was thrown against Sexton's bony frame. By the time they reached the Place de la Concorde two blocks away, the car was doing seventy. The driver slowed somewhat to navigate the Place—thankfully, sparsely trafficked at this hour—but resumed speed as soon as he reached the quais of the Right Bank. Landmarks flew by, the Eiffel Tower on the left, the Palais de Chaillot on the right.

"Where are we going?" André said.

"You'll see."

"Come on, Dick. What the hell's going on?"

"Boss's orders."

There was absolutely no question in André's mind as to the identity of the "boss": Charles Houghton, acting director of the CIA, father of Meredith Houghton and André's future father-in-law. Nor was there any further question in André's mind about who the terrorists' target had been. He pressed into the corner of the car, trying by force of will to quiet his suddenly shaking limbs.

Within minutes, they reached the Boulevard Périphérique, and in another few minutes the Autoroute du Nord.

"Le Bourget?" André asked. He'd taken this route to the airport countless times himself, for commercial flights in the early years, in later years for charters.

Sexton didn't answer. He kept turning to look through the rear window.

André rose to look out the window. "Stay down," Sexton said. He pushed André back into the corner, but not before André had seen that another car was following them, driving just as fast as they were, weaving in and out of traffic in an alarming fashion even by Parisian standards.

"Don't worry. It's our backup," Sexton said. "It won't let anyone get in behind us."

"How long have you been in Paris?"

"Three weeks."

"You've been tailing me all this time?"

"I didn't come here for the fashion shows."

"How come I didn't see you?"

"Because you weren't looking for me."

"Who tried to kill me, Dick?"

"Don't know."

They reached Le Bourget in fifteen minutes. For the next hour, as they waited in a corner of the parking lot for their transportation to arrive, André tried to answer the question for himself. But he was too wrought up to make the systematic analysis he knew the question required. It was nearly midnight when a man from the convoy car approached their car and whispered some words to Sexton. "Let's go," Sexton said. In a few minutes, they were aboard an unmarked Gulfstream III.

To André, the drive to Le Bourget had signified that he was being evacuated from France; given the shock of the attempted assassination, he was in no mood to argue. But he had thought that he'd be flown to a U.S. Army base in Germany; the Gulfstream—an executive jet capable of transatlantic flight—told him that they were almost certainly flying to the States.

He and Sexton were the only passengers. They took window seats across from one another. As soon as they were airborne, Sexton opened the bar, filled a highball glass with Scotch, drank it neat and went to sleep. André nursed a snifter of brandy that relaxed him but did nothing to change his mood. Had he drunk an entire bottle, it would not have obscured the recognition that his life was out of control. In a matter of hours, he had been plucked from his home of fifteen years with nothing more than the clothes on his body—appropriately, a tuxedo, he decided mordantly—and was flying to an unknown destination under the aegis of a man with whom he'd been in contact one day of his life. That day, fittingly, had been the most violent he'd ever experienced, embracing the rescue of Meredith Houghton in La Paz from an ex-Gestapo commander named Kurt Hoepner, who had kidnapped her in an effort to stop André from revealing that Camille Laurent had been his Resistance contact during World War II. And now André himself had just been rescued, and by the very same man who had run that earlier mission, a tall, thin, sixty-year-old cipher about whom he knew absolutely nothing other than his name, except that this was obviously the sort of thing he did for a living. At least, he did it well. Thanks to Dick Sexton, whoever he may be, no one could kill André Kohl for however long it took them to fly wherever they were going.

He was cold, he suddenly realized. The interior of the plane was chilly. On transatlantic flights he usually traveled with a special sweater, a blue wool cardigan he'd purchased years ago in Rome, which he put on before he slept. He wanted to sleep; he wanted the sweater. But he had no sweater, no clothes, not even a toothbrush. He felt completely dispossessed, a man without a country, dressed in a monkey suit.

He got up to stretch and use the bathroom. On his return, he saw that Sexton was still asleep. He found two blankets, draped one of them over Sexton, then took his seat and covered himself with the other. He tilted the seat back, hoping he could sleep. Within minutes, he knew that he wouldn't. His mind was too filled with thoughts, and now that the alcohol had succeeded in calming him, he was at last able to attempt to sort through them.

Who *would* want to kill him? Supporters of Camille Laurent who knew the truth about why he had resigned? Ex-Nazis, colleagues of Kurt Hoepner, whose paramilitary operation had been destroyed by André's story? Colleagues of Hoepner's sponsor, Virgil Craig, the former CIA agent who'd been killed along with Hoepner during the struggle in La Paz? Or, as farfetched as it might seem, KGB colleagues of Gennady Gondrachov? It was Gennady who had brought to Paris the evidence that Laurent had been an informer during the war, evidence in the form of a dossier kept by the Gestapo, a dossier seized by the Russians at the end of World War II along with all the Gestapo's records, and later removed to Moscow. The memo incriminating Laurent had turned up in a routine computer check when the Russians decided that they would have to take his presidential candidacy seriously. They were so astounded by what they found that they didn't think anyone would believe them. So they had planted the information on an unsuspecting Shlomo Glaser of the Mossad, the Israeli intelligence service, certain that Shlomo would leak it to André, his favorite Western journalist. The mastermind of that scheme had been Gennady Gondrachov, the Russians' "disinformation" specialist, and an old acquaintance of André's.

Gennady. The Communist with the taste for all of life's good things: powerful cars, English suits, fine cuisine, great wines. The KGB colonel who loved to come to Paris and do business at the Crazy Horse Saloon. André had joked once about doing a profile on him. It would ruin him, Gennady had joked back. You could always defect to the West, André had said. You'd have a wonderful life. Nothing in the West could compare to the life I already have, Gennady had said, and it probably was true. A large Moscow apartment, filled with paintings his artist friends would never show in public. A dacha outside Moscow with tennis court and swimming pool. Three cars in the driveway, one of them a Mercedes. And a live-in housekeeper.

Twenty years he and Gennady had known one another. In the strictest sense, they had not been friends. But he had held Gennady in the high regard one feels for a skilled opponent, and he was as certain as he could be that Gennady had felt the same regard for him. He knew better than to trust Gennady, because the Russian had prospered in a society that believed, at its very core, that the ends justified the means. But there had always been a saving grace about him, a good-humored cynicism which hinted that he was without illusions. It emerged in his banter, as well as in that light, enigmatic smile suggesting that he possessed some private and especially funny knowledge. Once, just once, he had been serious, in a covering letter he'd written when his increasingly perilous situation dictated that he make arrangements to pass the original of the Hoepner dossier to André, should anything happen to him. Yes, he'd acknowledged, Russians were a difficult people, intransigent, stubborn and xenophobic. But would Americans be any different if every hardship foreigners had inflicted on the Russian people had been inflicted on them, as well? Yes, there were differences, but it was imperative nonetheless that the two powers find *something* they could agree upon, because the alternative wasn't very nice. So let them begin by agreeing that a man who assisted Nazi murderers should not become President of France.

That belief, André was certain, had cost Gennady his life. It might yet cost him his own. Who had tried to kill him? Frenchmen? Germans? Russians? Americans?

"Arabs," Charles Houghton said.

The last time André had seen Houghton had been in Lima five weeks before, as he was taken from the plane in which they'd made their escape from Bolivia. During their struggle to find Meredith, a stray bullet had lodged itself in Houghton's chest. Had you not known it had happened, you would not have guessed from his appearance that he'd had such a recent brush with death. He was a comfortably handsome man with a full head of wavy brown hair uncompromised by gray. From the waist up he had the build of a weight lifter, a consequence not only of a religiously observed conditioning program but of the vigorous manner in which he propelled his body, crippled legs and all, with the aid of metal canes, the kind with a brace for the forearms and handles for the hands. The crippled legs were the yield of an OSS parachute drop into France ambushed by the Germans; a bullet fired from far away had hit him in the back. French Resistance fighters had rescued him, then hid him after his surgery. Forty years later, following up a tip from the Mossad, André found a photograph of the Resistance group taken at the end of World War II. In the middle of the group, standing with the aid of two canes, was Charles Houghton, and next to him was the group's leader, Camille Laurent. Prior to André's discovery, he and Houghton had met several times, but did not really know one another; they had gained vast knowledge of and respect for one another since. Willy-nilly, a synergy had developed between them. In mid-May, Houghton had been fired by the President for refusing to find a way to quash André's investigation of Camille Laurent; two weeks later, in the wake of André's exposure of the secret network within the CIA, the President had called Houghton at the hospital in Lima to offer him his old job back.

Now André stared at Houghton in silence. At last, he said, "That makes no sense at all."

It was 9 A.M. The two men were seated alone in a ramshackle farmhouse surrounded by land that André assumed was in Virginia only because an old pickup truck next to the barn had Virginia license plates on it. Neither the people who had brought him to the safe house early that morning nor those who ran it would tell him where he was. Houghton had arrived at eight-forty with some clothes, including a pair of cotton slacks with an elastic band, a polo shirt and a sweater. "Give me fifteen minutes," André said. He showered, shaved and dressed, and felt somewhat restored. But Houghton's identification of André's attackers completely undid him. He would have been almost comforted to learn that the assassins had been from a group whose enmity he could understand.

"It doesn't figure," he said. "In the first place, I haven't done a story on the Mideast in more than five years. If the last story I did had offended anyone, they would have acted long before this. In the second place, I've gone out of my way to be impartial on that story. I'm friendly with the key people on both sides."

Houghton shook his head gravely. "Any impartial story on the Middle East is bound to make someone mad. They don't want you to be fair. They just want you to be on their side. What was your last big story there?"

"The Sabra and Shatilla massacre."

"What line did you take?"

"I didn't take a line."

"Did you report that any certain faction was to blame?"

"It was clear that the massacre was the work of renegade elements on both sides. That's what I broadcast—but I never heard any complaints from either the Lebanese or the Israelis."

Houghton looked intently at André, as though he might be able to divine the answer by seeing inside his head. "There's always the possibility that those two guys were mercenaries—which means that anyone could have hired them."

"There's a comforting thought," André said.

Houghton sighed. "I'm afraid I don't have much comfort to offer you."

Now it was André's turn to be silent. "I haven't heard of Arab mercenaries before," he said at last.

"The word's a bit misleading. They rarely work just for the money. They get political favors, instead."

"How does that work?"

"Let's say I'm Abu Nidal. I have the best-trained terrorists in the world. To put that training to use, I have to have opportunities. The greater the area in which I can operate, the more opportunities I have. So some Germans come to me and ask me to settle a score for them. I say, 'I'll take the assignment, provided you can make it easy for my people to get into Germany.' "

"What kinds of Germans would make a deal like that?"

"The kind who'd like you killed."

"Why hire Arabs to do it?"

"It's handy. It's efficient. It takes the suspicion away from them."

"*Do* you think that friends of Hoepner hired the Arabs?"

"Could be. Could be Camille Laurent, although I strongly doubt it. I'm guessing now, but I assume that whatever deal you made with Laurent included a proviso by which the story of his collaboration with the Gestapo would be told by your network if anything happened to you."

No one, not even Meredith, knew about that. So unless Laurent himself had told Houghton, a totally unlikely possibility, Houghton really was guessing. He could keep him guessing, André knew, but at the moment coyness didn't seem wise. He needed all the counsel Houghton could give him. "You're guessing extremely well," he said.

Houghton nodded. "It could also be people in my shop," he went on. "Four weeks ago, I would never have thought so, but after what you turned up I have to consider it a possibility. Your tip led me to Virgil Craig and his secret network in Latin America.

There could be similar networks in every sector we run. What motivated Craig and probably those who worked with him was a single obsession about saving the world from communism. The Nazis always saw communism as a Jewish conspiracy. They weren't the only ones. The Argentine military became convinced that they were engaged in a life and death struggle to save the world from communism, and that anyone who was Jewish was by definition a Communist. For all I know, Craig and his allies thought so too. It's only one step from that belief to hiring some Arabs to kill you."

"Because I was indirectly responsible for Craig's death?"

"Because of that. Because you ruined their setup in Latin America. Because you destroyed Camille Laurent. Because they believe it was the Israelis who got you started. Because the Israelis helped you along the way. Because you're half-Jewish. Who knows?"

"What you're saying is that my life isn't very secure."

"I'm saying you have a serious problem."

Do you have any suggestions?"

"None that you'd be likely to listen to."

"Try me."

"We could arrange to hide you for a spell."

"Do you think that would work? I'm a fairly visible fellow."

"I'm sure we could come up with an adequate solution."

André shook his head. "I don't even want to think about what that means." He stood and went to the window. Outside, dogs were sleeping in the sun. Beyond them, and for as far as he could see, there was nothing but fields and woods. He was hidden now. He might as well be dead. On the other hand, if Meredith were with him, he really would have reduced the world to a size so small that everything in it could be genuine. But did he have the right to ask her to enter such a world? And would she agree to come? Even the questions punctured his heart.

He'd known Meredith such a short time and they'd been together less than half that time, yet she had invaded his senses in every possible way. The taste of her full lips was in his mouth, the smell of her freshness in his nose, the sound of her mellow, assured voice in his ears, the feel of her skin in his fingertips. Her face was engraved in his mind, its cool, classic, patrician lines, so reminiscent of Grace Kelly, set off by long straight blond hair held at the back by a bow. Her manner was equally vivid, the directness and openness with which she looked at him, the serenity of her expression in repose, her tall, lean athlete's body, not muscular, simply fit, her utter comfort being nude, her eagerness and honesty in bed. This is what I want. Tell me what you want. Is this good? Oh yes, again. I love you, André. Will you marry me?

At last, he turned back to Houghton. "Why don't you say what you're not saying?"

Houghton shook his head. "I've said what I came to say."

"You haven't said anything about Meredith."

"No, I haven't. And I won't. All I can do is assess the situation for you."

"Have you assessed the situation for her?"

"There was no situation to assess until last night."

"But you thought there was enough of a possibility to warrant keeping an eye on me in Paris."

"I could have been wrong."

André stared at Houghton, not knowing what the man was to him in this moment. "You want me to make the assessment because you know the decision I'll make. You know I'll call the wedding off. And that's what you want, isn't it?"

At once Houghton's eyes softened. Assured and vital just seconds before, he suddenly seemed old and vulnerable. For a moment he looked away. Then he turned his gaze on André. In his eyes was a plea for forgiveness. "I owe you so much, André," he said. "But I must be blunt."

"Please."

"What I want is her happiness. What she wants is you. If you ask me, am I sorry you're the one she wants, I have to answer yes. I admire you greatly as a journalist and a man, particularly after what you did in La Paz. But you're twenty years older than Meredith. And, much more important, you're a man other men, all of them professional killers, would dearly love to kill. It's true you saved Meredith's life in La Paz. But you're the one who took her there in the first place. If she hadn't gone, she wouldn't have been in danger. As long as she's with you, she's going to be in danger. If she's not with you, she won't be." Houghton shrugged. "Poetry to the contrary, no one ever died of a broken heart."

André stared at Houghton, crestfallen. "I wouldn't be too sure about that," he said, his voice barely audible. He hesitated for another moment. "Okay, the wedding's off."

Houghton smiled weakly. "I'm afraid it's not that simple. I've known Meredith longer than you have."

3

She arrived within the hour. A car drove her to the farmhouse door, and she was in the room before André realized she was there. She sailed into his arms without a word, and clung to him in silence, as her father left the room with as little noise as he could.

For these few moments, André permitted himself not to think about the future. He was with Meredith again, and nothing else truly mattered. He could feel the blood surging through his chest and out to his limbs and into his head. It was chemistry, pure and simple. Feeling her pressed against him with a strength that never failed to surprise him, André could still not understand why Meredith had chosen to love him. It wasn't that he didn't feel worthy. It was those twenty years. Why men fell in love with younger women was so obvious it didn't need consideration; why young women would fall for older men was the mystery. Let it remain a mystery; André was content simply to have the real person supplant those sensual memories on which he'd had to exist for the last several weeks. For another moment, he held her, feeling the firmness of her tall athlete's body. Her strong, steady heartbeat gave him the sensation that a new life support system had been attached to his.

"All right, what's going on?" Meredith said at last.

"You'd better ask your father," André said.

"I might just as well ask the Sphinx. He won't tell me."

"I think he will this time." André went to the door and motioned Houghton inside. Meredith listened in silence while her father brought her up to date. Her breathing seemed to deepen

31

with each passing detail; only when he had concluded did she take her eyes from him to look at André. "It's no good," André told her then. "I'm not going to put you in jeopardy."

She looked at him with such intensity that he could feel his adrenaline begin to flow. There was love in her gaze, but far more: strength, the advertisement of a will that he had suspected might exist but had never seen before. Her blue eyes were magnets fastening his gaze to hers. He knew that if she held his gaze much longer she would strip him of his own will just as surely as if she had hypnotized him. Yet he couldn't bring himself to look away. No one, man or woman, had ever looked at him that way. It was a wordless affirmation of a resolve so firm that nothing could possibly shake it. Her words, when she finally spoke, did not surprise him; they simply defined her resolve. "If you don't want to marry me because you don't love me, I'll accept that. But that's the only condition I'll accept. I'll decide for myself what risks I'll take and won't take. I refuse to live my life on the possibility that something bad might happen." She had been speaking slowly, to be certain she was completely understood. Now she paused a moment for added emphasis. "I have only one question, André. Do you love me?"

It flashed through his brain that he should lie, and say that he didn't love her. But the lie would be transparent and more than that, he couldn't say it if his own life depended on it. "You know I love you," he said at last.

"Then let's get married," Meredith said. And then, suddenly, she laughed, and her eyes shone with the singular incandescence a woman displays when she knows, for the first time, that she is going to be a bride.

They were married the next day in Fredericksburg, Virginia, fifty miles south southwest of Washington. Houghton did not like the idea at all—he had wanted to bring a judge to the farm to preclude any possibility of André being recognized—but after Meredith had insisted on a church wedding he chose Fredericksburg over some hamlet on the theory that a small wedding party could get in and out of a medium-size town without attracting attention, whereas strangers in a community any smaller could hardly go unnoticed.

André had wanted to invite his children to the wedding, as well as Mike Paul and several colleagues from the network. But Houghton had vetoed all guests, and André, after thinking about it, had decided that it was just as well. He was in no mood to explain himself to anyone at this point. As for his son Gene and daughter Paula, meeting their new stepmother for the first time at her wedding to their father was hardly ideal. It would be shock enough for them to learn that he was going to marry again after all these years, and to a woman only a few years older than they were; being flown to a clandestine wedding that could not be adequately explained might color the marriage for them with a darkness that might never be expunged.

Once agreement was reached, Houghton took care of everything. That very afternoon, one of his men showed up with a marriage license. André knew better than to ask how it had been obtained. The man also had a suitcase for André, filled with an adequate, if not elegant, wardrobe of summer clothes. The next morning two cars arrived to take them to Fredericksburg—not agency cars, André noted with interest. Probably rented from Hertz or Avis. Their drivers were cordial but uncommunicative, as were the women who accompanied each of them. Both men were about fifty, and neither looked remotely like CIA agents. In their dark suits, white shirts and expensive-looking silk ties, they looked, rather, like two friends of the groom who had taken the day off to attend his wedding, accompanied by their wives.

Inside the church, however, they paid no attention to the ceremony. The two women stood with their backs to the altar, watching the two doors to the nave, one at the end of the aisle, the other at the side of the pews. The two men posted themselves just inside the front and side doors of the church.

Houghton gave the bride away, and then stood by André as best man. André wondered briefly if any other man had performed such a double function at a wedding; in any case, the circumstances of this wedding were so bizarre that it seemed like an appropriate touch. To complete the picture, the minister was a black man, no older than Meredith, with a resonant voice and a speech pattern that defied racial or regional categorization. He was black only by definition; by the standards of his race he was pale. Whatever his shade, a black minister in a white man's church in Virginia, even in its more progressive northern regions, was the last thing André expected; it told him how out of touch he was with all that had happened in America during his sixteen years in Europe. As André heard the minister intone the familiar words, he looked over at Meredith. Her blue eyes were fixed intently on the minister. A gentleness André had never seen before had settled into her face. Her smile seemed beatific. What was happening was exactly what she wanted, and in the way she wanted it. It had been so easy to say yes when she'd asked for the church wedding; anything to make it happen, even though to André it held no special meaning. Obviously, it represented something important to Meredith, but what that was he didn't know. There had been no time to talk about religious convictions—no time, really, to learn about the hundreds of things one generally knows about an intended prior to the marriage. The truth was that almost everything would have to be learned post facto about the woman he was in the process of marrying.

The minister was looking at Meredith. "Will you have this man to be your husband, to live together in holy marriage? Will you love him, comfort him, honor and keep him in sickness and in health, and forsaking all others, be faithful to him as long as you both shall live?"

"I will," Meredith replied.

Now the minister turned his gaze to André. No man had ever looked at him more seriously. Had he divined somehow that even as he was being married André was wondering if he was in the process of committing some awful error?

"Will you have this woman to be your wife, to live together in holy marriage? Will you love her, comfort her, honor and keep her in sickness and in health, and forsaking all others, be faithful to her as long as you both shall live?"

To all those questions, the answer was yes. But the most vital question, in this case, hadn't been asked: Would he—*could* he—protect her? For that question, he had no answer. André turned from the minister to Meredith. She was looking at him, her eyes bathed in love and trust. "I will," he said. God help him if he failed.

Very little that had happened in the previous twenty-four hours had concerned itself with anything but their future safety. For a few hours, it looked as though they might be spending their honeymoon at the farmhouse, because Houghton simply refused to provide them with transportation until he was satisfied with the arrangements.

"I can't hide forever," André argued.

"But you *can* hide until I can set up something safe for you—and that's going to take me a few days."

"Daddy," Meredith said, "I'm not starting married life in this place under any circumstances. If you won't drive us out we'll walk."

"Wait a minute," André said. "I've got an idea." He turned to Houghton. "Mike Paul has a house in the Dominican Republic that he's been trying to get me to for years. I remember his telling me that it's in a guarded compound and that there's a private airstrip on the compound big enough for jets. I'm sure he'd be happy to lend us the house."

"I'll call him," Houghton said.

Ten minutes later, they had not only the loan of the house from a surprised, delighted and much relieved Mike Paul, but also a private jet to fly them from Virginia to the resort. The plane belonged to Jacob Jones, who had flown in from Paris the previous day on business and, still shaken by the terrorist attack at his party, had contacted Mike to find out about André.

At last, Houghton gave his blessings, but only on the condition that André and Meredith would remain in the compound at all times, and for however long it took him first, to make adequate arrangements for their return and, second, to identify, if at all possible, the people behind the assassination attempt in Paris.

That was the key, André knew: to find and neutralize whoever had tried to kill him. To that end, he had, with Houghton's permission, placed a call to Pierre Gauthier in Paris. Gauthier was the number-three man in the Direction Générale de la Sécurité Extérieure, or DGSE, the CIA's counterpart in Paris. He was also a close adviser to Camille Laurent, and would have become chief of the DGSE had Laurent become president. Gauthier had been the only other man in the room on the day that André had called on Laurent, given him a copy of the script he had written exposing Laurent as a World War II Gestapo informer and told the President-elect that he would broadcast the script if, within twenty-four hours, Laurent had not announced his irrevocable decision not to take office.

There was that other circumstance in which the broadcast would be made: if André was killed or injured or if he disappeared, either that day or at any other time. It was this circumstance André reminded Gauthier of when he got him on the phone.

"I assure you that the general has no interest in seeing your story made public. He had nothing to do with the attempt on your life."

"Do you know who did?"

"Not as yet."

"What do the terrorists have to say?"

"For the moment, nothing. But we are urging them to cooperate."

The same way you probably urged Gennady Gondrachov to cooperate, André thought. What a strain the desire to survive put on one's principles. Nothing could make him favor torture, yet he would give almost anything to have a confession from these men. "If anything happens to me, Mr. Gauthier, I'm not going to be in a position to tell the network not to broadcast—even if the general wasn't involved. So I hope you can find out who those guys are working for and how they got into France."

"I understand, Mr. Kohl."

I'll bet you do, André thought. He hung up wondering why he should feel concerned about what was about to happen to two men who had tried to kill him.

As they cleared U.S. airspace in Jacob Jones's Gulfstream III—a more luxurious version of the same aircraft that had flown him from Paris two days before—André did his best to put his worries to rest. With his new bride beside him, he tried to believe that he was flying away from an old life and toward a new one. If anything bad was to happen to him or Meredith, it would not occur during the next weeks as they honeymooned in Casa de Campo.

That was the name of the resort to which they were heading. It was a seven-thousand-acre development near the town of La Romana on the southeastern coast of the Dominican Republic, built by Gulf and Western. Uniformed guards manned the gates to the resort on a twenty-four-hour basis, admitting only registered guests and property owners and those they vouched for. The world inside was self-contained, with small electric trains—golf-cart-style tractors and wagons—that ferried visitors back and forth from villas or bungalows called "casitas," to one of two golf courses, the hotel or restaurants.

"Oh, boy," Meredith said as their train drove them along the fairways of the Teeth of the Dog golf course toward their villa. It was after 6 P.M.; the low angle of the sun put a mirror on the water, and deepened the textures of the tropical vegetation—thick clusters of royal palms, lime trees, cascades of bougainvillea and hibiscus so bright it seemed to be on fire. The lush fairway of the golf course looked more blue than green in the late afternoon light. Beyond the course, to the south, lay crescents of white beaches; between each crescent was a mound of coral rocks, against which the surf crashed with metronomic rhythm, shooting strands of glistening spray high into the air.

To honeymooners craving not only privacy but anonymity, the situation could not have been more perfect. They had landed ten minutes before on the 6,800-foot private airstrip, which cut through the second nine of the Teeth of the Dog golf course. Immigration was perfunctory; if the officer reacted to André's name, he gave no sign; he appeared to check only the date of issue of André's passport to make certain the document was still valid, then turned to a blank page and stamped it. Meredith's passport received the same treatment.

"How did you happen to have your passport with you?" André asked as they were waved through customs.

"Daddy told me to bring it."

"He does think of everything."

"Almost everything. What about you?"

"Habit. Keeping his passport with him is the first lesson a foreign correspondent learns."

Mike Paul's house was in the middle of a line of eight "golf villas" called Costa Verde. The house was white, with a red corrugated roof. Windows and sliding glass doors framed views of the rolling green fairways to the north and the blue Caribbean to the south. The sea was no more than fifty yards away, past small sand dunes that descended to the beach. Mike had obviously called ahead, because when they entered the villa, they found the doors open, breezes sweeping through it aided by an old-fashioned ceiling fan, and flowers in profusion on every table in every room. The interior, like many of the other homes, was designed by Oscar de la Renta, a Dominican. It had an airy spaciousness, with floors of hand-fired reddish-brown tiles, wooden shutters, woven furniture on wooden frames and cotton fabrics with blazing flowers on a white background. On the coffee table in the living room was a bottle of champagne in a bucket, with a card that said, *"Esta en su casa,* which means this is your home for as long as you like. Mike." When they walked into the bedroom, Meredith took one look at the king-sized bed, already turned down, and said, *"Now* I feel like a bride." They came to one another and kissed. André immediately sensed a difference, but for a moment couldn't define it. Then he knew. There had always been an urgency to their kissing, as though they didn't know how long they would be together and had to make up for both the past and the future. Meredith's words confirmed it. "I want to really be a bride," she said. "You go into the living room and wait. I'll be out in ten minutes."

He went into the living room and in a moment heard the shower. He walked through the dining room to the kitchen, hoping that someone had stocked the refrigerator. He opened it, and smiled. Two cold, boiled lobsters sat waiting. On the shelf above was a salad, and a bowl of fresh sliced fruits. Mike had thought of everything, at least for their first night.

In ten minutes, Meredith appeared, wearing a floor-length lacy white robe and matching nightgown. "It's a bit early," she said, "but I figured why waste time?"

"My turn," André said.

He showered and shaved quickly, threw a bath towel around his middle and stepped into the bedroom. Meredith was propped on the bed, smiling. On the table next to her was the champagne and bucket, and two glasses, already filled. "C'mere, buster," she said. She handed him his glass, and raised hers to his. "To André and Meredith Kohl, and to their glorious children."

"Wait a minute," André said.

Meredith touched her glass to his, smiled and said, "Drink up and get to work."

Hours later, after their lovemaking, after they'd eaten their cold lobster and salad and fruit and finished the bottle of champagne, after they'd made love again and Meredith had at last gone to sleep in his arms, André lay awake evaluating this latest of the sudden and profound changes in his life. For the last twenty years, at least, he'd believed that it was he who created and controlled the circumstances of his existence. True, he'd been at the mercy of world events. But in all other respects he lived where and in the manner he chose, and did what he chose to do. Now, suddenly, choices were being made for him in every category of his life. He hadn't chosen to be evacuated from Paris, or to marry abruptly and in secret and in a church, or to have a cold lobster dinner on his wedding night or to conceive a child with his new wife.

The other choices he could comprehend, but this last one confounded him. The thought of having a child or children with Meredith had never entered his mind. They'd certainly never discussed it; it was simply one of dozens of matters that should have been considered by a couple planning marriage, yet impossible during their brief and fragmented courtship. What he could not get over now, as they lay together, was his lack of protest on realizing that Meredith wanted a family, and at once, and the way in which he'd gone along. He'd felt in that moment that he was the captive of a force he could neither resist nor direct.

For two days, he'd done nothing but worry about how to avoid being killed, and then three hours ago he'd acted to produce a life. Was that why he'd gone along, to affirm life in the most fundamental of all ways?

Meredith stirred. He looked down at her. She was naked, as was he. Beauty and the beast, he thought. If they had, indeed, just made a child, he prayed that it would look like her.

A breeze drifted into the room. He withdrew his arm, reached down and pulled a sheet over them. He turned onto his side, then pressed backward until he could once again feel Meredith. Just before he closed his eyes, he saw the sea, bathed in moonlight. Peace, he thought. For once, let life run you.

At nine the next morning, two Dominican women, one forty, the other no more than twenty, arrived. They were mother and daughter, they explained to Meredith; the mother, Luisa, would cook, and the daughter, Carmen, would clean.

Just past the veranda on the ocean side was a pool, and it was there that André and Meredith spent the morning. At one o'clock, Luisa called them to lunch, a tossed salad with shrimp and avocados, a sautéed fish covered in a spicy onion and chili sauce and a rum cake for dessert. A white Argentine wine accompanied the meal, served by Carmen. "Let's," Meredith said to André when the meal was over. She stood, held out her hand and led him to the bedroom.

Except for the servants, they spent the rest of that day and evening in isolation. The next day was the same. On the third day, they explored the beaches, taking care to steer clear of other tourists. For good measure, André wore a cap and a pair of sunglasses he'd found in one of the drawers. By the fourth day, he was restless.

"Bored?" Meredith said.

"Not bored. Frustrated. There's a golf course on the other side of this house. I'm a golfer. A miserable, inept golfer, but a golfer. To be living next to a golf course and not be able to play is a torture only a golfer can understand. Furthermore, the last time I played was the day my friend from the Mossad walked along with me on the golf course at Dieppe and told me the story of Camille Laurent. What history will judge important about that day is not that it initiated the circumstances leading to the fall of Camille Laurent, but that something awesome happened to my game. I hit shots I had never hit before. I had a birdie. A birdie. For five holes I was like a man possessed. I would give a great deal to discover whether that was a one-time thing, or a gift from God in anticipation of what he was about to put me through."

"Then why don't we play?" Meredith said. "Daddy didn't say we couldn't."

"You didn't tell me you were a golfer."

Meredith patted André's cheek. "I wasn't until I married one."

That afternoon Meredith went to the clubhouse to rent clubs and shoes. There were no shoes to rent, but there were some to buy, and after conferring with André by telephone, she bought a pair for him and another for herself. She also arranged for a late morning starting time the next day, during a period when no one else was signed up, explaining that she was a beginner and didn't want to hold the other golfers up.

As André had instructed, she brought a five iron back to the house, along with half a dozen golf balls. In the early evening, while it was still light and after all the golfers had finished their rounds, they walked across the road to the second hole of the Teeth of the Dog course. "Let's see what you can do," André said, setting the balls down.

"Just show me the right grip," Meredith said. He did. She swung. The ball shot from the ground and flew directly to the green. André watched in silence. "It's not fair," he said at last.

She was, it became clear the next day, one of those adepts who slip instantly and naturally into a sport, and she set about her round with good humor and relish, which did not diminish even when she made the classic beginner's errors. She made fewer and fewer of those as the round progressed, a consequence not only of her aptitude but of the constant presence at her side of her caddy, Francisco, a man of indeterminate age who, except for his lack of an education, might have been a golf pro, and who constantly demonstrated shots to her along the way.

Golf carts were available, but Meredith had refused to use them, and insisted that André walk, as well. He employed the only other caddy available, a boy named Domingo, who couldn't have been more than twelve, and who was so small that he kept falling behind. At one point, André carried the bag himself to give Domingo a rest. Remembering the lesson he'd learned that day on the Dieppe golf course with Shlomo Glaser of the Mossad—"think of something else"—André started out where he'd left off, hitting the ball extremely well, but his good performance—he was only three over par by the sixth hole, the best score to that point he'd ever had—paradoxically proved his undoing. His high expectations made him anxious and his anxiety impaired his game.

"At least it completely absorbed me," he said of their round as they sipped cocktails on the oceanside veranda that evening.

"I can see how it would," Meredith said.

"You enjoyed it?"

"Can't wait for tomorrow."

At ten-thirty the next morning, Francisco and Domingo were waiting for them on the first tee, which was otherwise abandoned, other golfers preferring to start much earlier in order to beat the midday heat. For André and Meredith, the solitude was an ample trade-off for the discomfort, and because no one was playing behind them, they could stop briefly for a bite of lunch at their house, which lay just to the north of the eighth green. Francisco and Domingo were delighted with the arrangement; while André and Meredith ate under an umbrella on the veranda, Luisa gave the caddies lunch in the kitchen.

Each day they played it became more apparent to André that, as improved as he was, Meredith would soon be the better golfer. He couldn't have been happier. It meant that when, as and if their life ever returned to normal, he would have a golfing partner. He could visualize them now, playing at the Dieppe Country Club on their vacations.

They'd talked about that as one of a dozen ways in which they might spend their new life together. They had agreed that, for the moment at least, it would be a mistake to dispose of André's properties in France, either the Paris apartment, or the house in Varengeville-sur-Mer, a dozen kilometers from Dieppe. They would start out in New York, of course, in Meredith's loft in Soho, which André had never seen but which he assured her would do just fine.

"Don't be too sure," she'd said. "You're a front-of-the-airplane fella."

"Not necessarily," he'd said. "I'm an unemployed writer. We'll have to watch our step." It was not exactly true. He wasn't rich, but he was in good shape even without a salary, and there would be income from the writing he would undoubtedly do—magazine articles, of course, and almost certainly a book; he had, after all, made his reputation initially as an author—as well as a monthly check from USBC, which had generously construed his resignation as an early retirement. On the other hand, he had no idea how much life in New York would cost them. He'd been to New York a hundred times, at least, but always on an expense account. He'd never lived there, paid rent there, kept a car there or fled from there on weekends. For that matter, he'd never experienced married life there, and having lived alone for so many years, he wondered most of all what that would be like.

"Grand. Just grand," Meredith assured him. During the day, he could write or practice piano—there was plenty of room in the loft for one, and the walls were thick—while she went to her gallery, and evenings they would dine in Soho or the Village, or go to plays or concerts, or entertain their friends. Between her friends and his, they would never want for companions.

It did sound grand—fresh, vibrant, stimulating—which was why they talked about it at such length, along with the trips they might take and their visits to France, as though planning the future somehow guaranteed its existence. Not once since arriving had they spoken of the threat hanging over them, even though all of their movements were made with that threat in mind. They'd deliberately refrained from listening to the radio or watching television or even buying a newspaper, knowing that if anything important happened that affected them Houghton would call them at once. If for some reason he didn't, Mike Paul certainly would. But no one had called during the entire week that they'd been there.

Nor had anyone at Casa de Campo bothered them, although by this point, they realized, some of the other guests must have known they were there. Playing golf, there was no way to avoid other golfers for an entire round, even though they teed off long after the others had started. Several holes on the first nine bordered holes on the second nine; at some point on the first nine they were bound to pass golfers finishing their rounds. They did each day, and still their luck held. No one stopped to stare or came over to shake André's hand.

On their sixth day of play, André hooked his drive on the ninth hole. Walking to his ball, he realized that he was headed directly toward a man who had sliced his drive on the eighteenth hole, which paralleled the ninth. They met in the rough between the two fairways. The man was in his sixties. He had a drinker's face, the skin red and mottled, with a cluster of tiny veins visible on his nose. Either he took his golf seriously and was at the end of a terrible round, or else his life had been joyless. As he stared in silence at André, André wondered if he had ever seen a meaner, more hostile face. After what seemed an eternity, the man hit his ball and moved on. He had not said a word. The degree to which that brief encounter shook André, who had suffered his share of unfriendly stares, told him how vulnerable he still felt. But he said nothing to Meredith, and for the rest of the round and the rest of the day he tried hard to forget the encounter.

He couldn't. What the encounter had reminded him of was that he was on a honeymoon not just literally but in the larger, more figurative sense. Very soon now, he—and Meredith with him— would have to reenter the real world.

4

For Charles Houghton, the honeymoon had ended almost the moment he returned from Lima. The President had sent a plane to fetch him the very day that Augusto Perez, his Peruvian surgeon, had pronounced him fit enough to travel; early the following morning the plane was on its way back to Washington with the rehabilitated CIA deputy director and his daughter aboard. Houghton had been pleasantly surprised by the President's gesture, but that was nothing compared with the surprise that awaited him at Andrews Air Force Base when they landed that evening. His boss, William Coughlin, the sixth political appointee for whom he'd worked, came aboard the plane and, after greeting Meredith, asked her to deplane ahead of her father. "If you feel at all up to it, the President would like to see you first thing tomorrow morning," he said as soon as they were alone.

"What's the rush?"

"I'm quitting, Charlie. The President wants to name you acting director and then, if all goes well, give you the job."

Houghton stared at Coughlin, noting for the first time the utter weariness in the seventy-one-year-old former admiral's round Irish face. "Why? And why now?"

"I know the timing's lousy. But I don't have any options. Janet's doctor says another month in Washington could finish her off."

Janet was Coughlin's wife. She'd had a heart condition for years. She was, Houghton well knew, the kind of woman who absorbed her husband's tensions. "This last week has been unbelievable here, Charlie," Coughlin went on. "You have no idea what a sensation this story has produced. The President's as upset as I've ever seen him. Between him, Congress and the media, I've been working twenty hours a day. There's no way I can shield Janet from that kind of pressure."

"But why me?" Houghton said. "He knows I never wanted to be the director."

"I think he should explain that to you himself."

"We need a professional in there, Charlie," the President was saying, "someone who knows how the agency operates and isn't going to be fooled by his own people. I'm not saying Bill was fooled, or couldn't have gotten to the bottom of it if he stayed. But he's a political appointee, not an intelligence professional, and it's a professional with vast experience and impeccable credentials who can reassure the American people about the CIA. You agree with that, don't you, Bill?"

"Absolutely, Mr. President."

The three men were seated in armchairs at the west end of the Oval Office. The last time Houghton had been in that room the President had been so angry with him that he'd left him standing in front of his desk, crutches and all, while he dressed him down for his role, as inadvertent as it was, in the Laurent affair. Outwardly, at least, this was a totally different man—solicitous, reasonable, subdued. Could he have changed so fundamentally, and so quickly? Yes, if he'd found out in the interval that this matter of the secret network could kill him politically. Obviously, that was exactly what he'd discovered. The morning papers, which Houghton had scanned before coming to the White House, had reported a 20 percent dip in the President's overall approval rating from the previous month. Even more significantly, the same poll showed only 31 percent of the public believing that he was doing a good job in foreign affairs, a drop of twenty-seven points. "Who's Running the Country?" the *Washington Post* had headlined its lead editorial that morning, which concluded: "When middle-level bureaucrats can make decisions that affect our relations with foreign governments, it is not only this President's position that is under-mined and weakened but the presidency itself."

"The American people don't approve of anyone breaking the law, no matter how laudable their objectives," the President went on. "They won't stand for it. I won't stand for it, either. Christ knows, I want to prevail over the Communists every bit as much as this so-called secret network does, and maybe knowing that gave those characters an open invitation to act. But I hate what they did."

"Mr. President," Houghton said, "this network has been oper-ating at least since 1959."

"Then how the hell didn't anybody know about it?"

"It beats me, sir, but I'm going to do everything I can to find out."

"Then you'll take the job?"

Houghton sighed. "I'd like to have a day to think about it."

"What's your objection? Why do you hesitate?"

"I'm very tired, sir, and I don't like to make decisions when I am. I'm also surprised. Two weeks ago you canned me, and now you offer me the directorship. But the most important reason is that I'm not sure I'm qualified. As deputy director, I'm practicing a profession I'm trained for. As the director, I'd have to practice politics, and that's something I'm not only not trained for, but don't particularly like."

"I didn't know anything about politics, either, Charlie," Cough-lin said. "But you learn damn fast."

"Look, Charlie," the President said, "I know you're tired, and I apologize for getting you in here, but I've got to get my ship tight. This is no time for me to be worrying about the kind of intelligence I'm getting. I've got decisions to make before I leave office that could affect the fate of all mankind."

Ah ha, Houghton thought, the hidden agenda. "Are you speak-ing of the Russians, sir?"

"Exactly. You know how I feel about them. But if there's some-thing to this so-called peace offensive of theirs, I'd never forgive myself if I missed it. The problem is, is it genuine? Is that guy for real? What do we make of these stories that he's unstable and hits the bottle? What happens if I negotiate with him and make a deal

47

and he's all of a sudden out on his ass and the hard-liners are back in power? I'll have given something away that we might need, and we'd have a helluva time at that point getting it back." The President paused for a moment. "An emotionally unstable Soviet leader could be the gravest imaginable danger to the future of the world. I've got to know who I'm dealing with. I've got to know if those reports are true—and so far, you guys haven't come up with diddly."

The problem to which the President referred was a relatively new one that had surfaced within recent months, following the election of the new Premier. After years of belligerence abroad and tight rule at home, the Soviets were issuing multiple signals suggesting fundamental change: the release of political prisoners, the publication of once banned books, the screening of once banned films, a provision for the election of certain officials who had previously been appointed. In foreign policy, the Soviets were letting it be known that deals could be made to scale down missile deployments, deals that might lead eventually to disarmament. Confounding these developments was the question of how deep the commitment to them was in the party hierarchy. Would the new Premier prevail? Or would he meet the fate of Nikita Khrushchev? A story alleging that he had a drinking problem and was given to emotional tantrums had been widely circulated in the West earlier that spring. Houghton had been trying to establish the validity of the story at the time the Camille Laurent matter surfaced but had not had any success. Now he turned to Coughlin, who held his hands out, palms up, in resignation. "We're workin' on it," he said. "That's all I know."

"Let me tell you something, Charlie," the President said. "If the Russians do want to deal, it's because I've been so tough on them. You can't negotiate from weakness with those bastards. Only hard-liners like myself can cut a deal. Look at Nixon and China. If Kennedy had tried to cut a deal with them he would've been crucified. But if the Premier is anything like those stories say he is, shit, I'll be the one gets crucified." He leaned forward and grabbed Houghton's arm. "Don't let that happen. It won't help the country."

"I'll do my best, sir."

"Then you'll take it?"

For a moment, Houghton hesitated, just long enough to ask himself once more what was really going on. Why did the President want him? Because the President needed him. Why did the President need him? Because he'd been involved in the discovery of the secret network, along with André Kohl, and would therefore be credible to the American people. Ultimately, it was the people, not him, the President needed. "Before I answer that, Mr. President, I have two questions to ask you."

"Shoot."

"First, why the delay in nominating me to be the director? Why name me acting director?"

"Two reasons, one political, the other practical. I *think* I'm right about how the public will react to a professional at this moment to deal with this problem, but I could be wrong. If I *am* wrong, no harm done, I can look for a nonprofessional. The practical reason is that I can't have you tied up in confirmation hearings right now. There's too much to be done. As acting director, you won't need to be confirmed, but you'll be able to act as though you had been. That good enough for you?"

"Yes, sir."

"What's your second question?"

"Two months ago, you hinted that someone within the CIA was telling you about my involvement in the Camille Laurent affair. Knowing who that was could make my job a lot easier. Will you tell me?"

The President shook his head. "I'm sure it would, but that's not the way it happened. I got a call from Laurent himself. He told me you'd been to France investigating charges that he'd been a Gestapo agent during the war. He said the charges were ludicrous. Said he'd saved your life during the war. I asked him how he knew what you were up to. He said that someone in his intelligence service had been tipped by one of your people. He wouldn't tell me who."

Houghton sighed. "Too bad," he said. It was too bad, as well, that there was no way to know if the President was telling the truth. In their last meeting, the President had been ready to dismiss Laurent's Gestapo informant's role as the work of "a kid."

Today's realities, the President had argued then, dictated the need for Laurent to be elected president of France. Any other outcome —meaning the election of Laurent's leftist opponent—could create too many imponderables, he'd said, beginning with the defense of Europe. There was also the matter of France's commitment in Africa, its role in the UN, the intelligence problems created when a friendly power becomes an antagonist.

"Too bad about Laurent," the President said now. He was referring, certainly, to the French President-elect's accident several days before. According to reports, he had suffered a grave head injury while on a brief postelection vacation.

"We understand he'll never take office," Coughlin said.

"I'd be surprised if he did," Houghton said. There was nothing more he could say, because he didn't know for certain, but he did know from long experience that events like this didn't just happen. Of the identity of the man who had precipitated the event he was absolutely certain. The only questions remaining were how André had pulled it off and how many more enemies he'd made.

The President was silent for a moment. "Maybe it's just as well," he said then.

What did *that* mean? Houghton wondered. Did the President know, or suspect? So many mysteries. The one advantage of the director's job was that it would put him in increasing contact with the people who might give him the clues he would need to solve them—beginning with the President. For a moment, he was tempted to tell the President that the man who had saved his life in World War II had also destroyed it by tipping the Germans to the mission in which he was paralyzed. But telling him that could lead to questions he might not want to answer.

"Well, Charlie?" the President was saying.

"Okay, Mr. President. You're on."

The President held up the announcement for a week to give Houghton time to recuperate. From that moment forward, Houghton was besieged both by Congress and the media. A joint committee of the House and the Senate, which had opened an investigation into the CIA's secret network within days of the André Kohl disclosures, invited Houghton to testify in executive session at the earliest possible moment. At the same time, the committee, in time-honored fashion, initiated a stream of leaks to the media designed to make his refusal impossible. The leaks hinted that the secret network extended far beyond the Latin American elements covered in the USBC exclusive.

The media, for its part, scarcely contented itself with leaks. Reporters from every major newspaper, the news magazines and the networks had dug into the story before it was hours old. Since André Kohl was one of theirs, he could hardly have been expected to tell them how he'd gotten onto the story, so their efforts to get to its origins had focused on Charles Houghton. Had *he* tipped André to the story? Houghton's categorical denial did not keep several newspapers from speculating that André enjoyed a special relationship with his prospective father-in-law. Those newspapers that didn't print such a story employed reporters and editors who believed it.

No reporter likes to be beaten by another reporter, and for the print media, it was especially galling that they had been beaten by television. And so, since early June, Houghton had not only been besieged for interviews, but had seen the effects of his refusal in a variety of critical stories, most about the agency, some about him personally.

The stories about him didn't trouble him unduly. Every career public servant knew that sooner or later it would be his turn for scrutiny. Actually, Houghton favored such scrutiny. Unlike his predecessors, and most public officials, he had a genuine respect for serious reporters as well as their outlets, and did his best to inform them at background briefings, consistent with the inherently secret nature of his work. He was also zealous about quietly informing members of Congress whose committees served as watchdogs over the nation's intelligence activities. It was Congress, after all, that wrote the laws and paid the bills.

But Houghton hated testifying before committees of Congress, even in executive session. To his mind, everyone's interest could be far better served through private channels. That belief had never been more pronounced than during the preceding weeks, when his agency—the work of his life—had come under such heavy attack.

The overriding problem was that he had almost nothing to tell anyone. Partly this was because he could not divulge much of what he did know, particularly the portion relating to the greatest mystery of the entire affair: how and why it had begun. Everyone —congressional investigators as well as the media—was speculating, but none of them had the answer. In not a single case had a reporter or commentator or government official linked the secret network disclosures to the resignation of Camille Laurent. The people who knew the answer were not about to disclose it. André had sworn not to, and—in a call to Houghton the morning after his return to Washington—had received his pledge that he would say nothing, either. As to Laurent and the few people in his entourage who knew the truth, the revelation would destroy their cause.

The other reason Houghton would have so little to contribute to a congressional inquiry was that he knew nothing more about the extent or identity of the secret network than he had known when its existence was first revealed. It galled him to admit that. All he knew for certain was that deep in the bowels of the CIA there existed a small cadre of men committed to an agenda that was not authorized by their government. It was possible, even likely, that the agenda of this network *had* coincided with the objectives of their president, but that didn't make it legal. Members of the CIA were obliged to uphold the law, not invent it. They were not sanctioned to forge unofficial alliances with like-minded agents in other countries, as they had obviously been doing. The question was, who in the CIA was running this secret network of intelligence agents exposed by André that was attempting to impose its own law on international affairs?

For Houghton, knowing such a man existed was worse than discovering that your wife had been unfaithful. An unfaithful wife was a disappointment, but an unfaithful agent was dangerous. How he would catch this man he still didn't know. The man wasn't a double, working for the other side, meaning that Houghton could learn nothing about him from defectors. He was a zealot, a superpatriot, believing, like Virgil Craig, that means of any kind were justified in the war against the Communists. Until he acted again, there was simply no way to find him.

For all these reasons, an appearance before a congressional committee—even one behind closed doors—struck Houghton as pointless. Nonetheless, the day finally came when he went up to the Hill, was sworn to tell the truth and then sat before the joint committee to tell as much as he knew.

"Mr. Houghton, why don't you give the committee an overview of what you know and how you came to know it," Sam Harper, the committee chairman, offered. He was the senior senator from Tennessee, a Democrat, and in his physical aspect and courtly demeanor so reminiscent of his namesake, Sam Ervin, that half a dozen veteran reporters would comment on it in their stories the following day.

"I'll do my best, Senator, but in a few cases, it will be a good bit easier to tell you what I know than it will be to tell you how I came to know it. My involvement began when André Kohl came to see me. That would be about mid-April. He had information that prompted me to go back in our files to the interrogation of certain ex-Gestapo officers in our custody at the close of World War II. What I found in one of the files disturbed me greatly. It suggested that someone within the American intelligence community had tampered with the file."

"Can you tell us whose file it was?" Harper asked.

"Kurt Hoepner's."

"The man known as the 'Executioner of Clermont-Ferrand'?"

"Correct."

"And what was it about that file that suggested tampering?"

"The name of a Gestapo informant had been blacked out."

"What did you do after making this discovery?"

"I paid a call on Virgil Craig."

"The same man who was killed in La Paz?"

"That's correct."

"And why did you see him?"

"He was the intelligence officer who had interrogated Hoepner following the war. It was his report that I read. I thought he might know something about the tampering."

"Did you suspect that he had done the tampering?"

"After I questioned him, yes."

"Did he admit it?"

"No. But my visit made him extremely uncomfortable. And

then a whole series of events led me to believe that he had informed a number of people about my visit."

"Can you tell the committee about these events?"

"Only in a general way. Any number of people became knowledgeable about my visit with Mr. Craig within days and even hours."

"What kinds of people?"

"Again, I can tell you only in a general way. They were people of sufficient importance to lead me to believe, first, that Mr. Craig had contacts in very high places, second, that these places were both in and outside of the United States and, third, that these people did not want me to know what I had begun to find out."

"Did what you were finding out precipitate your trip to Europe?"

So they knew about that, Houghton thought. Was it conceivable that they knew about Camille Laurent? If not, they wouldn't find out from him.

"That's correct."

"And what was the purpose of your trip?"

"To meet with André Kohl." It was not a lie; meeting with André *had* been the major purpose of the trip.

Harper frowned. "Isn't it a little strange for the deputy director of the Central Intelligence Agency to fly three thousand miles to meet a reporter?"

"Not if the reporter has important information that the deputy director doesn't have."

"What was that information?"

"It had to do with Kurt Hoepner."

"Mr. Houghton, did you have a personal interest in this matter?"

Alarms went off in Houghton's head. Someone who knew something was feeding it to the committee. "What do you mean, Senator?" he said, his voice and manner unchanged as always.

"It just seems to me that you were going to enormous lengths to make a personal investigation of something that could have been handled by some other member of your agency."

"I didn't see it that way."

"Why? Because you had a personal stake in the matter? What was it?"

"I didn't say I had a personal stake in the matter."

"You haven't said that you didn't."

Houghton stared for a moment at the committee chairman. "Senator," he said then, "it's well known that I have worked in intelligence for my country ever since World War II. When it begins to appear that the branch of government to which I have given my professional life may include an element that presumes to take matters into its own hands irrespective of the laws of the land or the will of its people, I would say that, yes, most definitely, I have a personal stake in the matter."

Houghton knew he had scored. From that point on, Harper let him tell his story uninterrupted by questions: how he had reread the interrogation file on Hoepner, along with the files of numbers of other Nazis interrogated by Craig, all of them, like Hoepner, second-rank Gestapo men, not one of them tried for his crimes against humanity, all of them having escaped to South America; how he had then contacted a number of men who had worked, like Craig, in American intelligence in Europe after the war; how they had, to a man, told him a story that seemed consistent and plausible and held up under his questioning. It was their job to learn everything that they could about the Russians and their agents throughout Europe. If the Russians were to attempt to seize Western Europe, as was commonly believed at the time, the only force against them was the Americans. But the Americans knew almost nothing about the Russians. Who did? The Germans. And so the American intelligence officers, desperate for information, began to seek it from the very men they had been fighting less than a year before. Yes, these men were war criminals, but the assignment of the Americans was to obtain knowledge, not justice. And so it developed, little by little, that the American intelligence officers were forced to protect their sources, even when Allied prosecutors were looking for them. Eventually the Allies caught on, and the presence of Hoepner and the others became a political embarrassment. There was no way the Americans could surrender their sources; they now knew too much about their operation and could give compromising information to French intelligence, for example, which the Americans were sure was riddled with Communist agents. One day, the word came down: "Get rid of them." And so U.S. Army intelligence organized a "rat line" to get its sources out of Europe, moving them first to Austria and then to Italy, where they boarded boats for South America. And who had supervised their movement and subsequent resettlement? Virgil Craig.

"And then what, Mr. Houghton?" Sam Harper said.

"And then someone got the idea to put all that experience to use."

"Was that Virgil Craig?"

"Perhaps. But I have no proof that he was the instigator, and I would be surprised if he worked alone. I'm speculating now, but what I believe happened is that some people of like mind in the CIA and perhaps in the State Department, reacting to the rise of Fidel Castro in Cuba and his popularity throughout Latin America, saw this population that had been resettled as an asset that could be put to use."

"In what way?"

"To deal with the threat of Marxism wherever it emerged."

"Could you be more specific?"

"Well, let me tell you what happened. This—let's call it a subgroup within the government—arranged to have Virgil Craig transferred from Europe to South America in 1959. That, as you'll recall, was the year in which Castro overthrew Batista. This subgroup persuaded the CIA to form a dummy company, which was listed as a subsidiary of an American real estate development firm specializing in high density housing. Virgil Craig was the president of this subsidiary, but he remained on the CIA payroll. Craig was ideal. He knew Germany, he spoke German, he'd worked with these ex-Nazis, he'd arranged for their transfer to South America. He was the man to recruit the Nazis and help them set up an effective organization."

"To do what?"

"To do whatever they were hired to do. Basically, to terrorize or eliminate any elements deemed dangerous by those people whose retention of political and economic power seemed to be in the democratic interest."

Sam Harper exchanged glances with members of the committee,

many of whom were shaking their heads. "Mr. Houghton, I've heard some pretty cynical statements in my time on the Hill, but that statement of yours just about takes the prize."

"Senator, let me remind you that I'm giving you a history. I promise you that I find the ideas more abhorrent than you do. It's my family, as it were, that we're talking about. You must understand that everything I'm telling you was going on unofficially, without official knowledge. I, for example, knew absolutely nothing about it."

"I find that hard to believe."

Houghton's eyes narrowed almost imperceptibly. "You're just going to have to believe it, Senator. I have no way of proving it. I can only give you my word. We've known one another for twenty-five years. You know that I've never lied to you. If I haven't been able to tell you the truth, I haven't told you anything."

Harper shook his head, a sorrowful expression on his face. "Mr. Houghton, I apologize. I didn't mean to impugn your honesty. Our relationship has been exactly as you've described it. What I said was an involuntary response to your disclosure. It was simply a figure of speech. Let me clarify what I meant for the record. I find it hard to believe that an operation of this nature could be carried out without the knowledge of *someone* within the hierarchy of the CIA or the Department of State."

Houghton nodded. "So do I, Senator. I believe that someone must have known about it and sanctioned it. My problem—and I might say my intense embarrassment—is that I don't know who it was, or is."

"But you are trying to find out?"

"Senator, that is an understatement."

The investigation had not started well. A critical increment of impetus had been lost while the President tortured himself about how to handle the situation with the least amount of political damage. In that brief period before the President decided that he needed Charlie Houghton after all, whoever was running this secret network moved swiftly and efficiently to control the damage to itself. By the time the CIA's internal security division moved to seal Virgil Craig's house in Virginia, someone had already been there and cleaned it out. No one but the people who had done the job would know whether Craig had collected any incriminating materials or not.

Then Houghton had returned to Langley. His first act was to call in Billy Markham, his young, trim assistant with the crew cut, who looked as if he'd just finished a tour of duty with the Marines. "Billy, have you ever done a phone bill check?"

"No, sir."

"Nothing to it. Just a lot of hard work. Call the Virginia telephone company. Ask for copies of Virgil Craig's phone bills for the last year. When you get them, run a check on every number. The phone company will tell you who they belong to. If they give you any trouble on unlisted numbers, let me know, and we'll go to the top. Nobody knows about this but you and me, understood?"

"Yes, sir."

"And, Billy, don't call the phone company from here, or anywhere else in Langley. Come to think of it, don't even call them from home."

The moment Billy left, Houghton dialed the CIA's director of personnel. "Harry," he said, "I want files on ten extremely bright career men or women who joined the service in 1980 and are presently working at Langley. People not only bright, but highly motivated both in behalf of the country and the Company. And don't give me ten clones; I want all kinds." An hour later, the files were on his desk. Before day's end, he had selected his candidate, a woman of thirty named Madeline Martin, and that evening he called her from his home. He was pleased that she was neither astonished nor flustered by his call, and grateful that she should be willing to be at his Watergate apartment in an hour, regardless of what she might have been doing.

Madeline Martin, her file disclosed, had majored in political science at Cornell. Following her graduation, she had gone to the Thunderbird School in Arizona, where she had studied foreign trade and other business subjects, and taken a crash course in Portuguese, with the objective of joining an American company with a business subsidiary in Brazil. She received two offers before graduation, and a year later was living and working in São Paulo. The following year, she applied for employment in the Central

Intelligence Agency, listing as her reason the belief that unless progressives became involved in the workaday efforts to bring social justice to Latin America, the democratic cause in the area was lost. Her criticism of current policy, as well as its implementation by American diplomats, was scathing.

"What made you think that you could achieve your objectives through the Central Intelligence Agency?" Houghton asked Miss Martin a few minutes after she arrived. She was a compact, pleasant-looking woman whose understated tan gabardine suit only emphasized a well-proportioned and well-conditioned body. He had been surprised by her sedate appearance; it did not seem to match her forthright attitudes.

"Intelligence is what policy is supposed to be based on. Somebody's been telling the government what it's wanted to hear. I thought that there ought to be at least one voice crying, 'Bullshit.'"

Houghton nodded. "How much do you know about this secret network that's supposed to exist in our shop?"

"Nothing."

"Do you believe it exists?"

"I could nominate half a dozen candidates."

"Really. On what basis?"

"They think policy's too slow, too careful, that it'll all be over before we've formulated the right policy and passed the right laws. They think they know what to do."

"Do you think they're right?"

"I think they're crazy, dangerous, stupid and hopelessly uninformed. They don't know a damn thing about what the world's like out there."

In his mind, Houghton had set two rules for investigating his organization: trust no one, and use back channels. But if he was going to get anywhere, he would have to take some chances. "I've got a job for you, Miss Martin," he said. "It comes with some pretty grim conditions. First, you've got to accept it before I tell you what it is. Second, if you ever disclose its nature to anyone either deliberately or inadvertently, you're out of the agency. If you don't like those conditions, we can have a pleasant visit and you can go back to work tomorrow morning with absolutely nothing changed. Well, what do you think?"

"I can't wait."

"Good. I want your help in finding this secret network." He paused for a moment, watching for a reaction. There was none. "You don't seem surprised."

"I'm delighted, but I'm not surprised."

"Why not?"

"Why else would the deputy director, a man I've never seen, who inhabits a world I've never been in, call me out of the blue and ask me to come to his home—just as I'd finished watching the evening news, which had virtually nothing on it but stories about the CIA's secret network?"

Two days later, Madeline Martin was transferred to personnel, where she began a search of the records to discover which employees of the CIA had ever had contact with Virgil Craig, or had dealt with the kinds of operations in which he had been involved. In processing these records, she was also to look for agents and other personnel who had affiliations with ultraconservative political groups or who had otherwise expressed a fervent anti-Communist outlook. The man she was looking for, Houghton advised, would probably be in his fifties. Miss Martin worked without assistance, and reported directly to the deputy director, who instructed the director of personnel to refer any questions about her activities to him.

Three of Charles Houghton's most important lieutenants in the CIA—the deputy director of operations, the deputy director of intelligence evaluation, and the deputy director of administration —had been his friends and colleagues for more than thirty years. Not once in all that time had it occurred to him that any of the three might at any time have operated at cross purposes to his. Now that he had been compelled to think about it, the very idea sickened him. And yet, operating on the premise that everyone was suspect, he had to accept that even these men, to whom only weeks before he would have entrusted his life, could be involved.

"I don't have to tell you what a threat this whole affair is to the agency," Houghton began as the three men settled into chairs around the conference table in his office. To his left was Tom Haseltine, who was in charge of intelligence evaluation. To his right was Harry Coffee, who ran operations. George Stone, the director of administration, was on Coffee's right. All three men were in their late fifties and looked as though they might have come off the same campus thirty-five years before. To judge by their speech and their dress, the campus would have been part of the Ivy League, a suspicion reinforced by the knowledge that both the Foreign Service and the CIA were looked upon in the forties and fifties as appendages of the eastern Establishment. Physically, as well, they bore a remarkable similarity. All were lean and approximately six feet tall, had the ruddy coloring of joggers and wore their hair, or what was left of it, short.

"That's too bad," Haseltine said, "because I've got to believe we're dealing with a very tight little operation."

"Tumors start out pretty small," Stone said.

"What do we know for sure?" Coffee said, looking at Houghton.

"We know that whoever it was knew absolutely every move I made from the time I went out to see Virgil Craig, including the fact that my daughter was helping André Kohl in Paris. That's why the President fired me. He told the director that if I couldn't control my daughter, I wasn't fit to run the CIA." He waited until the others had finished laughing, then went on. "The last thing we know is that the head of this network is working with people in other services. No question about a French connection. That's how he found out about Meredith helping André."

"What the hell *was* she doing, Charlie?" Haseltine asked.

Houghton shook his head. "Can't do it, Tom. I gave Kohl my word."

The statement had been as fast and without thought as a reflex, and yet it had been historical. Never, not once, no matter what the situation, had any of the four men in this room held anything back from one another, or shaded the truth. For all the years that they had worked together, an understanding had existed between them that informed all of their discourse: Secrets were what they kept from the outside world and shared with one another. Now, with a single statement, Houghton had demolished that unverbalized bond.

There followed an uncomfortable silence, in which none of his three lieutenants would look at him. Finally, Coffee said, "Well, I hope *you're* talking to him, Charlie. You want to be sure he's told you everything he knows."

"Look, you guys," Houghton said, "there's only one person in this agency I don't suspect of being part of this secret network, and that's myself, because I *know* I'm not in it. But that doesn't mean you shouldn't suspect me. You should."

There was not much anyone could say after that. They talked on in desultory fashion for another few minutes. Then the three lieutenants left, leaving Houghton to reflect on the remark of one of them: "Tumors start out pretty small."

5

On the eleventh day of their honeymoon, a familiar feeling over-
came André. It was a desire for action, to be once again in the
center of events. He always experienced the same feeling at the
same time and under the same circumstances—at the halfway
point of a vacation. Motion had been his narcotic for so long that
remaining in one place for any length of time was equivalent to a
withdrawal. The great question mark of the one-year leave of absence he'd taken from USBC to practice the piano—the leave
aborted by Shlomo Glaser's tip about Camille Laurent—had been
whether André would be able to "attach his seat," as he'd put it at
the time, to a piano bench in a village in Normandy three hours
from the nearest international airport.

This time, of course, there was more to the feeling than a craving for motion. It was a craving for information, which, although
he had never thought of it before, had been as great a narcotic as
motion. Motion, after all, simply led him to information; it was in
pursuit of information that he moved. Now he had neither narcotic to sustain him; he was not only immobilized, but cut off.
Even that he might have overcome, were it not for the nature of
the information. Surely, Houghton had learned something by now
about the identity of the assassins, and perhaps who had hired
them. No other word could convey what André felt; he *craved* to
know.

Ever since their arrival, he'd been eyeing the telephone, fighting
off an escalating desire to pick it up. With one call he could get

reconnected to the world. He would also destroy the cocoon in which he and Meredith had managed to envelop their honeymoon. For ten days, it had been a standoff. On the eleventh day, he called.

"They're from a group we never heard of," Houghton told him. "They call themselves 'The Popular Front of the Arab World.' We think the group may have been invented for the job, but we have no way to prove that or disprove it. We know that they traveled on Jordanian passports, and that the passports were phony. We checked with the Jordanians. They said the passports were part of a group of a hundred blank passports that had been stolen from the Foreign Office several months ago. All of the passports were numbered, and the passports of our boys fit those numbers. We know that our boys started out from Damascus, and that their last stop before coming to Paris was Frankfurt. They had a four-hour stopover, although they could have made a much better connection, which ties in with their story that they had been instructed to meet someone in the transit lounge. In any case, they never left the airport. We're reasonably certain that they had a meeting in the transit hall with a West German, in which money was exchanged."

"Ah ha."

"Once we got his name, we did some checking and found out that the same West German had been in Damascus ten days before."

"Well, that's it, then."

"Could be. They say he gave them a hundred thousand Deutschmarks at the Frankfurt airport, which is entirely possible, because ninety-six thousand Deutschmarks were found in their room at the Ritz. They said they were to receive another hundred thousand Deutschmarks on completion of the job."

"Where'd you get the information?"

"From your friend Pierre Gauthier."

"He's no friend of mine."

"I gather you inspired him."

André shivered involuntarily. There was no denying the truth of what Houghton had said; he had undoubtedly inspired Gauthier, to what acts he preferred not to know. What else was he capable of in pursuit of his own survival? "Did Gauthier inspire them to tell him who they were working for?" he asked at last.

"He did. They said a man named Khalel el Hassan."

"Never heard of him."

"Neither have we, which is why we suspect the group was invented for the job."

"And what sort of explanation did Khalel el Hassan give them for going to Paris to kill a man?"

"That you were an enemy of the Arab nations."

A sudden tremor passed through André. "That's ridiculous. And that's all the explanation they needed?"

"That's all."

For a moment André couldn't speak. Then he said, "Who's the German?"

"His name is Alex Eichmann. No relation, but apparently a great admirer. He has a long history of right-wing associations. Interestingly enough, he was in Munich during the 1972 Olympics when the Arabs seized the Israeli athletes."

"You think there's a connection?"

"We've always wondered how the Arabs got into Germany. Someone had to have helped them."

"How'd you identify Eichmann?"

"We asked some of our West German colleagues to make a check of arriving and departing passengers during the period when the Arabs were in the airport. Then we gave the list to the Israelis. They came up with the Munich connection."

"Did the West Germans pick him up?"

"Yes, but they had to release him. They had nothing to hold him on."

"Too bad."

"Not a wipeout, however."

"Did Eichmann have any connection to Hoepner or any of the other Nazis in South America?"

"Nothing direct that we know of, but we're working on it."

"I guess the big question is whose money it was. Was it Eichmann's, or was he fronting?"

"We're working on that, too."

"Any theories?"

"I don't want to disappoint you, André, but I doubt if it's that simple."

"Meaning that you still don't know who wanted me killed."

He could hear Houghton sigh. "I'm afraid that's true." There was a brief silence. "How's Meredith?"

"I'll let her tell you," André said. He motioned to Meredith, who had been seated in the living room, listening in silence. When she took the phone, André walked out to the south veranda and watched the Caribbean. It was eleven o'clock; the last fishing vessels were returning for the day to the marina west of Casa de Campo. André watched them for a moment, trying to evaluate what Houghton had told him. It seemed almost certain now that Germans had been behind the plot to kill him. He wasn't surprised; they'd been the most natural suspects. Yet the knowledge gave him no comfort; there was too much that he still didn't know. Who, exactly, were these Germans? Would they try again? And what should he do in the meanwhile? Did he really have any options?

"Don't tell me. Let me guess. We're to stay here indefinitely," André said to Meredith when she joined him on the terrace.

"He didn't use that word but, yes, he wants us to stay put. Incidentally, he wasn't too happy when I told him we were golfing."

"He really doesn't have to worry. There's no way that a terrorist could get in here."

"That's what I told him. But you know Daddy."

Another week passed, a week of more golf, and long walks at sunset along the beach—it was a measure of André's increasing fitness that he would want to walk after golfing—heavenly meals and, each evening without fail, at least an hour of lovemaking. That had become a fitness event, as well; by now, André was convinced that an absence of stimulus was far more responsible than aging for a diminishing of desire. With Meredith, he was as eager as he could ever remember being, and he had the added advantage of the staying power of an older, experienced man. He did not believe she was trying to make him feel good when she told him he made her happy.

That she made him happy was undoubted. She produced in him a zest for living unlike anything he'd ever felt. Without benefit of words, she persuaded him that chronological age meant virtually nothing if one felt young in heart. Physical acts he would have scoffed at months before seemed suddenly within his power. One day he even accompanied her on her ritual morning jog.

Feeling as he did, and expressing it in every way that he could, he was surprised, therefore, when she asked him late one evening how he could have given up his dream life in Paris. They were in a deserted bar at the hotel, having decided spontaneously to go for a walk in the light of a full moon. Their walk had taken them to the main building of the resort, which until now they'd scrupulously avoided. Seeing that the bar was empty of all save the bartender and that it also had a piano, they'd ventured inside, and now André was playing softly, a mixture of classics and ballads. "Do you know that Peggy Lee song, 'Is That All There Is?'?" he said after a moment's reflection. "It's about a young girl who can't feel anything. Nothing impresses her, not fires or circuses or even, when she's older, the prospect of death. Well, in a way, that's what I was like in Paris. I had no more worlds to conquer or pleasures to experience. I felt that I was meeting myself coming around the corner. And then the Laurent story happened, and I was suddenly an agent of change rather than a reporter of change, and I felt alive for the first time in my life. When it was over, I realized that I'd been living a passive life, reacting to events rather than creating them." He played a series of random chords that carried his hands up the keyboard and then down again. "I likened what I'd been doing to the difference between a composer and a performer. The performer plays the composer's works. He interprets but doesn't create. It's the composer who makes something out of nothing, something that didn't exist before he made it and would never have existed except for him. We all can't be composers. But it occurred to me that the only authentic way to live was to make something happen that wouldn't have happened except for you." He stopped playing and looked at Meredith. "If I could love you in a way that would make you love me, then I'd have created a love that wouldn't have otherwise existed. That meant a lot more to me than living comfortably in Paris."

For a moment, Meredith didn't speak. Then she said, "This is the place where I normally make a joke, but I seem to have forgotten my line."

They looked at one another in silence. Then André took Meredith's left hand, drew it to his lips and kissed it. "Now I'm really going to get schmaltzy," he said. He released her hand and, hardly taking his eyes from her, played his trademark piece, the "Moonlight Sonata," the one that had indeed—as Jacob Jones had put it—closed so many Parisian parties.

On the twentieth day of their stay, Meredith beat André for the first time. "Are you sure it doesn't bother you?" she asked as he toasted her that evening with champagne.

"Why should it?" he joked. "Now you'll have to give me strokes."

Meredith tried to make light of her accomplishment, perhaps thinking that he was more upset than he made out, but she could not conceal her pleasure. In the morning, she was ready to leave for the clubhouse half an hour before he was. They teed off at eleven o'clock. Meredith, playing the women's tees, invariably put her ball in the fairway; on the holes when André managed to hit a straight drive, their balls wound up nearly side by side. After seven holes, they were each five over par, meaning that if they continued to play as well they would wind up in the mid-eighties, an exceptional score for them both.

The eighth hole was a slight dogleg that ran along the ocean and took them almost to their house, where, as usual, they planned to stop for lunch. "If I sink that putt I may be too excited to eat," Meredith said, as she watched her approach shot land on the green and move close to the pin. André turned to smile at her just in time to see her frown and suddenly sink to the turf. He heard the muffled report at the same time he saw the wound open up in her chest and the foamy blood spurt from it. For an instant, he was too surprised to act, and in that instant, a sound passed his left ear. A second later, he fell on top of Meredith, shielding her body with his. At almost the same moment, he heard a loud ping, and felt his head explode, and then felt nothing at all.

6

The two caddies, Francisco and Domingo, ran for the house. They burst inside, where Luisa was just finishing the lunch and Carmen was setting the table. Their words were incoherent, but their wild eyes and frantic gestures conveyed the sense that something terrible had happened. Luisa began to cross herself; Carmen grabbed the telephone and called the security police.

The first car arrived, siren wailing, in less than two minutes, drove across the lawn and onto the golf course. Two policemen emerged with guns drawn. The driver took one look, then got back into the car to call for an ambulance. The other man crouched over the motionless forms of André and Meredith. But he was shaking so badly he could hardly hold his gun, and after staring at the bloodied bodies for a moment, he turned his face and threw up.

The bullet that hit Meredith had cut through her chest to her lung, and each breath she took sucked air through the hole in her chest. Although she was conscious, she did not know what had happened to her. She knew only that each time she inhaled, she heard a gurgling, wheezing sound, and that for some reason André had fallen on top of her and wasn't moving. His body was very heavy. She was sure she would feel better if she could move him, but when she tried the pain in her chest intensified, as did the terrible sound. Then she heard a car and saw the two policemen above her, and an instant later she passed out.

It was another twenty minutes before an ambulance arrived.

The paramedics separated André and Meredith, and checked for vital signs. Satisfied that both were still alive, they immediately inserted intravenous lines in their arms and began to administer fluids. One of the paramedics ripped the plastic wrapper from a thick bandage and clamped it over Meredith's chest wound to try to stop the bleeding as well as to keep her from breathing dust directly into the wound. The other put a pressure bandage over the wound on André's head. But neither had dealt with bullet wounds before, and if they had ever been taught they had long since forgotten what else they were supposed to do.

By now the rest of the Casa de Campo security force had arrived, along with a good-sized crowd. Through the crowd came the manager of Casa de Campo, Jorge Rodriguez. He took one look at André and Meredith, still lying on the fairway, then turned and ran for the house. In another minute, he was talking to Mike Paul in New York.

Charles Houghton was eating lunch in his office at the CIA's Langley, Virginia, headquarters when Mike Paul called him. He reacted just as he had on hearing two months earlier that Meredith had been kidnapped: with utter calm. He could not permit himself even a second of sorrow; there was too much to do.

Within a minute, he had Arleigh Dexter, the chief of naval operations, on the line. In another minute, Dexter had the information Houghton wanted: a Navy task force was on maneuvers less than a hundred miles from the Dominican Republic. Even as the two men were speaking, Dexter was ordering communication with the task force.

Ten minutes after Mike Paul's phone call, Houghton was in a helicopter en route to Andrews Air Force base for a flight to Santo Domingo.

The CH-46E "Sea Knight" helicopter, off the carrier USS *Coral Sea,* set down on the eighth fairway of the Teeth of the Dog golf course at Casa de Campo forty minutes later. A detachment of armed Marines jumped from the helicopter the moment its wheels touched the ground and set up a perimeter around the bodies. Four Navy corpsmen, carrying stretchers, and two Navy doctors followed the Marines out of the helicopter. "Out of the way!" one of the corpsmen screamed. Few in the crowd understood his words, but the message was clear.

One of the doctors examined André, the other Meredith. Then they looked at one another, and nodded. "Let's go," one of the doctors told the corpsmen. Seconds later, Meredith and André were on stretchers, and a minute later they were aboard the helicopter.

By the time the helicopter reached the Santo Domingo airport, eighty miles away, a U.S. Air Force DC-9 hospital plane, based in Puerto Rico, was already there, guarded by a detachment of Dominican Republic troops. The helicopter set down next to the plane, and the corpsmen transferred the two patients.

With the exception of its contours, the inside of a hospital plane looks exactly like a standard operating room: white walls, bright overhead lights, operating tables and trays with instruments laid alongside them, the room populated by a dozen doctors and nurses clad in green smocks. The moment André and Meredith were lifted onto the operating tables, they were given anesthetics, Meredith a much heavier one than André. Of the two, she was the more gravely injured. Superficially, the need seemed obvious—to remove the bullet from her lung and then repair the lung, and this the surgeons set about doing at once. But until more elaborate x-rays could be taken, there was no way of knowing whether that was the only problem. The bullet might have fragmented on hitting a bone, and a fragment could have lodged itself next to a major artery or, even worse, the spinal column. If such a fragment were to move, either now or at some future time, she could be paralyzed for life. Given that prospect, the surgeons ordered a heavy sedation for Meredith as soon as the operation ended.

André's head wound appeared to have been caused by a bullet fragment that had ricocheted off whatever the bullet had hit. The blow had knocked him out and given him a concussion. There would be no telling whether it had also produced some brain damage until they could hear him talk and watch him move, and could perform a CAT scan once they got him to a hospital. In the meanwhile, there was nothing to do but make certain the wound was clean, then sew it.

By the time the surgeons finished, Houghton had arrived from Andrews Air Force Base, and been lifted into the hospital plane. The moment the door slammed shut, the big DC-9 began rolling to the takeoff runway. In minutes, they were airborne, en route to Washington.

"She's doing fine," one of the surgeons told Houghton, "but she won't wake up for a while." He explained the purpose of the heavy sedation. Houghton nodded, then turned back to his daughter and rested his hand on hers. He could feel her pulse. Or was it his own he felt? Did it matter? Were they not commingled? Would his heart not stop beating if hers did? He was certain that it would, in spirit if not in fact. For almost three hours, he had sat alone with his thoughts in an Air Force jet as it sped him to Santo Domingo. In those hours, life had suddenly become exquisitely clear and simple. His own life, he saw, was near its useful end. If he was to extend himself in time, it was through his daughter. If she lived, it would be his job to ensure her survival.

There was no longer any question that the present circumstances of her life were unacceptable. The only question remaining was how to change them. As he sat, his hand still covering hers, he sorted through his options. When he had made his choice, he pushed himself to his feet and lurched forward on his canes until he was next to André.

André had awakened half an hour before, while the plane was still on the ground. He saw a nurse in green at the foot of the gurney, making adjustments on an instrument. He did not recognize the instrument, and for another moment he did not comprehend the surroundings. The scene was unconnected to anything else in his life.

And then, suddenly, it was. "Where's my wife?" he said.

The nurse looked at him and smiled. "About twenty feet away. She's doin' fine." She came to him. "How you feelin'?"

"My head hurts."

"I'll bet it does."

As the plane began to taxi to the runway, she told him as much as she knew about what had happened. Only when she'd finished reassuring him about Meredith did he permit himself to doze, but the motion of the airplane once they were airborne, coupled with the lingering effects of the anesthetic, made him feel as if he were in a boat, riding up and down on wave after wave of guilt. For the second time in as many months, he had jeopardized the life of the woman he loved. His conduct might well be faultless—he'd opposed the marriage, she'd insisted—but the responsibility was his. Now, sensing another presence, he opened his eyes and saw Houghton. The sight of his father-in-law staring grimly at him snapped his mind to attention. "I'm so sorry," he said.

Houghton nodded in acknowledgment of André's apology, but did not otherwise comment. "Do you feel like talking?" he asked.

"Yes."

"Did you see anything?"

"No."

"The Dominicans caught the terrorists."

"Arabs?"

"Yes."

"Sent by Khalel el Hassan?"

"Yes."

"How'd they get in?"

"Boat."

"Of course," André said. How stupid, he thought. Of course they could get in by boat.

"They rented a boat at the marina, and ran it onto the beach just below your house. Then they apparently wedged themselves into the rocks at the end of the beach, and waited for you to show."

"They knew where I'd be?"

"It would seem so."

André was silent for at least a minute. "You know more about this sort of thing than I do," he said then, "but doesn't it seem that there's something more involved than revenge?"

"Go on."

"If revenge alone were the motive, whoever's trying to kill me would wait until I were someplace more convenient and less costly to get to."

"What other motive is there?"

73

"Maybe somebody thinks I know something that I'm not supposed to know."

"Do you?"

"If I do, I'm damned if I know what it is."

They stared at one another in silence. "Whatever the reason," Houghton said then, "and whoever's behind it, he is very determined. I have to tell you that when a killer is unknown and his target is unprotected, the killer will eventually succeed."

André stared at Houghton, trying to find the least measure of hope in his eyes. There was none. "Go on," he said at last.

"If they could find you here they could find you anywhere. There's no way in the world that we or anyone else can protect you. André Kohl is a dead man."

As groggy as he was, and as much pain as he was feeling, André could not help but note Houghton's curious reference to him in the third person. "I think you're trying to say something but haven't really said it."

Houghton stared at him, unblinking, not a trace of emotion on his face. "For you to understand what I'm about to say, you've got to accept that it's only a matter of time before they kill you. Do you accept that?"

"Barring a miracle, yes."

"There won't be any miracles. There's only one way you can save yourself."

"And that is?"

"To let André Kohl die."

As their plane flew north, Houghton made an argument so incredible that at first André wouldn't even consider it: To save himself, he must assume a new identity. This was the perfect time, and perhaps the only time, for him to do that. On landing, André would be spirited not to an Air Force hospital, but to one used by the CIA. There he would "die." Two days later, there would be a memorial service for André Kohl, whose body would have been cremated. Over the next several months, he would be prepared for another life. His face would be remodeled and his body remade, through diet, exercise and surgery, into that of a much younger

74

man. He would be trained to alter his voice and manner and given an entirely new identity.

"And then what?" André said. "What will I do?"

"Whatever you like. If you need our help, we'll set you up."

"There's only one reason I don't dismiss the idea is madness, and that's Meredith."

"I'm sure that's true. I counted on it."

"What you're really saying is that Meredith will be in danger as long as I am."

"You can make that judgment for yourself."

"What if I left her?"

"You know she'd never permit that. She'd insist on being with you."

It took several moments for the full impact of what Houghton had just said to register. "But you'd tell her, wouldn't you?"

"No. Same problem. She'd insist on being with you—and then it wouldn't work. Her picture's been broadcast and printed all over the world. There's only one way to make it work, and that's to cut it clean."

"Christ, that's so cruel."

"If you've got a better solution, I'd be happy to hear it."

He had none, and he knew it. Houghton's solution was madness, but a solution. If he didn't pursue it, what would he do? There was only one possible outcome: death. Perhaps next week, perhaps next year. But each day that he lived would be a hostage to the possibility that a shot or an explosion would suddenly kill him. He would never be able to stand with comfort next to a window without wondering if someone was out there, seated in a car, or standing across the street, waiting for exactly such a moment when he would unwittingly make himself a target. He would never be able to open the door to his apartment or house without wondering if it had been wired. He could never start a car without wondering whether a turn of the ignition would detonate an explosion. He could never go to a restaurant or a theater or a racetrack without fearing an ambush. In most of those scenarios, Meredith would die with him.

Everything that had happened to him since Shlomo Glaser's telephone call three months before had led inexorably to this time and place and condition. For just a moment longer he held himself from the acknowledgment he knew that he must make, feeling, he was certain, like a man who is about to jump from a bridge. Perhaps he had figured it wrong, and there was hope, after all. But there was none, and he knew it, and now he had to tell himself: Life as he had known it was over.

There arose in him then an anger so profound it exceeded anything he'd ever felt. For exposing an international network of fascists *this* was his reward—to never again be with his wife, his children, his friends? How could any Great Design encompass anything so cruel and manifestly unjust? As weak as he was and as much in turmoil, he was seized by an overpowering desire to create his own justice.

"How soon do you need my answer?" he asked then.

"Right away. If you agree, I'll have to radio ahead."

"I need ten minutes alone."

Without a word, Houghton struggled to his feet and swung away on his canes.

For the next ten minutes, André thought, not about the past because that truly was irrevocable, not even about the present because the past controlled its conditions. What he thought about was the future, and the minimum conditions he would expect from it in order to make it worthwhile. When he had finished thinking, his list was very small.

"There are only three things I want," he said when Houghton returned. "The first is to survive. The second is to find out who's trying to kill me, and deal with him. And the third is to be reunited with Meredith. I know you'll help me with the first two. How do you feel about the third?"

Houghton stared at André, his face as always void of emotions. "I can't make any commitments," he said.

"You'll have to, or I won't do it. Look, I know you'd prefer to have me out of her life. But I'm in her life by her choice. I love her. I will never again do anything that could hurt her. I want your promise that if this makeover is so successful that no one knows who I am, you won't stand between us."

Houghton was silent. "It would be better my way."

"For you. Not for me."

76

"Then you must promise me to let me decide when it's safe."

"I'd be crazy to do that. What I will promise is that I won't reveal myself to Meredith until I'm certain beyond doubt that it won't put her in danger."

For at least ten seconds, the only sound was the steady hum of the jet engines. "We'll just have to trust one another, won't we?" Houghton said at last.

"A very great deal." André waited. "Well?"

"All right. You have my word. Now I've got to get to work."

Houghton turned and made his way forward, toward the pilot's cabin. Watching him, André felt a sudden, desperate urge to cry out, "No! Stop!" But he fought it down. It's over, he told himself. André Kohl is history.

7

Mike Paul, USBC's president of network news, was an intensely physical man. The restlessness contained in his short but powerful body expressed itself with movement at the slightest provocation. An idea could provoke such movement, sending him pacing around his spacious, eighteenth-floor office, its walls covered with awards. Frustration—as often a consequence of inaction as the inability to gain his objectives—could produce physical expression, as well. In such cases, Mike would drop to the floor and do fifty of the two hundred push-ups he managed each day, or a hundred of the five hundred daily repetitions of various stomach exercises.

The one event that would catapult him from his chair, no matter how often it happened, was the beep-beep-beep signal from the computer in his office, which told him that a news bulletin was about to move. In seconds he would be at the terminal, punching the button that would bring the bulletin onto the screen. Most of the time, the bulletins required no response from him; his deputies, Charles van Damt and Saul Geffin, would be reading the same information and doing what was necessary. But every so often the signal heralded a major breaking story, and on those occasions Mike took charge himself, deploying a significant segment of his staff to cover, process and prepare the story for broadcast. Running a network news operation with bureaus throughout the United States and abroad and a nucleus in New York was a major enterprise characterized by enormous pressures and irregular hours. It was Mike's conviction that one had to be physically fit to do the work; the more fit one was, the better he would do it. Thus his early morning runs around the reservoir in Central Park and the weight-lifting in the gym of his co-op apartment building, in addition to what he did in the office. As a consequence, he almost always radiated good health.

But when he arrived at his desk the morning after André and Meredith had been shot, he looked as haggard as a man fighting a battle against serious illness. Yesterday's news had cost him dearly. He was the man who had wooed André Kohl away from print journalism and into television. It was under his guidance that André's career had prospered. In the process, a bond had formed between them. They were more than colleagues, more, even, than friends. They were brothers—or so, at least, Mike felt. André didn't acknowledge his feelings publicly or even, Mike suspected, to himself. But Mike knew they were there.

It was this bond between them that had compounded Mike's concern ever since the first attempt on André's life. André had not wanted to take on the Camille Laurent story, preferring to remain on the just-begun year's leave of absence he had taken to attempt to regain some of the prowess he'd possessed as a child piano prodigy. It was Mike who had coaxed him into checking out the story on the grounds that no one else on the staff could do it. It was true; Europe—France, in particular—was André's turf. As the chief of network news, it was Mike's job not only to cover the news in the most comprehensive way, but to beat the other networks; to have done less would have been irresponsible. (How ironic that the story they'd used hadn't dealt with Laurent at all, but rather with the fallout from that investigation, the discovery that American intelligence had ferried Nazi war criminals to Latin America following World War II, and later used them, in the name of anticommunism, to repress any and all progressive movements.) There was no question in Mike's mind that the story would win at least half a dozen new plaques for his wall. There was no doubt that the enterprise had already covered both André and the network with honor whether it won awards or not. What Mike had been unable to shake since the assassination attempt at the Ritz was the realization that he had intervened in another man's life to that man's potential detriment. That the man was one for whom he felt a brother's love made the realization all the more difficult to live with.

And now André was wounded, along with his new wife. No one could possibly blame him, Mike knew, yet he might live the rest of his life with André's and Meredith's blood on his hands. And what would happen to them now?

The beeper on the computer began to sound even as Mike asked himself the question. It was, he would recall much later to his grieving colleagues, one of those memorably terrible collisions of negative thought and dire event.

BULLETIN

WASHINGTON—André Kohl, wounded yesterday in an attack by terrorists at the Dominican Republic resort where he was honeymooning, died this morning at a suburban hospital after being rushed to the U.S. for treatment.

"Oh, no, no," Mike whispered. He closed his eyes and gripped the computer. He grew dizzy, and for several seconds could actually feel the blood draining from his head. Then he went to his desk, and said into his intercom, "Get Jeff and Gordon up here, and tell Chuck and Saul to come, too." Behind his desk was a table, and under the table a safe. He bent down, opened the safe and extracted a large manila envelope. Then he began to pace furiously as he waited for his men.

Jeff Grissom was the director of special events for network news. Gordon Sobol was the executive producer of the USBC evening news. They would have learned of André's death at the same moment that Mike had, as would Van Damt and Geffin; he was grateful, at least, that he wouldn't have to tell them.

All four men arrived together in less than two minutes. The heaviness in their faces confirmed that they knew.

Mike started to speak, and then stopped, undone by a sudden rush of emotion.

"I'm not sure I'm going to be able to say this all at once," he began, and then had to stop again. He took several deep breaths, trying to regain control. He began to pace the room more rapidly than he ever had. "Okay," he said, "let's lead the evening news with André. Three, four minutes, whatever you need to do it right.

About a minute on the shooting and his death, a minute on André's career, capped by the CIA-Nazi exposé that undoubtedly led to the attack, then say that André Kohl's greatest story was one he couldn't tell, and then another minute or two on this, ending with a tease for a special on André at ten o'clock tonight." With that he slid the envelope across his desk to Sobol.

Sobol frowned. "What is it?"

"It's the script of a story André wrote about Camille Laurent. He made a deal with Laurent not to broadcast the story if Laurent would refuse to take office. That's why André resigned. He felt he couldn't suppress a story and keep his job."

Their faces betrayed the surprise and pique they felt at not having been let in on the secret. Watching them, Mike knew that he had to say something. "I couldn't tell you. André wouldn't let me."

"But why didn't he just do the story and force Laurent out?" Van Damt said.

"Because he'd found out that the Russians had set him up. They were the ones who originally found out that Laurent had worked for the Gestapo. They didn't want him elected president of France. They knew that no one would believe them if they broke the story. So they went through an elaborate charade to plant the story on the Israelis in the expectation that the Israelis would take it to André. They were right. That's exactly what happened. Checking out Laurent led André to Kurt Hoepner in Bolivia, and that led, in turn, to the story of how Hoepner got to Bolivia after the war with our help, and how our crazies had used him, and the whole business about the secret network. But it all began with a tip from the Mossad that Camille Laurent had been a Gestapo agent."

"And it's all in here?" Sobol said.

"Yes."

"I still don't get it," Saul Geffin said. "So the Russians set him up. A story's a story, if it checks out."

"André didn't want to be used by the Russians. What the Russians wanted was not only to keep Laurent from winning the election but to discredit the conservative movement. André felt that's what would happen if he broke the story—which, in his mind, would have made him a tool of the Russians. But he didn't want a

Nazi collaborator to be president of France any more than the Russians did. So he did it his way."

"And André's death removes our obligation to Laurent?" Geffin asked.

"It's more than that. When André sent me the story, along with a copy of the dossier incriminating Laurent, he sent a covering letter stating that if he was injured or killed in a manner that looked like foul play, or if he disappeared, I was to broadcast the story."

"But doesn't that defeat his purpose?"

"It would have if the election hadn't been held. But it has been, and the French have a new president."

"Hang on a minute," Gordon Sobol said. The others turned to him. In his hands were the contents of the envelope Mike had given him. "André's case against Laurent rests on the Gestapo dossier he found in Moscow. What we've got here is a *copy* of that dossier. We can't indict a man with a copy. Did he ever get the original?"

"Yes. He got it out of France and put it in a safe at the Connaught in London. Then he went back to Paris and gave the key to Tom Shaw along with a letter instructing him to get the dossier and bring it to New York if anything violent happened to him. I'll be very surprised if Tom doesn't walk in here within the hour. But just to be safe, let's call Paris and see where he is."

He picked up his phone and dialed direct. In less than a minute he had the word: the bureau's most junior correspondent had taken the first flight to London that morning, and then boarded the Concorde for New York.

Mike hung up, and announced the news with grim satisfaction.

"It sounds like André thought of everything except how to stay alive," Van Damt said. The others nodded their agreement.

The noise of the traffic at Columbus Circle filtered into the room as each man spent time with his thoughts. At last, Mike spoke. "Jeff, let's call that special 'André Kohl: The Untold Story.' We'll preempt the 'News Magazine' at ten o'clock. Start with the event. Then go to a straight obit, ending with how he uncovered the Nazis and the secret network. Then the assassination attempt at the Ritz, and then yesterday's shooting. Tease at the first break with the untold story. Use that line, 'André Kohl's greatest story was one he couldn't tell.' Break for commercial. Come back. Anchorman holds up the dossier, says, 'This was left to be opened only in the event of an attack on André. The contents will explode in France and reverberate through the rest of the Western world.' Tell the story in segments two and three. Then do a two-way with the highest French Government official you can get, the Foreign Minister, maybe even the Prime Minister or the President. Try for a two-way in Moscow with the Foreign Office spokesman. Why did the Russians believe they needed to plant the story?"

"They'll never answer," Geffin said.

"Doesn't matter. The question's the answer." Mike was silent for a moment, getting his thoughts back on track. "Okay, Paris, Moscow, how about a two-way with a friendly ally, the Brits? And then Washington. Houghton?"

"It'd be great, but he'd never do it," Geffin said.

"For Christ sake, André was his son-in-law."

"But he's still running the CIA."

"Okay, the best you can get. Maybe someone who was in the OSS during the war. But somebody in Washington. Finally, update the investigation, speculating on why Arabs were hired for the job —were they contract players?—and close with André Kohl's last words."

"Which are?" Grissom asked.

"The letter he wrote me. Incidentally, Harrison should anchor. Will he be too tired after the evening news?"

"He can do it."

"Good."

His visitors rose, yet hesitated, as though waiting for some word that would send them on their way.

"There's one thing André would be pleased about," Mike said at last. "It'll be a helluva special."

The hospital to which André and Meredith had been taken following their arrival at Andrews Air Force Base was one the CIA had used for years to care for personnel who might not be able to reply with candor to a civilian doctor's questioning as to where they had been and how they'd acquired their medical problem. It was a private hospital thirty miles from Langley, Virginia, all of whose small staff had been cleared by the CIA, and whose experience had long since accustomed them to unusual decisions. The doctors, in particular, rationalized their conduct on the grounds that their actions undoubtedly contributed to the health and well-being of their patients. Describing the circumstances of André's death to reporters was a classic case in point; paradoxically, the doctors had been told that for André the charade was a matter of "life and death." No other explanation was needed.

So it was that André, seated once again in the living room of the Virginia farmhouse to which he'd been brought from Paris less than a month before, learned on his network's evening news broadcast, that his "death" had been the consequence of a cerebral hemorrhage, undoubtedly associated with the head wound he'd received two days before at Casa de Campo.

Whatever trauma the wound might have produced was nothing compared with what he experienced as he watched USBC news. That was his friend and colleague, Gregory Harrison, telling lies to 15 million viewers. Greg didn't know they were lies; he believed them to be truths. So did Mike Paul, Chuck van Damt, Saul Geffin, Gordon Sobol, and all the other men and women who had prepared this evening's broadcast. Only now did André comprehend the dimension of his deceit.

Deceit. There was no other word for it. His entire professional life had been dedicated to the revelation of truth; in one moment of weakness, he had approved the dissemination of a lie so overwhelming that it negated everything he'd ever done. Or so, at least, he felt as he watched and listened to the four minutes dedicated to the story of his life and death. Perhaps he might come to feel otherwise; at the moment he didn't see how he ever would. Here was Gregory Harrison announcing that at ten o'clock, the network would broadcast an hour special called, "André Kohl: The Untold Story." The deceit would go on and on, the false legend of André Kohl would grow, enlarged and enriched by the imaginations of friends and colleagues attempting to outdo one another in service to his memory.

How easily they had all been deceived. Why wouldn't they believe doctors who told them he was dead? It was clear to André that his friend Rafer Rothwell had been right. Rafer was a news-paperman, the kind they called a journeyman reporter. He'd worked for four metropolitan dailies in four different sections of the country, his way, he would explain, of seeing the United States. When André met him, Rafer had finally landed on the Washington *Post* as a reporter on its elite national news staff. A Southerner, divorced, without children, Rafer took his greatest delight in exposing those politicians and bureaucrats who made the mistake of not telling him the truth. "Never believe anybody about anything for any reason whatsoever," he told André one evening. "That's known as Rafer Rothwell's Maxim."

What lies had he unknowingly perpetrated in his time? André wondered. What sources had gulled him into reporting stories that served their interest but simply weren't true? He'd always been meticulous in his reporting, always questioned intently, then re-viewed the interview to see what he might not have covered or where his source might be leading him astray. He'd always gotten at least a second source for any controversial information. And yet, what good were second sources if they were part of a conspir-acy? Two doctors had confirmed his "death." The "untold story" of André Kohl, indeed. It was a story of deceit.

"Oh, my God," André said aloud, although there was no one in the room to hear him. He put his hands to his head in anguish. It had flashed into his brain what the "untold story" was: his script on Camille Laurent. Broadcasting that story violated his agree-ment with Laurent. Not technically, because he'd warned Laurent that the story would air if anything happened to him. But the assumption at the time had been that any violent acts against him would have been ordered by Laurent or his followers, and André was as certain as he could be that of all the people who might have wanted to kill him, Laurent was the least likely suspect. He had no interest in seeing the story made public. But now it would be, and there was nothing André could do. "Oh, God," he moaned again. Whoever had suggested that death was preferable to dishonor must have known something about the pain associated with shame.

He wondered if Meredith had recovered sufficiently to have been told, or whether she was still in intensive care. He was no longer worried about her recovery—Houghton himself had assured him that she was out of danger—but he prayed that her father would wait a few days, until she was stronger, to tell her the story.

Whatever pain she would feel would pass in time, he knew. It would, in effect, pass to him, to become part of his burden. The bottom line for him, and the only thought that saved him, was that he had done what he had to protect her. He made a silent vow, that someday, somehow, he would do something that might make up, in some way, for this awful event he had caused. It was the most amorphous thought imaginable, without specifics of any kind —just as amorphous as he was, a man with no name, no identity, no past, present or future, and a face that would soon be a stranger's.

For the second time in less than two months, a story by André Kohl led all news broadcasts and dominated the front pages of newspapers throughout the world. What made the story irresistible to editors was the knowledge that it was being told, in effect, from the grave. In France, especially, the story was a sensation— more so the second day than the first, after Camille Laurent's wife found his body. The general had put on his dress uniform, affixed all his medals, then put a bullet through his head.

A memorial service for André—whose remains, it was reported, had been cremated—was held in Washington three days after the announcement of his death. It was covered live by USBC, and taped by the other networks for broadcast on the evening news.

Meredith was still far too weak to attend, but Houghton was there, along with two hundred mourners whose ranks included Jacqueline Onassis—her first husband had been the subject of André's prizewinning biography—Senator Ted Kennedy and several other members of the Kennedy family; half a dozen other senators and as many former cabinet members; the entire executive staff of USBC News, led by Mike Paul; André's first wife, Katie, and her husband, John Morgan, who had come from California along with the children of her marriage to André, Gene, a stockbroker, and Paula, a reporter on the San Francisco *Chronicle*. Jacob Jones had flown from Paris on his private jet to attend the service, and Shlomo Glaser of the Mossad had come from Tel Aviv.

It fell to Mike to conduct the service for André, the lapsed Catholic and nonbeliever. There had been some sentiment in favor of retaining a minister, but to Mike that would have been solely cosmetic, not something André would have wanted. Since he could not discuss the matter with Meredith, he checked with Gene and Paula, who agreed with him. As the man who knew André best, he gave the principal eulogy, after other colleagues and friends had spoken.

"When our network was planning its special on André the day we received word of his death, I said to my colleagues that the one thing André would be pleased about was what a great special it would be. Anyone who knew him knew how much he loved a good story, particularly if he could cover it. Other than the obvious, what would most disappoint him about this story, I'm sure, is that someone else got the assignment."

The audience laughed quietly at Mike's jest, as they had at the reminiscences of the other speakers. By the time Mike had finished speaking, many of them had tears in their eyes, and as the organist played the "Moonlight Sonata" they began to cry openly. Then the mourners filed from the chapel, where they lingered to embrace old friends and exchange mutually consoling words. As the crowd began to drift away, Mike Paul approached Houghton.

"How's the investigation coming?" he asked.

"Slowly."

"We're extremely interested in knowing who ordered André killed. We don't think the Arabs did it on their own. We're offering a hundred-thousand-dollar reward for proof of who set them up."

"I don't think that'll do much good."

"What will?"

"A lot of hard work. We're giving it our best shot."

"Do you think a private investigator working full time might come up with something any faster than you would?"

"It's not impossible. Depends on who you get."

"I was hoping you might be able to suggest someone."

Houghton looked intently at Mike Paul. "There *is* someone who might be able to help you. He's very special. Makes a virtue of anonymity. We've used him ourselves, from time to time when we couldn't handle something officially. The problem is he's on something right now and won't be off for at least three months. If nothing's been resolved by the time he's free, I'll give you a call."

They shook hands. Then Houghton turned and swung on his canes to his car for the ride back to Langley. Only when he had settled into the back seat did he realize how tired he was and what a strain the last two hours had been. Uncounted times he had caught mourners staring at him in perplexity, as though they could not interpret his presence, and did not know how to feel about him. Should they sympathize with him as the father of André's wife? Should they be angry with him for not protecting André? Should they blame him for André's murder, since it was a consequence, ultimately, of wrongdoing within the CIA?

But even without such stares, it would have been an uncomfortable time for Houghton. No deception he had ever perpetrated in all his years in intelligence remotely compared with this one. He had conceived it out of a conviction that it was the only solution. He had meant it when he'd told André that there was no way he could protect him. What greater proof did André need than what had happened?

By his sacrifice—the only word that described what André had done—he had stopped the danger to Meredith, or at least alleviated it considerably. For that, Houghton owed him an incalculable debt that could never fully be repaid. At the very least, he intended to make certain that André's life would pass in as agreeable a manner as possible—in whatever form it took.

And yet, one thought kept repeating itself to Houghton: how convenient it would be if André could see the possibilities available to a man who, knowing as much as he did, and with such a talent for amassing information, suddenly assumed another life.

8

The morning after the funeral, Shlomo Glaser had breakfast with Houghton at the CIA deputy director's apartment in the Watergate, the residential and commercial complex next to the Potomac River. As long as the two men had known one another, and as often as they had cooperated on intelligence matters affecting their mutual security, it was the first time either had been in the other's home, a circumstance that said a great deal about their relationship. Each held the other in the highest respect, but they were not friends. Neither mistrusted the other, yet both knew that duty might require them at any time to be less than forthcoming at best, and devious at worst.

In honor of his guest, Houghton had arranged for a breakfast of soft-boiled eggs, smoked fish, cheeses, tomatoes, cucumbers, dark breads and coffee. That was the traditional breakfast served at the kibbutz near the Sea of Galilee where Shlomo had grown up; there, work began at daylight, and the first meal of the day was not until several hours later, when the sun made it uncomfortable to continue. When Shlomo, a short, stocky, powerfully built man in his early sixties whose cherubic features made him look ten years younger, saw the spread on Houghton's table, he could not repress a smile.

"I hope you approve," Houghton said as they sat.

"I approve not only of the menu and your thoughtfulness, but the thoroughness of your research."

Houghton nodded, but didn't smile. He was too intent on his

purpose, and began the inquiry that had brought them together before Shlomo had cracked his first egg. "It would help me a great deal if you could tell me what your people showed André in La Paz when he went to them for help. He never would tell me."

Shlomo shook his head, and concentrated on his egg. "I had a feeling you were going to ask me that. A very difficult question. Officially, I shouldn't answer."

"Will it make it any easier for you if I tell you what I think you showed him?"

"It might."

"Will you be able to tell me if I'm right?"

"That depends on how well you guess."

"It's extremely important, Shlomo. I have to proceed on the assumption that the attacks on André were related to his exposure of the secret network within my organization."

"I understand."

"Then you can understand why it would help me to know what he learned. It could give me some leads."

"It could also make a great strain on relations between our countries."

"Whatever you can tell me will never be mentioned to anyone."

"How can you make such a promise?"

Houghton looked intently at Shlomo. His question had gone to the heart of their relationship. It implied that the Israeli could never make the same promise, given who he was. How then could Houghton do it? An answer was required that would move them to new ground in their dealings with one another, ground uninhabited by mistrust of even the most perfunctory kind. "Because André Kohl was my son-in-law. Because I'm still concerned for the safety of my daughter."

Shlomo looked away. When he turned back to Houghton, his look was transparent, so different from any he had ever given Houghton before that it might have come from another person. "All right," he said. "That I understand. For that you shouldn't guess. I will tell you the story, and you will understand why we are so reluctant, and why nothing has ever been said, and why I must ask you, as I asked André, to never ever mention this to anyone. Give me just a moment to finish this nice breakfast."

He finished his meal in a few minutes. The story took half an hour. It was no secret, he said, that the Israelis' search for ex-Nazis had been relentless since the formation of the Jewish state. The trail made by the Americans in spiriting ex-Nazis like Kurt Hoepner from Europe to South America in exchange for services rendered against the postwar Communist movement had been a broad one, easy to follow. Once these former Gestapo officers had relocated, their lives were readily monitored. Some thought had been given to kidnapping them, as had been done with Adolf Eich-mann, and taking them to Israel for trial, but that had been deemed too costly. Money was not at issue; the price was political support. Those were the years when Israel, finding itself virtually alone in the world, considered it prudent to seek friends. For this reason, the country had launched a program of assistance to Third World nations even while it was desperately in need of aid for its own development programs. The hope was that a country assisted by Israel would not vote against it in the United Nations. If Israel would go to such costly extremes to gain political allies, it followed that usurping the sovereignty of these countries in a manner that would cause a rupture in relations made no sense at all—except, of course, in the case of Eichmann, whose role in the extermination of the Jews had been so critical it had to be dealt with regardless of the cost. So, the Mossad had bided its time, in the meanwhile keeping tabs on all the Nazis who had been relocated by the Americans.

Imagine the agency's surprise, therefore, when it discovered that the Americans had organized the Germans into a paramilitary group for use in achieving "politically desirable" objectives.

"When did you first find this out?" Houghton asked.

"In the early sixties."

"Why in God's name didn't you tell us?"

"We did not want to be the ones to give you such embarrassing news."

"We would have gotten over our embarrassment."

Shlomo put his right hand out, palm down, and rocked it back and forth. "Maybe yes, maybe no. What we knew was not only embarrassing. It was the worst kind of revelation."

It was for this reason, Shlomo explained, that even he had been against telling André everything they knew about Kurt Hoepner when he had asked. Finally, after André had begged for whatever information they had in the hope that it might help him free Meredith from Hoepner, Shlomo personally had gone to the Prime Minister to obtain approval. Once he had it, he had thermofaxed to La Paz a copy of a report called "Kurt Hoepner: From Clermont-Ferrand to La Paz, Including 'Operation Detox.' "

"Was that the operation we supposedly ran to make certain the Communists didn't capture the French Resistance?" Houghton asked.

"Not supposedly. You ran it."

"I still find it hard to believe that we actually employed Hoepner during the war."

"Why do you find it difficult? I understand that Hoepner confessed it just before he was shot."

"That doesn't matter. It still seems incredible."

"Any more incredible than that you would use them in Latin America in the manner that you have?"

"There's one critical difference. We were at war during Operation Detox. Craig was paying off an enemy."

"Is a Nazi butcher any less an enemy because the shooting stops?"

"Officially, yes."

"Is he any less a monster?"

"Of course not." Houghton held up his hands. "Look, you're putting me in the position of defending something that horrifies me."

"I know you're not defending it," Shlomo said. "I understand what you're saying. What I don't understand, and never will, is how you Americans permit your obsession with the Communists to destroy your own values."

Houghton sighed. "Tell me why you wouldn't tell us."

"I have told you."

"It doesn't make sense."

Now Shlomo sighed. "Look, suppose we give you the report on Hoepner. Now you know that some of your people have been working in Latin America with ex-Nazis to repress progressive movements. There have even been murders of promising young radicals, murders performed by Hoepner's paramilitary organization but traceable to the Americans, who just happen to be present or former members of the CIA. You clean house. The word gets out, if not from you, from some bitter former agent who feels he's been unjustly fired, or from someone else within your organization who decides, for God knows what reason, that the story ought to be told. One way or another, the story leaks. The media develops it. You can't blame them. That's their job. But the United States is made to look terrible before the nations of the world. Who made the United States look terrible? The Israelis, that's who, the people whose very existence depends on the United States. That, my friend, is a poor way to show our gratitude. Who knows what backlash this could produce?"

Houghton drummed his fingers on the table. The information Shlomo had just given him satisfied him only in the sense of explaining what he hadn't understood. What made him even more restless than he had been was the possibility that there might be other secrets out there, secrets known by others but kept from the Americans on the same basis. He didn't expect a straight answer, but he had to ask the question. "Tell me," he said, "are we in for any more bad surprises?"

"From us?"

"Yes."

"I don't think so. Are we?"

Houghton took a deep breath. "I wish I knew, Shlomo. I just wish I knew."

Shlomo looked at Houghton with commiseration. "I'll make a suggestion. I'm sure you have your hands full with your internal investigation. Let us look into the murder of André. We're probably a little stronger than you are in the Arab department. And we would like to know ourselves who was behind it."

"You were close to André, weren't you?"

"He was a good friend. We worked well together. We just did it once too often." Shlomo faltered. "I feel responsible," he said then. "I was the one who brought him the Camille Laurent story."

Once more, Houghton was confronted with sorrow, as he had been so many times in the last several days. It was sorrow he had provoked by a subterfuge, no matter how justified that subterfuge had been. "Shlomo, I am as sure as I can be that André would not hold you responsible. He would not have had it any other way."

"I hope so," Shlomo said.

Houghton rose then to say good-bye to his guest. Steadying himself on his canes, he put out his hand. Shlomo shook it firmly. "A sad business," he said. "If I can be of any help, please let me know."

Houghton hesitated. "As a matter of fact, you could be. If you knew what was going on down there, you must have known the names of the Americans involved."

"Only Craig's. They were very careful."

"That's too bad."

Now Shlomo hesitated. "There *was* one suspect. I can't remember his name. It sticks in my mind that he worked out of Buenos Aires."

"If you can get the name, I'd be grateful."

"I'll see what I can do."

Madeline Martin, the young woman Houghton had enlisted to help him find the secret network, had been immersed in the company's personnel records for almost two months now, and had at last reduced an overwhelming task to manageable proportions. First, she had made an analysis of Virgil Craig's career, from college until his death: undergraduate studies at Amherst, majoring in history; graduate studies at Rutgers in German history; appointed to the faculty there after earning his Ph.D.; enlisted in U.S. Army the day after Pearl Harbor, at the age of thirty; gone to Officer Candidate School following basic training; commissioned a second lieutenant; recruited at once by the OSS; service in European sector; remained in Europe after the war, transferring to CIA following disbandment of OSS; stationed in Germany until 1959; moved to Latin America in 1959 to run a proprietary company of CIA, whose overt operation was joint development with indigenous firms; remained in Latin America until his retirement in 1976. It was a long trail, but clearly marked; her job was simply to follow it. Had Craig encountered Amherst classmates along the route? Colleagues from Rutgers? From the Army? And so forth, through the years. What impressed her immensely was a singular characteristic of Craig's that permeated virtually every evaluation of him in his record. The man was a loner. He had never married. He identified no family, nor did relatives ever appear. He made no close friendships. He lived by himself. His vacations were brief, and taken alone. His one abiding passion was his work, which he pursued incessantly. That characteristic was remarked upon by every one of his superiors, all of whom extolled his dedication and patriotism.

Cross-checking personnel records at each of Craig's posts, Madeline found no obvious connections between him and his colleagues—no hometown acquaintanceships, no old school ties, no colleagues from Amherst or Rutgers. But beginning in the early fifties, Craig's career did begin to intersect more or less regularly with a number of men his age or younger, many of whom were still in the agency, and the list grew with each passing year. How to determine which, if any, of these men were as committed in their anticommunism as Virgil Craig? Houghton himself had listed the criteria: participation in the same kinds of operations in which Craig had been involved; affiliations with ultraconservative political groups, or strong ideological affirmations at work. To these, Madeline added a few criteria of her own: a comparable intelligence; similar social patterns; and an abiding sense of duty.

Looking through these hundreds of dossiers, Madeline could only wonder at the vast variety of backgrounds from which members of the Company had come. If there was one characteristic they appeared to share, it was a taste for the unconventional. Their earliest evaluations contained references to prospective careers in business or law as "a waste." Almost all, conversely, expressed enthusiasm for politics and international relations. The same tastes and convictions showed up in their vocational and aptitude tests. The words most commonly used to describe what they were after were "excitement," "stimulation" and "intellectual challenge." In exchange, they were more than ready to accept a lower standard of living than they might obtain through more conventional careers in the private sector.

As she read through these life stories, Madeline could not help but feel a kinship; she'd felt the same things. Whatever else they might be, these men—all of them were men—were, in part, kindred spirits. At base, they all considered themselves servants of their country, soldiers in the war against a totalitarian ideology that threatened freedom and individual liberty throughout the world. The obverse of that, the principal side of the coin, was the desire to protect and promulgate the American way of life. At what point do the means to those ends become inimical to the ends themselves? And who was she to sit in judgment of men whose motivations were so similar to her own, and at least as principled?

Well, she'd been out there—only to Brazil, true enough, but so intensively there that she was certain she had located the point of diminishing returns. It was the point at which U.S. objectives prevailed over the aspirations of the host country. Do it our way, or we cut off aid. It simply didn't work. It always ended with a win-the-battle-lose-the-war result.

So, who were these men whose youthful evangelism now expressed itself as arrogance, either by word or deed? Had they ever been involved with Virgil Craig? And were they sufficiently well placed either geographically or within the Company to be of consequence?

When her work was finished, Madeline Martin had five names. Her choices were all tentative, of course, based on circumstantial evidence and subjective judgments. Each would have to be extensively checked. But at least she had some leads, and a gut feeling that one of these men was running the secret network within the CIA.

Madeline delivered her packet to Houghton at his Watergate apartment on a Saturday morning. He wanted to tear it open at once, but he did not want her there when he did, and civility required him to offer her a cup of coffee. Madeline poured the coffee herself, then asked if she might smoke.

"I don't remember you smoking the first time you came here," Houghton said.

"I wasn't. I'd stopped."

"And now you've started again. I'm sorry."

"No problem. I'll kick it in a couple of weeks."

"Do you have any vacation time coming?"

"No, but I'm planning to be ill."

Houghton smiled. "I wish you a speedy recovery."

She left a few minutes later. He opened the packet at once. There was a short covering note.

Dear Mr. Houghton:

I enclose the dossiers on five men who appear to fit your specifications. I've taken the liberty of summarizing their careers, and including a few subjective impressions.

Madeline Martin

The dossiers, with covering summaries, followed.

PHILIP LOOMIS—Current age: sixty-five. Brilliant college student. Recruited into OSS during World War II. Assigned to OSS office in Bern, Switzerland, coordinating relations with French Resistance. After war, returned to college for master's degree in international relations. Recruited into CIA in 1951. Served twice in Paris, first as CIA line officer in late fifties, then as station chief in early seventies. In Saigon 1966 to 1969, assigned to clandestine operations. Following second tour in Paris, returned to Langley in 1975. Assigned to the counterintelligence division. Presently heads one of the sections in that division. Contacts with Virgil Craig: Multiple contacts during World War II, mostly re French Resistance. Right-wing connections: While serving in Southeast Asia became close to group of CIA agents and military personnel with known far-right, fundamental, anticommunist views. Maintained contact with group after transfer to Paris, and continued contacts after return to Langley, despite departure or retirement of others from CIA and military.

CARL SANDERS—Current age: fifty-one. Son of a former United States ambassador to Chile. Born in that country. After father's tour ended, returned to U.S. with family. Returned to Latin America at age ten when father appointed ambassador to Peru. Became bilingual in Spanish. After college (University of Arizona, B.A., 1955) married daughter of a Peruvian senator. Recruited into CIA in 1961. First assignment, Operation Mongoose, undercover operation to destabilize Cuban Government. After Operation Mongoose, officially left CIA, but continued with Company under deep cover, setting up proprietary companies in Latin America used to fund CIA operations. Currently president of Banco Casa Grande in Buenos Aires, a proprietary company of CIA. Connection to Virgil

Craig: On trips to Washington, usually stayed in Craig's home. Right-wing connections: Extremely close relations with General Juan Perez Carlos, Chilean intelligence officer who helped bring General Pinochet to power. When visiting Chile, stayed in Perez home.

CHRISTOPHER SLOVOTKIN—Current age: fifty-six. Parents were Russians who emigrated to U.S. following Bolshevik Revolution and settled in New York City area. Attended city schools, graduated from New York University. Drafted into Army during Korean War. Attended OCS, commissioned second lieutenant, assigned to intelligence services. Recruited by CIA after discharge from Army. Assigned to Berlin office because of Russian-language proficiency. Specialized in counterespionage work, primarily against Soviet agents. Persuaded top KGB agent to defect to West. Next assignment, U.S. embassy in Sofia. Following that, station chief in Warsaw. Presently, chief, Soviet section, CIA, Langley. Connections to Virgil Craig: On several occasions retained Craig as consultant re counterespionage measures in Third World countries. Right-wing connections: Grew up in circle of hard-line Russian émigrés who organized anti-Soviet political clubs in New York City area, which attracted Russian and East European émigrés. Slovotkin a member of these clubs since college. Still active. Frequent speaker at major gatherings. Speeches profoundly anti-Soviet.

ERNEST MCDONALD—Current age: fifty-four. Born in San Francisco. Graduated from University of San Francisco in 1953. Attended Institute of Chinese Studies, Harvard University. Speaks and reads Chinese well, but not bilingual. Recruited into CIA immediately following graduation. Assigned to Hong Kong, where he remained for twelve years. Special assignments in Laos and Vietnam during Vietnam War. Returned to Langley in 1970. Assigned to Chinese section. In 1978 appointed national intelligence officer. Connections to Virgil Craig: On recommendation of Phil Loomis, hired Craig to write analysis section reports. Right-wing connections: Basic connection is to Loomis, with whom he served during temporary duty in Vietnam. Ran with same anticommunist group. Currently maintains contact with group through Loomis.

For Houghton, the first four dossiers contained few surprises. Had he been asked to make an impromptu list of ten likely suspects, the names of Loomis, Sanders, Slovotkin and McDonald would have been on it. They were all old-timers, all Cold Warriors.

The fifth name was Harry Coffee's.

For several minutes, Houghton stared at Madeline Martin's analysis of the director of operations' career, too disturbed to read it. Yes, he had told himself that everyone was suspect, but in truth he had excluded Harry. He had known Harry Coffee almost from the moment Harry had entered the Company thirty-five years before. He knew, or thought he knew, everything about the man. His work had been impeccable. He had never failed. He was one of the men younger men in the Company looked up to. Between himself and Harry Coffee, it was a toss of the coin as to which of them deserved to be the director.

His eyes skipped down the report, past the all too familiar details of Harry Coffee's Establishment upbringing and Ivy League education:

> Graduated Yale, magna cum laude, 1939; enrolled in Russian and Soviet studies at Harvard as World War II broke out; enlisted in U.S. Army December 8, 1941; commissioned second lieutenant, 1942; assigned to OSS; remained in Army following war, helping to restructure Germany; assigned to team interrogating former Nazi officials; recruited by CIA following discharge from service; assigned to Moscow as second secretary in political section of embassy; subsequent stations Berlin, Rio de Janeiro, London; reassigned Moscow 1967 as station chief; returned to Langley in 1971 as assistant deputy director of operations; named deputy director of operations in 1975, the post he presently holds.

His links to Virgil Craig? So obvious that Houghton should have remembered them. They'd both been in Germany following the war. They'd both served on interrogation teams.

His right-wing connections? None. Not a single affiliation of record. No evidence whatever of casual contact with conservative extremists—not even with Virgil Craig.

It was the link with Craig that had flagged him. But that had been nearly forty years ago. A case of sheer coincidence.

Still.

On Monday morning, Houghton asked Billy to obtain copies of personal telephone bills paid in the last year by Philip Loomis, Chris Slovotkin, Ernest McDonald and Harry Coffee. Carl Sanders' bills could not be checked, of course, because he still lived in Buenos Aires. But Houghton was reasonably certain that he would be able to find out what he needed to know about Sanders from Shlomo Glaser.

9

"The object," the surgeon was saying, "is to make the nose fit the face. A little button nose with a low bridge and a turned up end would hardly fit a strong face like yours." He was about fifty, André judged, a thin, sporty-looking man in tweeds, with an unusually burnished face for an Englishman, suggesting hours on a horse or driving country roads in a Jensen convertible or, perhaps, a great deal of drinking. He looked much more like a prototypic country squire than he did a Harley Street plastic surgeon. His name was Collins, or so he said. André was certain of very little having to do with his new life. He did know that he was in the Cotswolds, a few hours from London, living on an estate near Broadway, in a spacious stone house on a hill, from which he could look across seemingly endless rolling fields covered in the deepest of nature's greens and populated by dense flocks of thick-coated sheep. He knew, as well, from watching television and reading the newspapers and periodicals brought to him by his keepers, that four weeks after his supposed death the story of André Kohl had at last passed from prominent attention. And he knew that he would be imprisoned in this chilly stone house until he had been transformed by Dr. Collins and the several other people employed by Charles Houghton to rid him of any resemblance to André Kohl.

Houghton himself had accompanied André on the flight from the States to England. They'd traveled on a private jet. André had no idea whose it was, and he knew better by now than to ask. No one on these flights volunteered his name. When the crew members on the flight to England spoke to him, they addressed him not as André or Mr. Kohl, but as "sir," or "Peter."

His new name, in full, was Peter Burke. He'd chosen it out of a Virginia telephone directory the morning after the memorial service. He'd simply opened the directory at random and let his eyes settle on a name. "You'd better get used to it," Houghton had urged on the flight over. "Don't even think of yourself as André any more."

"Look, I'll go along with this charade, but don't ask me to play games with myself," André had replied.

"But that's what it is, a game, and you'd better play it if you intend to win it."

As upset as he was, he knew that Houghton was right, so he'd done exactly that, writing the name a hundred times, repeating it aloud as he looked into a mirror, repeating it silently as he talked to himself. Well, Peter old chap, this is a jolly bloody mess you've fashioned for yourself. What in the jolly bloody old hell are you going to jolly bloody do? Eh, Pete? Or do you prefer, Peter? I think so, Peter. What do *you* think, Pete? Each of these interior monologues was laced with the same invective, the same self-contempt, the same anger, repressed just below sight. He had to gain control of himself, and he knew it. The problem was that, long after he had recovered from his head wound, the psychological wounds remained raw, with no indication whatever that they might heal.

"You have a nice chin, which under normal circumstances we wouldn't touch," Collins was saying, "but given our objective we really have to do at least a little something to every part of your face. So while we're lowering the bridge of your nose a bit, we'll also augment the chin. But why am I just talking? Let me show you."

The doctor had brought a computer with him. Its screen was the size of a television set. Next to the computer was a keyboard and a joystick exactly like those used in arcade games. He turned it on, waited for his program to appear, then punched a series of keys. "What you're about to see will explain why we slipped you into hospital in the dark of night last week. That CAT scan we made gave us a specific set of facial contours we could program into the computer. Ah, here we are."

An image of a face appeared on the monitor, made up of a hundred small, multicolored patches, that, despite its many hues and shades, André recognized as his own. "You see," Collins said, moving the joystick, which in turn moved a white cursor on the screen, "this nose line could lose a little without any harm at all. Actually I think you might like it. And then we'll give the chin a somewhat firmer line, and slim down the area under it. The nice part of it is that there's very little guesswork. I can show you what you'll look like." With that, he punched in some information; in moments, the bridge of André's nose had receded, his chin had grown and his jowls had disappeared. "What do you think?" the doctor asked.

André stared in silence at the image on the monitor. Its multicolored squares combined into the profile of a strong-looking face, yet the image seemed so remote and foreign to him it might have been from some twenty-first-century cartoon. "What I think wouldn't be helpful," he said at last.

Collins frowned, and looked at André, first out of the corner of his eyes, and then full on. "Well, we don't want to do something you don't want to do, now, do we?"

"That's not the point. I have to do it."

"I see. Well, yes, in that case, we should carry on." He hesitated for a moment. "There *is* one thing I'm obliged to tell you before we start, and in view of your apparent ambivalence about the undertaking, perhaps I should tell you now." He was, André could see now, a good deal more the serious physician than he was the sporting Englishman, which meant that his burnished complexion was almost certainly not from drink. "Plastic surgery is the safest surgery there is. One reason is that the people who have it aren't ill. Another reason is that the surgery usually involves the upper body, which is rich with blood, which means, in turn, rapid healing. There's absolutely no need for you to worry about not being in hospital, because everything I'll be doing to you here I do as a matter of course in my office. Actually, *not* going to hospital is very much in your favor, because it greatly reduces your prospects of infection. Nonetheless, I am obliged to remind you that plastic surgery *is* surgery. Something *could* go wrong. You *could,* conceivably, die. That is the remotest possibility, and I don't for a moment expect it to happen, but as a matter of principle, and particularly since this is elective surgery, I say the same thing to all my patients. Now, then, having made my little speech, what is your pleasure?"

"Let's do it," André said.

"Splendid. I'm sure you'll be pleased."

"I'm sure I will be."

"Good. Now the eyes. Nothing can make you more youthful-looking than a little work around the eyes. You won't object to being more youthful-looking?"

André knew the doctor was trying to be helpful, and that his question undoubtedly reflected a mild state of confusion. At all other times he dealt with people who saw him precisely because they wanted to be more youthful, or beautiful, or have some disfigurement transformed. Dealing with a man who wanted no such service had to be a first. What inducement had brought him from a busy practice in London to spend several hours with a stranger who didn't want to see him? Without question a great deal of money.

Where was all the money coming from to finance this venture—the plane from the States, the car and driver, the house, the cook and maid, the food, and above all the experts involved in his makeover: this plastic surgeon, the dentist who was bonding his teeth, the physical therapist who supervised every minute of his three-hour-a-day exercise program, the dietician whose meals, together with the exercise, had set in motion a two-pounds-a-week weight loss, and the ubiquitous trainer, undoubtedly a former CIA man, who, in whatever free hours were left, was supposed to teach him how to survive? Other tutors would appear in the coming months. Peter Burke had to have a past; as soon as they decided what it should be, the tutors would arrive to fit André to it. Already, a dozen people were involved; there would be more. Who was paying them? Under whose aegis had they been hired? Houghton had refused to tell him. "The less you know, the less you can give away and the safer you are," he'd said when he deposited André in the Cotswolds. That, it quickly became clear, was the operating principle on the estate. No one asked him questions. Only his CIA trainer knew his real name and his new last name. To everyone else, he was simply "Peter."

"What we'll do," Collins went on, "is cut away some loose skin and then trim these small patches of fat that cause drooping in the upper lid and bags under the lower lid. Actually, I'm prepared to do that today, if you like."

It had been a remark so offhand that Collins might have been suggesting lunch. But it had the effect on André of moving him to the edge of a chasm. Either he retreated, or jumped across the chasm. "Sure. Why not?" he said.

"Good," Collins said emphatically. "I'll only be a minute." He was back in not much more than that, carrying a tray of instruments wrapped in sterile cloth. Behind him came a young man—presumably the driver of the van in which the surgeon had arrived—carrying a high intensity lamp. Over the next few minutes the young man returned with a portable operating table, a suitcase filled with equipment, a portable anesthetic machine and a bag of sterile linens.

"How permanent is plastic surgery?" André said as the doctor was setting up.

"You've asked the right question. A while back, it wasn't very permanent. Our work went only skin deep, you might say. But today, we work with what's under the skin—the fat and muscle and even the bone. When you remove fat, it's gone forever, because the fatty tissue's gone with it. Filing a bone's permanent, too. Getting rid of wrinkles is another matter. We can't get rid of those permanently. Still, we're light-years ahead of where we were ten years ago. In the old days, we used to make an incision around the ears and inside the hairline, pull the skin tight and cut away the excess. That was good for about five years, at which time you'd have to repeat. Now we cut deeper so that in addition to tightening the skin, we can tighten the muscles and connective tissue. That way we don't have to pull the skin so tight to get the effect we want. I'm sure you've seen some faces that look like they belong to a pilot in a 9-G power dive. We don't do those any more."

"What's the bottom line?"

Collins laughed. "Good American question. Some of the first

patients on whom I used the procedure look almost as good as they did ten years ago."

"And the others?"

Collins laughed again. "They don't look quite that good." He regarded André with a twinkle. "Ah, well, nothing's *really* permanent, is it, Peter? We're all dust in the end."

There was no need for bandages, only a cold compress applied overnight. In the morning, the area around his eyes was swollen and discolored, but he couldn't see any scars. Within a week, the swelling had abated, and the discoloration had disappeared. André looked at himself with wonder, understanding at once why Collins had suggested changing his eyelids as the first procedure. The area around the eyes not only displayed the scars of aging, it was also the most visible battleground of the emotions. Just this procedure had removed years of wear and tear from his face. Nothing Dr. Collins might have done could have been as convincing. That very day, André sent word to the doctor that he was ready to proceed with the rest of the surgery. It was scheduled for late the following week.

This time there was a considerable amount of pain and soreness, both lingering long after the swelling had subsided. For two days, he wore a whole-face bandage that kept pressure on his wounds. Then his head was wrapped in a long piece of gauze that covered everything but his eyes and nostrils and mouth. His head would remain bandaged for two weeks, and he was glad that it would because it postponed the moment when he would have to confront his new face in a mirror. He knew what a shock it would be when he finally did. Each increment of his transformation meant a corresponding loss of his former self; although he made a conscious effort to "play the game," as Houghton had suggested, knowing that he had no alternative and that his survival depended on it; he knew as well that part of him was trying to hold on for as long as possible to the person he had been.

The second bout of surgery provided two immediate, if inadvertent, benefits. The first was a change in his schedule. The second was time to be alone. Until the surgery, the mornings since his arrival had been devoted to his fitness program: a session on a stationary bicycle that had begun with fifteen minutes at a slow pace and low resistance and was now up to an hour at a more rapid pace and stress; a second hour with weights, working on upper body one day and lower body the next; and a third hour of stretching every muscle, joint and ligament, with the objective of restoring flexibility to his tissues and changing his body's alignment so that he stood straighter and taller. Convinced that he would hate it, he had surprised himself by the eagerness with which he threw himself into the program after getting over the initial aches and pains. The results were immediate and gratifying; he felt better, physically, than he could ever remember. The only deficit to the enterprise—and a major one it was—was the sadness he felt at not being able to share his sense of rejuvenation with Meredith. In any case, now that the makeover program had come to a standstill until his wounds could heal, he had several hours a day to read, stroll the grounds of the estate, or work on his journal.

The journal, begun three days after arriving in England, had quickly become his salvation. He wrote in longhand, on a lined pad he had found in the study of the house. And he wrote because after all the pain and anguish had finally been assimilated, it had occurred to him that what he was experiencing was, at the very least, an extraordinary story. At first he had asked himself why he should write something no one could ever read. Then he discovered that putting pencil to paper slowed and focused his thoughts, and the journal gave him a framework with which to attempt, at least, to come to terms with all he'd been through.

Did Houghton take advantage of me? I was wounded, drugged. I should never have made a decision under those conditions. But he pushed me. He made me believe that if I didn't decide just then there wouldn't be another chance. Admittedly, it was the ideal time, when the fewest possible people knew about my condition, and when Meredith was still unconscious.

But what good does it do me to think like this? It's done. It's over. If Meredith's face hadn't been known to the people trying to kill me, they could have changed me and then resettled us together. But after all the publicity it never would have worked—and, Houghton was right, she would have never stood for a separation. Under the circumstances, I made the only decision I could.

But, my God, the pain. I could go mad from it. I know now what it must be like for men who are widowed when they're young, men who loved their wives and believed that marrying was the best thing they had ever done. That's how I felt with Meredith. I had never felt it before. And now, nothing, emptiness, a void as vast as the universe.

How do I keep my sanity? The answer may well be this interior monologue. For Christ's sake, don't compose as though someone's going to read it someday. That may never happen. Just get the thoughts down. And try to find something positive.

How many men, after all, get a chance to start life over with a tabula rasa? How many men, given the opportunity to walk away from all their frustrations and mistakes, would snap it up in a second? How many men would volunteer to be made to look ten years younger, cost free? Face it, if it hadn't been for Meredith, and someone had offered you the opportunity to lose ten years and start with a clean slate, you might have very well jumped at it yourself. So you were André Kohl. Big deal. Living alone. Flying a thousand miles to do a fifteen-second standup in Helsinki or Beirut or Timbuktu, then spending the night in an empty hotel room. You found out three months ago that you'd spent your life as an observer, watching life from the press box. You decided you wanted to try it for a while as one of the players. Well? You got your wish, Peter, old man. You got it in bloody spades.

The hell of it is that this is a marvelous story, the best story I've ever had. No one can possibly beat me on it; it will be told only if, when and as I decide to tell it. So: make notes, lots of notes, every chance you get, and maybe someday, who knows?

The one part of André's rehabilitation program he was most pleased to avoid during his recuperation was what he referred to as survival training. He'd been at it less than six weeks but he already hated it, partly because of the secretiveness but mostly because of his trainer.

Jack Fleming—if that, in fact, was his name—had arrived at the estate three days after André. He was an imposing man, well over six feet tall, with broad shoulders and a ramrod posture suggesting more than a few years in the military, undoubtedly during World War II. A two-inch rim of sandy hair ran from ear to ear; otherwise he was bald. With one exception his features seemed so mainstream American as to be unmemorable; that exception was his brown eyes, which seemed never to waver or blink. André judged him to be between sixty-five and seventy, undoubtedly a retired CIA agent, and almost certainly a CIA station chief at an embassy at one point in his career. It was nothing Fleming had said, because he said absolutely nothing about himself; it was the sense of detachment he maintained in spite of the intimacy of their surroundings. André had seen the same trait in station chiefs throughout the world. They were pleasant to one and all, certainly, but not once in André's presence had any of them ever loosened up. At breaks during working hours Fleming would simply disappear, to reappear again only when it was time to resume their work. Their conversations during dinner were perfunctory. After dinner, he invariably took a book into the study and attacked it with that same absorption with which he regarded André during their training sessions. In every way he could—his tone, his language, the pedantry of his lessons—he drove home the message that he was the teacher and André the pupil, he the superior and André the inferior.

The tension between them had been evident from the first day, when they settled into the study for what André had supposed would be an orientation. But Fleming had plunged right in.

"The very first thing you must learn to do is make yourself innocuous," he'd begun. "The last thing in the world you want is to be noticed. You have to convince the opposition that you're ineffective. Do you read spy novels?"

"Sometimes."

"Did you read *Funeral in Berlin?*"

"Yes."

"Remember what Deighton wrote? 'The best compliment you can give a secret agent is to take him for a fool.' Perfect. I'll give you an example."

"Wait a minute," André had interrupted. "What's this about a secret agent? I'm not going to be a secret agent."

"Figure of speech," Fleming had said. "Your basic task is the same, to avoid detection, or suspicion. You want to blend into the woodwork, so that no one has reason to wonder if you're someone other than who you say you are. Understood?"

"Understood," André said, but he was not at all comfortable. If André Kohl was dead, and he was going to be transformed, why the need for the spy lessons? The thought of being indoctrinated into the ways of spying chilled him. Intelligence agents had been among his major sources, and been responsible for leads to some of his best stories. Inevitably, his success had given rise to rumors that he was on the CIA payroll; for that reason alone, he had had to work harder than most foreign correspondents to maintain a distance between himself and his intelligence sources. The worst thing that could be said of any journalist was that he had compromised himself in behalf of any interest. And the worst interest a journalist could be compromised by, without question, was the CIA. Not even the motive of patriotism was sufficient to excuse a journalist, in the eyes of his or her colleagues, who believed that any such contamination of their independence infected them all. It didn't matter to André that he would no longer be practicing journalism; his reaction was instinctual. From that moment forward, there would be an edge to his encounters with Jack Fleming.

If Fleming knew that he had touched a sore spot, he did not let on. He was exactly like Houghton in this respect; no matter what was going on in his mind or what he was feeling, nothing, but nothing, showed, and his voice remained the same. "The most important thing you're going to learn from us in terms of keeping yourself alive is to be able to determine whether you're under surveillance," he went on. "And the most important thing you're going to learn about surveillance is to be aware of it without giving any indication to the surveillance team that you know you're being followed. The moment you begin to take identifiable countermeasures the surveillance team will know that you're someone who's been trained, and they'll pick you up. Remaining natural while under surveillance is more difficult than you might imagine. The average person walking down the street sees nothing. A trained person sees everything, regardless of which side of the law he's on. Undercover cops, and thieves and pickpockets, can often spot one another simply by watching the eyes. When I was just out of college, I worked for a spell as a store detective in San Francisco. After two weeks I could spot shoplifters as they walked into the store simply by watching their eyes. The first thing they did when they walked in was to scan the floor, looking for security. If you walk the streets obviously looking for stakeouts, you'll give yourself away in the same manner."

Fleming rose, stood over André and fixed him with his gaze. "The point is, Peter, that you have to see everything that is going on without appearing to see it. Not easy, not easy at all. The trick is to keep your eyes moving and a pleasant expression on your face. I remember another time early in my training, in a bar with some friends. My thoughts started to drift, and for some reason my eyes settled on some fellow at a nearby table. After about a minute of this he bolted from the bar. I'm sure he thought I was a narcotics agent."

For the rest of the day, Fleming drilled André on all the ways he could determine if he was under surveillance. Primary among them was learning to recognize irrational or inconsistent acts: for example, a man standing by a store counter that sold women's sanitary products, or a man waiting in a bus line who does not board the bus when it arrives. Using a chalkboard, Fleming diagramed for André—whom he invariably addressed as "Peter"—how surveillance could be carried out by agents using what was known in the trade as an "ABC pattern." Agent A walks either ahead of or behind the target. Agent B is ahead of the target on the opposite side of the street. Agent C is also on the opposite side of the street, but behind the target. By watching one another and passing prearranged signals, they can keep the target boxed in without making him aware that he is under surveillance. To further allay suspicion, they might rotate positions, or be spelled by another team. A clumsy, easily spotted team might be covering for a second, more subtle team. At times, clumsiness can be deliberate; the Russians, in particular, are often obvious about surveillance in order to see how their quarry will react to the psychological pressure.

Over the next few weeks, André was initiated into other basics of what intelligence agents call "tradecraft." One lesson was devoted to learning how to communicate in a passive way if he sensed that he was in danger. "What you want to avoid at all costs is sending up a red flag, so that your adversaries know that you know they're onto you," Fleming told him. "The best signal is to stop doing something that you normally do. I've noticed that you always wear a handkerchief in the breast pocket of your jacket. Is that something André did?"

"Yes."

"Then you'll stop doing that as of right now—and the next time you put a handkerchief in that pocket we'll know that you're in danger."

In the same manner, they agreed that wherever André established himself, he would buy a potted plant and put it on a windowsill facing his street. He could signal a need for assistance by removing the plant from the window. Together, they wrote out a message that André would place in the personal column of the morning newspaper of whatever city he settled in should other means of communication fail. The ad would read: "Harry: Come home. We can work it out. Sue." Some ally in that city would be assigned the task of reading the personal column every day.

Over and over again, Fleming stressed to André that his best protection against assassination was to develop an unpredictable life-style devoid of set routines. "What your adversaries will be looking for, should they ever discover who you are," he said, "is a pattern that will permit them to get at you. You've got to constantly scrutinize your own behavior, so that you can pick out before they do what habits you've let yourself slip into." To help André determine whether his premises had been entered, he taught him one of the oldest tricks in the business, putting a matchstick on his door ledge that would dislodge if the door was opened. The intruder wouldn't see it, but André would. "Never trust a mechanical lock," Fleming told him. "There isn't one that can't be opened within ten minutes by a man who knows what he's doing."

Fleming showed André a large sample of the kinds of electronic bugs that could be planted in his lodgings, as well as more sensitive parabolic microphones that could pick up conversations a hundred feet away. "The best way to counter room bugs is to turn your radio on and walk out. Most bugging is done with voice-activated microphones. If the radio's left on, it will create miles of tape that whoever's doing the monitoring will have to listen to. At some point, that character's going to lose patience and enter your digs to turn the radio off. When that happens, you'll know for certain that you're being bugged." He warned André that playing music loudly would not protect him against eavesdropping, because sophisticated electronic equipment can filter out music frequencies and isolate the live voices in a room.

In a course he referred to as "Flaps and Seals," Fleming taught André how to open letters surreptitiously, and how to determine if his own mail had been tampered with. Of the three basic ways to open mail, the most common was to steam the letter open. A second technique was to slice the end of an envelope open and then glue it back together again. A third technique was to use a razor to cut a small slit at the end of the envelope, then insert two knitting needles into the envelope, roll up the letter and slip it out through the slit. Once the letter had been read, it could be reinserted by reversing the process.

Fleming also showed André how to hide a piece of microfilm in a tube of toothpaste or shaving cream, or under the inner sole of his shoe, and he gave him a pen with a hollow compartment. "When it comes to hiding microfilm, nothing's really foolproof," he warned. "If you get caught by professionals, they'll know where to look."

André could not resist this intimate glimpse into an arcane world about whose techniques he had always been curious, but he did not take it seriously because he couldn't imagine any circumstance in which the techniques themselves would prove useful. But each day, he could feel his resistance mounting. The more complex the course became, the more personal Fleming became, until finally he was boring in on the very nature of André's identity.

"Now I know what André Kohl did in his past, Peter," Fleming began on the morning of their twenty-third day together, "and I'm sure he fancied himself quite a verbal poker player, but I must tell you that the techniques he used as a reporter would be a handicap to him in this game."

"How's that?"

"Overconfidence, mostly. I'm sure André believed that the reportorial process could gain him access to almost any information. The fact is that most of what reporters learn is given to them by people who stand to profit in some way by public disclosure of the information, either by exposing a political enemy, or arousing public emotions over specific conditions they wish to change, and so forth."

"And how do your techniques differ, if I may ask?"

"To begin with, the objective, in your particular case, isn't to obtain information. It's to avoid divulging it." Fleming frowned. "You're from New York originally, aren't you?"

"No. California."

"Really? Where, exactly?"

"Los Angeles."

"Oh, that place. How could you stand it?"

"Well, I haven't lived there for a very long time, but whenever I've gone back to visit my children it's struck me as a vastly underrated place."

"How many children do you have?"

"Two."

"Sex?"

"One of each. Son's a stockbroker. Daughter's a reporter on the San Francisco *Chronicle.*"

"And their mother?"

"We're divorced. She lives in Palos Verdes."

Suddenly, Fleming stopped asking questions. He looked at André with a grim but satisfied smile. "Well, now, Peter, you've just given me the family history of a man who's dead. You were told when you got here to forget that that man ever existed. And you just gave him away."

"But we were just talking."

Fleming drew himself up. His smile vanished. "We are not just talking, Mr. Burke. We are training you to maintain an identity."

"Oh, ease off, Fleming."

"Call me Jack, if you like, or Mr. Fleming, but don't call me 'Fleming,' all right?"

André stared at Fleming with ill-concealed distaste. "Fine," he said at last.

There was no way that Fleming, his eyes fixed on André, could have missed his look. Yet he continued as if he hadn't seen it. "There are four basic ways in which a trained agent can disarm a person like yourself and get him to reveal what he shouldn't. The first is by use of false declarations. That's the method I just used. I knew you were originally from California, as would every operative looking for you. But when I asked you if you were from New York, your involuntary response was to correct me. That gave me the opening I needed to engage you in further conversation. The second method is exaggeration. I might say something to you about your age, tell you you don't look a day over forty. That might provoke you to say, 'I wish,' or something else that would tell me that you're probably the age of the man I'm looking for. The third method involves references to shared experiences. When people are under stress they tend to look for common links to others around them. Suppose you've been followed for several days and you've at last shaken your tail. You stop in a pub to get a drink and relax a little and, being alone and not wanting to seem conspicuous, you strike up a conversation. Perhaps about a game that's on the tube, or about a show, if they're watching one. Eventually it comes down to what you think of this and that, and before long, unless you're on to him, the person you're talking to, if he happens to be an agent who's deliberately placed himself next to you, is able to put together a mosaic with the pieces of information you've given him."

André had listened with increasing incredulity. "I mean, it's just so improbable that I'd do something like that. I don't go into bars or pubs . . ."

"André Kohl didn't, but you are Peter Burke, a completely different man, and each and every thing you do must be the virtual opposite of, or at least, not resemble, the acts of André Kohl."

Fleming's sudden rebuke carried the surprise and sting of a slap. André could feel the heat in his face. He sat staring at his trainer, refusing to look away, hating him for making him feel foolish.

But suddenly Fleming was all charm. His sternness melted, he smiled, his body seemed to relax. "That's enough for today. I'm getting paid to get you in shape, and I give my clients their money's worth. But we don't have to get it all done by the weekend."

For the first time since they'd been working together, other than when they took their meals in the dining room, Fleming sat down in André's presence. He pulled out a package of cigarettes. "Smoke?"

"No, thanks."

"I forgot. You don't smoke, do you?" He lit the cigarette and then drew on it, letting the smoke stay in his lungs several seconds before exhaling it. "Hope this doesn't get you down too much. I'm kind of enjoying myself. I was really struggling in the dark when Charlie Houghton called me."

"What doing?"

"Well, to tell you the truth, I was trying my hand at your racket. Sort of. I get so many calls for training from security agencies that I decided I'd produce a video tape. Figured it would be a snap. Brother, was I wrong. Didn't know the first thing about it."

André chuckled, another first in Fleming's presence.

"What would be the first thing *you* would do if you were going to produce a tape?"

"Get a script written. That's always first."

"And then?"

"Get a director, some actors and a narrator."

"And then?"

"Help them in any way they ask—and watch them like a hawk, preferably without their knowing."

Fleming wasn't smiling any longer. He was looking at André as though he were a child who had done something naughty. *"I understood that your career has been entirely in international finance, Mr. Burke. How is it that you know so much about producing videos?"*

"Oh, shit," André said. "I've had enough." He stood and moved for the door.

"Just a minute," Fleming said.

André stopped, not because he'd been commanded to, but because he wanted to have it out. "Just who the hell do you think you are, Fleming?"

"That's not the question," Fleming said, his voice suddenly mild. "The question is who you think *you* are. And the answer,

I'm afraid, is that you think you're André Kohl. You're not. He's dead."

"Look, you can change my body, but you can't change *me.*"

"Oh, but we can, if you'll let us." Fleming paused for just a moment, with an actor's exquisite timing. "If you don't, Peter Burke is dead, too."

For some seconds, André stood there, breathing deeply, feeling ridiculous. He knew that his pique was unwarranted, that whatever Fleming was doing was being done for his benefit. He suspected that Fleming was deliberately baiting him in an effort to beat him down. Why that was necessary he didn't understand, and he couldn't accept another person's judgment that it *was* necessary just because that person was supposed to be an expert.

"In case you're wondering," Fleming said, "the fourth way in which a trained agent can get a suspect to reveal himself is to ask him for advice. Everyone loves to give advice. Once they start to give it, it's no trick at all for the agent to move them onto ground with which they're familiar, just as I did with you. Before long, the agent knows a great deal that he shouldn't, if the person dispensing the advice is interested in maintaining a cover. It was my impression that that's what I'm here for, to teach you how to do that."

André spent that afternoon with the dentist, Terence Dover, a tall, freckle-faced redhead who looked even younger than his thirty-eight years and spoke of tooth bonding with an evangelist's passion. Like Dr. Collins, the plastic surgeon, Dover had driven up from London, and brought with him everything he needed to do the work in the seclusion of the manor house. It was, in a small way, a providential bit of timing; dentistry of any kind, even having his teeth cleaned, made André so uneasy that it preempted his thoughts. For a few hours, at least, he was spared the further anguish of thinking about Jack Fleming and everything he had said.

Of all the physical changes proposed to André, the bonding of his teeth was the only one to which he had responded. While he hated his time in the chair, he had always been self-conscious about his teeth, which were poorly formed and irregular, the result being that his smile had always been rare and guarded. Perhaps that was why he struck so many people as dour, and had looked so fierce on television.

"You won't recognize your teeth when we've finished," Dr. Dover told him.

"All I want to know is, will it hurt?"

"You might feel it a bit. I'll need to roughen the surfaces with a drill before I make an impression. If you think that might bother you, I can inject the nerves of each tooth."

"Novocain?"

"Xylocaine. It's better."

"Which will hurt more, the drilling or the injection?"

"The injection won't really hurt at all. Before I give it, I'll use a Xylocaine ointment on your gums, which will deaden the area. You'll feel pressure, but no pain."

"Do it," André said.

"What do you think?" the dentist asked after he'd given the injections. "Shall we leave a little space between the front teeth, or close them all the way? Women seem to find a small space sexy."

"I've spent my life with a space between my front teeth," André said. "Close them."

"Very well. Now, let me explain what's happening. The reason I need to roughen your teeth is to give the bonding material a good surface to stick to. After I finish, I'll make some impressions for the lab. The lab will make porcelain caps and I'll be back in a week to fit them." For the next thirty-five minutes, as he abraded a dozen of André's teeth with a portable drill and then made the impressions, the dentist hummed all three movements of the Tchaikovsky violin concerto. When the concerto was finished so was he.

"Congratulations. You didn't miss a note," André said.

"Ah, you know it, do you?"

"Well enough to know if a note is missing when I hear it, but not remotely as well as you do. Are you a musician?"

"My mother thinks so. I'm not sure how musicians would respond."

"What do you play?"

"Violin, actually."

"And do you play the Tchaikovsky?"

"As a matter of fact, I do."

André thought for a moment. "By any chance, do you have any music for violin and piano?"

"I believe I do, yes."

"If you have the time and interest, perhaps we might play some when you return next week."

"Oh, you play piano, do you?"

"I used to. I'd been hoping to get back to it."

"Well, that might be very nice. I'll see what I can find."

André showed him to the door and then watched his car move down the road toward the gate half a mile away. Even after the car had disappeared into some woods, he lingered, not wanting to move out of the mood that had seized him. Ever since the attempted assassination at the Ritz in Paris, every conversation he'd had, even those with Meredith, had dealt either overtly or by implication with his predicament; for the first time in almost two months, he'd had a normal, unstrained, uncalculated conversation with another human being. And just the thought of playing some duets on the dentist's return next week was more intoxicating to him than the most potent cocktail.

"I see you've made a friend."

André wheeled. It was Fleming. He hadn't heard him approach. "Yes," he said. "And a dentist, to boot."

"Most unfortunate," Fleming said.

André frowned. "What do you mean?"

"There's not going to be any concert."

André glared at Fleming. "How did you know what we talked about?" He hesitated. "Did you bug that conversation?" Even as he asked the question he knew that it was needless. He knew the answer already. A fury rose in him, just as it had that morning. But this time he said nothing, waiting instead for the lecture that was sure to come. He did not have long to wait.

"André Kohl played piano. Peter Burke doesn't. The reason he doesn't is that if he did, he'd play just like André. Peter can't do anything that André did. He can't talk like him, or stand or walk like him, or eat like him. If André poured wine or held a glass in a special way, Peter has to do it differently. If André was neat, Peter must be sloppy, or vice versa. When Peter gets his new teeth, he's going to have to brush them in a manner different from the way André brushed his."

"That's fucking ridiculous!"

Fleming smiled. He moved very close to André. "You'd think that, of course. But let me explain why it isn't, and I hope you'll listen very carefully because it's your heart we're trying to keep beating." The last seven words were punctuated with a stiff index finger poked into André's chest. "Only when Peter Burke is thinking at all times about *being* Peter Burke will he start *thinking* like Peter Burke and not like André Kohl. And only then will he have a chance to survive."

10

Lying on the table, her feet in the stirrups, her knees bent, a sheet draped over them, Meredith could not see the doctor but she could certainly feel his probing as he sought to measure her uterus. She remembered an admission by her mother that she found pelvic examinations so embarrassing she had never gotten used to them. It didn't matter whether the doctor was male or female. "I just feel that it's something another person shouldn't be doing," she'd said. "Every woman I've ever talked to feels the same. We know we should go more often, but we don't, and that's why." The admission had been made as an explanation, following an emergency, of why she hadn't been more diligent about her checkups. Meredith had sympathized with her mother and thought she understood her; her generation had been raised to think of that part of the body as being exclusively bound to the mysteries of sex. Meredith had no such hang-ups; to her it was simple biology.

Three weeks after the shooting, and a week after she'd returned to her loft in Soho to convalesce, Meredith had sent a friend to the drugstore to buy an early pregnancy test kit. The chemical was already in the test tube in which she was to urinate. Two hours later, a ring of sediment had settled at the bottom of the tube, the sign that she was pregnant. That very afternoon, she'd called to make an appointment with Dr. Lee, her Chinese gynecologist. "You're in luck," his cheery receptionist said. "The call just before you was a cancellation. Can you come tomorrow morning? Otherwise, it's three weeks."

"I am so sorry," Dr. Lee had said the moment he saw her, taking both of her hands in his.

She knew then that he had read about the story of the shooting, or seen it on the news broadcasts, like almost everyone else she knew. "Thank you," she'd said.

"How are you feeling?"

"As well as can be expected."

"Let's have a look."

Now she could feel Dr. Lee's hand retracting. In a moment his head appeared over the sheet. "Yes, you are pregnant," he said with a smile, "and you are about six weeks along. I hope that was what you wanted to hear."

"Yes, it was," Meredith said. "Now just tell me everything I should do to deliver a healthy baby."

"There is only one thing to tell you: Be healthy yourself. No drugs of any kind—no alcohol, not a drop, no caffeine, no smoking. I want you back as soon as possible for a complete examination. In the meanwhile, try to put yourself in a more positive frame of mind. I know that's a lot to ask, but think of this: It's a miracle that you didn't abort."

Driving back to her loft in a taxi, Meredith stared trancelike at the passing scene. It was a hot, dusty August day. The air was foul with exhaust fumes. The city badly needed a rain, as much to refresh its inhabitants as to clean the air and the streets. Not a good atmosphere in which to raise a child, Meredith decided, not just for the child but also for a mother whose thoughts, inevitably, would return to the way it was all supposed to have been. That kind of melancholy wouldn't be good for the child, either, and might even endanger the pregnancy. That's what Dr. Lee was saying. Yet, how could she shake it? Her last conscious moment before the shooting had been filled with heady thoughts and rhapsodic visions: the lush grass of the golf course, her ball rolling toward the hole, her husband cheering it on, and a conviction, born of her inherent optimism, that, regardless of the frightening reality that had forced them to take refuge at a guarded resort in the Caribbean, somehow their life together would always be the way it was right now, filled with surprise and beauty. And then, so suddenly it was like the next frame in a film, the picture before her began to disappear, and she heard a sharp, popping sound not unlike that made by a picture tube that explodes. Save for the briefest, disjointed moments, first on the ground and later in intensive care, when she would flit in and out of consciousness, there was no memory after that until she awakened in her hospital room and saw her father. "How is André?" she'd said. And her father had said, "He's gone." In three months that corresponded to absolutely nothing else in her life, she had met her man, married him and then lost him. It had all been so swift, and their time together so brief, that the memories had almost no texture and thus scarcely any power to endure.

She thanked God for the child, who would be the living, breathing proof that her time with André Kohl had been real. Now, she knew, and would have even if Dr. Lee hadn't told her, it was her job to will her mind into a positive phase so that she could send messages of welcome to her womb. C'mon, old girl, let's get on with it, she told herself as she stepped from the taxi and entered her building.

The moment she turned the key in her lock, she knew that something was wrong. She always double-locked; this time, however, a single turn of the key disengaged the tumbler. Very slowly, she pushed the door open just enough to be able to see inside. What she saw sent tremors through her limbs. Drawers had been pulled from desks and dressers and their contents dumped on the floor. Her closet had been emptied; her clothes lay in a pile in front of it. Even her dishes had been removed from cabinets; the only reason they, too, hadn't been strewn on the floor, she surmised, was because of the clatter they would have made. All this Meredith processed in a few seconds; in another second she had closed the door softly and was running down the stairs. Whoever had been there might still be there; she had better sense than to search the house alone.

Heart pounding, feeling weak, she called the police from a street pay phone. It took them twenty minutes to arrive. There were two of them, neither inspiring. One was in his late thirties, the other in his late forties. Both looked soft, and not at all happy about the prospect of entering a building where a burglar might be present. To judge from the way they eyed her, they seemed to resent that they'd been called. Finally, perhaps to avoid her increasingly hostile eyes, they began to mount the steps, as she watched them from below. At the doorway they unsnapped their holsters, then, hands on the butts of their revolvers, quietly stepped inside. A minute passed. Then the younger policeman appeared in the doorway. "You can come up," he said, more than a trace of sarcasm in his voice.

She made a hasty inventory, but could find nothing missing. The thief had found her jewelry case, but had overlooked the only item of any value in it, a strand of pearls. Her television set, VCR and stereo equipment were all still in place. "Musta scared him away when you came home," the older policeman said.

"I don't think so," Meredith said. "He would have had to get past me to escape."

"What about the back door?"

"It's locked."

The policemen looked at one another unhappily. "Whatever made him leave, he ain't here, so there's nothin' more for us to do, ma'am," the older policeman said. "Be glad he didn't take your stuff."

As soon as they left she locked the door, then rechecked the windows and the back door to be certain they, too, were locked. Then she checked the closet and the bathroom, knowing it was irrational, yet incapable of anything further until she did it. That was what New York did to you; living there, to begin with, was an irrational act.

She felt unclean, as though she, not the apartment, had been violated. Suddenly, she began to shake. This was no moment to be alone. She thought of who she might ask to come over, but all the men she knew would be working. More important, she didn't want any of them to see her in this state of mind.

Independence had always been her badge. She'd read all the statistics about the probability of marriage for women who were still single after reaching thirty. At thirty, they had a 20 percent chance. By their late thirties, it had dropped to 1 percent. She had never believed those statistics, never worried about marriage. She could have married a dozen times, but no man until André had ever rung her bell, and she simply wasn't going to settle. Not once had she entertained the thought that failure to marry was a sign of her unworthiness, the common thread among the unmarried past-thirties. They trooped to the therapists' offices, saying, "What's wrong with me?" and, "Change me." She liked herself and believed in herself; all she'd asked for was a man, not a boy, for a husband. Males threatened by proficient women, males looking for a mother or a housekeeper were boys, not men. That's why André had rung the bell. He was an entity, he'd made a life, he had something to say. Because he was secure in who he was, he wasn't afraid of her. That was the key right there; that's what set him apart. Understanding that about him was what had convinced her to marry him. She hadn't understood it at first; she'd worried that he wouldn't be able to relate to the kind of self-sufficient women America had developed while he'd been living in France. She'd even confessed that concern to him. But her concern had been unwarranted. André, who had divorced an old-fashioned woman and not married since, had been looking for an equal.

She did not feel equal now. Rather, the feeling that welled within was so unfamiliar that at first she couldn't identify it. "Oh, André!" she cried, suddenly overcome. She sank into a chair, despairing not only over his loss but the knowledge that, for the first time in memory, she was immobilized by doubt and fear.

It was nearly five o'clock when the private telephone rang in Charles Houghton's office at the CIA's headquarters off the George Washington Memorial Parkway in Langley, Virginia. It had not been a good day. The low point had been a testy call from the President, wanting to know how the investigation into the secret network was coming ("Slowly, sir.") and when he was going to get some reliable intelligence on the Soviet leader. ("Soon, we hope, sir."). Not unsurprisingly, the President hadn't liked the answers.

In point of fact, Houghton hadn't had a good day since he'd returned from Lima nearly three months before. It had been a steady succession of bad days, interspersed with a few that had been memorably terrible. Those few related to the shooting of André and Meredith, her recuperation and what Houghton thought of as André's "disposition." That last matter hung over him like the effects of too much drinking: At the time, he'd felt it had been the thing to do; the result had not been so awful that he wouldn't repeat it; yet he felt suffused with a feeling that, except for brief spurts, left him constantly uncomfortable and wouldn't go away. The future looked to him as it must to the metronomic drinker: staying with the habit, rather than trying to kick it, seemed the lesser pain. There was no turning back. André's new life was launched. To undo what had been done was inconceivable.

Houghton had correctly calculated the pain his decision would cause Meredith. What he hadn't counted on was how vulnerable her pain would make him. Seeing Meredith suffer had almost unhinged him. What else could he have done? he'd asked himself at least a dozen times. And always the answer was the same: nothing. Casa de Campo proved just how likely it was that Meredith would have been killed along with André in any subsequent attack. Of the two likelihoods, the one involving Meredith disturbed him infinitely more. He wasn't in the least ashamed of that. The corollary to that, however, was that the primary purpose of André's disposition was to save her, not him. At the time of his decision, Houghton had managed to shield that knowledge from himself. But within days, he'd had to admit the truth.

Houghton did not have a clue as to how the assassins had found André. Neither threats nor bribes had worked to get them to reveal more than the identity of their group, and Houghton could not bring himself to order the kind of treatment that had obviously worked for Pierre Gauthier in Paris in his interrogation of the terrorists there. Mysteries don't get solved unless there are acts that leave clues, and now, with André's "death," there would be no further acts from the people trying to kill him.

It was with all these matters running through his head that Charles Houghton picked up the telephone and, after his first alarm over the anguish in his daughter's voice, listened with great care to her account of the robbery. After he put the receiver down, he sat for a long while, drumming his fingers on the table. He'd said nothing to Meredith, of course, because he couldn't be sure. But if the prowler took nothing, perhaps it was because he'd been looking for something that wasn't there.

11

In a further effort to change André's mind-set during the first month of his training, Jack Fleming had ordered an absolute news blackout. There were to be no newspapers or news magazines, and Fleming had extracted a grudging pledge from André not to watch any news programs on television.

To André, the prohibition was simply the latest in a series of unending discomforts and insults relating to his transformation. Since his blowup with Fleming, the ledger he used to calculate his state in life had come to resemble that of a man favorably contemplating suicide—its debits grossly outweighing its credits. An entry in his journal, written just prior to the initial surgery, gave some clue to the cost of this accounting.

There is an insidious temptation inherent in this transition, and that is that somewhere along the line the previous person loses responsibility for the actions of the present and future one. Should I ever succumb to this temptation, there could come a point when I will have forgotten who I really am or was, and what I stand or stood for in a moral way. At that point, André will be dead.

Against these fears stands the matter of survival. Whatever person is evolving in me tells me that my mentors are right. If I don't go all the way, if I don't manage somehow to bury André Kohl and become Peter Burke, this enterprise is never going to work—and all of André's fears will have become academic.

But who *was* Peter Burke? What were his antecedents? And what was to become of him? Those were the questions that not only preoccupied André, but were bringing Charles Houghton back to England six weeks after establishing him in the Cotswolds. Or so Houghton had informed him by telephone that afternoon; as before, there was that unwillingness in André to accept anything that had to do with his new life for what it appeared to be. In part, this was due to training, to his acceptance of "Rothwell's Maxim," and its corollaries, "never assume," and "never take anything for granted"; in part it was due to his belief that nothing involving intelligence agencies was ever precisely what it seemed.

The impatience with which he awaited Houghton's arrival was literally painful. He ached to be in touch with a living, breathing representative of his authentic past. He craved to know about Meredith. And he felt so helpless he had contracted a headache that aspirin couldn't cure.

Protocol required that the head of an intelligence agency notify his counterpart in a friendly country that he was arriving in that country, whether he was or wasn't on official business. Prior to leaving for England with André, Houghton had informed Jeremy Croft, the head of MI-6, that he would be visiting the Cotswolds on a private matter, and he asked Croft as a matter of personal courtesy to convey the information to his staff on a strict need-to-know basis. His message was as much a consequence of prudence as it was of protocol; if someone in British intelligence were to discover that a safe house and training center had been established near Broadway, Houghton did not want the operation to be mistaken for that of Irish terrorists. But while he wanted Croft to know he was there, he gave him no specifics, and he ruled out MI-6's assistance. Ever since the defection of Kim Philby to the Soviet Union, the CIA had been leery about letting the English know too much about internal business; this being a private affair, conducted outside CIA channels, the need for security was even greater. Would Croft honor his American counterpart's request? Houghton couldn't be sure; the temptation to know would be great. But it was a risk he had to take, and it compared favorably with the risk of attempting to conduct the operation in the United States.

From the outset, Houghton had recruited specialists who had worked for the CIA with distinction in the past but had since retired or moved on to other employment—people like Dick Sexton, and now Jack Fleming. It was Sexton, the man who had set up the rescue operation in Bolivia and later the surveillance of André in Paris, who subsequently arranged for the estate and staff in the Cotswolds. It was Fleming, once the station chief in Berlin, the CIA's most sensitive foreign post, who had run the Cotswolds operation since then. All of the people employed so far had not only worked within top secret operations in the past; they understood that their continued service in such generously funded positions depended on their absolute discretion.

So André—or Peter, as Houghton, too, insisted on calling him—was safe so long as he remained at the estate. But he could not be kept there indefinitely, and would not stay there if he could. Thus the subject that had ostensibly brought Houghton back to England.

"Let's talk about cover," he said on the first afternoon of his visit, as he and André settled into deep chairs in the sitting room of the manor house. They'd just finished a hearty lunch in the dining room and now the same elderly man who had served them there put a pot of coffee and two cups on the coffee table and disappeared, mumbling, "Thank you, sir." It was late-August, but a fire crackled in the fireplace to ward off the chill of a rainy summer day. "It will have to be deep cover, as deep as any we've ever used. We'll have to create a history for Peter Burke not just in our minds but in fact."

"How do you do that?" André said. The question seemed straightforward enough, yet the manner of its delivery gave it a rough texture, and Houghton could only guess at this point about the depth and nature of the hostility beneath it. Despite all the efforts of Jack Fleming, and perhaps because of them, André was still resisting the André-to-Peter transition. It was concern over his attitude, reported to him by Fleming, that had, in part, prompted Houghton's visit. In their first half-hour together, André had demanded information about Meredith with such vehemence that it became impossible for Houghton to bring up the business he had come to discuss.

"You're really angry, aren't you?" Houghton said now.

"How the hell do you expect me to feel?"

"Relieved to be out of danger. Grateful that Meredith is."

"I ask myself at least a dozen times each day whether there wasn't some less extreme way to do it. I ask myself whether you didn't take advantage of me at an unimaginably vulnerable moment."

Houghton nodded, as much in acknowledgment of the truth of what André had just said as in his understanding of the source of his son-in-law's hostility. "I've thought about that, too. The moment was almost that vulnerable for me. I grant you that my interest in Meredith was paramount, but I figured that yours was, too. For what it's worth, I've been over it all many times since, and concluded that there was no other way. I realize that may not help you."

"It's just very hard to come to terms with."

"You may never come to terms with it. On the other hand, if we do what we've come here to do, that might bring you a little closer to those three objectives you set out on the day you made your decision."

"You remember those, do you?" André said bitterly.

Houghton sighed. "Please, Peter. I'm very mindful of what I've done. I've vowed to help you in every way I can."

André stared at his father-in-law, feeling absolutely helpless, pulled to the breaking point by conflicts within him, wanting to believe that Houghton was on his side, yet not really trusting him, wanting to believe that there really was a way out of the void in which he was trapped, yet unable to see a path. "Okay. Let's get on with it," he said at last.

"As I indicated, the cover will have to be comprehensive, from the cradle to the present, and it will have to be backed up at every step of the way. For example, if we agree that Peter Burke went to Harvard, then we not only put that on your CV, we get a transcript of Peter Burke's academic record into the Registrar's file."

"You can do that?"

"Not easily. But, yes."

"What else?"

"Absolutely everything. Birth certificate. Vaccination certificates. Grade school and high school records. Social security number. Driver's license. Bank accounts. Credit cards. Credit rating.

And then, of course, we have to manufacture an employment record, and find several people you can list as references who will vouch for you."

"How tough is that?"

"Let's say that we've done it before. The real challenge is figuring out an occupation that doesn't in any way correspond to what André did but is something with which Peter would be comfortable. How does finance strike you?"

"I did a lot of stories on the subject in my day."

"You mean André Kohl did."

"Have it your way," André said, not even trying to disguise his contempt for the make-believe Houghton insisted on practicing even in their dialogues.

"How does this sound? Peter Burke worked out of San Francisco for a group of investment bankers, specializing in the Far East. Hong Kong. Japan. Thailand. Singapore. Indonesia. South Korea. Formosa. Even mainland China."

"You realize I have virtually no experience out there."

"Peter, Peter," Houghton scolded.

André sighed. "Have it your way," he said again.

Houghton reached into his briefcase and pulled out a folder. "In the hope of a favorable reply, we've created a background for you." He pushed the folder across the table. "If you approve what's in there, you'll want to be able to rattle it off as readily as the alphabet. Why don't you look it over while I excuse myself for a few minutes."

Alone, André opened the folder, and had the immediate feeling that he was prying into the personal affairs of a stranger. It was all there: Peter Michael Burke, born April 19, 1937, to Catherine Cardman Burke and William Joseph Burke, at New York Lying-in Hospital; no brothers or sisters; family home, 1070 Park Avenue, Manhattan; grammar and high school, the Dalton School, honors graduate, 1954; B.S., Harvard, 1958, summa cum laude, major in economics; entered U.S. Army, 1958; six months' special training in Korean at Army language center in Monterey, California; one year in Korea as language specialist; discharged, 1960; joined Pacific Far East Line as trainee at company headquarters in San Francisco; in 1962, moved to Dotson & Agee, shipping brokers; in

1965, named vice president for sales, Far East Transit Corp.; 1968–83, chief, Far East investments sector, World Bank of North America; married Marilyn Anne Hastings of San Francisco, July 14, 1961; divorced, 1978; no children.

"Well, what do you think?" Houghton said as he settled back into his chair.

"What happens if anyone looks up my parents?"

"They were killed in an automobile crash in 1980."

"And my 'wife'? What about her?"

"They won't be able to find her."

"What if someone sees through this cover?"

"Then you'll use a fallback cover."

"Which is?"

"It could be a lot of things. The only requirement of a fallback cover is that there has to be a plausible reason for not having used it in the first place. In other words, it has to involve something that you would have wanted to hide."

"For example?"

"If you were involved in industrial espionage, or smuggling dope or fine art, or were homosexual."

"Which one have you picked out for me?" André said, his tone caustic.

Houghton smiled. "None of those. I have a suggestion that you might find easier to sustain. It's also considerably more flattering."

"Go ahead."

"You could tell your interrogators that you worked for us."

André stared at Houghton, his face growing dark and his skin prickly as the blood rushed through his body to service his anger. "I had a feeling you were going to say that." He regarded Houghton balefully. "I want to ask you something. Do you have a hidden agenda?"

Houghton returned André's stare, certain that he had at last reached the source of André's resistance to Jack Fleming and his training program. He chose his next words with care, while at the same time attempting to sound offhand. "It has crossed my mind that, with a little training, Peter Burke might become a rather useful fellow."

"As an agent?"

"Not formally, no. Let's say, someone who might be interested in taking on some special assignments."

"Never. That's absolutely antithetical to everything I've ever stood for. Look, I don't mean to offend you. I don't condemn the CIA, and I don't hold it in contempt. Given what the world is like, I doubt that we could do without it. But, as far as I'm concerned, the agency lives by a set of rules that are in total conflict with mine. At the risk of sounding pious, I've always been for openness, access to information, a free flow of ideas. The agency is closed, rigid and undemocratic by definition. More than that, the day you guys compromise one journalist and he gets discovered, foreign powers could rightly suspect all of them of being CIA agents, and their effectiveness would be finished."

Houghton nodded. If he was angry, André would never have known it from his expression or voice. "What you've just described are the values and outlook of André Kohl. We are deliberately trying to remove you completely from that person. It won't do us a bit of good to create a background for Peter Burke unless we also create a persona, as well. We can remake you physically and fail if your personality stays the same. Don't you understand what's going to happen to you if you hang on to these convictions? You're going to be discovered because you're going to start functioning like André Kohl. If you want to live out your years, we—you—have to create a new personality that is completely consistent and coherent and totally supplants the old one."

André felt himself being drawn down a path he knew he should not be on. Yet he was helpless to resist it. "So, the opposite of truth-telling being lying, you want Peter Burke to be a liar?"

Still Houghton showed no sign of anger. "In the strictest sense, you're already living a lie," he said quietly. "We're making you into a man who didn't exist."

André glared at Houghton. When he spoke he could almost taste the venom in his words. "I am mindful of that every waking moment."

"Why are you being so hard on yourself? If ever a subterfuge was justified, this was that time. There's not a person breathing today who, given your circumstances, wouldn't have made the same choice." Houghton paused for a moment. "Everyone tells lies at one time or another," he went on. "The difference is that where most people tell lies carelessly, an agent is absolutely scrupulous. He knows that if he's caught in a lie, even one that's seemingly inconsequential, he risks being imprisoned or killed. As a result he trains himself to be scrupulously honest, much more so than the average person, until the critical moment when a lie becomes essential. And even then, there's a difference. The civilian lies to help himself. The agent lies to help his country."

André nodded. "Show me a public servant who believes he's lying in the interest of his country and I'll show you a dangerous man. That's just one step away from an 007 license to operate outside of society's laws. When your agent has done it enough times for his country and gotten away with it, he'll begin to do it for himself."

"We're more aware of that danger than anyone," Houghton said patiently. "To guard against it, we try to recruit either extremely moral people or people who are in such desperate trouble that they'll do exactly what they should." He smiled. "You qualify on both counts."

"No way, Charles."

Houghton pursed his lips, and nodded, as though in recognition of the problem. "Let me ask you something," he said. "When we decided on this disposition, you listed as one of your objectives finding the people who were after André. Is that still your objective?"

"Absolutely."

"How do you propose to go about it?"

"By doing what I've always done, asking questions and using logic and piecing the parts together by talking to a lot of people."

"What kind of people?"

André shrugged. "People who might know something about it."

"Why would these people have any interest in talking to Peter Burke? He's not a reporter. He can't be, because if he were he'd have a public record. The fact is that as Peter Burke you don't have the resources any longer to find out who killed André Kohl. André had the resources, but he's not alive to use them. And there's no way the intelligence agencies that helped him are going to work with a stranger named Peter Burke."

André was trapped, and he knew it. Houghton was saying what he had resisted admitting to himself ever since coming to England. And yet he could not bring himself to acknowledge it to Houghton. "Look, you guys have your high tech methods, but beyond that, the deep hard work of an investigator isn't any different from that of an experienced investigative reporter."

"If you think that you can find out who killed André Kohl by using reportorial methods, you are very foolish, indeed."

"I've done pretty well with those methods."

"That's true. But you've never solved a murder, particularly a political one."

"I'd think that would be a lot easier to solve than a murder perpetrated by criminals."

"Why?"

"The motive would be more suggestive. A man is murdered for his money, it could be any one of a hundred thousand criminals with the generalized motive of greed or profit or whatever you want to call it. When a man is murdered for political reasons, the people opposed to what he represented are pretty easy to identify."

Houghton shook his head. "André Kohl could never have found out who tried to kill him. If you want to find André Kohl's killers you'd better understand how to do it. You're not going to be officially inscribed. You're just being trained to protect yourself, and possibly to enable you to make some headway." Houghton paused. When he resumed speaking, he looked like he had aged a year. "You are very much on my conscience. I want to protect you in the best way I know how. But unless you help us, you're never going to make it."

"I can't do it. I've tried. You can change my face and my body and my voice, but in my mind, I'm still André."

Houghton nodded. He was silent for at least a minute. When he spoke, his voice was very soft. "Would it change your mind if you knew there's someone out there who may not be convinced that André Kohl is dead?"

As the light faded in the study, Houghton told André about the break-in at Meredith's apartment and why he suspected that agents might be on his trail. "If they didn't take anything, that

135

suggests to me they were looking for something they didn't find—evidence that you're alive."

"Such as a letter from me written since I supposedly died."

"Exactly," Houghton said, then added almost apologetically, "We're all in the same business. We all know one another's tricks."

André looked blankly at Houghton, too disappointed to speak. If what Houghton said was true, this whole charade had been in vain. No, not all. He *had* managed to extract himself, and thus the danger he represented, from Meredith's life. That thought was all that consoled him.

12

The first thing Charles Houghton had learned as a young investigator was to start with telephone calls. If you could get hold of a person's telephone bill you could determine a great deal about the kind of life he led: the nature of his business, the extent of his activities, the degree of his success or failure and, of course, the identity of virtually everyone with whom he dealt. On the personal side, the revelations could be just as devastating. The leads were all there, not simply to the construction of a history but to the creation of a psychological profile.

Virgil Craig's phone bills, which Billy, Houghton's assistant, had obtained from the telephone company, were something of an exception. What was missing on them told Houghton at least as much about the man as what was present, more than confirming Madeline Martin's impression of him as a loner who had led an ascetic's life. Retired persons tend to spend a great deal of time on the telephone; to judge by his toll calls, Craig wasn't like that at all. They were relatively few, and bunched together. Days would pass without any charges at all. When he did make calls, the man appeared to be all business. There was not a single identifiable toll call to an individual who could be characterized as simply a friend; there was not a single identifiable call to a woman. He was just as obviously a man who worked in mysterious ways. Almost half the calls were to the main switchboard at the Central Intelligence Agency, even though the men he would logically be calling would all have direct lines. Why call in such a manner? To avoid creating a traceable record. The same objective undoubtedly held with reference to most of the remaining calls. With several significant exceptions they had all been made to half a dozen telephone booths in and around Washington.

The exceptions were a series of overseas calls Craig had made beginning in mid-April until just before his death near the end of May. Those calls, for the most part, *had* left a traceable record. Had Craig become careless? Not likely. Had he decided that because the calls were overseas they wouldn't be traced? That wasn't likely either. The probable reasons were that he considered time of the essence, and the gains worth the risk. Whatever the explanation, the calls enabled Houghton to reconstruct a great deal of what Craig had done from the day that they had met.

Four months had passed since their encounter, but the memory of it was as intact as if it had happened an hour ago. He could remember asking himself, as he swung on his canes across the sickly lawn and onto the sagging porch of the old colonial house, its wooden siding badly in need of paint, what kind of man would spy for thirty years and then squirrel himself away a quarter of a mile from a country road in the rolling hills of Virginia? His first look at Craig had given him at least a partial answer. The slack face, mottled skin and rheumy eyes laced with tiny red lines suggested that this lifelong bachelor had a companion after all: alcohol. Craig confirmed that impression within minutes; although it was not yet 11 A.M., he poured Scotch into a teacup and sipped it throughout their interview.

"I haven't the vaguest idea what this is about," he'd said nervously after sitting in a paisley-covered wing chair and attempting to look Houghton in the eye.

"Would it help if I identified myself?"

"No, no. I'm well aware of who you are. Tell me how I can help you."

"You interrogated Kurt Hoepner in 1945."

"Good Lord, is this about Hoepner?" Craig said. His eyes suddenly focused, his features froze, his body pressed against the back of his chair. "I hope you're not going to ask me to remember something that happened forty years ago."

"I'm afraid I am," Houghton said. He drew a piece of paper

from his pocket and handed it to Craig. "That's a copy of the last page of your interrogation report. As you see, a name's been blacked out. I'd like you to supply it."

Craig studied the report long past the amount of time it would have taken him to read it. Twice he raised his teacup to his lips and sipped without looking from the page. His hands were trembling, but that, Houghton knew, could be from age or the alcohol rather than from surprise. At last Craig looked up. "I can't remember. For the life of me, I can't remember."

"Would you remember the name if I told you?"

"Try it."

"Camille Laurent."

Craig frowned so deeply that he loosened flakes of dried skin. "The general? Whatever would make you think that he could have been a collaborator?"

"I won't answer that for the moment. Do you know why this document was sanitized?"

"No."

"Did you sanitize it?"

"No."

"Do you know who did?"

"I haven't the vaguest idea."

To his horror, Houghton felt his control slipping. "Why are you lying to me?" he demanded, knowing it was the worst thing he could say, yet unable to stop himself.

"I beg your pardon."

"Come off it, Craig. Who else would know what's in that report but you? I want the name of Hoepner's man in the Resistance."

Craig sipped from his teacup. His hand no longer shook. His watery eyes held steadily on Houghton's. He smiled lightly, revealing stained and crooked teeth. "I believe you're out of order, Mr. Houghton," he said in a voice now glacially calm. "I'm not in the agency any longer."

The feeling of helplessness that crept through Houghton in that moment was like nothing he had experienced before. He was the nation's top intelligence professional, with Orwellian forces at his disposal, but at that most crucial moment in his life he had suddenly been rendered powerless. He could not force Craig to tell him what he so desperately wanted to know. The man, as well as the information he certainly possessed, was beyond his reach. "Please!" he implored. "This is a matter of great importance to me. You see the way I am. I got it during a clandestine jump in France during the fall of '43. Someone betrayed the mission, probably the man Hoepner named. I'd like to know who it was."

"Why now?" Craig said.

"I can't tell you."

"And I couldn't tell you who the man was, even supposing I knew."

"Why not?"

"Because it's not in the national interest. That period opened up some terrible wounds, and many of them haven't healed yet."

Even now, Houghton could remember searching Craig's face for some clue as to what he meant. He saw a man who would have spent his years in retirement seeking to validate his existence from the perspective of enforced obsolescence, angry that he no longer mattered, critical of any policy that did not extend the line of history he had helped to draw. That line was the Cold War. By his definition, the national interest meant dominance over the Soviet Union. What could a minor league betrayal involving the French Resistance and the Gestapo during World War II have to do with the Cold War? he had asked himself at the time. He knew that the answer wouldn't come from Craig.

Now, of course, he had the answer. In Craig's mind, and the minds of those who thought like he did, the election of Laurent to the French presidency had been vital to the security of the United States. It was their belief that only he could have rooted out, once and for all, the insidious socialist tendencies that had festered in France since the end of World War II. His steadfastness in this regard had been evident even during the war, when he had collaborated with the Gestapo for the sole purpose of making certain that Communists didn't capture the Resistance—and thus the vehicle to political power in postwar France. At the time of Houghton's visit to Craig, Laurent had been on the verge of capturing that power, but the knowledge that he had collaborated with the Nazis—no matter how farsighted his reasons—would have destroyed his chances, and therefore had to be suppressed.

140

Within moments after Houghton left his house that April morning, Craig had been on the telephone, spreading the alarm. His first overseas call, the record showed, had been placed to Pierre Gauthier of the French secret service, the DGSE, the man who would become head of the department should Camille Laurent be elected. A number of toll calls to the Washington area followed, several to the switchboard at the CIA, and later to the various telephone booths in and around Washington. Several more calls were made in the following weeks to Paris, most of them to Gauthier, two to Laurent himself. And then Craig had made two calls to La Paz, both to Kurt Hoepner. Both calls had been made just days before André Kohl had gone to La Paz with Meredith, to confront Hoepner with a copy of the dossier he'd found in the Gestapo archives made available to him by the Russians. In that dossier was a statement André had relayed to Houghton and Houghton would never forget:

> Leading *réseau* in this sector has now been successfully infiltrated by placement of sympathetic man of military background, Camille Laurent, code name "Felix," in important leadership position. Information furnished by "Felix" enabled us to meet and destroy American intelligence mission. Future successes likely as no suspicions aroused.

Two more overseas calls had been made by Craig just before he'd left for Bolivia. Both calls had been made on the morning of the same day in May, minutes apart. The second call, to Paris, had been made to Pierre Gauthier. But coming right after the first call, it made no sense at all.

That call had been to Moscow.

The question was, to whom? The identity of the phone in Moscow simply could not be established. It was in no computer files on Moscow. It was not the number of any American official. It was not the private number of any American in Moscow. It was not the number of any embassy part of or friendly to the West. Nor was the number in the unofficial yet accurate and comprehensive directory published several years before by the British-born wife of a high-ranking Soviet official in the foreign ministry. That directory, the likes of which had never previously existed in a city whose telephone numbers were notoriously hard to come by, had been a godsend to diplomats and journalists alike. It listed the office and often the home telephone numbers of virtually every important official in the government. The telephone numbers of foreign diplomats and journalists were in there, as well. But none of those several thousand numbers matched the one Craig had called on that day in May, just before his departure for Bolivia.

Lacking that specific fact, Houghton had to work by reason. Why would Craig call Moscow at a moment when so much was going on? To judge simply by the proximity of the calls to one another, the call to Moscow definitely had had something to do with the call to France. Was there someone in Moscow he had had to consult before telephoning Gauthier? If so, it would have to be someone with whom he'd had dealings at an earlier time in his life, someone who had been instrumental in setting up the informal network and now, even though posted far away, still acted as a consultant. It was the only explanation that made sense.

Who could this consultant be? The most obvious possibility was the CIA's station chief in Moscow. Houghton could scarcely believe that one. The man, David Anderson, was twenty-five years Craig's junior, and totally dissimilar in temperament. Although geopolitics was his life, he was not himself political. Houghton could not conceive of Anderson acting in any way outside official boundaries where the United States or agency business was concerned. All right, everyone was suspect, but there were certain people you knew just couldn't be involved. Besides, the phone number wasn't his. That didn't mean he couldn't have an unlisted phone, but given all the other factors, it simply didn't figure that Anderson was the man.

Who else, then? From his home that evening, Houghton called Madeline Martin; an hour later, she was at his apartment. "I'm sorry to trouble you," he said.

"It's no trouble," she said.

He handed her a piece of paper. "Here's a roster of the American embassy in Moscow. Everyone's on it, our people as well as State's. I'd like you to see whether any of these people ever had dealings with Virgil Craig."

Madeline studied the list. "I'll double check tomorrow, but I can tell you right now that the answer's no."

"Damn," Houghton said under his breath.

"What's up?"

Houghton shook his head. "I wish I could tell you. I really do."

"I understand," she said. She let herself out the door.

Once more he was alone with his question: *If not an American, who?*

In a simple and trusting world, the answer to that question could be simply obtained. All one had to do was dial the number and ask whoever answered to identify himself. But that approach, which would stand little chance of working in a country as open as the United States, stood no chance at all in a country as closed as the Soviet Union. Houghton's last realistic chance, therefore, was the National Security Agency, which for the last three decades had been monitoring every overseas call made from the United States. Key words spoken by either party to the call would trigger a computer response and record the call for eventual analysis by NSA.

The following morning, Houghton put in a search request to NSA, but he was not hopeful. It was extremely unlikely that Craig, who had been so careful to avoid creating a traceable record of his domestic calls, would be careless with his vocabulary in his calls abroad.

That proved to be the case. NSA had no record of any overseas calls made from Craig's Virginia home.

In the context of so much frustration, Billy's analysis of the phone bills of Madeline Martin's suspects, which arrived on Houghton's desk the same day as the NSA response, could not have been more timely. The results were fragmentary and inconclusive, but powerfully suggestive. Three of the men, Loomis, Slovotkin and McDonald, had been in constant touch with one another. All three, in addition, had made multiple calls from their homes to countries dominated by ripe and active internal conflicts: Chile, Peru, Nicaragua, Guatemala, El Salvador, the Philippines, South Africa and half a dozen others. While the identity of the persons they had called had not yet been established, the conclusion was inescapable that these men were involved in efforts beyond their official duties. Moreover, the calls had produced telephone bills running in some cases to several thousand dollars a month. It was hard to believe that these men could pay those bills on their government salaries. The money had to be coming from somewhere; it was not unreasonable to suspect that the suppliers were individuals or groups interested in specific outcomes in each of those countries. For the moment, it was all conjecture, but at the very least, Loomis, Slovotkin and McDonald all had to be suspected of being members of the network.

By the same measure, however, Harry Coffee was *not* suspect. The deputy director of operations hadn't made a single overseas call from his home. He hadn't called any of the other three men. Nor had any of them called him. It was conceivable, of course, that the most adept intelligence agent in the agency had just been super careful, but it did seem more likely now that his long-ago encounter with Virgil Craig—the event that had flagged him as a suspect—had been nothing more than circumstantial.

Well, there was a way to make sure of that. It was risky, but the risk was worth it. The CIA could never regain its health so long as its director of operations was suspect.

Within minutes, Coffee was in Houghton's office. "I've got a job for you, Harry," the director said, "and I want you to take personal charge. There are a lot of loose ends on this Latin America business, and we may never tie them up, but the one I really want to know about is how the whole deal was financed. We know that Craig set Hoepner up, but he had to have money to do that. Where did it come from?"

"Gotcha."

"Can you get right on it?"

"Not full time for the moment, but I can certainly get it started."

"Fair enough."

"I'll keep you posted," Coffee said.

When he was gone, Houghton wheeled his chair around and twirled the knob on the safe behind his desk. From the safe he removed a folder containing a report from Shlomo Glaser of the Mossad. In midsummer, Houghton had asked Shlomo to investigate Carl Sanders, the man who had operated for the CIA out of a bank in Buenos Aires, and who had been on Madeline Martin's list of suspects. Just yesterday, the report had come in. As Houghton reread the memo, he reflected with satisfaction that Carl Sanders had one last duty to perform for the Company before he was fired.

At five o'clock that afternoon, Houghton called Madeline Martin. "By any chance, are you free for dinner?"

There was a moment's pause. "I could arrange to be free," she said.

"I don't want to inconvenience you."

"No, no, it's quite all right."

"Good. Then be at my place at eight."

"Are you cooking?"

"Of course."

"Then let me bring dessert."

Three hours later, she stood in Houghton's kitchen watching in admiration as he sautéed two filets of sea bass, then garnished them with anchovies and capers. Throughout the dinner he gave no clue about why he had invited her. "The suspense is killing me," she said as she served the dessert, kiwi tarts.

"Better that than getting killed on assignment. I asked you here to discuss an assignment, but now I'm not so sure it's a good idea."

"Why don't you let me be the judge of that?"

"Because I'm not sure you're qualified."

"Try me."

"All right. We have it authoritatively that the Arab terrorists who tried to kill André Kohl in Paris last June were paid by a German. We need to know who put up the money."

"That doesn't sound so dangerous."

"It could be if you disturb the wrong people."

"Then I'll be sure not to do that."

"Is this something you think you'd know how to handle?"

Madeline smiled. "Let's say it's an opportunity to grow in the job."

13

In the end, it was not Fleming's bullying or Houghton's entreaties or even the enhanced sense of jeopardy that brought André around. It was a woman named Kate Berrigan. She was an acting coach, a former actress of ample girth who'd once played leads for Dublin's Abbey Players but had surrendered to her love of food, which she now indulged in London. She arrived two days after André's second surgery. "Well, now," she said in a booming broguish voice, a reassuring smile on her robust face, "I don't know who you are, or what you look like with all those bandages on you, which is a bit of a handicap when one has been asked to help one create a character completely different from the person one was. But, God, how delicious, to be remade into anything one wished! Do you know who I'd be? Audrey Hepburn—slim and elegant and screwing Gary Cooper. Did you see them in *Love in the Afternoon?* My very favorite-most picture. Be a dear, Peter, and walk across the room."

They were in the drawing room of the manor, a large space dominated by an enormous open fireplace, with a low ceiling supported by darkened oak beams and walls covered with a vertical stripe to add an illusion of height. Walking across the room was not that simple a matter, for it was densely furnished in early Victorian style, with a bulky sofa, assorted upholstered chairs, a games table, a coffee table, a circular table, a sitting stool, several footstools, two "what-nots" and even a basket on the carpeted floor filled with painted ceramic balls. Nonetheless, André did as bidden.

"Whoever you were didn't dance much, did he?" Kate said.

"Not too much."

"As in, not at all."

"He was known to dance."

"But maybe once every three years?"

"How did you know?"

"Your walk is a bit, well, plodding, not like a dancer's at all." She rose and moved toward him. "Dancers walk with grace, lightly on their feet, their heads high and carriage erect."

He could see at once that Kate had been a dancer. For all her weight, she seemed to glide his way. "Dance with me, Peter," she said, and before he could protest that he really didn't feel up to it she'd led him to the stone floor of the foyer, taken his arms, positioned them correctly and gently initiated a waltz as she sang the theme music from *Dr. Zhivago*. "Very good!" she said, as André found the rhythm. "You could be a *good* dancer."

"I'm pretty clumsy."

"In your previous life. But the man we invent will be graceful. And suave, very suave, a cross between Fred Astaire and Cary Grant. Would you like that?"

"Why not?" André said, catching, in spite of himself, her infectious mood.

That very afternoon, they began to build a character for Peter Burke, literally from the ground up, creating before anything a distinctive walk of short, rapid steps on the balls of his feet, the walk, Kate said, of a man used to moving and changing directions quickly. They pushed a table in the foyer into the library to enlarge their floor space, then pretended they were skating together, their left hands joined, his right arm around her waist, swinging their weight fully onto their left feet, then their right, as they circled the foyer. Playing tapes Kate had brought, they danced for hours, waltzes, fox trots, rhumbas, tangos, sambas, merengues, until André did truly begin to feel like another person, if only in the smallest way, during the time they were together.

Little by little, Kate introduced him to the actor's world of make-believe. She gave him exercises designed to move him in tiny increments from the inflexible mold of his reality to the boundless universe of fantasy. They played dozens of games in which they pretended, first, that they were children, then teenagers, then college students, then adults of countless varieties. Ever so gradually, she brought him to the point where he might begin to play Peter. This was the point beyond which Fleming had been unable to take him. He knew exactly where he was, and what was expected of him, and to Kate's credit, he truly wanted to succeed. The key was her stress on make-believe. Fleming and Houghton were telling him to be Peter Burke. Kate was telling him to pretend. He could never *be* Peter, but he might be able to make believe that he was.

There was an additional factor in Kate's favor. Fleming had proposed that Peter be innocuous. The character Kate was helping him to invent was suave, debonair and charming. To a man who had always felt ill at ease with strangers and in unfamiliar surroundings, conquering such discomfort was a heady prospect.

There was yet another factor helping Kate. For more than a month now, he had been emotionally alone, so shocked by everything that had happened to him that he had trusted no one and been incapable of receiving or rendering even the smallest degree of affection. Kate had managed to penetrate that wall as incrementally as she had introduced him to make-believe. At first he had resisted, but then, seeing how much she cared about helping him without even the faintest idea of why this transformation had been undertaken, he had let himself relate to her in the tiniest degree. The result had been as consequential as a pin in a balloon. Once he understood what had exploded in him, he came to view her, almost instantly, as friend, confessor, mentor, mother, everything short of lover. Yet there was nothing he could tell her, and no affection he could overtly give her. The only way in which he could express his gratitude was by helping her to succeed in what she had come to do.

Each day there was progress, but they both knew that he had yet to make that imaginative leap that would enable him to play his role on demand and with conviction. Never once did Kate scold him, however, or express the slightest doubt as to his ultimate success, even though failure piled upon failure. One day, at last, she said, "Now, Peter, you're on a boat, all alone. The boat has been tied to a dock for ever so long, to the point that you've become restless and decided to put to sea. One by one you undo the lines that moor the boat to the dock, and then, ever so gradually, the boat begins to edge from the dock, and then to slip into the channel and out through the channel to the ocean. And very gradually, the land falls away until it's no longer in sight, and even more, no longer part of your life. There's nothing out there, Peter, just you and your boat, and you can set your course for Never Never Land. And when you reach Never Never Land, your past will no longer be with you, and you will be whomever you wish to be. Are you sailing, Peter?"

"Yes."

"Where are you bound?"

"For Never Never Land."

"Can you see the shore?"

"Yes."

"Are you landing?"

"Not yet."

"Land, Peter."

"I can't."

"You can! Imagine! Believe!"

He stood there, immobilized in the center of the room, staring at this overweight yet voluptuous woman whose face had suddenly turned dark with emotion. Her arms reached out to him imploringly, her wide eyes beseeched him. "Close your eyes!" she cried. "Breathe deeply, Peter. Focus on your breathing." He did as bidden for at least a minute. With each breath he felt less foolish. Soon he began to feel a lightness, and then a tingling in his limbs, and then a motion, as though he were really on a boat, riding up and down on the swells. And suddenly he was rising on a swell so steep that when he reached the top it carried him across an invisible reef to the shore. It was a delicious feeling, unlike any he had ever experienced before, of being suspended in time, in a round enclosure that isolated and protected him from everyone and everything. In this enclosure, the loudest sound was his breathing, which had deepened and slowed. He knew he was somewhere he'd never been, and he didn't want to leave. Minutes passed.

"Where are you, Peter?" Kate whispered.

"In Never Never Land."

"What's it like?"

"Beautiful."

"Are there people?"

"Yes."

"What are they like?"

"They're lovely."

"What are they doing?"

"They're smiling."

"Yes. Go on."

"There's a young woman, very beautiful. She's coming toward me, holding out her arms."

"Hold your arms out, Peter."

He held out his arms, and felt Kate in them, and felt her arms go around him. He buried his head in her shoulder. Only then did he feel the wetness on his face, and realize that she understood the joy and sorrow he was feeling.

During the second week of Kate's visit, the actor Richard Hampstead arrived, to begin with André the long process of changing the timbre and style of his speech. Peter Burke, André knew, had gone to the kinds of schools that made boys sound like George Plimpton—the kind of upper-class Eastern accent that almost passed for British, and as far from the neutral, plebian speech of native Californians as were the Atlantic and Pacific seaboards. Hampstead, tall and thin, in his fifties, with a good-looking face known to countless millions of film-goers who would not be able to tell you his name, had played characters from every part of the United States. His American accent was uncanny, and he could do a perfect imitation of Plimpton, whom he'd seen only a few times on television. Given André's own ear for languages, it was not long before his accent was a reasonable facsimile of Plimpton's. But Hampstead wasn't satisfied. "It will get you by with strangers. They'll immediately assign a class and origin to you. But it won't play with anyone who knew you. There's a difference between one's speech and one's voice. We can have you speaking Eskimo and your *voice* will still sound the same. In your case, I fear, the voice is very distinctive."

"What do you propose?"

"It's out of my field, you understand, but I should think that if one wanted to really pull it off, one would seek out a throat man and have a small adjustment. It's really quite simple, from what I understand, an injection of Teflon in the vocal chords. Several of my colleagues whose voices were going prematurely have had it done, and the result is rather marvelous."

It was a measure of the change in André that he took the advice seriously. He could feel the change, himself, and he knew exactly what had produced it. For him, the game had turned from negative to positive. Instead of destroying André, they were creating Peter. It was a matter of emphasis to be sure—each fresh mannerism would replace an old one—but to André the difference was critical.

Besides, he liked Hampstead, who confessed after several drinks one evening that he had wanted to be a historian but had become an actor, instead, in order to flee the reality he found too grim to confront. André, once a naval officer, was won over with Hampstead's story of how he went through Sandhurst and earned a commission in the Royal Navy, only to discover that the slightest pitch of a ship made him seasick. The psychiatrist assigned to cure him only made it worse; instead of suggesting, under hypnosis, that Hampstead would not be seasick any more, he fixed it so that he would no longer throw up.

André laughed until he ached and, for the first time since he'd been wounded, forgot his misery, if only for an hour. For the first time, as well, he had the tiniest glimpse of a new world, populated by new people. It wasn't much, but it was something.

And then Dr. Dover returned to bond the porcelain caps to the front of André's teeth. When it was over, the dentist handed him a mirror so small all André could see was his mouth. He parted his lips, and stared at his teeth in wonder. They bore no resemblance to what he'd seen in his mirror throughout his life, and yet they looked as though they'd been that way forever.

"Are you pleased?" Dr. Dover asked.

He was, but couldn't bring himself to say so. Instead, he asked, "How long will they last?"

"Depends on you. Years, if you're careful. No spareribs, and don't bite into anything hard, like a Granny Smith apple. Best to cut those up. Brush gently, as well."

Half a dozen times that evening, André went to a mirror to study his teeth, much as a child might gaze at a new toy, feeling, at last, a sense of renewal in spite of everything that had happened. It bothered him that neither he nor Dr. Dover mentioned the music they would not be playing together—he was sure that Fleming had passed the word to the dentist—but he did not let it get to him.

And finally there came the moment that André had both dreaded and anticipated more than any other, when Dr. Collins removed the bandages from his head. He looked André over meticulously before pronouncing his verdict. "You've healed extremely well. I doubt that you—or anyone—will notice the scars at all. Would you like to have a look?"

André could not help but smile at the doctor's classic British understatement. Yes, indeed, he wanted to have a look, more than he had ever thought possible when this transformation began. There was still much to do: more pounds to lose, more iron to pump, thousands upon thousands more sit-ups and sit-backs and crunches and torso twists and side bends to further slim and solidify his waist, as well as a lipectomy to vacuum the excess fat cells from his love handles should all other efforts to remove them fail; applications of phenol acid, which would produce a smoother and lighter skin; that surgical procedure on his vocal chords, which, he'd learned, would give him a softer, more mellow voice; contact lenses to change the color of his eyes; and a session with a stylist, who would give his hair a short but full look and color away the gray. There was a difficult new task to master: learning to be left-handed in everything he did, a stratagem devised by Fleming principally to make certain that André's and Peter's handwriting did not match in any way. There were more acting lessons, as well, and weeks, perhaps months, of study ahead in Korean as well as international finance before André could play the role of Peter Burke with the degree of confidence that would place him beyond suspicion. And there was an important new addition to the curriculum: computers. They'd all agreed, on reflection, that no master of international trade would be operating today without benefit of computer programs, a subject about which André Kohl had known nothing.

But even as he had waited impatiently for Dr. Collins' invitation, André already knew that the gap between reality and make-believe had shrunk to such a degree that at times there was no space between them. He no longer fought the idea of being called Peter. In his mind, it was no longer André internalizing, it was Peter Burke. When he talked to himself on his walks around the estate, which he took at least once a day in order to be able to practice his George Plimpton accent out of the earshot of others, he addressed himself as Peter. And when he thought of the future, it was as Peter Burke, not André Kohl. When he thought of André, as he did less and less frequently, it was as a close friend who had died.

Dr. Collins stood aside as André walked slowly to a full-length mirror pinned to a wall. A figure came into view, that of a bearded man one might judge to be in his mid-forties, erect, if not quite lean certainly not fat, with scarcely a wrinkle in his long and classic face. It was a handsome face, as well, the face of a keen and self-possessed man. The man looking at the image smiled, revealing two rows of even, healthy teeth. "Hello, Peter," he said.

II
PETER

14

Peter Burke left England in a driving rain on a foul November day. At Heathrow, he presented himself at the emigration desk, where a pleasant man in his late thirties, dressed in civilian clothes, compared his face with the photograph in his passport, stamped the passport and returned it with a smile. "Hope you had a nice stay with us, Mr. Burke," he said.

"Lovely," Peter said, taking his passport.

The emigration man frowned. "May I see that again, sir?" he said, reaching for the passport. He opened it to the first page, the one with the vital details, studied it for a second, then smiled. "Ah, yes, birthplace New York," he said as he returned the passport.

"Something wrong?" Peter said.

"No, no. From the way you spoke, I thought for a moment that you might be one of us."

"I'm English at heart."

"That's very nice to hear, sir. Have a nice trip."

Peter walked around the desk and put his tote bag on the moving belt of the x-ray machine, then walked through the metal detector. A moment later, he was inside the passenger lounge, a tall, slim man with the graceful, slightly pigeon-toed stride of an athlete, dressed in a sport coat whose tweed material, natural shoulders and narrow lapels immediately placed him to anyone who noted fashions as an Ivy League American. His shirt was white, a color making a comeback, his collar a button-down and his tie a regimental stripe. His slacks, an expensive gray flannel, were cuffed at the bottom and rode slightly above a pair of well-shined cordovan penny loafers. A full head of hair, neat and closely cropped, completed the picture of a youngish middle aged member of the American Establishment. It was his bearing and expression, more than his dress, that projected this sense of youthfulness. His head seemed to stretch toward the ceiling, and his body to move effortlessly under it, the curves of his spine reduced to a minimum, shoulders carried naturally on his frame, chest high, stomach flat. No compromising indulgences for this man; he was obviously someone who put great store in fitness, and had invested the time and effort to achieve it. As he moved through the lounge toward the newspaper and book racks, his brown eyes, soft yet keen, surveyed the room with the eagerness of a man so in love with life that he did not wish to overlook its smallest details. His smooth, cleanly shaven face seemed unmarked by struggle, its pleasant expression, almost a smile, advertising an inner peace.

He seemed no less tranquil or composed ninety minutes later as he passed through immigration at Charles de Gaulle Airport, outside of Paris, even though the young uniformed policeman who examined the tourist card he'd filled out aboard the plane and then matched the photograph in his passport with his face did so with deliberate care, unmindful of the long line of arriving passengers waiting to enter the country. After collecting his bag—a tan Hartmann whose battered condition seemed an appropriate match for the many stamps in his passport—he passed through the "nothing-to-declare" portal at customs and emerged from the terminal into weather that was at least as foul as the climate he'd left in London. There were taxis waiting, and he was tempted, but—as a reminder to himself of who he was—he boarded the shuttle bus and rode to the RER railway station, where he transferred to a train for the half-hour ride to the Gare du Nord. From there he took the Métro to St. Germain des Prés. He emerged from the Métro on the north side of the Boulevard St. Germain, less than two hundred yards from his destination, the Hotel St. Germain des Prés at 36, rue Bonaparte, the street leading from the boulevard to the Seine.

He walked those yards as though he had never walked them before; in truth, he could not remember the last time he had, or whether he ever had. Certainly, he had never walked them with a suitcase slung from his shoulder and a tote bag in hand. He hadn't taken the Métro in years, and other than a taxi, the only means of transportation he had used to get from Charles de Gaulle to Paris was a private, chauffeur-driven car. But that was then and this was now, and everything now was different.

Paris, above all, was different, as familiar as a favorite reverie, yet as fresh as a tourist's eyes. He had determined to see it in that way, but he would have, in any case, whether he had consciously tried to or not. In the forefront of his consciousness was the realization of how grooved had been that life now relegated to an attic of his mind: a car from home to office, or to the homes of a few close friends, or to one of a dozen restaurants, or to the Ritz Hotel —the same patterns each day, each week, each year. This time there would be no car, no office, no friends, and only three calculated visits to those restaurants, and one trip to the bar of the Ritz. Staying at the Ritz was out of the question. It did not fit the budget of Peter Burke, American, forty-six, investment banker, presently between positions, in Paris as a visitor for the first time since graduation from Harvard a quarter of a century before.

The Hotel St. Germain des Prés did. It was one of those small, three-star hotels on the Left Bank that made up in charm what it lacked in amenities, and gave its patrons the feeling that they were part of le vrai Paris. Peter's room would cost the equivalent of seventy dollars a night, service and tax included. The manager of the hotel, a tall and striking brunette whose dark hair, olive skin and straight nose suggested an Italian ancestry, gave him his key and wished him a pleasant stay. She spoke to him in heavily accented English, which surprised him before it pleased him. Of all the things he had learned to do in the last four months, the most difficult, perhaps, was to speak French like an American who had learned it in college and had scarcely used it since. The hotel manager's response persuaded him that he had succeeded.

Before going to his room, he made a quick inventory of the ground floor. The entry was a corridor ten feet across and no more than thirty feet long, small enough to be dominated by a spectacular floral arrangement that sat on a table across from the reception desk. Beyond the corridor was the small lobby, approximately thirty feet square, which doubled in the morning as a breakfast room, and in the evening as a bar. It was a cozy room, with muted light and comfortable chairs and sofas. What most distinguished it was an enclosed garden visible through the row of windows at the far end of the room. At eye level, not more than four feet wide and tiered against a wall, it was laden with rows of yellow and white chrysanthemums, as well as shrubs and fuchsias.

His room, on the fifth floor, was equally cozy, but very small, with a low beamed ceiling, a bed that took up most of the floor space, an armoire, and a desk next to a small window looking to the west onto the roofs of the neighboring buildings. There would be no point in putting a potted plant on the windowsill to signal that all was well, as Jack Fleming had suggested months ago in the Cotswolds; it could not be seen from the street. That thought put another into his head, Fleming's warning that he must always think like Peter Burke. In that sense, this room was perfect; there was no danger, as long as he occupied it, that he would mistake his position in life for the one once enjoyed by André Kohl.

The next several days persuaded him that he truly had entered another life. He had no destination, and no initial purpose other than to ease himself comfortably and inconspicuously into the flow of the city. Later, in ten days or two weeks, there would be tests to pass, but until then he was unpressured for the first time in months. All he was obliged to do was remember that he was Peter Burke. And so, he toured Paris in ways that linked up with few if any memories, riding the Métro and buses, walking the streets, strolling through the city's many parks, visiting museums he'd never had time for, examining the street markets, a harvest for the eyes with their mounds of bright produce, trays of glistening fish, and—this still being fall—racks of game, and taking his meals in restaurants that he had either never heard of or hadn't patronized in years. In the latter category, La Coupole, a Parisian institution, was ideal. It was on the Boulevard Montparnasse, about a mile from his hotel, as cavernous as a railway station, with high ceilings to match, its walls yellowed with age, its hundreds of tables filled with Parisians at their animated best. Peter returned to La Coupole night after night, knowing that, seated in the midst of the boisterous patrons and scurrying waiters, he would feel as much a part of the city as he could, given his exceptional circumstances, and assuage, if only somewhat, his terrible loneliness.

Nothing anyone might have done could have prepared him for that. He had lived as a bachelor since his divorce, and suffered empty hotel rooms during his travels, but the circumstances in both cases had been mitigated by days with his colleagues, and evenings with friends in that same lively spirit to which he was a spectator each evening at La Coupole. Eating alone was the worst; he could not remember the last time André Kohl had done so; nor could he imagine a more joyless experience. The one positive thing that could be said about his four months in the Cotswolds was that he had never dined alone.

A companion was out of the question at this juncture, even if he could find an agreeable one. The only solution was to keep himself as occupied as possible, and to that end he was out of the hotel by 10 o'clock each morning, venturing to parts of Paris he hadn't cultivated nearly as well as he would have liked to, hoping that discovery might somehow fill his void. It was in this manner that he found himself early one afternoon in the Marais, the city's oldest quarter, on the narrow winding streets lined with art galleries, boutiques, tailor shops, delicatessens and kosher butcher shops. The streets were heavily trafficked, not with cars but pedestrians. Occasionally, a young Hasidic Jew would walk by wearing the traditional long black coat and flat, broad-brimmed hat edged in white fur, black pants and shoes. But most of the Jews seemed as contemporary as other Parisians, a point poignantly emphasized by a hand-lettered sign in white letters painted on the windows of one of the delicatessens. Its message to passersby was that despite the ancient beliefs that Jews were agents of the devil who devoured the blood of Christian children, they were, in reality, decent, kind, loving people, worthy of the respect of all.

Reading the message, Peter felt a sudden resonance. Whoever had written it or caused it to be displayed wanted understanding, community with others not like themselves, peace. Alone, adrift, he understood something he had never thought about before: the primary need for acceptance.

On an impulse, he stepped inside, and was immediately overwhelmed by odors of spiced meats and fresh baked breads, and the sound of passionate discourse. All the tables were full; although many of the customers had finished eating, they were absorbed in their conversations and gave no sign of leaving. When ten minutes had passed and no one had left, the cashier asked Peter if he would like a vodka. He declined. After another ten minutes, a man in his sixties who seemed to be the owner came out from behind the counter and asked if he would please accept a vodka. This time, Peter agreed. "Good," the owner said. He went behind the counter again, returning a moment later with a bottle and two shot glasses. He filled them both, raised one and when Peter had raised his said, *"L'chayim."* They drank, Peter a sip, the owner the entire contents. "Do you know what that means, *'l'chayim'?"* he asked after exhaling in satisfaction. "It means 'to life.' The most beautiful toast there is."

"I agree," Peter said.

The owner leaned toward him, a twinkle in his eye, and smiled conspiratorially. "You're Jewish?"

"No."

The owner shrugged. Then he patted Peter's arm and said, "That's all right. You're a nice man." Despite Peter's protest, the owner filled his glass to the brim.

Finally, it was time to determine whether he was now the man who had been so assiduously created over the last four months in the Cotswolds, or whether those who knew him well would see through his elaborate and comprehensive disguise. He had designed the tests for himself, yet the mere thought of them sent tremors to his stomach, even though his previous experience had given him reason to be optimistic. In England three weeks earlier, Jack Fleming had invited him to dinner. "A graduation present," he'd explained. Except for his middle-of-the-night visit to a London hospital for a CAT scan just after his arrival, it was Peter's first foray off the estate since arriving in the Cotswolds. They'd gone to Buckland Manor, in Buckland, a hamlet a few miles from Broadway. "I think you'll like it," Fleming said as they drove onto the graveled driveway.

The manor, built in a vernacular style that had predominated in the region since the seventeenth century, was more prototypic than typical, a work of art in stone somewhere between cream and brown, its colors and texture so in harmony with the surrounding hillside that it almost seemed like an outcropping. The building was three stories high, with a series of pointed gables, mullioned windows and a steeply pitched roof covered with thick stone tiles. Next to the manor was a small, graceful church, and behind it a croquet pitch and formal gardens. Inside, the manor was a traditionalist's delight, its wooden floors glistening with polish and covered here and there with deep red Persian carpets and runners flecked with blue, its public rooms furnished with soft upholstered chairs and sofas and antique wood tables, dark brown and deeply lustered. Portraits of regal-looking men and women in fifteenth- and sixteenth-century costumes adorned the wood-paneled walls.

Fleming led Peter down a wide hallway into a spacious sitting room dominated by a fireplace at least five feet high and filled with leaping flames. A thin, medium-sized man wearing spectacles, perfectly turned out in a blue blazer and gray flannels, whom Peter judged to be in his mid-forties, stood behind the sofa, next to a tea table bearing bottles of spirits, mixers, an ice bucket and glasses. He smiled at them and extended his hand. "I'm Barry Berman," he said.

"Ah, the owner," Fleming said. "I'm Jack Fleming and this is Peter Burke."

Berman and his wife, it developed, had tired of the professional life in London, where he had been an accountant, bought Buckland Manor in the seventies and restored it with loving and lavish care. The manor, which could bed twenty-two guests in eleven rooms and suites, each with its own name, had become so popular year round that one needed to book, as Berman put it, two months in advance to be certain of accommodations. All this Peter, Jack and a dozen other guests learned from Berman as he poured their drinks and served them, while Mrs. Berman, as gregarious as her husband and just as carefully turned out, passed among them describing the options for dinner and taking their orders. So ebullient were the Bermans, and such effective hosts, that the guests, most of them strangers to one another twenty minutes before, were conversing like old friends by the time the proprietors ducked into the dining room and kitchen to make certain that preparations for their famous meals were on schedule.

Barry Berman was back minutes later, however, obviously alerted by someone at the entrance to the arrival of a new set of guests. "Robert," Peter heard Berman say with obvious delight. Immediately, the owner began to mix an American-style gin martini. Moments later, Peter went cold, as the man addressed as Robert approached the tea table to claim his drink. His back was to Peter, but there was no mistaking him, even from that angle: his large frame and slight stoop, his full head of straight, prematurely white hair and his hoarse, gravelly voice. Not ten feet away stood Bob O'Rourke, the London bureau chief of *The New York Times,* alongside whom André Kohl had covered stories at least twenty times over the last dozen years.

He had only a moment to try to collect himself while Berman poured O'Rourke's companion a Cinzano on the rocks. In another moment, they had turned and were moving to a vacant space on the sofa in front of the fireplace. Peter and Fleming, seated just to the side, rose, and Barry Berman introduced them. The woman had an Italian name, which Peter, in his confusion, didn't catch. She was dramatic-looking, as were all of the women with whom O'Rourke had been involved through the years, a tall brunette with voluptuous breasts and hips, and a way of flattering men she favored with the unmistakable appraisal of her large brown eyes. That was the look she bestowed upon Peter as he resumed his seat.

For the next twenty minutes, until Mrs. Berman mercifully called Fleming and Peter to dinner, he heard himself speaking of another life as though it had been his own: investment banking, consulting, years in international finance. He listened to his own words with as much disbelief as to the words of Fleming, whose story carried as much invention. Throughout, not a flicker of either doubt or recognition appeared in O'Rourke's eyes. He might have been talking to a total stranger.

"Nice going," Fleming said after Mrs. Berman had seated them in the dining room. "You passed with flying colors."

"I 'passed'? Was that a test?"

"I thought a trial run might be a good idea before things got too heavy."

"You mean you set that up?"

"Let's say I knew that O'Rourke would be here. It's where he always brings his playmates."

For hours afterward, Peter shook from the adrenalizing effects of the encounter. Not even the Bermans' splendid dinner, the best he had eaten in months, or his share of a bottle of vintage Bordeaux, or even the knowledge that he had succeeded could calm him.

Now, in Paris, he would shortly discover whether that success had been a fluke—O'Rourke, after all, was an acquaintance, not a true friend, and someone he saw infrequently—or whether he really could pass for the rest of his life as the man he had become. He would make a series of visits to old haunts, whose staffs knew André Kohl well, and where he would in all likelihood encounter André's friends and colleagues. If anyone so much as raised an eyebrow or wrinkled a forehead or said something suggestive, he was dutybound to report it.

On the evening of his fifteenth day in Paris, he had dinner at Chiberta. He had made the reservation himself, two days before. The owner, Louis Noel Richard, who had taken the reservation over the phone, seated him with courteous indifference. It was a miserable evening, despite the splendor of the food. Chiberta had been the setting for André's first evening with Meredith. It was there that he'd felt the first stirrings of his love. Since his arrival in Paris, Peter had willed himself to think of her as André's widow, but being in a room they'd once occupied together disarmed his will and sent his mind reeling backward to that first meeting—her little joke when he'd suggested they meet at his apartment: "Don't I get dinner first?"; how she'd entered the apartment with such extraordinary self-possession; the acuteness of her perception and the candor of her questions. "How long have you been divorced?" she'd asked. "How did you know I was divorced?" he'd said, and she'd replied, "I saw the pictures of your children on the piano. Since there doesn't seem to be a Mrs. Kohl around, I took an educated guess." "And why did you ask?" he'd said then, and she'd replied, "Because you still sleep on your side of the bed." "Do you always get so quickly to the point?" he'd asked after pouring some champagne to cover his confusion. "Don't you prefer it that way?" she'd said in a tone indicating that his answer had to be yes. "Men and women think nothing of screwing on their first night together, the most intimate act imaginable, and yet they wouldn't dream of opening their minds to one another, which is just as much fun and a lot more rewarding." "Cheers," he'd said, for lack of an alternative.

Now, sitting alone in Chiberta, Peter silently lifted his glass.

At one o'clock the following day, he entered Fouquet's for lunch. He asked for a table on the terrace, the one facing Avenue George V. That was where André Kohl had always sat when he had lunch at Fouquet's, which was fairly often because the USBC office was just across the street, on the north side of the Champs Élysées. The maître d'hôtel, who had seated André several hundred times, obliged him with the same courteous indifference Peter had been shown the previous evening at Chiberta. A second success, this one mitigated somewhat by the absence of anyone from the bureau. But this time, at least, there were no memories to haunt him.

Saturday lunch would present a far more serious challenge. On that day, he planned to go to Lipp, on the Boulevard St. Germain, a minute's walk from his hotel. There he could count on the presence of at least two dozen friends from the city's inner circle, in addition to the inimitable Roger Cazes, who had run the brasserie for forty-seven years and was there every day except Sunday to make certain, above all, that the best people sat at the best tables. They would be there, these "best people," just as they had been virtually every Saturday for years, eating exactly what they had eaten on every previous visit: either a *Salade Lipp* with tuna or pickled beef to start, followed by the Saturday special, *gigot d'agneau,* or the house special, *choucroûte garnie.* With the meal they would drink either wine or a *serieux,* a half liter of beer.

Peter had two choices, to arrive very early, promptly at noon, or very late, at two-thirty or even three. If he arrived at twelve-thirty or one o'clock, he knew that he would have to wait at least an hour and a half for a table, and by then all of André's friends would have gone. Fortified by an aperitif at the Deux Magots across the street, he arrived at precisely twelve o'clock, with his scenario firmly in mind and his lines well rehearsed.

Monsieur Cazes was guarding the door, just as Peter had expected, a short man in his mid-seventies who had inherited the restaurant from his father in 1936. "One, please," Peter said, his French accent as much a giveaway to his identity as his Ivy League clothes.

Monsieur Cazes appraised him and, without a word or a smile, signaled for him to climb the stairs to the *salle* on the floor above.

"I'd prefer to be in the main dining room," Peter said.

"Not possible, monsieur. The tables are taken."

"But they told me on the phone that you don't take reservations."

Once again, Monsieur Cazes appraised him. "If you wish to sit in this room, you will have to wait."

"How long?"

For an answer, Monsieur Cazes simply shrugged.

Peter hesitated, just long enough to draw Monsieur Cazes's attention to him once again. Then, with a look of resignation, he turned to mount the stairs. The moment he was certain Monsieur Cazes couldn't see him, he broke into a smile. It had gone exactly as he'd planned it; Monsieur Cazes had looked at him—really looked at him—without the slightest glimmer of recognition.

An hour later, after finishing his *gigot,* Peter left his table, walked downstairs and proceeded down the aisle toward the bathroom at the rear. He walked at a deliberate pace, gazing directly, and one by one, at a host of people he'd last seen as André Kohl: Philippe Labro, the head of RTL; Philippe Grumbach, the former editor of *L'Express,* who now worked for the media giant Robert Hersant; Roger Frey, the former head of the Constitutional Council; Jacques Guillaime, an aide to the President; and Jean-Didier Wolfromm, deputy director of the École des Beaux Arts. To a man, they looked his way, directly at him, and with attention, because he was violating their privacy, the most precious possession of every Frenchman. Just as he reached the end of the aisle, Monsieur Cazes was behind him, uttering a stream of invective. He was in the way, the waiters couldn't pass, he was disturbing the guests. Peter turned, smiled sweetly, held his hands out, palms up, in the universal sign of nonunderstanding, and continued to the toilet. Without any doubt, every eye he'd wanted to gaze on him had now been turned his way. There hadn't been a single sign of recognition, and not a single exclamation of "André!"

At five o'clock Monday afternoon, he was in front of the Ritz. He timed his entry so that he would walk right by the doorman, the one with the round and ruddy face who had always taken charge of André's car. "Bonjour, monsieur," the doorman said, lifting a finger to his cap. But no smile creased his face.

Moments later, Peter was through the revolving door, and there, of course, just as he'd known he would be, was Josef, the security guard, the tall and husky Slav with the soldier's bearing who, on the night of Jacob Jones's surprise party for André Kohl, had probably saved the guest of honor's life. "Good evening, sir," he said in English. "May I help you?"

"Just wanted to look around," Peter said.

"The hotel is reserved for registered guests."

"I had hoped to have some tea."

"Our salon is small, and reserved for our guests."

"What about the bar?"

There was an instant's pause on Josef's part, while the security guard reappraised him. "If it would please you, you could take tea in the Vendôme bar."

"That would be fine."

Josef smiled, turned and led Peter to the entrance of the Vendôme bar, a dozen steps away. When Michel Bigot, the chief barman, came to take his order and didn't recognize him, either, he decided to forego the tea in favor of a split of champagne.

Only an hour later, when it was too late, did he remember that alcohol, rather than banishing cares, deepens the mood one brings to it. Up from his bowels rose a melancholy so profound that it drowned the triumph and exhilaration he felt at having run the gauntlet and emerged intact as Peter Burke. Yes, he had made his little scene at Lipp and gone unrecognized, but the fact was that as Peter Burke he was not, and would never be, a member of the inner sanctum to which André Kohl had belonged. And now, here he was at the Ritz, where André Kohl had entered to the smiles of the staff, and not half a year ago been feted by *tout Paris.* An hour before, it had been problematical whether Peter Burke could get in to buy a cup of tea.

What a splendid triumph, he told himself as he beckoned to Monsieur Bigot for another split of champagne.

15

Thirty minutes later, overcome with sadness, Peter left the Ritz. It would soon be time for dinner, but the prospect of eating alone once again so defeated him that skipping the meal seemed the less painful of his options.

In his mood, he was as helpless as an iron filing in a magnetic field. As he began to walk away from the hotel and out of the Place Vendôme, he could feel himself being drawn inexorably toward the Fifth Arrondissement, the area that for André Kohl had always been the heart of Paris. Down the rue de Castiglione he went, then east along the rue de Rivoli and south again on avenue du Général Lemmonier through the Tuileries, the branches of its trees as bare as his spirit, and across the Seine to the Left Bank. The end of November had always been the worst time for André in Paris, its chill winds forecasting the months of bleak winter ahead, with week upon unbroken week of gray skies and damp, penetrating cold; it was then, and only then, that he would contrast Paris with Los Angeles, where November was the beginning of the best time of the year—skies clean, air fresh, days warm, evenings crisp. November also meant Thanksgiving, the one holiday he truly loved, when a dozen good friends, American expatriates all, would gather at the home of one of them to remind themselves who they were and where they had come from. There would be no Thanksgiving this year, no gathering of friends, no warm reminiscences. He was, and would be, alone.

Walking along the quai, he came abreast of Lapérouse. Some

years before, the restaurant, one of the most notable and redolent of atmosphere in all Paris, had passed unaccountably from three-star greatness to no standing at all. He stopped walking, and stared at the patrons on the restaurant's second floor, visible through the windows, who were just beginning their dinner. *That's* where he would feel at home, he decided. What could be more fitting for a has-been than a has-been restaurant? Abruptly, he crossed the street and went inside.

Ninety minutes later, he had finished a glorious and classic dinner of *escargots* and steak *marchand de vin,* accompanied by a half bottle of splendid Bordeaux, and then a *soufflé au Grand Marnier.* As he sipped a demitasse of rich and fragrant coffee, he took a notebook and pen from the wallet pocket of his jacket, and made a one-word entry: COMEBACK. Clearly, the restaurant was trying. The odds were considerable, but its staff promised the most important ingredient of all, the will to overcome adversity. Without that there was nothing.

Perhaps it was his age, but at this point in life, everything seemed serendipitous. Whatever force had led him to Lapérouse and then drawn him inside to discover this analogy, he was exceedingly grateful. No more feeling sorry, he told himself. The important ingredient is the will.

As he had countless times in the months since his decision to assume another life, Peter once again made a mental inventory of his predicament. All the same debits and credits were still on their respective sides of the ledger; now, however, buoyed by his dinner and the reflections it had induced, he made two new entries. On the debit side was the frustration he felt at being cut off from all sources of information. That was the true nature of the deprivation, not the tables he couldn't have at Lipp or the access denied him at the Ritz, not even his exclusion from the magic circle of Paris life to which André Kohl had belonged. What, after all, could being inside the magic circle do for him in his quest to find André's killers? What could those within the circle do? In both cases the answer was "nothing." The circle he needed to penetrate was the one surrounding intelligence agents and experts on terrorism. That was where whatever information existed was located. And that—just as Houghton had predicted—was the circle to which he lacked access, as well. For a journalist to be denied access to information is like having the blood cut off to his limbs. Information had been the lifeblood of André's professional existence; to have been engaged in the work of the world, and then suddenly not to be, was akin to a total loss of circulation. So much for the debit side. On the credit side, he understood the problem now, and understanding it was the absolutely essential prelude to solving it. If he could reconnect himself to the sources of information, he would have the beginnings of a solution. Or so, at least, he concluded in his postdinner euphoria as he paid his check and departed.

On the quai again, he resumed the eastward march that had been interrupted by dinner. By now, he knew where the magnetic force was drawing him: back to André's apartment on the Quai d'Orléans of the Île St. Louis. For days, he'd been avoiding it. Two hours ago, he had undoubtedly been pulled toward it in some unconscious desire to deepen the pain he was feeling, to convince himself that he had descended to the absolute depths of human anguish. Now, in his altered mood, his march seemed like a pilgrimage, a way to tell himself that—Houghton and Fleming be damned—someday, somehow, some way, he would be installed there once again.

Then he saw the light in the window.

Not for a second did he consider that the light might be coming from another apartment. He'd seen his apartment so many times from the same vantage point directly across the river that he was absolutely sure. He was equally certain that the light had only one explanation.

He half-ran to the nearest telephone booth on shaking legs. Inside, he searched his pockets frantically for a coin, then, fingers trembling, inserted it with difficulty into the slot. He punched his number, then waited. One ring. Another. Then the ringing stopped, as someone picked up the receiver. "Hello," a woman's voice said. His heart exploded.

"Une erreur," he mumbled in French. Then he hung up, and stood in the shelter of the booth for a minute, trying to compose himself.

The shock of Meredith's voice, the knowledge that she was just across the river, less than two hundred yards away, had emptied his mind of all other thoughts. Why had she come? What could he do? The questions, impossible to answer without information, besieged him nonetheless as he walked slowly back to his hotel, and then tormented him through half the night. When he looked at his watch for the last time before falling asleep it was past 3 A.M. At 6, he awakened, and was on the street long before 7. A taxi took him to the Île St. Louis, to the café on the corner nearest his apartment. He took a table at the window, ordered a coffee and waited, praying that Meredith would take a morning run.

An hour passed, during which he drank three small cups of coffee. He had just finished the third, and was about to give up, when Meredith came in view, fifty feet down the quai.

The first thought that struck him was that she wasn't running. The second was that she had forsaken her jogging suit for a sweat suit. In another moment, he understood why she was walking, as well as wearing oversized exercise togs.

The shock was so profound that for a moment his mind could do nothing more than assimilate the information. It processed no judgment whatever. Immobilized in body as well, he could only watch her approach, his focus on her movement deepening his trance. Now she was abreast of the café, no more than ten feet from him. And then, perhaps conscious of his stare, she turned to look into the window of the café. For a moment, their eyes caught, and in that moment he was certain that his heart had stopped. Then she smiled—a defensive smile, meant to disarm and hold off —and turned away, and in another moment she was gone.

In all, he had seen her for no more than ten seconds, but in that time he had memorized every feature of her face. In the four and a half months they'd been apart, she appeared to have aged as many years. A hollow darkness lay underneath her eyes, along with the first suggestion of lines. The eyes themselves, once so radiant, seemed almost lifeless. The spirit of eternal optimism that had once suffused her face had vanished; in its place was the resignation of a woman without illusions.

Sitting there, it occurred to him that what he'd just seen might as well have been an illusion. There was no running after her, no crying out, "It's me. I'm alive. I love you."

No torture or sense of deprivation he had experienced in the months since they'd been shot had prepared him for the intensity of the pain and anger he now experienced. Why hadn't Houghton warned him that Meredith was coming to Paris? Why, in God's name, hadn't he at least told him that she was going to have his child?

He left then, unable to contain his rage, needing to move in order to somehow give it physical expression. He walked swiftly back to his hotel, having nowhere else to go, knowing that it would be hours before he could call Houghton. Only the knowledge that he would be addressing a mind fogged by sleep kept him from calling now.

He waited until twelve-thirty Paris time—six-thirty in Washington—and then he called. "This is Peter Burke," he said, his voice trembling and acidulous.

There was just the slightest pause at the other end, and then Houghton said, "You've seen her."

"Yes."

"I should have told you."

"That, my friend, is an understatement."

"Did you speak to her?"

"Not yet."

"Please. I beg you. Don't do it."

"Give me one good reason why I shouldn't."

"I'll give you three. Her life. Your life. And the baby's."

For some seconds, Peter listened to his own tremulous breathing. He felt that he might break down at any moment. "Christ," he said, and then he did break down, holding his head in his free hand. "That wasn't a robot you made in the Cotswolds, you know. I still have feelings."

"And I had reasons not to tell you."

"Yeah, you and your goddamned reasons."

"That's not fair."

"What the hell is fair?" Peter asked bitterly.

"Look," Houghton said, "Paris was Meredith's idea. Knowing you'd be there, I tried to discourage her, but you know her once her mind's made up." He hesitated. "I was planning to come over next week to see how both of you were doing. I had hoped to tell you in person. Do you think you could sit tight until tomorrow? If so, I'll come tonight."

"What's the point?"

"To bring you up to date. To explain what's happened."

"What is there to explain?"

There was a moment's silence. "I can't tell you from here."

Peter inhaled deeply, and rubbed his face. "I'm not sure how much more of this I can take." He hesitated. "Can you tell me if it's bad?"

"It's not good."

They agreed to meet for lunch the next day at Chez André, a bistro on the rue Marbeuf below the Champs Élysées. The choice, in part a mordant jest on Peter's part, suited their purpose well; the restaurant was crowded each day with a clientele of regulars, *gourmands* too intent on consuming the traditional but spectacularly well-prepared food to pay attention to two out-of-place Americans. Even Houghton, the striking cripple with the muscular upper body, full head of hair and handsome looks, scarcely merited a glance when he hobbled in on his canes. For at least fifteen seconds, he stood uncertainly, looking about the room. At one point, his gaze went right past Peter. It was only then that Peter realized Houghton wouldn't recognize him. He raised his arm and waved it. The gesture caught Houghton's eyes. He smiled and began to move awkwardly on his canes through the jammed dining room toward their table. Peter stood to greet him. They shook hands, but Houghton made no move to sit. For a second Peter didn't understand, and then suddenly he did. "I'm Peter Burke," he said.

Houghton smiled. "Thought you might be." Then he sat.

Once he was settled, he wasted no time. "There was a second break-in. The gallery this time. Same result: nothing taken. I don't have the slightest doubt now that someone's looking for evidence that André's still alive."

Peter stared at Houghton. "Then there's no doubt about why. They believe he knew something that he wasn't supposed to know."

"Any idea what that might be?"

"None."

Peter continued to stare at Houghton. Somehow this information, as threatening as it was, managed to take Houghton off the hook. He could feel the anger, carefully stored since yesterday, slipping from his body. "Did you say anything to Meredith?"

"Of course not."

"Did she figure it out?"

"Not unless she's playing games with me, and you know that's not her way. I think she's still so shocked by everything that's happened that the connection simply eluded her."

A waitress came to take their order, a short, attractive woman of forty with pitch-black hair, a soft body that hinted at a weakness for pleasure, and a pleasant manner that suggested she'd had her share. "Something in the breakfast line," Houghton said. "It's 7 A.M. stomach time for me."

"Eggs and bacon?"

"If you can get them."

Listening to Peter's tortured efforts to make himself understood, Houghton could not repress a smile. "My compliments on your French," he said when the waitress had gone.

"Thanks," Peter said.

"How has it gone for you? Have you had any problems at all?"

"You mean being accepted?"

"Yes."

"None."

"To the rest of the world you're Peter Burke?"

"Absolutely."

"You're certain?"

Peter recounted then all of the tests he had arranged for himself since he'd come to Paris. As he spoke, Houghton listened attentively, nodding with approval. At last Peter came to his brief encounter the morning before with Meredith. "And she didn't frown or hesitate or anything like that?" Houghton asked.

"No," Peter said. "Nothing. Not a flicker." For some moments, he couldn't speak, and Houghton pondered his eggs. Peter tried to eat, but couldn't. At last he said, "She doesn't look well at all."

"I know that. So does she. That was one reason she decided to come to Paris."

"Paris in the winter is no place for a rest."

"I think it will be an improvement over New York. The second break-in persuaded her that she didn't want to raise a child there."

Whatever residue of anger had lingered in Peter was dissipated by that remark. Since learning of Meredith's pregnancy, he'd been unable to deal with it in a concrete way. Here, suddenly, was an issue that would shape his child's life: where it should grow up. "Does she plan to stay here?" he asked, not knowing which answer would disturb him more. Her proximity might drive him mad, yet now that she was here he would be devastated if she left. Both responses would be magnified once their child was born.

"I don't think she knows," Houghton replied. "Not the least overwhelming aspect of these last months is that she's apparently become the owner of two substantial properties in France. Another reason for coming was to sort out her options."

"What do you mean, 'apparently'?"

"André didn't leave a will, so it's not entirely clear who has a claim to what. The fact that the properties are in France further complicates the proceedings."

Peter laughed involuntarily. "What a joke," he said. "What a colossal mess." Suddenly, he was overcome by a desperate desire to fix it, to solve the mystery of who killed André Kohl, as if that single feat could somehow set not only his own world but Meredith's right again. But how could he do that without resources? The question caused him to abandon any further attempt at eating. "Look, can you bring me up to date?" he said after the waitress had cleared his virtually untouched plate with a disapproving look. "Where do we stand?"

Houghton shook his head. "Not very far from where we were when André bowed out of the picture."

"Why? What's the problem?"

"To be perfectly frank, with everything else going on at the Company, I can't arouse much interest in the question of who killed André Kohl. Especially since, superficially, the question appears to have been answered. We know who fired the guns. Both men involved are in custody. One day, presumably, they'll be tried. The word has gotten around that they were paid by a Ger-

177

man, so everyone just assumes they were hired by some angry ex-Nazis and is quite prepared to drop the matter."

"And the fact that someone's still looking for André—that doesn't impress anyone?"

"It would if anyone knew about it, but I'm not about to tell them. The last thing in the world we need is a lot of speculation as to whether André Kohl is really dead."

"Then I don't see any alternative. I've got to get in the game. The question is, how do I do that?" It was more a plea than a question.

Houghton studied Peter for a long time before replying. "There's one way," he said, "if you think you can pull it off. But it could blow your cover."

"Go ahead."

"I believe I could arrange it for you to investigate the death of André Kohl in behalf of his old employer."

16

Long after Houghton had told Peter about his conversation with Mike Paul following the memorial service for André Kohl—Mike requesting a recommendation for someone who could investigate on the network's behalf, Houghton suggesting a man, presently occupied, who might become available—long after Peter and Houghton had left Chez André and gone their separate ways, Peter continued to play the possibility over and over again in his mind. To him, the question was not whether he could get away with it; it was whether he could permit himself to do it.

Could he really go before Mike Paul, whose respect had mattered more to André Kohl than that of any other man—a respect predicated on integrity and trust—and pose as a man he wasn't? Yet what alternative did he have? From the moment in the hospital plane when he had accepted Houghton's solution, he was committed to a life of deception. His only hope for moral salvation was to put that life to good use.

He had asked Houghton for time to think it over, and given him the number of his hotel as well as his room number, so that if Houghton had to call in Meredith's presence he would not need to use Peter's name. Houghton would call that evening. If the answer was yes, he would then call Mike Paul in New York to ask if USBC was still interested in hiring an investigator. If Mike said yes, Houghton would put the two men in touch.

By late evening, the matter was settled. Peter was to fly to New

York the next day on the Concorde, his ticket prepaid by the network. Houghton would remain in Paris until his return.

From that point on, Peter tried to think of the experience not as history relived but as a quintessential *déjà vu:* the ride to the airport in a chauffeured car; the familiar faces aboard the Concorde; the tight seats; the muffled boom as the airplane reached supersonic speed; the sumptuous food and glorious wines; the 8:45 A.M. arrival in New York, more than two hours earlier on the clock than when he'd left Paris; the waiting car and driver; the escalating sense of discomfort at being in the States; and, finally, the walk into Mike Paul's office on the eighteenth floor of the USBC building across from the southwest corner of Central Park.

As he shook hands with the man who had been André Kohl's best friend, and felt the familiar powerful clasp, he instinctively tightened his hand to match it, remembering that André's handclasp had been softer. As Mike looked him over, he was surprised by his utter calm. He answered Mike's stare with a pleasant smile, his own eyes fixed on Mike's to detect any sign of recognition. There was none.

"Houghton tells me you have a craving for anonymity," Mike began.

"It's really much better that way."

"Am I going to be able to check your references?"

"Of course."

"On the other hand, if Houghton vouches for you that ought to be good enough."

"Whatever makes you comfortable. My only request is that my employment—if you decide to retain me—be a matter between us."

"I'll have to tell the person who'll be paying you."

"Can you list the expense as 'research'?"

"I'll think of something. How much am I paying you, incidentally?"

"Seven-fifty a day, plus expenses. A fifty-thousand-dollar bonus if I succeed."

"That's high."

"The work is difficult, and dangerous."

"Okay. Deal."

"You don't want to check my references?"

"Nah. Knowing you guys, they're probably phony." Mike laughed, then, seeing that Peter didn't join him, said, "That was a joke, Mr. Burke."

"I'm sorry," Peter said. "I'm afraid I take myself too seriously."

"I would, too, if I did what you do. Now, how can I help you? What would you like to know about André?"

Peter had anticipated the question. From his breast pocket he produced a piece of paper. "Here's my shopping list." There were half a dozen items: biographies of André Kohl, any notes he kept in the process of working his final story, any memos he wrote, any pertinent internal memos written by others at the network, a copy of the dossier that had incriminated Camille Laurent and half a dozen original letters of introduction from Mike stating that Peter Burke had been retained by USBC to investigate the death of André Kohl.

Mike studied the list for twenty seconds. "I see no problems, but I'm puzzled why you'd want a letter of introduction if you're trying to remain anonymous."

"Anonymity is an ideal, Mr. Paul. I have to be realistic. There are people I'll need to see who will want to know for whom I'm working as a condition of helping me. In such situations, they tend to respect my wishes and keep our business between us."

"Sounds right," Mike said. "Let me get this started." He summoned his secretary and gave her instructions. "What are your plans?" he asked after the door had closed behind her.

"I'd rather not say. I hope that doesn't offend you."

Mike moved from behind his desk and began to pace. "It doesn't offend me. Do it any way you like. I'm just eager for results, and extremely frustrated. We've gotten nowhere ourselves." He went to the window and looked below at the traffic on Columbus Circle. "This is a personal matter, Mr. Burke. André Kohl meant a lot to me. I loved him like a brother. I know that's a cliché, but it happens to be true. More than that, I'm the guy who got him into this business, and I'm the guy who talked him into aborting his leave of absence to do the Camille Laurent story. If it wasn't for me, he'd be playing piano today at that house of his in Normandy."

Mike fell silent, but continued to stare out the window. The strain in his voice had told Peter how much he was suffering. "You didn't force him to take the assignment, did you?" he asked.

"Of course not."

"Then I don't see that you're to blame. Kohl was a grown man. He made his own decisions. From what I've read of him, I'm sure he wouldn't have blamed you."

Another silence passed. At last Mike said, "Thank you. I'd like to believe that." A moment later, he turned and walked back to his desk. When he was seated he said, "I know I'm asking the same question, but I'm really curious to know where you intend to start."

Peter smiled. "I won't know for a few days. What I'll probably do is what I always do—just follow my nose."

In fact, Peter knew exactly what he would do first. That very evening, he boarded TWA Flight 800 for the return to Paris, intent on collecting his clothes—he'd traveled only with an overnight case to New York—seeing Houghton once more and flying on to Israel for a visit with Shlomo Glaser of the Mossad.

The prolonged day had so exhausted him that he had no trouble sleeping on the plane. But he was still tired when he reached the Hotel St. Germain at 10 A.M. Paris time. He put a "Do Not Disturb" sign on his doorknob and crawled into bed. An hour later, he was still awake. Another historical vibration to treat as a *déjà vu:* jet lag so profound that his body's clock seemed to have lost all sense of time.

Even without the physiological confusion he would have had trouble sleeping, so excited was he over the prospect of getting to work at last. Providentially, Houghton called shortly before noon. "I had a hunch you'd come right back. Congratulations."

"You talked to Mike?"

"He called to thank me after you left. He was very impressed. Said you were very convincing."

"It wasn't hard to be convincing."

"Look, I have to get back tomorrow. I'm here unofficially. Haven't even gotten in touch with the French. Could we meet this afternoon? I could come to your hotel at three."

"You don't want to meet for lunch?"

"I'm afraid I can't," Houghton said. In the silence that followed, Peter knew what he hadn't said, that he was having lunch with Meredith. It flew into his head to say, "Give her my love." Two days before he might have said that as a means of hurting Houghton, but he no longer wanted—or needed—to do that.

"How is she?" he asked when they met in the sitting room of the hotel. They were alone in the room, at a table next to the window behind which rested the enclosed, eye-level garden, incongruously bright and spring-like in the gloomy late November weather.

"Better," Houghton said. "She says my presence here has helped."

"Has she found a good doctor?"

"She thinks so. He's affiliated with the American Hospital."

"Good. When's the baby due?"

"March 11."

"Will she have it here or in the States?"

"Here." Houghton paused. "She's here indefinitely, Peter. I thought it would be tough on her to be in André's home, but it seems to be just the reverse. She says it's a comfort."

Peter did not know how to reply. He could not afford to think about it. "Let's get on with it," he said. "I want to get to Tel Aviv as soon as I can."

Houghton nodded. "I was sure you would, and you may still want to after we finish, but I doubt that you're going to learn anything there that I can't tell you here. I've been working pretty closely with Shlomo."

"And?"

"They finally found out who's behind Khalel el Hassan." Houghton hesitated, as though reluctant to continue.

"Not the Germans?" André asked.

"I'm afraid not."

"Who, then?"

"The Russians."

For some seconds, Peter sat in silence, too stunned to speak. "Are they sure?" he said at last.

"They say they are."

"What about that payment from the German?"

"I asked the same question. They said they don't understand it, either, but there has to be an explanation because they're dead certain the Russians set up the Arabs." Houghton hesitated for a second. "I'm looking into it," he said then.

Peter stared at Houghton. "How long have you known this?"

"A few months."

"Why didn't you tell me?"

"I felt you had more important things to do. I didn't think you'd be able to do them as well if you were thinking about André Kohl."

Peter knew dimly that Houghton's reasoning made sense; if he felt anger at having been deprived of this seemingly crucial piece of information, it was mitigated by his dismay at the destruction, with a single blow, of the structure of logic he had built around his problem. For months, the facts had seemed to arrange themselves in such an orderly manner. André Kohl had exposed a ring of ex-Nazis running a for-hire paramilitary organization in Latin America. The ex-Nazis had been set up by a secret network of present and former U.S. government employees, mostly CIA agents. Both groups wanted revenge. Someone from one of those groups had used a German named Alex Eichmann as an intermediary to hire some Arab killers. Find out who hired Eichmann, and you've found the guilty party. Now, a single piece of information had demolished that possibility. There was no way in hell that Russians, no matter how angry they might be with André Kohl over the death of Gennady Gondrachov, would contrive with either the CIA or a bunch of ex-Nazis to gain revenge.

That Russians were involved with Arab terrorists, however, did not surprise Peter at all. A case could be made that without Soviet support Arab terrorism as the world has come to know it would not exist. Helping terrorists upset the status quo in Third World countries went hand in glove with the Soviets' geopolitical policy of strategic encirclement of the industrial democracies; by creating uncertainty in those countries, they could affect and even cut off the flow of vital materials to the West. But it was a long way from using Arab terrorists to advance a provocative foreign policy to hiring them to kill an American television journalist. It wasn't characteristic, and more than that, it simply made no sense. If they wanted to kill André Kohl, why hadn't they done it themselves?

Then, suddenly, Peter turned to Houghton. "Wait a minute. Maybe this does make sense. Whoever wanted André dead went out of his way to kill him, as though more than revenge was the motive. Right?"

"Right."

"Whoever wanted him dead believed he knew something he wasn't supposed to know. Right?"

"We don't know that. But it's certainly a possibility."

"It's the *only* possibility, because nothing else makes sense. Okay, what is it that he supposedly knew? I don't have a clue—but it would have to be something that he alone would know because somebody told him. I don't know what that *something* is, but I'm beginning to think I may know who the *somebody* is."

"Who?"

"Gennady Gondrachov."

Houghton frowned. "You've got me," he said.

It occurred to Peter only then that in all this time, he had never told anyone—not even USBC—from whom he had obtained the original Hoepner dossier incriminating Camille Laurent. The only person who knew was Meredith, and she knew because Gennady had insisted on keeping the dossier in his possession while it was being authenticated by the expert Meredith had provided. There was no longer any need to protect his source, of course, because the source was dead. So, in a sense, was the reporter.

"You knew of Gondrachov, of course?"

"Of course."

"Did you know he'd been killed?"

"Our people in Moscow reported that he'd disappeared. We figured something had happened. Do you know what happened?"

"He was killed in France, in all probability by Laurent's people."

As he told Houghton the story, Peter could feel his excitement mounting, his thoughts outracing his words. For the first time in more than five months, he believed he might be getting somewhere, even if it was taking him further into a labyrinth. At least he was in the flow once again. "Whatever it was André learned had to have been during the last story he did," Peter explained, "so it had to have come from one of the parties with which he was involved. From whom did he learn something he wasn't supposed to know? Not the French, because they knew what he knew, and they'd struck a deal. Not the Germans, because he'd already broadcast everything he knew. Not the Americans, for the same reason. So that leaves the Russians. The *only* Russian André saw during that entire time was Gennady Gondrachov.

"Gennady and André had a very special relationship. It's very hard to describe. André didn't trust him, but he liked him. And because he knew him so well, he always had a feeling that he could get what he needed from him without getting hurt. There was the regard Gennady felt for André, first of all. And then there was the knowledge on his part that each time they did business together would be the last time if he wasn't straight with André. He wanted to maintain that relationship because it had been very good for him in the past. He made a potful of money arranging for USBC's interview with Khrushchev. That led to *Khrushchev Remembers,* which he ghosted, and from which I'm sure he made another potful of money. André helped on that deal. So, you can see there's an unusual *quid pro quo* here: André gets exclusive stories, Gennady supports his lavish tastes."

"Are you saying André paid a Russian for information?"

"Technically, Gennady didn't supply information. He supplied access. And André didn't pay Gennady, USBC did—just like it would pay a stringer anywhere in the world. That, more than friendship, is why André knew Gennady wouldn't burn him. If he did it was all over."

"Did the KGB know about Gennady's special relationship with André?"

"There's no way they wouldn't. His job with the KGB was to plant stories with Western journalists. André was his biggest success. He asked for the Khrushchev interview just at a time when the Soviets wanted the world to know that they hadn't executed him. They made their point and USBC got a great interview. Everybody was happy. From that point on, André used Gennady whenever he needed strings pulled in Moscow to get to an important source, or to go somewhere that required special permission.

Gennady came through every time. Then came the Camille Laurent story. As the Soviet's disinformation specialist, it was Gennady's job to plant the story—or try to. He could have chosen any Western journalist. He chose André. It was Gennady's idea, as well, to plant the story first on Shlomo, figuring on the basis of past history that Shlomo would almost certainly bring the story to André. The plant was a beauty. One of the KGB's agents in Israel was a German woman who'd gone underground during the war, gotten phony papers and wound up working for the Gestapo. The KGB sent her to the Mossad with the story that she'd seen a memo from Kurt Hoepner to Gestapo headquarters in Paris, which had then been sent on to Himmler in Berlin. That was the memo in which Hoepner identified Camille Laurent as his contact in the Resistance. The woman's story was phony, of course, but the memo, as we well know, was real. The whole scenario was Gennady's idea, but he would have needed high-level approval; he couldn't have acted without it. And then, finally, there was the matter of getting the dossier to Paris so André could get it authenticated. Gennady *had* to go to the top to get that one approved, as well. So, no, I don't know for a *fact* that the KGB knew about the ties between Gennady and André, but it figures that there's no way they wouldn't."

Peter paused, and locked eyes with Houghton. "What if *Gennady* knew something very special? What if he passed that information to André?"

"Wouldn't that have been totally uncharacteristic?"

"Yes. But what if he sensed that his life was in danger?"

"Did he sense that his life was in danger?"

"I think so. But whether he did or didn't doesn't really matter. What matters is what the KGB believes he might have been thinking. They had no idea what he was up to in Paris. The way their minds work, they might have worried that just before he died, Gennady—maybe in a moment of weakness—passed some kind of information to André."

"Which brings us back to what that might have been."

"Right. The questions are, one, what did Gennady know, and, two, who didn't want him to say anything?"

Houghton shook his head back and forth for several seconds. "I wouldn't begin to know how to answer either of those questions. Would you?"

"Not now. But I just have a strong conviction that the clue to who killed André Kohl is to find out what Gennady might have told him."

The room had grown dark. A woman came in to turn on the lights. "Oh, but this is terrible," she said in English. "You cannot see a thing." Peter saw that it was the tall, attractive manager. His concentration had been so intense that her presence, her voice and the lights she illuminated hit him like successive shocks. When she left a moment later all Peter could hear was the ticking of a clock.

Then Houghton spoke. "There's still that other question, isn't there? Why, if the Russians hired Arabs to kill André Kohl, were the Arabs paid by a German?"

"There's got to be an answer. It's all got to tie together. The big problem is that most of the loose strings are undoubtedly in Moscow."

Houghton held up his hand. "Just a second. *I* have a loose string in Moscow." He told Peter then about Virgil Craig's mysterious telephone call to the Soviet capital, and of their fruitless efforts to identify the number. He explained, as well, about Craig's call, minutes later, to Pierre Gauthier in Paris. "From the proximity of the calls, you have to believe that Craig had to consult with someone in Moscow before calling Gauthier."

"That's right."

"But who was it? That's the question—and we just can't come up with the answer." Houghton shook his head. "I find it hard to believe that that loose string will tie up with yours, but I suppose that anything is possible."

"What was the date of those calls?"

"I believe it was May 24."

Peter thought for a moment. "Would you be willing to give me the number?"

"With pleasure." He drew a small note pad from the wallet pocket of his jacket and wrote the number out, then passed the paper to Peter. "But do you really expect to be able to work in Moscow?"

Peter smiled ruefully. "It's going to be tough without a Gennady Gondrachov running interference."

"How will you manage?"

"I have no idea—wait a minute." He smiled. "Yes, I do. Jacob Jones."

17

Jacob Jones was away—in Moscow, not surprisingly, where he conducted so much of his business. He would certainly be happy to see Mr. Burke on his return in ten days, a sweet-voiced Frenchwoman assured Peter when he called Jacob's office the morning after his return from New York. She had answered the phone in French but switched to English as soon as she heard Peter's accent. There had been few things to laugh about since André was shot, but Peter did find that amusing. It was not the first time it had happened, but he was comforted each time it did, because it told him how well he had learned his lessons. It was especially comforting this time, because André Kohl, the man Jacob Jones thought so highly of that he had hosted a farewell party in his honor, had spoken to this particular French woman countless times before.

Peter had explained to Jacob's secretary that he was calling at the suggestion of Mike Paul. He was certain that as a stranger without sponsorship he would have gotten nowhere. He was pleased by her assurances, but the prospect of a delay distressed him. Now that the hunt was on, he wanted to be moving. He let it bother him for a day, until he remembered that he was acting exactly as André Kohl would. That would never do. Jack Fleming had been right, damn him; in order to be Peter Burke, he had to think like him at all times, and act like him as well.

The next morning, Peter went to the library at the Pompidou Center, a place where André Kohl had never been. All of André's background research, as distinguished from his reporting, had been done by members of his Paris bureau. Moreover, libraries in Paris were not places one simply walked into. Special permits were needed by those with legitimate needs. Almost the only legitimate need, in the eyes of France's academic elitists, who controlled the libraries, were those of scholarship. The result was that the overwhelming majority of the populace was excluded from library resources. The facility at the new Pompidou Center, or Beaubourg, as it was popularly known, was a brilliant exception; it was also, far and away, the most controversial, a building turned inside out, the work of two London-based architects who had submitted their design as a joke in an open competition, and to their consternation won. Joke or no joke, the building, its ducts and pipes and girders and escalators exposed to the world, had fostered a teeming cultural center from the moment its doors opened. The library was often so crowded that readers would sit on the floor between the stacks, absorbed in their books. Thousands milled outside the building each day, taking in the action.

It was midmorning when Peter arrived, but a crowd had already gathered on the broad, cobbled area sloping down to the building's entrance, most of them forming circles around one or another of half a dozen street artists—a mime, two clowns, a juggler, a sword-swallower, a flame-eater. Peter stopped to watch one of the clowns for a few minutes, hoping to lighten his mood. His biggest laugh came when the clown, who had been speaking French, delivered an aside to a friend in English forged in Brooklyn.

In the library, Peter asked first to see newspapers published in Paris during the last week in May. Within fifteen minutes he had found what he was looking for. It was a small story, in the editions of Friday, May 25—a story André Kohl had read on his return to Paris from Bolivia—about the death of one Milos Novotny, a Czech businessman, whose battered body had been discovered in the Bois de Boulogne, near the Auteuil racetrack, in a region, the story pointed out, that was frequented by transvestites. The story also noted that in addition to multiple bruises on his body, there was evidence of a sexual attack. A picture accompanied the story. It was a picture of Gennady Gondrachov, from the phony Czech passport he'd been using.

What had the Russians done, Peter wondered, on learning of Gennady's death? Surely they would have recognized a setup when they saw one. But had they made an inquiry? A diplomatic protest? In both cases, the answer was probably no. Gennady had entered France illegally. The French knew that he had come as part of an effort to influence their presidential election.

Peter knew that his job at this point was to deal with the facts objectively. But it was tough to do that. He could not keep from thinking how different it all might have been had André and Gennady chosen to meet in London. The authentication André had insisted on as a condition of using the story could have been done there just as readily as in Paris. Who could have dreamed of the difficulties that would ensue? Gennady had said nothing to André about how he planned to sneak into France, only that he was delighted for the excuse to come. And so, on that slim twist of fate, that choice of cities, he was dead, and André's life had effectively been ended, apparently by order of Gennady's KGB colleagues.

Why? *Could* revenge have been the motive? Objectively, that just didn't make sense. Yes, it was André who had insisted on the authentication of a document that was, in fact, authentic, so a sorrowing colleague of Gennady's could technically blame André for initiating the chain of events that had led to Gennady's death. But surely the Russians had deduced, just as André had, that Gennady had died at the hands of Pierre Gauthier of the French secret service. Why, if revenge was the motive, hadn't the Russians pointed their Arab terrorists at Monsieur Gauthier, as well? The more Peter thought about it, the more convinced he became that the key to the entire mystery lay in what secret Gennady knew.

It was late morning, still too early for lunch. With time on his hands, Peter decided to look through back issues of the leading newspapers and magazines—not one of which he had read since his abrupt departure from France more than five months before—to see how they had handled the Camille Laurent story following the announcement of André's death.

Every newspaper, without exception, had devoted its entire front page to the story the day after USBC broke it. Laurent's suicide the next day had produced another rash of stories. Every newspaper and periodical had sent reporters and photographers to

Laurent's funeral in Rodez, a small city of rose stone houses in the Aveyron, his birthplace. At the cemetery, the media far outnumbered the mourners.

As Peter leafed through the back issues, he was struck by how rapidly the story had died. In the States, a comparable story about a comparable American would have endured for years, passing from the news pages to the editorial pages, where columnist after columnist would return to the subject again and again to explain, evaluate and draw morals. From there it would pass into the vocabulary and the lexicon of analogy. Not here. Within a month the Camille Laurent story had disappeared.

It was only after he'd finished his search that Peter realized what else was missing. Not a single newspaper had written an evaluation of the role of André Kohl.

Nothing. Reports on André's death. Reports on the story he'd written. Explanations of why he hadn't broadcast at the time of his discovery. But not a single sentence that said, one way or the other, whether André had done the right thing. Not a single commentator recalled that American reporters were used to doing stories that destroyed their leaders. Not a single commentator noted that French reporters would go only so far in an investigation and then back off rather than tear apart a nation. Not a single commentator had suggested that one of the French press or broadcast associations award André Kohl a posthumous prize. No stories announced plans for a book about André Kohl and the Camille Laurent affair. *Why?*

He took this and his other questions with him as he left the library for lunch. Walking aimlessly, he passed innumerable restaurants, none of which seemed right. Fifteen minutes later he found himself in the heart of the Marais, at the delicatessen where he'd had lunch soon after returning to Paris, and realized that his unconscious had made his choice.

Once again the restaurant was crowded, but when the owner saw Peter he moved at once from behind the counter and beckoned for him to follow. In a moment, he had seized an empty chair and made a place for Peter at a table occupied by six middle-aged men, not one of whom questioned the owner's right to do exactly as he pleased. All greeted Peter with friendly smiles. "This is my friend from New York," the owner announced. He looked at Peter. "You are from New York, aren't you?"

Peter shrugged. "More or less."

"You're from New York, you should have pastrami or corned beef. Which would you like?" Before Peter could reply, he said, "I'll give you half and half. After you've eaten the pastrami and corned beef here you'll never eat them again in New York."

Three minutes later, he returned with the sandwich, cut in two, each side piled high with meats. In his other hand, he carried a bottle of vodka. He set the bottle and sandwich down, then pulled two shot glasses from the pocket of his apron.

"Aha," one of the men at the table said. "He really must be a friend for Cohn to pour him a drink."

"Ignore him," Cohn said. He poured the drinks, and raised his glass. *"L'chayim."*

"L'chayim," Peter repeated.

Another of the men leaned toward Peter. "It means 'to life,' " he said.

"He knows what it means," Cohn said.

"I do, indeed," Peter said.

"You're Jewish?" someone asked incredulously.

"You don't have to be Jewish to translate *l'chayim,"* Cohn said.

When the lunch hour had passed and the others had gone, the owner came to sit with Peter. "So, I'm glad you came back. You're in Paris a long time for a tourist. Maybe you're not a tourist. It's none of my business, but what are you doing here?"

What the hell, Peter thought. "Does the name 'André Kohl' mean anything to you?"

"Are you kidding? Of course. He was a *mensh.* You know what means a *'mensh'?"*

"A man."

Cohn's eyes narrowed. "You're sure you're not Jewish?"

Peter laughed. "I speak German."

"Ah. So why do you ask about Kohl? Were you some kind of friend of his?"

"In a manner of speaking. I'm here looking into the circumstances surrounding his death."

"You're a writer?"

"In a manner of speaking."

"Okay. I won't ask no more."

Peter grabbed his arm. "No, no, I want you to. It's just that it's a little complicated. I do hope to write something eventually. For now, maybe you can explain something. Here's a guy who saves France from having a Nazi for a president, and they turn their backs on him." He told Cohn then about his findings at the library.

Cohn raised his hands, palms up. "Ask me something hard." He reflected for a moment. "You want an answer, I'll try to give you an answer. The French people don't want to know from the Resistance. They don't want to talk about it. You know why? They were all Camille Laurents. After the war, they made a big *tsimmes*—you know what's a *tsimmes?* A big stew—over how they'd all been this and that in the Resistance, when the fact is that not one in ten thousand of them did a thing except try to save their *tuchises.* You know what's a *tuchis?*" He dropped a hand and patted his behind.

Cohn leaned forward, and clutched Peter's arm. He was whispering now. "The French want that time forgotten, to go away, disappear. They want to destroy that part of their history."

Cohn leaned back. He poured two more shots of vodka, and put the bottle back on the table, but made no move for his glass. "They hate André Kohl for reminding them."

"But André Kohl *didn't* remind them. He made a deal with Laurent: he'd keep quiet if Laurent would resign. It was the network that broke the story after Kohl was killed."

Cohn waved him off. "I know that. I read that. Doesn't matter. It was André Kohl's story—and for that they won't forgive him, because he made them remember something terrible they had pretended to forget." Cohn looked away, his eyes focused on a past that only he could see. "In a way, they're lucky. Sometimes I wish I could forget." He was silent for a moment, and then abruptly he turned to Peter, lifted his glass, and waited for Peter to raise his. They touched glasses. Cohn said: "To André Kohl."

18

Each evening for a week, Peter fought and lost a battle. He would eat his dinner and drink a modest amount of wine, fully intending to return to his room at the Hotel St. Germain and read until he fell asleep. But the moment he would leave the restaurant, he was once again like that iron filing in a magnetic field, helpless to resist the force pulling him toward the Île St. Louis. He knew it was foolish; what good would it do to stand and watch a light burning in a window across a river, two hundred yards away? Yet, night after night, that was what he did.

And then one morning, as he was shaving, he looked at his image in the mirror and said aloud, "What the hell are you doing?"

The image was of a man named Peter Burke. He was so used to it by now that it not only didn't surprise or shock him, it had supplanted the other image of himself he had previously carried in his mind. He *was* Peter Burke now, in fact as well as in name. He had been retained by the United States Broadcasting Corporation to investigate a crime. The basis of all investigations was the interrogation of informed sources. What more informed source could there be than the wife of the victim, who had herself been shot during the attack on her husband?

Did he dare? Why not? Mike Paul, André Kohl's closest friend, a man André had known for a quarter of a century, had accepted him as Peter Burke. Why wouldn't Meredith accept him?

André Kohl had always acted on instinct. Peter, feeling the

turbulence in his body, determined to let the idea settle, so that he could consider it in a more reflective mood. But it obsessed him through the day, and then tossed him through the night. By the next morning he knew that he would act.

He rehearsed for half an hour, and finally he called. "Is this Mrs. Kohl?" he said, trying to still the tremor in his voice. He could tell himself that it wasn't André's voice any longer, not in pitch or timbre or volume or tone or accent. It was the voice of another man. And yet, the uncertainty in the voice so reminded him of André's audition for television that he was sure he would give himself away.

"Yes," Meredith said. Her answer was almost a question. Why shouldn't she be wary after all she'd been through? he asked himself. Besides, she knew almost no one in Paris. A call out of the blue, and from a stranger, even one who spoke English?

"This is Peter Burke," he said quickly. In an instant, no more than a millisecond, he knew that he'd made a colossal mistake. André Kohl's telephone had been tapped for fifteen years. It seemed inconceivable that the French would still have a tap on it —but not at all inconceivable that someone else could be listening in. Twice intruders had entered Meredith's premises, looking for evidence that André Kohl still lived. Their surveillance wouldn't end simply because she had moved to Paris. At the very least, he should have checked out the area around the apartment before anything so rash as this call. Now it was too late. If the phone was tapped, his name was already on a tape. "I'm a friend of Mike Paul," he said quickly, throwing away his mental script. "He suggested I call to see how you were getting along."

"Oh, how thoughtful," Meredith said. "You can tell him I'm just fine, all things considered."

The script had called for an invitation to lunch that day or the next, but now Peter didn't dare. "How long will you be in Paris?" he asked instead.

"A long time, I think."

"Well, perhaps we might meet for a drink or a coffee one day."

"It wouldn't be either of those, because I'm busy making a child."

"Well, then, a lunch, perhaps?"

"That's very kind, but I wouldn't want to inconvenience you. I'm sure you must be here on business."

"Let me call you in a few days, if I may. By then my business may be settled."

"Please do."

He sat immobilized for several minutes, damning himself for his carelessness, yet thrilled all the same by her voice. Then, quickly, he finished dressing and took a taxi to the end of the street at the north side of the Notre Dame Cathedral, got out and walked across the Pont St. Louis to the Île St. Louis and turned right onto the Quai d'Orléans, which ran along the southwest side of the island.

It was then that he saw the stakeout.

They were seated in a gray Peugeot parked forty yards west of André's building, two men wearing business suits, one reading a newspaper, the other smoking, his head lined up with the building's doorway. Peter couldn't see their faces, but from the back of their heads they seemed to be in their thirties. As he approached the car, still behind it, he looked inside and saw that the newspaper was Arabic. There was a pack of cigarettes on the dashboard, its letters also in Arabic. He continued on, without breaking stride, until he reached the bar on the corner. He went inside, ordered a coffee and sat at the same table he'd been at the first day he'd seen Meredith.

He couldn't be positive that the men were there on a stakeout. But he had to assume that they were. Why else would two men of working age be seated in a car during working hours? They were obviously Arabs, but they could be employed by anyone. The question now was whether they were there simply to watch the apartment, or whether they would follow her when she left. Even if they didn't follow, he couldn't assume that she wouldn't continue to be under surveillance wherever she went. There could be another team.

Shortly before noon, Meredith emerged and walked down the Quai d'Orléans. As she approached the bar, Peter turned away, not wanting her to remember that she'd seen him there before. When he turned back, she was crossing the Pont de la Tournelle to the Left Bank. He left the bar and followed, giving her plenty of room. At the center of the bridge, he stopped and turned to his right, to all appearances an American tourist admiring the view of the flying buttresses of Notre Dame. Out of the corners of his eyes he could see an uninterrupted line of automobiles parked along the Quai d'Orléans. The gray Peugeot was among them.

He turned south again and continued across the bridge. Meredith had turned right at the end of the bridge and was walking toward the Boulevard St. Michel. He remained behind at a discreet distance, until he was certain no one was following her.

Meredith crossed the boulevard, then began edging into the Latin Quarter on ancient streets so narrow that traffic could be impeded by one carelessly parked car. When she reached the rue Christine, she turned right and walked fifty feet to a bistro. Peter waited for several minutes to make certain yet again that neither of them had been followed. Then, heart pounding, he approached the bistro, praying she was alone.

She was.

A minute to rehearse. One more look to be certain he wasn't being observed. A few deep breaths to try to slow his pounding heart. Then he went inside.

"Mrs. Kohl?" He stood a few feet from her table, trying to speak as gently as he could. Yet at the sound of his voice her head jerked up, and she looked at him with that same wariness he'd heard on the telephone earlier that day. As her eyes enlarged, he could see her fright. Oh, Meredith, he thought, what have I done to you? "I'm Peter Burke," he said. "We spoke on the phone. May I sit for a moment? I have something to tell you."

For a moment, he was not at all certain that she would accede. Her eyes narrowed, and she looked at him as though he might be an enemy. Then, at last, she said, "Please," and indicated the chair opposite her. The invitation could not have been more tentative. The moment he was seated, she said, "I've seen you before." She thought for a moment. "The café on the Île. St. Louis."

The speeches he had rehearsed died on his lips. He reached into his wallet pocket and withdrew Mike Paul's letter. "This will explain it," he said as he handed it to her.

As she read, deep lines creased her forehead. With her eyes

diverted, he could feast his own eyes on her face. Joy and pain in equal measure coursed through his body.

Then she looked at him. "I knew nothing of this," she said.

"It just happened, as you can see by the date on the letter."

"Why did they wait so long?"

"I believe they were working on it but didn't come up with anything."

"And so they've hired you."

"That's correct."

"Who are you?"

He smiled, as much to cover his nervousness as to express his appreciation for her aggressive question.

"I'm a private investigator."

"Do you work for my father?"

He smiled again. "I know your father. He recommended me for this job. But I'm not employed by him."

"Why weren't you hired right after André was killed?"

"I wasn't available until now." He smiled again, hoping somehow to melt the hostility still visible on her face. "I was otherwise engaged."

Meredith looked at him in silence for some time. He tried hard to keep his eyes locked with hers. If confession was the price he had to pay to transform the anger and hostility in her eyes, he was almost ready to confess. At last, she broke the stare. Then she picked up a menu. "Here," she said. "I've already ordered."

André had favored meat and poultry. Peter ordered fish. When he turned his eyes to Meredith once more, the look of hostility was gone, but she still appeared grim. "I'm sure you're going to want to talk about André, and Bolivia, and the Dominican Republic. That's not going to be easy for me, because that's not the way I want to remember him. As you can imagine, I've had a very bad five months. Being here has helped more than anything, because living in his apartment, I'm surrounded by his memory. That's all I've got, and not very much of that. We were together a very brief time."

Her eyes were shining, but no tears escaped. Nor did she try to hide her pain. As she spoke, she continued to look at him in that same unflinching way that had first attracted André. "I suppose it's important to find out who killed my husband, and I'll help you if I can. But I have to say, Mr. Burke, that I don't know how much good it will do. It certainly won't help me. Now, if you're not too discouraged and would like to ask me some questions, I'll try my best to be helpful."

He asked questions to which he already knew the answers. As routine as the questions were, her feelings for André crept into everything she said. The worst moment, by far, came when she reconstructed the shooting. "I just remember being so very happy. It was a beautiful day, and I was with the man I loved in one of the most glorious spots on earth, and my ball had just landed on the green and was rolling toward the pin. We were going to break for lunch after that hole, which was right next to our house, and I remember saying that if I sank the putt I might be too excited to eat. From that point on, it's all very disjointed. I remember things now that didn't register at the time. I felt this sudden tear in my chest, and for an instant I thought that I must have been hit by a golf ball. And then I was on the ground, and André was on top of me. I couldn't understand why he would do that but I realize now that he was shielding me. I'm sure that's when he was hit, because I saw his head snap." She stopped then, unable to continue. Then she turned her head and closed her eyes.

He watched her in silence, anguishing over the pain she was experiencing, wishing with all his might that there was something he could do to reprieve her. A minute passed. When she turned back to him, she managed a small smile. "I'm sorry. That's the toughest part."

He wanted to take her hand and comfort her, but he didn't dare. He knew that he had to do something, however, if only to assuage his guilt. "I hope you won't be offended by what I'm about to say. I can understand why your husband loved you. I'm sure that he was deeply grateful for whatever time you spent together."

She waited some time before replying. "I'm not offended," she said, "even if you don't know what you're talking about."

He carried that remark with him through the day. More than anything that had passed between them, it told him the best thing he could have learned, that beneath the hurt and loss there still existed the wry and resilient woman André Kohl had married.

But their time together had passed so quickly, and she had left so abruptly—after insisting on paying her share of the lunch. Other than suggesting that she call him at the Hotel St. Germain —and cautioning her to use a pay phone when she did—there had been no talk about meeting again. Having covered everything that an investigator might logically have asked her, he didn't know what pretense he could use to see her again. Now that he had made contact, the thought of not seeing her was unbearable.

For the rest of the afternoon, he replayed their conversation in his mind, his recall as vivid as though he had taped it. When he came to her recollection of the shooting, he had to bite his lip. He was assailed by conflicting emotions. On the one hand, he empathized with her pain to the point that he could feel it. On the other, he rejoiced at her obvious love for André.

And then, suddenly, an awful truth was before him: Meredith's memory of André was and would always be Peter's rival for her affections.

Until this moment, he had never considered the possibility that he might be unable to reveal his identity to Meredith. But the cumulative effect of his knowledge led inexorably to that conclusion. For reasons he did not understand, people whose identity he didn't know were determined to make certain that André Kohl was dead. As long as that condition prevailed, revealing the truth would imperil Meredith's life, and the life of their unborn child. Only if the mystery was solved and the danger removed could he become André Kohl again. That might never happen.

If it didn't, and if Peter was ever to have a life with Meredith, he would have to vanquish his alter ego. The very prospect plunged him into gloom.

19

Charles Houghton, asleep in his Watergate apartment, awakened on the first ring of his bedside telephone. As he reached for it he automatically noted the time on his radio alarm clock: 4:40 A.M.

"I knew you'd want this as soon as possible," Harry Coffee said without apology and without bothering to identify himself. "Chris Slovotkin blew his brains out about one o'clock this morning."

Houghton was used to middle-of-the-night calls; he'd received hundreds over the years. He was also used to surprises; twists of fortune were the currency of the trade. Years of practice had trained him to remain impassive regardless of what news was brought to him. But this news, at this hour, jarred him to his marrow. "Did he leave a note?"

"The police say there was none on him, but they haven't searched his house."

"Wait a minute. Why not?"

"Because he wasn't in his house. They found his body in front of the Washington Monument."

For a moment, Houghton could not think of a response. "Are they sure it was a suicide?" he asked then.

"I asked the same question. They're satisfied it was. The angle of the bullet and proximity of the shot suggest it was self-inflicted."

"How'd you find out?"

"The police called the duty officer. The duty officer called me."

"Where are you now?"

"At the morgue."

"You'd better get to his wife before the press does."

"It's my next stop."

Twenty minutes after Harry Coffee's call, Houghton knew he would get no more sleep that night. Why would Chris Slovotkin commit suicide? His health was good. His marriage was good; at least Houghton had never heard anything to the contrary. He'd had an outstanding career. The son of Russian parents dispossessed by the Bolshevik Revolution, he had dedicated his own life to righting that wrong in the most effective manner imaginable. What more effective manner *could* be imagined than running the CIA's Soviet desk, charged with counterespionage work primarily against Soviet agents?

Slovotkin's suicide at the base of the Washington Monument was a declaration if ever there was one: a statement of love for country. Why would he feel the need to make such a statement? He'd been on Madeline Martin's original list of suspects; his phone calls suggested a link to the secret network. But *only* suggested it; they didn't constitute proof. Had Slovotkin compromised himself in some further manner that had produced unbearable guilt, and was this fact about to surface? It was the only explanation.

There was nothing about Slovotkin's death in the morning papers. The story had broken too late to make even the final editions. Nor, to judge by the fragmentary story on the eight o'clock news, which Houghton heard as he was being driven to Langley, had the media quite discovered what it had. That, he knew, would change within two hours at most. By then, he would have to be prepared.

Harry Coffee walked into Houghton's office at eight-thirty. He looked exhausted, and deeply troubled. Like Houghton, he did not normally wear his feelings on his face, but today his features were as raw as an open wound.

"How's his wife?"

"Terrible."

"Does she have any ideas?"

"None. She did say that he'd been depressed in recent weeks, but he wouldn't discuss it with her."

"Do you have any theories?"

"Yeah, but I want you to understand that it's a theory, nothing more. I don't have a shred of proof. I think Chris was scared out of his mind that he was about to be exposed as part of the network."

"Why do you say that?"

"Because my gut tells me he was part of it. It was all he'd talk about whenever we were together. He'd pump me, trying to see what I knew. He spent an entire lunch one day in a theoretical defense of anyone who might have worked for the network. Said he couldn't accept what they'd done but he could certainly understand why they'd done it."

"Do you think he could have been the ringleader?"

Coffee shrugged. "We'll never know now, will we?" he said. He looked unhappier than Houghton had ever seen him.

After Harry left Houghton sat at his desk, immersed in thought. When Harry had proposed his theory, Houghton had stopped himself on the verge of saying, "That's exactly the conclusion I came to." But he hadn't said that because he didn't want Harry Coffee to know what he was thinking. Why he still held back with Harry he couldn't understand. Absolutely nothing other than their having served in Berlin together after World War II had linked Harry and Virgil Craig. Absolutely nothing casting suspicion on Harry had been turned up in the internal investigation; to the contrary, his name or telephone number *hadn't* appeared on any lists. Whereas McDonald, Loomis and Slovotkin had all continued their same suggestive pattern of telephone calls, Harry's list of calls still looked lily-white. The clincher was—or certainly should have been—Harry's work on Carl Sanders. Two months after receiving the assignment, Harry had returned with a nailed-down case: Sander's bank in Buenos Aires had been the financial conduit for the secret network's activities in South America. All fees paid for the services of Hoepner's paramilitary group had found their way to the bank; all disbursements of the proceeds had been made by the bank. It was even possible that U.S. aid money had been illegally diverted to the network's account. Coffee's secret file on Sanders had enabled the agency to demand, and get, Sanders' resignation. At last, Houghton had been able to report some progress to the President; for this alone, he should have been grateful to Harry.

But what Houghton felt had no more to do with gratitude than it had to do with logic. The operating force was instinct. He'd learned long ago that when he didn't trust his instinct, he inevitably made an error. Thus it was instinct that had kept him from revealing his thoughts to Harry.

Houghton knew that the more people he brought in and the wider he made the investigation, the more risk he took of alerting the network to his moves. But he knew, as well, that there are never perfect choices, and that every choice created possibilities that would not otherwise have existed. His mind at last made up, Houghton picked up the telephone, called the director of the FBI and asked for an investigation into the death of Chris Slovotkin.

Late that afternoon, Houghton was back in the Oval Office, answering to a visibly agitated President. "What do you mean, you have no idea why he killed himself? If he was at the office every day, like you say, how the hell was it that no one noticed any odd behavior in the last weeks? A man doesn't just say, 'Have a nice evening,' to his colleagues and then go blow his brains out."

"That's why I've asked the FBI to investigate, Mr. President."

The President started to speak, then stopped. "Wait a minute, what are you saying?"

"Nothing for the moment. I just want to satisfy myself that he wasn't killed."

The President sat back and looked blankly into the distance. "Well, shit, I hadn't even thought of that. Why would someone kill him?"

"I haven't the vaguest idea."

"Damn!" the President said. "Just when I needed all the help I can get." He turned to Houghton. "Things are moving fast, Charlie. The Premier's putting out a lot of smoke. I don't know whether it's a screen or a signal. I still don't have a reading on him. Wasn't it Slovotkin who was supposed to be checking out those rumors?"

"That's right. And he never got anywhere." Houghton hesitated for a moment. "If I may ask, sir, what things are moving fast?"

"Between you and me for the moment?"

"Of course, sir."

"A proposal for an international peace conference on the Middle East, sponsored jointly by the United States and the Soviet Union."

"Their idea?"

"Nope."

"Ours?"

"Nope."

"Whose, then?"

"You'll never guess."

20

At last, Jacob Jones came home from Russia. His secretary telephoned Peter at the Hotel St. Germain on December 12. Could Mr. Burke come to Mr. Jones's office at ten o'clock the next morning? He could.

For Peter, the call could not have been more propitious. It didn't take his mind completely off Meredith, but it did reorient his thoughts into a more positive framework. Jacob Jones meant access to the Soviet Union.

For the moment, he didn't want to think of what he would do once he got to Moscow. The truth was that he didn't have the faintest idea. To an outsider, an American especially, Moscow was virtually impenetrable. If Russians mistrusted foreigners in general, they reserved a special suspicion for Americans. Every Russian schoolchild knew that President Woodrow Wilson had sent an expeditionary force to the country's eastern boundary at the end of World War I, its mission to guard the Trans-Siberian railroad so that supplies could be shipped in to White Russian troops fighting the Bolsheviks. Nearly seventy years after the revolution, the Americans, in the minds of most Russians, were still fighting the Bolsheviks. What chance, then, did an American without contacts, a private investigator looking into the death of an American television journalist, have of learning anything that would solve that mystery? None at all. Why, then, was Peter staking everything on a trip to the Soviet Union? Because André Kohl had known well the feeling of helplessness that occurred at the outset of every assignment when, for the life of you, you could not see how you could come to understand it or crack its secrets. What kept you from being fully paralyzed by doubt and fear was the knowledge, gained from years and years of experience, that one source could get you started. For Peter in this critical instance, that source was Jacob Jones—a man who, in some extraordinary manner, had managed to break through the xenophobic barriers and become the Russians' favorite capitalist.

"Be careful," Charles Houghton had told Peter after he'd thought of trying Jacob, "he may not be everything he seems." It was an odd remark, coming from the director of the CIA. Peter had watched Houghton closely, trying to gain some interpretation of the remark from the look on his face. But as usual Houghton's expression remained inscrutable. Was it simply a caution about a man whose business dealings had aroused suspicions for more than thirty years? Or was there more to it than that? Lord knew, everyone had suspicions about Jacob Jones; even André Kohl had always assumed that the commercial favors he'd obtained from the Russians had not been without their price. All that anyone knew for certain was that the man was a fantastic charmer whose charisma rested on two formidable assets: his powers as a raconteur, and his ability, when not talking, to concentrate all of his attention on the person to whom he was listening. He had used that combination to great effect on political and business leaders throughout the world, creating the kinds of deals that made them want to come back for more. The commissions on those deals had made him a wealthy man. His worth had been estimated by *Fortune* at more than $100 million, small potatoes to the likes of an Armand Hammer—with whom he was often compared because of their commercial dealings with the Russians—but more than enough to finance a splendid life in France: a three-floor apartment in a nineteenth-century building on Avenue Foch, its roof incongruously boasting a satellite dish that brought in Ted Turner's Cable News Network and other American programming; a small château near the English Channel in Normandy, just outside of Deauville, where he stabled a string of racehorses; and a house in the style of Le Corbusier on the water at Cap d'Antibes, where he also kept an oceangoing yacht. For the trip to the Riviera, Jacob was flown from Le Bourget airport just outside Paris to Nice in his Lear Jet. Door to door, it took exactly two hours. In the same amount of time, his Corsican chauffeur and bodyguard could drive Jacob's black Mercedes to Deauville from Paris on the autoroute; if Jacob didn't have two hours to spare, he went there by helicopter.

For his longer trips—to the United States or the Soviet Union—Jacob had his Gulfstream III. Wherever he went, he usually traveled alone. His firm, the Soviet-American Trading Company—or SATCO, as it was known—had a small office in New York and another in Moscow, so he didn't need to travel with an assistant to either of those places. As to women, he seemed to have a plentiful supply no matter where he was. After his fourth divorce, he'd been quoted in *People* as saying, "Some people aren't good at certain things. I'm obviously not good at marriage." Since then he'd played the field. To judge by the beautiful women he courted—all of them significantly taller than he—he did rather well. What he lacked in height he made up for in possibilities.

When he wasn't traveling Jacob worked out of an office on the top floor of a classic building on the Faubourg du St. Honoré almost across the street from the Élysée Palace, the most exclusive business location in Paris. The office consisted of only two rooms, one for him and another for his secretary—he was a deal-maker, and deal-makers did not require big staffs or elaborate record-keeping data—but his part of the office was as impressive as any in Paris. It faced south and west, giving him a view not only of the pomp and circumstance outside the palace and in the graveled courtyard, but also of the Grand Palais and the Eiffel Tower. Into that room had gone antique furnishings and paintings valued at well over a million dollars. No contemporary decor for him; he had surrounded himself with suggestions of old money. The impression, of course, was completely misleading; Jacob's father and mother had run a ma-and-pa grocery in Hoboken, New Jersey.

"So you're investigating the death of André Kohl?" he began after Peter had been shown into the room.

"That's right," Peter said, handing him one of the letters of introduction given him by Mike Paul. His hand shook imperceptibly, a consequence of the rush of adrenaline marshaled by his body in anticipation of this encounter. It would always be this way,

Peter knew, every time he invaded André's past. He would always wonder whether someone who had been intimate with André would pick up on a familiar phrase or gesture, or see through the reconstruction. To his relief, it had not been Jacob Jones.

Jacob read the letter in a few seconds. "Well, if Mike hired you, you must be pretty good. He told you, I'm sure, that André and I were close."

"He did."

"How can I help you?"

"Before I answer that, there's something I have to tell you. Can I do so in absolute confidence?"

"Absolutely."

"Telling anyone what I'm about to tell you could not only ruin my chances but create problems for Mrs. Kohl, as well."

"I understand. Shoot."

"Since one of the attacks took place at your party, I'm sure you know that the assassins were Arabs."

"Right."

"It was assumed by everyone that they were hired by Germans."

"The Hoepner connection. Right."

"The fact is that they were hired by Russians."

For the next ten seconds, Jacob simply looked at Peter in silence. "You're sure?" he said then.

"Sure enough to want to go to Moscow."

"I see," Jacob said with a nod of his head. "That's where I come in."

"That's right."

He kept nodding his head in silence. "I'm really stunned by what you've just told me, but I'm trying to think of how I can help you and I'm damned if I know the answer."

"There's a man I'd like to see."

"Go ahead."

"Do you know the head of the KGB?"

"Vassily Krylov? Of course. But why would he be willing to see you?"

"Because I have something to tell him."

"That his people shot André Kohl? That's not something he's going to want to hear."

"That's not the way I would tell him," Peter said.

"How *would* you do it?"

"Would you mind if I didn't say?"

Jacob leaned back in his chair. He was grinning but he was angry. "Hey, what d'you take me for, pal? A *shmuck?* I set you up with Krylov and you upset him, then Krylov's upset with me. You do business in the Soviet Union, you don't upset the chairman of the KGB."

"He'll get upset, all right, but not with you, and not with me. He'll want to know what I have to tell him."

"No he won't, because you're not gonna get a chance to tell him. At least not through me you're not." For some seconds, Jacob tossed his head and waved his hands, as though conducting some inner monologue. "Look, what's the point?" he said at last. "André's dead. Finding out who killed him isn't going to bring him back to life."

The two men stared at one another. Peter felt that he was seeing Jacob Jones in a manner Jacob had never let André see him. Jacob Jones had professed love and friendship for André Kohl, but clearly his affection did not transcend convenience. Peter knew he was at a turning point, that if he didn't convince Jacob his only entrée to Moscow was closed. What would make Jacob want to help him? The answer was suddenly very plain: if there was something in it for him. He was the author of the statement that the best friendships are those in which there is profit for both parties. André Kohl had questioned that, but Peter Burke could use it. "Have you ever wondered why the first attack on André occurred at your party for him?" Peter said.

Jacob's eyes narrowed. "What are you getting at?"

"Didn't it seem odd that the terrorists would attack him in a place where they were almost certain to be captured, when they could so easily have shot him on the street?"

"Go on," Jacob said uncomfortably.

"Well, one possibility is that André wasn't the only target."

"Who else, then?"

"You."

For at least thirty seconds, the loudest sound in the room was Jacob Jones's breathing. "Are you making this up, or do you have something to go on?"

"I'm analyzing what's there. And what's there, inescapably, is that whoever wanted André shot wanted it done in a manner that would involve you. Whether they wanted to shoot you, too, or just to scare you or discredit you is something I'd like to find out."

Jacob regarded Peter balefully. "This is nonsense," he said. His words did not sound convincing.

Peter knew that he'd scored. But he hadn't won. "There's something else. Do you know how André Kohl got the Camille Laurent story?"

"Only what was broadcast, and what was in the papers."

"His most important source was a KGB agent who passed himself off as a journalist."

"Gennady Gondrachov?"

"You knew him?"

Jacob's eyes narrowed once again. "What do you mean, 'knew' him? Is he dead?"

"He was killed here in Paris while working with André."

The look of astonishment on Jacob's face could not have been more genuine.

"You didn't know?"

"I hadn't heard a word."

"But you knew him?"

"Everybody in Moscow knows Gennady." He shook his head. "Knew him. He came to my apartment, I went to his. He was a helluva nice guy. Who killed him?"

"*That's* what I want to ask Krylov. I don't know what it is yet, but I've got a powerful hunch that there's a relationship between the death of Gennady Gondrachov and the death of André Kohl. I've just got to believe that Krylov and I have something to talk about."

For a moment, Jacob was silent. Then he said, "The way to do it is to have a little gathering at my apartment in Moscow."

"Then you'll do it?"

Jacob nodded. "Yeah. I'll do it." He gave a plaintive laugh. "I guess I *am* a *shmuck.*"

21

But he would not do it for a month, at least. He was going to the Bahamas for the holidays, and would not return to Paris until the second week in January. Having just been to Moscow, he explained to Peter, he had no need to return at once. Without a legitimate need, there was not only no point in going, his trip would raise some Russian eyebrows. "In the meanwhile, get yourself a tourist's visa and some extremely warm clothing. While we're there, we're going to make a little side trip."

Peter didn't ask for specifics. Once again—as they had been after his encounter with Meredith—his emotions were confounded by gain and loss. On the one hand he had succeeded in winning Jacob Jones to his side. On the other, he would be incapable of progressing for another five weeks. Because there was nothing else in his life now but solving this mystery, the delay meant not only that he would be idle, he would be in the same city with the woman he loved for all that time without being able to see her.

The first hours of his limbo were the easiest because he had something constructive to do. At lunch at Chez André—where he had become such a regular that he now got the same table and waitress—he forced his thoughts away from Meredith by making notes of his conversation with Jacob. The turning point, clearly, had been his suggestion that Jacob, too, might have been a target. The idea had come to him out of the blue, surprising him as much as it had Jacob. But it had been neither cavalier nor calculated. It had obviously lain in his unconscious all these months, undigested or evaluated, waiting for the right moment. It *had* to be more than a coincidence that the terrorists had orchestrated their attack in the manner they had. There *had* to be some connection to Jacob.

The second surprise of the encounter had been Jacob's reaction to the news about Gennady. If he hadn't known, given all his high level contacts, it was because the Russians had chosen to keep Gennady's death a secret even within the government. The knowledge reinforced Peter's suspicions that Gennady had been involved in something very special at the time of his murder; it also deepened his conviction that the something special, whatever it was, had bearing on what had happened to André.

Peter finished his notes just as he finished his meal. He put his paper and pen away with regret. Before him lay the prospect of endless meals alone and nights in an empty hotel room.

The next night, Meredith called.

It was nine o'clock, but he was already in bed reading. "I hope I'm not bothering you," she said.

"Not at all," he said, thrilled by her voice.

"I found something that I thought might be helpful."

"Where are you calling from?" he said quickly.

"The Deux Magots."

"But that's a hundred yards from here. Look, would it be all right if I joined you? I could be there in ten minutes. But perhaps you're with someone."

"No. I'm alone. I'll see you in ten minutes."

He dressed quickly and, too excited to wait for the elevator, raced down the stairs two at a time. On the street, he half-walked, half-ran up the block toward the Boulevard St. Germain.

He saw her from thirty feet away. She was sitting in a corner of the café, the sidewalk portion enclosed for the winter. The sight of her made him shake. He had always believed that women were never more beautiful than when pregnant, and Meredith was no exception. Whatever happened, he was so very grateful that Meredith had seduced André into having a child. That was how he thought of it: as an event in another man's life. He had to think of it that way. He could not afford to slip.

He took a minute to collect himself, as well as to check out the surroundings and then the café from his vantage point on the sidewalk. He went table by table until he had covered all of them within sight of Meredith's. Every table, without exception, was occupied by patrons engrossed with one another. After a final check of the area near the café, he went inside.

Meredith looked up and smiled. "I'm glad you could come," she said. "I wasn't very nice to you the other day, and I wanted to apologize. Also, I was feeling pretty lonely."

"No apologies necessary. I was feeling lonely myself."

She reached into her purse. "Here's what I found." She handed him a letter.

Opening it, he saw at once that it was the covering letter Gennady had included in the packet containing the Gestapo dossier incriminating Camille Laurent. Why Gennady had asked his friend Tricia Boogaloo of the Crazy Horse Saloon to help him hide it and later to deliver it André had never figured out. He'd simply assumed that Gennady, being an experienced operator, needed to put it somewhere where he could retrieve it without alerting a lot of people. To protect his source, André had removed the letter from the packet before putting it in the safe at the Connaught Hotel in London, and then taken the letter to his apartment in Paris. Now, as Peter reread the letter, memories surged from storage.

Dear André:

Well, old man, if you're reading this, it hasn't gone well for me. Don't blame yourself, whatever you do; it was I who got careless. In any case, here, as you would say, is the one I owe you. My great regret is that I might not be around to find out what you'll do with it. Since part of my job was to know your mind as well as you, yourself, knew it, I'm pretty certain that I know what you're going through. Given the circumstances in which I'll have probably found myself by the time you have this letter, I think I can safely say that your thoughts are not without merit. We Soviets *are* a difficult people, intransigent, stubborn, xenophobic. I would ask you only to consider what you Americans would be like if everything that had happened to us at the hands of foreigners had also happened to you. As I said that night at the Crazy Horse, somewhere, somehow, at some time we have to agree on something. The alternative isn't very nice. So let us agree that a man who collaborated with Nazi mass murderers shouldn't become president of France.

Gennady

P.S. The mirror behind which I hid the dossier was the very one that reflected Miss Boogaloo's indescribably marvelous bottom.

"Powerful stuff," Peter said when he had finished the letter.

"Do you know what it means?"

"Not entirely, but I'm beginning to have an idea."

"What happened to Gennady?"

"André never told you?"

"No."

"He was killed."

"Oh no," she said. She bit her lip and let her eyes fall.

"You knew him?"

"I'd met him. I was with him for a day when the dossier was being authenticated. I helped set that up." She paused. "Still, it's a shock."

"I wonder why André never told you."

"I'm sure he had his reasons." She paused. "Does the letter help you?"

"Very much." He could not resist a smile. "It's already filled a gap."

For an instant, their eyes locked. Then, quickly, Peter looked away in turmoil. It would not do to read more into that look than was there. It must be comforting to her to know that someone was concerned about what concerned her. That was it. Period.

"Your work must be very lonely," Meredith said.

Peter nodded. "A series of empty hotel rooms."

Her head cocked. "How odd that you would say that."

"Why?"

"My husband used to say that."

Oh, God, Peter thought, am I slipping? Am I losing it?

"He told me once how lonely the job of a foreign correspondent was," Meredith went on. "The worst part, he said, was when you went to your room at night."

"I'm sure he knew what he was talking about."

"You're away a lot?"

217

"I'm always away."

"You have no home?"

"Not really. Home is where I am."

"I take it you're not married."

All sorts of answers flashed through his head: "I was." "I'm separated." "Marriage isn't possible given what I do." But he said, simply, "No."

"How do you stand the loneliness?"

There it was again, that directness of Meredith's André had found so startling the first night they'd met. Thank God she still had that; it meant that she was becoming herself again. "I try not to think about it," he said.

She looked away. "I think about it all the time." She was silent for a minute. He wanted to touch her, to communicate that he understood, that he was suffering too. Her hand, the hand that had explored every inch of André's body, was only a foot from his. But he didn't move, or speak.

"Would it be helpful if I told you about my husband?" she said, turning to him at last.

"Very much."

"Good. I think it would help me to do that." She took a breath. "We met here in Paris. It was sheer coincidence. I'd come in April to look for painters—I have a gallery in Soho—at the same time André was getting started on the Camille Laurent story. When André found that wartime picture of my father with Laurent, he went to Washington to see him. My father mentioned in passing that I was in Paris, and asked if he could help me make some contacts in the art world. André gave him his number and he gave it to me. So I called, and left word on André's answering machine, and he called back and invited me to dinner."

She smiled, the warmth of the memories obviously suffusing her. "I can tell you exactly when I knew that it wasn't going to be just an encounter: when I walked into his apartment. What I sensed at once was a man with an identity. Not something that had been superimposed on him by society, but something he'd made himself."

"Why do you say that?"

"Because of how he lived. There were his books and his paintings and his piano, and that incredible view of the Seine and Notre Dame. I thought to myself, here was a man who knew what he wanted and got it. And what it was was totally unconventional— and absolutely, exactly what I wanted, the fantasy image of my own life I'd carried in my head."

"Are you saying that you fell for his life-style and not him?"

"Aren't the two inseparable?"

"I wouldn't think so."

"Oh, but in this case, I think they were. His life-style told you exactly who he was."

"His age didn't bother you?"

"The only thing I worried about was whether, being from the generation before mine, he would be able to relate to a woman who wanted her own identity. We had long talks about that. He said he understood, but there's a difference between understanding something and approving of it or wanting it in your own life. His first wife had been traditional, and I'm not, and I wasn't at all sure that he'd be able to compromise. But then he more than compromised, didn't he? He quit his job and even though he was well established in France, he was about to move back to the States so that I could build my career."

He could see that her eyes were glistening. She dabbed at them with a tissue she'd quickly pulled from her purse, and said, "Boy, I'm really a crybaby tonight."

"We don't have to continue," Peter said.

"No. I want to continue. I'll be all right." She put the tissue back into her purse and snapped it shut with authority. "There," she said, as though she had placed her sadness inside the purse and wouldn't let it out again. "The chronological age difference just didn't bother me because he was so young in his ways, but I think it bothered him. Once, after we'd been together, he looked at me so strangely that I asked him what was the matter. He said, 'I don't understand what you're doing here.' I'm sure he meant by that that I belonged with someone younger. But from the moment I'd felt myself falling in love I'd realized that the reason I'd never found anyone before was because I'd been dating men my age or just a few years older. They didn't have that definition that André had. Or maybe it was that the definition they did have was one of nondefinition. They all seemed to be in transit toward some amorphous future that they hadn't even designed for themselves. It was as though they'd gone along for the ride in a car someone else was driving, without even knowing the destination. The destination didn't matter all that much, so long as they kept moving." She laughed, clearly at herself. "Am I making any sense?"

They talked until midnight, at which point Peter took her across Boulevard St. Germain, to the taxi stand in front of Lipp. When they shook hands her grip was firm. "Can I call you when *I* feel lonely?" he said.

She smiled. "Please do."

"Actually, I know when I'm going to feel lonely. It will be at dinner tomorrow night."

That made her laugh. "Then let's have dinner tomorrow night," she said.

He thought quickly. "Meet me at Duquesnoy at 30, rue des Bernardins. It's just a few blocks from your apartment."

"You seem to know Paris well."

"I've worked here a lot."

She studied him for a moment. "You're a mystifying man, Mr. Burke."

"For heaven's sakes, call me Peter. How so?"

"You don't strike me as a man who would spend his life as a private investigator. I see you as married, with children, loving your family and your home."

He smiled. "That's very perceptive," he said. "That's what I wanted, but somehow, it hasn't worked out." He looked into her eyes for a moment, all that he would permit himself. "Eight-thirty tomorrow night," he said then. "Duquesnoy—30, rue des Bernardins."

"Eight-thirty," she said. "And thanks for tonight. It helped."

"Any time," he said. Then he put her into a taxi and watched the taillights until they disappeared.

Duquesnoy was a small, smartly furnished bistro run by a young couple of the same name, Françoise in the restaurant, her husband Jean-Paul in the kitchen. Peter and Meredith both elected to try the *degustation*, a sampling of four of the chef's specialties.

When Françoise asked if they would be drinking wine, Meredith patted her stomach and shook her head.

"Very wise," Françoise said.

Peter contented himself with a single glass of white wine, which he nursed through the meal. He did not want his senses to be compromised, not only to avoid mistakes but also to be able to appreciate and remember everything that transpired.

"André loved wine," Meredith said after he had ordered. "Red only, though. He didn't like white."

"I know," Peter said.

She looked at him incredulously. "Are you serious?"

"I don't mean to sound immodest, but there's very little that I don't know about him by this point."

"Let's not talk about him," Meredith said abruptly. "If we do, I'll only get depressed, and that's not fair to you."

"As you wish," Peter said, trying to maintain a normal voice. But her remark had startled him. Once again, he realized what an equivocal game he was playing. Each time she smiled at him or looked him in the eye he felt that he was gaining. Yet did not each advance for Peter mean that the memory of André was fading?

"What's the matter?" Meredith said. "Did I say something wrong?"

"No," he said with a laugh. "What you said touched a memory from my past."

"A good memory?"

"The best."

She smiled at him. "I'm glad that you have a good memory."

Her smile and her statement told him that she liked him. Could he like her any less for that? Suddenly he knew that he had it all wrong. He'd been focused on himself. The object was to focus on her. If he did that, everything would fall in place.

"May I ask one more question about André?" he said. "Then we'll drop him."

"Of course."

"How long do you think he would have wanted you to mourn for him?"

He could tell by her look that she knew what he was asking. Her eyes were suddenly shiny. "You're a nice man, Peter. I like being with you. But please don't try to tell me how to feel about my husband."

"I'm sorry," he said at once. Impulsively he took her hand and squeezed it. She squeezed back. He knew exactly what it meant. "Please forgive me."

"You're forgiven," she said quietly, as their first *degustation* arrived. "Now let's eat this gorgeous food."

As Christmas neared, Parisians left for the mountains and countryside in such numbers that both Peter and Meredith began to feel they had the city to themselves. Without further comment they had reached an understanding. Being together was good for both of them. That was all that was possible. But it was enough.

Incredibly, Meredith had managed, by her gentle rebuke, to put Peter's dilemma to rest. His interest had been acknowledged and André's memory had been honored. He couldn't ask for more.

Nor did he, as difficult as that was. As if in understanding of and appreciation for his tact, Meredith reached up and kissed him on the cheek as they said good night following their fourth dinner together. "You're very nice," she said, and squeezed his hand before she stepped into her taxi. As he had each evening he was with her, he watched the lights of the taxi disappear before taking the next taxi in line.

He never saw her home, and never called for her. Nor, since that first ill-advised call, had he ever telephoned. Each evening they were together, they made a plan for the next time—never repeating restaurants—and it was understood that if Meredith had to cancel, she would call him from a pay phone. It was also understood that she would arrive at the restaurants before he did. He would be watching from a secluded place to make certain she hadn't been followed.

"Why all the precautions?" she asked one evening.

Knowing that the question would inevitably come, he'd prepared an answer. "Habit. I work anonymously wherever possible, which means that I try not to identify myself to anyone who doesn't absolutely have to know who I am, or to let anyone but those who need to know know what case I'm working on."

She stared at him, and held his gaze. "Peter, are you telling me that *I'm* under surveillance."

"Let's say that the French police know you're here. I'm sure that they want to be certain nothing happens to you."

"Why would anything happen to me?"

"André made a lot of enemies. You were his wife."

She shook her head, stared into space for a moment, then looked back at him. "Is there something you're not telling me?"

He knew that he had to look her in the eye. If he didn't, she wouldn't believe him. But as the answer came to him, his own eyes softened. "There's a lot that I'm not telling you—for example, how you make me feel."

She was the first to look away.

"You know what I want to do?" Meredith said abruptly. "I want to cook a Christmas dinner."

It was December 23. They had just finished a delicious meal at the Petit Perigord on the rue de Tocqueville in the Seventeenth Arrondissement. They'd begun with *foie gras,* then had sliced duck breast in a dark sauce and finished with what Meredith described as the most sinful dessert she had ever tasted, a chocolate mousse cake with some mysterious ingredient that set it apart from all others. "Food just doesn't ever have to be any better than this," she went on, "but there comes a time when you want to eat your own. I want to cook a turkey, stuffed with bread and onions and chestnuts and apples and anything else I can think of. I want to bake a pumpkin pie. And I want to start the dinner with a salad, not have it after the main course. Maybe it'll be a Caesar salad, or a California salad with avocado and shrimp. Am I communicating, Peter?"

"Oh yes," he said.

"Will you come?"

His mind was whirling. Could he surmount the surveillance problem? Did he dare try? "What time would you like to serve?"

"I have always been partial to a Christmas dinner in the midafternoon. That lets you sleep in, have a late breakfast and still get the bird in the oven in time. One-thirty? Two o'clock?"

Peter thought for a moment. "Perfect," he said.

Meredith smiled. "You mean it?"

"Provided I can come early and help. Say around twelve-fifteen."

"If that's what you want."

"That's what I want."

"Deal."

The next morning at ten, Peter was at *Au Nain Bleu* on the rue St. Honoré, the premier toy store in Paris. He made three purchases, had them wrapped in separate boxes, then carried the boxes—all three large and unwieldy—from the store, drawing amused smiles from other shoppers as he proceeded.

That evening, he called Allo Taxi and ordered a car for 11:30 A.M. the next day, emphasizing the importance of punctuality by offering to pay a hundred francs above the meter charge if the driver arrived on time.

The driver arrived at eleven-twenty. At eleven-thirty Peter descended in the elevator with his packages. By eleven-forty, he had been deposited at the west end of the Quai d'Orléans on the Île St. Louis. He was at least twenty minutes early for his rendezvous, but he could not have afforded to be late.

At noon, the bells of Notre Dame pealed into the winter air. Five minutes later, the familiar figures of Monsieur Fildier, the ancient concierge of André's building, and his wife, Madame Fildier—in his ten years in the building André had never learned their first names—appeared on the other side of the Pont St. Louis, just as Peter had known they would. Monsieur and Madame Fildier were metronomic Catholics; on Sundays and holidays they never missed the eleven o'clock mass at Notre Dame. Today, thankfully, had been no exception. Peter waited until they crossed the bridge and started up the Quai d'Orléans, then fell in behind them at a pace designed to overtake them fifty feet from the stakeout car. It was still there, with two men seated inside.

"Good morning, sir and madam," Peter said to the concierge in excellent colloquial French.

"Good morning," they returned.

Peter continued walking until he was a few feet in front of them.

Then, abruptly, he stopped. *"Alors!"* he said loudly. "They're still there!"

Monsieur and Madame drew abreast of him, and followed his gaze. Their eyes narrowed in unison. "Who is still there, monsieur?" Monsieur Fildier said.

"Those men. There, in that car." The Fildiers followed Peter's gaze. "I have no idea who they are, or why they're there. All I know is that they've been there every day for the last two weeks."

They were still thirty feet behind the car, but now they began to move closer. When they were ten feet away, Monsieur Fildier looked at his wife, then at Peter, and whispered, "Arabs!"

Without another word, Monsieur and Madame advanced on the car. Monsieur rapped his fist on the window. "What are you doing here?" he demanded of the occupants before the man on the driver's side had had time to roll the window down. "What do you want? Who are you waiting for?"

Clearly startled, the driver opened his window and attempted to answer, but neither Monsieur nor Madame Fildier cared to listen. Instead, they continued to fire questions, and then to explain to the crowd that was beginning to gather that these two men had been sitting in their car for the last two weeks, spying on the residents. As Peter continued walking, his packages shielding his face from the car, the hubbub was so loud that he could hear only isolated words, such as "Kidnappers!" and "Assassins!" Knowing his former neighbors, he was sure they would have the police there in ten minutes, and knowing the police, he was sure they would occupy the two men for the rest of the day and evening, at the very least. In another thirty seconds, he was inside the door of André's building, and a minute later inside André's apartment, giving a peck on the cheek to André's smiling wife.

The next several hours were the happiest Peter had experienced since the shooting at Casa de Campo. From the look of her, he had the feeling that they were Meredith's happiest hours as well. Rather than being forgotten, André was a formidable presence; it was his life that had brought them both to this moment, a knowledge that underscored almost everything they did. "Do you understand now how I felt when I walked into this place?" Meredith asked as she showed him proudly around the apartment. "I knew exactly who he was—and I wasn't wrong."

"I do understand," Peter said, nodding appreciatively. "And also how you could see yourself in this setting."

In the next hour, as Meredith put the finishing touches on the dinner, Peter proved himself to be André's opposite in a number of ways. André had been at home in the kitchen; Peter confessed, after bumbling an assignment, that all he really knew how to make was ice. Meredith sent Peter into the living room to choose some music for the stereo; when she came out five minutes later to find out what had happened, she found Peter looking in vain through André's records. "They're all classical," he said. "I was hoping to find some jazz." When Meredith showed him André's library and paintings, he apologized for his lack of enthusiasm with the explanation that people in his line of work seldom made collections. "You're a Philistine!" Meredith said with a laugh, throwing up her hands.

But his presents—a teddy bear, a lion and a rabbit for Meredith's unborn child—were a tremendous hit, and got them to talking about the child's future as they ate their dinner in view of the Seine.

"You'll have the baby here?" Peter asked.

"I'd thought I would, but now I'm not sure. The American in me says have it in the States so that there'll be no ambiguity about citizenship. But André no longer thought of the States as home. He considered himself a transnational. Come to think of it, *he* used to say that home was where he was. You do have a few things in common with André, even if you are uncultured."

Peter laughed with Meredith, pleased beyond expressing that she felt comfortable enough with their relationship to be able to tease him.

"What about language?" he asked.

"Oh, English first, absolutely. But French, too."

"And education?"

"That's six years away."

"True." Peter paused on the verge of his next question, and then fell silent.

"What?" Meredith said. "Go on."

"No. Never mind."

"Go ahead. Say it."

"It's really none of my business."

"Peter! Say it!"

"Well, what about a father?"

She looked at him for a long time without speaking. "The baby has a father," she said softly at last. "He just happens to be dead."

He took her hand. "I'm sorry," he said.

"Don't be," she said. "It's a good question. A child needs a father." Her eyes glistened. "So does a mother." Then she withdrew her hand and went to the kitchen to get the pumpkin pie.

The telephone rang as they were finishing the dishes. It was Charles Houghton, calling from Washington to wish his daughter a merry Christmas. At one point in their conversation, Meredith beckoned Peter to the phone to say hello. Peter silently waved her off, and indicated with signs that she was not to mention his presence. From that moment on there was a change in the rhythm of her conversation, and when she hung up he could see that she was troubled.

"Any problems?" he said.

"All kinds," she said. "Daddy's got his hands full." She faltered. "He didn't tell me much, and the part he did tell me about he asked me not to discuss."

"I understand," Peter said.

For a moment, she looked at him strangely. Then she started back toward the kitchen, only to turn abruptly. "I'll tell you something, Peter Burke. If this baby in here ever does have a living father, I hope to God he won't be in my father's line of work, or yours. Too much mystery. Too many secrets."

22

Charles Houghton's telephone was ringing as he hobbled through the door of his Watergate apartment at four o'clock on the second Sunday afternoon in January.

"I've been trying to get you all weekend," Jack Fleming said without bothering to identify himself. "I was afraid to call the duty officer."

"I was visiting friends in Virginia," Houghton explained. "You sound upset."

"I am."

"Can it wait until morning?"

"It better not, and it won't take long. I can be there in ten minutes."

"Okay," Houghton said.

Eleven minutes later, Fleming sank his big frame into one of Houghton's easy chairs and began speaking without preamble. "There was a woman in the program, an actress and drama coach named Kate Berrigan. Good woman. I'd used her once before. The police found her body Friday morning in a country lane about forty miles west of London. She hadn't been sexually molested, but she had been tortured."

"How'd you find out?"

"Story in the London papers. My English liaison on the program saw it and had the good sense to call me."

"Any other reason why she might have been tortured?"

"I'd be dumbfounded if there were. The woman was a gem.

Didn't have an enemy in the world. I feel terrible. I'll feel worse if I found out she talked."

"How much did she know?"

"Only that she was to help someone learn a new role."

"Did she know his name?"

"First name only. The new one. Not the old one."

"Damn," Houghton said.

"We had a problem, remember? The graft wasn't taking. We had to get him used to the idea that he was Peter."

"It was good reasoning at the time. It doesn't look so good now." He chewed his lip. "How do you suppose they found out—whoever they are?"

"Let me ask *you* a question. How did you fund the program?"

"Through a proprietary company I set up."

"Name?"

Houghton hesitated.

"Come on, Charlie, this is me, Jack. I've got to know."

"Plymouth Rock, Limited."

"Had you ever used it before?"

"Once. Five years ago."

"For what purpose?"

"Strictly a money transfer. Pretty much like this one."

"And where did the money come from?"

"From the director's discretionary fund."

"When that much money moves how many people have to know about it?"

"Supposedly just me and the man who makes the entries in the books."

"Is he someone you can trust?"

"I thought he was. I'll know by tomorrow. In the meanwhile, could you go to London and find out what you can?"

"I was about to make that suggestion."

"Can you make the evening flight?"

"I've got a seat, and a bag in my car," Fleming said. He looked at his watch. "Better get going."

"Just a second," Houghton said. "When the people in your program billed you, you sent all the bills to me, right?"

"That's right."

"And, as I recall, you didn't use specifics. You just submitted a bill for services?"

"Right."

"And when you got the money, you simply disbursed it?"

"Right."

"No receipts?"

"None that anyone but me has ever seen."

"You're certain?"

"Unless I've been robbed since I left my place twenty minutes ago."

"So that even if someone stumbled onto Plymouth Rock, they wouldn't find any names?"

"That's right."

"Then how could anyone have placed this woman in the program?"

"That's what I hope to find out."

Jack Fleming took the 6:25 P.M. TWA flight from Dulles Airport to London. By 9:30 A.M. Monday, local time—4:30 A.M. in Washington—he was installed in his favorite room at a small hotel in Chelsea that he had used for years, and by 10:45 A.M., after a breakfast of kippers and bacon, he had begun to call on each of the people who had been involved in the makeover program. Ostensibly, Fleming's visit was to discover if each of them might be available for another, similar, assignment. Toward the end of the visit, he brought up his hidden agenda. "Any problems?" he would ask. The answers of Dr. Collins, the plastic surgeon, were fairly typical of all but one respondent.

"Problems? Wouldn't know. Haven't seen him since."

"How about yourself? Anyone curious about what you were doing in the Cotswolds?"

"Oh, that. Not that I know of. Wouldn't have done them much good if they were."

"No one—either directly or obliquely—asked you questions having to do with your work out there?"

"No. No one. Absolutely not. I say, the chap's not in trouble, is he?"

"Just double checking, Doctor."

230

"Good. Nice chap. Hope it all worked out."

Again, with one exception, not one of the respondents brought up the murder of Kate Berrigan, having failed, apparently, to connect her to the program, a logical conclusion since they had all worked with Peter at different times.

The exception was Richard Hampstead.

When Fleming called him on Tuesday morning, the actor refused at first to see him. "Is it because of Kate?" Fleming asked.

"You're bloody well right it is."

"Look, I'm as upset about that as you are."

"I would doubt that very much."

"I'm trying to get to the bottom of it. Won't you help me?" He paused. In the past, Fleming had always played a special card in dealing with reluctant sources. No Englishman, he'd discovered, could resist an invitation to lunch to the Connaught Hotel; it was the next best thing to a summons to Buckingham Palace. But it was also frightfully expensive. Well, this was no time to falter. "Can you meet me for lunch at the Connaught? One-thirty?"

Seconds passed before Hampstead spoke. "The dining room or the Grill?"

"I think the dining room, don't you? It's a little roomier."

Hampstead was fifteen minutes late. He didn't look at all well. When he sat he looked nervously around for a waiter, stopped the first one who came along and demanded a dry martini. When it still hadn't arrived by the time their regular waiter approached, he sent him out to look for it. At last, the drink came. He drank half of it in a gulp. Only then did he look at Fleming. "I knew I shouldn't have gotten involved in your dirty games."

"We were trying to help a man."

"At what price to ourselves?"

"I understand your feelings for Kate. What other price have you paid?"

"Look at me, for God's sake. I'm a wreck."

"Tell me."

"Christ! You people." He stared at his drink, then at Fleming. "Kate was a close friend. I loved that woman like a sister. What a rotten death."

"Do you have any idea who killed her?"

"You're bloody well right I do."

Just then, the captain arrived to take their order. He smiled at Hampstead. "How nice to see you, sir. I saw your last film. Excellent."

Suddenly, Hampstead was like a man transformed. He smiled warmly at the captain. "How kind," he said.

"We have some beautiful Dover sole today. I can sauté it on the bone if you like."

"Perfect," Hampstead said.

"That'll be fine," Fleming said.

"With some oysters to start?"

"Excellent," Hampstead said.

"Fine," Fleming said.

When the captain had departed it was as though the curtain had come down on a play. Once again, Hampstead looked stricken. "That man wouldn't know my name if I gave him a thousand guesses. It's the story of my life: to die anonymously." He looked angrily at Fleming. "And, apparently, prematurely."

The sommelier was right on the heels of the captain. He handed the wine list to Hampstead, who made gestures for him to give it to Fleming. "Go ahead," Fleming said.

Hampstead ordered a white burgundy. From the way the sommelier's eyebrows raised, Fleming figured it was expensive.

"You've just bought a beautiful wine," Hampstead confirmed dourly.

"That's fine," Fleming said. "Look, tell it any way you like, but please tell me. How do you know who killed Kate?"

Hampstead finished his martini, then stared into the empty glass. "I don't *know,*" he said. "I couldn't prove it in a court of law. I didn't see anyone do it." He lifted his face and looked at Fleming with hatred in his eyes. "But I would bet my life that whoever did it was trying to get from her the same information they've been trying to get from me."

"Can you take it one step at a time?"

The wine arrived. Fleming waited impatiently through the ritual of uncorking, smelling, tasting and pouring. At last they were alone again. "Go ahead," he prompted.

Hampstead let out a long sigh, then rubbed his face. Finally, he began. "I got a call a week ago from MI-6. Out of the blue. Said they wanted to see me. Two men came over to my flat."

"Names?"

"Didn't catch them. Too nervous. Didn't beat around the bush. Wanted to know what I'd been doing in the Cotswolds. Told them I was vacationing. 'At a private residence leased by the American CIA?' one of them asked. I said I didn't know it had been. 'Poppycock,' he said. 'What were you doing there?' Well, I had to tell him something. This was MI-6."

"You're sure?"

"Oh, absolutely. Showed me his credential. Mentioned laws against serving a foreign power. Made it sound like I'd been a bloody spy." Hampstead paused to take a long sip of wine. "You've got to understand, I was a naval officer."

"So what did you tell them?"

"I told them the truth."

"How much of it?"

"That I'd been brought in to give voice lessons to some bloke."

"Did you describe the bloke?"

"I told them he was bandaged all the time I was there."

"Did you give them his name?"

"What do you take me for? I said we never knew his name."

"We?"

The question stopped Hampstead cold.

Fleming waited. "They asked you how you got the job, didn't they?" he said at last.

"Yes." Hampstead looked crestfallen.

"And you told them Kate Berrigan recommended you?"

Hampstead didn't need to answer. His silence and remorsefulness were an eloquent response. At last, he said, "What could I do? He threatened me with an inquiry board."

Their oysters arrived. Fleming began to eat, but Hampstead ignored his plate. "Do you have any idea at all how they found out about you?"

Hampstead looked at Fleming miserably out of the corner of his eyes. "That wouldn't have been very hard, old man. I have one of the best-known faces in England. No one remembers my name, but there's not an Englishman or woman who doesn't look at me when I pass. I'm in so bloody many films that they can all place me in one role or another."

"But why would it be so out of the ordinary for you to be in the Cotswolds, and for someone to report that?"

Hampstead regarded Fleming with a look of sheer malevolence. "I don't know the answer to that question. I would suppose it has something to do with you chaps and your silly games."

The waiter came to their table, cleared Fleming's plate, then faltered as he moved to Hampstead's side and noted his untouched oysters. "Is everything all right, sir? May I bring you something else?"

"No, no, that'll be fine."

"Very good, sir. Thank you, sir."

Fleming waited until the waiter had moved away. Then he said, "You mentioned that there were two men, but from the sound of it only one of them did the talking."

Hampstead cocked his head. "That's right."

"Are you certain that the other man showed you his credentials?"

"Yes. No. I'm not sure. I told you I was extremely nervous."

"Are you sure the man was English?"

"Oh, God, I don't know."

"Then he didn't do any talking at all?"

"I suppose he didn't. What are you getting at?"

"Could you describe the man?"

"Yes, I think so. Late fifties, early sixties. Tall. Slender. Well, not slender, but nothing extra on him, as though he took care of himself. Short gray hair. Ruddy complexion, as though he spent a lot of time outdoors."

"English tailoring or American?"

Hampstead closed his eyes and concentrated in silence for several seconds. Then he opened them and looked directly at Fleming. "American, by God. No padding in the shoulders. Thin lapels. A button-down shirt. I played a Harvard professor once, and that's exactly what I wore."

Fleming nodded, but said nothing. A name had come to mind, based on Hampstead's description. He couldn't conceivably mention the name to Houghton until he knew more.

At Langley late Tuesday morning, Houghton listened in silence as Fleming, on the phone from London, told him the story. When Fleming had finished, Houghton said, "Okay, let's try to reconstruct this thing. Your hunch was right. It started with the funds. There was a slip on this end. The man who handles the Plymouth Rock account went on emergency leave. His mother was suddenly and seriously ill. He ran off without saying anything about Plymouth Rock to the man who sat in for him. When that man got the account, he asked around to see who could identify the expenses. There's no way the network would have missed it."

"So someone in the network asked MI-6 for assistance."

"That's where it should have stopped. MI-6 knew this was a private matter. I spoke to Jeremy Croft myself."

The next seconds passed in silence. "Are you thinking what I'm thinking?" Fleming said.

"Let me call Croft," Houghton said. "I'll get right back to you."

Five minutes later, Houghton had the head of MI-6 on the phone. "Never heard of it," Croft said. "Let me look into it and get back to you."

"It's rather urgent," Houghton said.

"Half an hour do?"

"Of course."

He called back in twenty minutes. "The request didn't come to us officially."

"But it did come to someone?"

"Apparently so."

Houghton thought for a moment. "Is it possible, Jeremy, that you've got the same problem we do?"

"It would seem so, wouldn't it?"

Houghton sighed. "Let's stay in touch."

"By all means."

He would want to go over it with Fleming, but Houghton was reasonably sure he had it. Someone in the Company heard about Plymouth Rock and called a friend in MI-6. The friend would have been well enough placed to have gotten the word about the private operation in the Cotswolds. A case of two and two. From that point on, it was even simpler. Ask around. Get the actor's name. Then the actress's. The only question now was whether she talked before they killed her. Somehow, Fleming would have to find out.

When the telephone in Jack Fleming's room rang, he thought it was Charles Houghton calling back. Instead, it was the hall porter. "Mr. Hampstead to see you, sir. May I send him up?"

"Yes, of course."

Fleming hung up, pleased. He'd given Hampstead the name of his hotel and asked him to come directly if anything further developed that he wouldn't want overheard by strangers.

A minute later, there was a knock at the door. Fleming opened it. The man who pushed himself inside wasn't Hampstead. He was tall, slender, looked to be in his late fifties or early sixties, with short gray hair and a burnished face. His clothes were exactly as Hampstead had described them. He pointed a gun with a silencer at Fleming.

"Well, well, as I live and breathe," Fleming said. In another moment he did neither.

The man bent to make certain Fleming was dead. "Sorry, Jack," he said.

Jeremy Croft himself called Charles Houghton at 11 o'clock Tuesday evening, London time, to tell him of Jack Fleming's murder. The night maid at Fleming's hotel had found his body at 9 P.M. when she came in to turn down the bed. He promised that he would move heaven and earth on his end to find out who had done it. "The only reason they killed Jack was because he figured out who killed the Berrigan woman," Houghton said. "Either that, or he was close."

"I agree," Croft said.

"Incidentally, you'd better get hold of Hampstead and get him somewhere safe."

There was a moment's silence on Croft's end. "I'm afraid we're too late, Charles," he said then. "He's disappeared."

"Damn!" Houghton said. "Let's hope that he took himself into hiding."

"Dead or alive, we know that he's still in England. He hasn't passed passport control."

"Keep me posted," Houghton said.

Twenty seconds after Houghton hung up—the time it took him to retrieve the number—he dialed Peter's hotel in Paris. The night clerk reported that he wasn't in his room. Houghton left word for Peter to call him at home the moment he came in. Then he left at once for the Watergate.

By 7 P.M., when Peter still hadn't called, he tried the hotel again. When the night clerk said that he hadn't yet returned, Houghton left a new message: "Urgent! Call at once, regardless of the hour."

At 10 P.M., with Peter still unaccounted for, Houghton called Dick Sexton, filled him in and told him to get to Paris as quickly as he could. In the office early the next morning, he asked Billy to arrange a flight to London on Thursday evening. If it weren't for an appointment with the President on Thursday afternoon, he would have left that evening.

23

Peter had spent the last two nights in Moscow, at Jacob Jones's apartment. Jacob had called him abruptly at eight on Monday morning and told him they would be leaving at ten from Le Bourget. Something had come up in Moscow that required his immediate presence. Peter should be at the airport at nine-thirty. The instructions were clipped and emphatic. He did not ask if Peter could make it on such short notice, and he hung up without giving Peter time to object.

Peter had been in his pajamas when Jacob called, sitting up in bed, just beginning to write in his journal. It was a new journal—he'd reluctantly destroyed the old one before leaving the Cotswolds—written in a deliberately nonspecific style. No names or dates or places or personal references, just thoughts and observations, most of them about such things as the impact of a single event—"an intrusion in time," he called it—on the course of a life, and sometimes far more. *What would the world be like today if Lee Harvey Oswald had missed, or if the bullets had been a few inches to either side?* he'd written. *Would it be a better place? A safer place? One would have to think so. It would be fascinating to try to calculate that. Someday, maybe.* Then the phone had rung, and moments later the thought, like the paper, was abandoned.

As he had packed, Peter cursed himself for not having made a contingency arrangement with Meredith. They'd had dinner together half a dozen times since Christmas, less often than he would have liked but as often as he'd considered prudent; they were to have had dinner that evening at La Barrière Poquelin on the rue Molière in the First Arrondissement. The last thing in the world he wanted was for Meredith to go to the restaurant only to discover that she'd been stood up. Then she would call the hotel and find out that he'd left Paris without an explanation. She was touchy enough, as it was, about the mystery and secrets that characterized their relationship; disappearing on her would just about do it as far as Peter Burke was concerned. But what could he do? Calling her directly was out of the question—he had to assume that the line was tapped—and having someone else call on his behalf would create even more suspicion on the part of the listener.

The solution had come to Peter as he finished packing. He grabbed the telephone directory, thumbed through it quickly, found the number and dialed. In another few seconds, Monsieur Fildier, André's old concierge, was on the line. In his most polite and eloquent French, Peter explained to Monsieur Fildier that the telephone of Madame Kohl was probably out of order because he had not been able to reach her at hours when he knew she was at home. Would the *cher* monsieur be so kind as to do him the enormous favor of asking Madame Kohl to call the Hotel St. Germain des Prés at once?

Peter had passed the next twenty minutes in agony, knowing how close he was cutting it. In another ten minutes, at the latest, he would have to leave for Le Bourget. Quickly, he wrote a note to Meredith, explaining that he had suddenly been called away. Then, once again, he called Monsieur Fildier.

"Madame was not at home," the concierge explained in an irritated voice.

"Could I impose upon you once again to deliver a message to madame?" Peter asked. "The message is that she should pass by the Hotel St. Germain at 36, rue Bonaparte today to pick up an envelope."

"Perhaps monsieur would be better off sending a telegram," the concierge suggested.

"It would be better for me to put two hundred francs in an envelope addressed to you," Peter said.

That settled the matter. It was chancy, Peter knew, but the best he could do. He repeated the message once more to the concierge, then grabbed his bag and went down to the lobby. At the reception desk, he gave the envelope to the clerk, then rushed for the door.

"Mr. Burke!"

The desk clerk's cry stopped him in his tracks. He turned. "Yes?"

She was looking at his bag in confusion. "Are you checking out?"

"No, no. I'll be back in a few days."

"You are keeping the room?"

"Yes, yes. I haven't time to explain."

"But the rent, monsieur?"

Peter exhaled in annoyance, put down his bag, reached into his wallet, extracted ten five-hundred franc notes and thrust them into the hands of the desk clerk. Then he turned once again for the door.

"Don't you want a receipt?" she called after him. But he was already out the door, rushing up the block to the taxi stand on the Boulevard St. Germain.

He got to the passenger lounge at Le Bourget at five minutes to ten. Jacob was visibly annoyed. "Another minute and you would have missed the flight, pal."

"I'm very sorry. It was such short notice."

"All the same, the man whose murder you're investigating would have been here an hour early. Let's go."

This was not the suave and gracious man that André had known. Jacob was obviously under pressure. Although he was six inches shorter than Peter, he walked so quickly that he beat him to the aircraft by thirty feet.

Jacob's plane was the same Gulfstream III that had flown André and Meredith to the Dominican Republic. Only now that Peter was about to board the plane did its significance strike him. They would be flying into the Soviet Union in a private aircraft. You could count the number of Western businessmen permitted to do that on the fingers of one hand.

On board, Jacob spread an array of papers on a table and worked on them until lunch was served. Even then, he gave no indication that he wanted Peter to join him, which suited Peter fine because he did not want to be questioned about his plans in

Moscow. He had allowed himself the period before lunch to worry about how Meredith would react to his abrupt departure. Then, knowing that all such worries would be at an end if he accomplished his objectives, he turned his thoughts to Moscow.

In truth, there wasn't much to think about. He had only two opportunities. He had to capitalize on both of them. If either of them fizzled, he was out of business.

Whether it was a blessing or not, Peter couldn't decide, but he quickly learned that he wouldn't have much time to think about his slim opportunities, either. An hour after they arrived at Jacob's apartment, Jacob announced that the gathering for which Peter had come to Moscow would be the following evening. Jacob would be spending the rest of the day at his Soviet-American Trading Company office. "Here's a key to the apartment. You've been cleared at the gate, so you can come and go as you please. Make yourself at home." Without another word, he left.

If any place in Moscow felt like home, the drab brick, ten-story building in which Jacob's apartment was located was it. The building was at Kutuzovsky Prospekt 13, one of the main arteries of Moscow. Jacob's apartment was on the top floor; three floors below was the combination apartment and office of the USBC correspondent, where André had worked on every trip to Moscow. Dozens of correspondents for the Western media had almost identical setups. It was no accident that they had been housed together; it made keeping tabs on their comings and goings that much easier. At the entrance to the building's grounds was a guardhouse manned twenty-four hours a day. Although the inhabitants of the building were not required to sign in and out, their movements were duly noted.

Contrasted with the depressing exterior, Jacob's apartment was truly another world. It was beautifully furnished in the same style as his Paris office, and fully equipped with the latest electronic equipment, including the first privately owned big-screen television set in Moscow. In addition to an ample living room overlooking the prospekt, there was a dining room, two bedrooms and a modern kitchen. In the kitchen was a gigantic freezer filled with meats, fish, vegetables and other foods flown in by a company in

Finland. While most of the apartment's contents had been brought in from the West, there were a number of Russian touches such as the lacquered boxes on the coffee table and a collection of multicolored decorative eggs. But without question, the most valuable possession in the apartment was a direct dial telephone from which Jacob could call anywhere in the world without going through an operator. Any foreigner who had ever tried to make a call to somewhere outside the Soviet Union would know just how precious that instrument was.

It was now late afternoon, time to make a move, as tentative as it might be. He was certain that whatever had brought Jacob to Moscow in such a hurry would keep him out through the evening, and equally certain that if he was to have been included in those plans he would have heard from Jacob by now. Being alone fit in perfectly with his own plans.

Bundling into his overcoat and fedora—the first hat he had ever owned, bought specifically for this trip—Peter took the drab and rickety elevator to the street level, then walked out through the gate and turned toward Kremlin Square. A block down the street was a *Beryozka,* a foreign currency store. Peter stopped to examine the displays in the window, surely a cornucopia to Muscovites. At the same moment, he turned his eyes as far to the left as he could without moving his head. Fifty feet away, a man drew to an abrupt halt.

Peter walked into the store and moved directly to a counter where fur hats were sold. His eye went immediately to a hat made of dark fur with ear flaps that tied at the top when not in use, exactly the kind of hat he had seen on thousands of male Russian heads in his trips to Moscow over the years. He found his size and bought the hat in a matter of minutes.

"Will you wear it?" a young saleswoman asked him in English.

"No, I'll carry it," Peter said. "Can you put it in a bag?"

A minute later, bag in hand, fedora back in place, Peter resumed his walk down the Kutuzovsky Prospekt. In another minute he came to a clothing store. Once again he stopped to examine the goods in the display window. Once again he looked out of the corner of his eye, with the same result. Someone—probably the same man—had abruptly stopped.

Satisfied that he was being followed, Peter meandered through the streets a while longer, then returned to Jacob's apartment. As he turned in the gate, he saw his tail watching from down the block.

The day he received his visa for travel to the Soviet Union, Peter had bought a detailed map of Moscow. In his room, he unpacked the map and studied it until he was certain that when the time came to create his second opportunity he would know where he was going and how he would get there.

Peter did not see Jacob that evening, and they were together only briefly the next morning. Jacob was still preoccupied, tense and very much in a hurry. "I've invited a dozen government officials," he said. "I'll try to arrange it so that you and Krylov have some time alone. He shook his head. "I'm really taking a chance," he said. "I hope to hell you know what you're doing."

Peter made a quick decision. "Would it ease your mind if I included you in the conversation?"

"That depends on what you're going to say."

"I won't know until I feel him out, but you're welcome to be there."

Jacob eyed Peter for a moment, seemingly lost in thought. "I'll play it by ear myself." As he turned away, he muttered, "I needed this like a hole in the head." In another moment, he was gone.

The menu that evening was eclectic—familiar enough to make the Russians feel at home, foreign enough to make the meal seem like an adventure. To start, there were slabs of glistening smoked sturgeon accompanied by Russian caviar and a variety of salads. Then came strips of American-style sirloin steaks with sautéed potatoes, and asparagus with hollandaise sauce. The guests served themselves from a buffet, then found places at the table, where they could fill the several glasses before them with vodka, brandy, wine or beer, or all four if they wished, which a few of them did. There were many toasts throughout the meal, to "peace and friendship," to the people of the United States, the people of the Soviet Union, the leaders of both countries and, of course, to the health of the host. At each toast, Jacob raised his glass to his lips and tilted it, but Peter noticed that he didn't drink. After a preliminary sip of the wine, he himself had done the same thing.

The dozen men ranged in age from forty to sixty. They wore surprisingly well-cut Western-style suits, with well-chosen shirts and ties. As a group, they were somewhat heavier than upper-echelon American bureaucrats, and several of them revealed some gold teeth when they smiled; aside from those two distinctions, and considered individually, they might well have passed for their American counterparts. There was, however, the matter of their companions. At a similar gathering of American bureaucrats, the males would have brought their wives. Most of the men had brought women ten to twenty years younger than themselves. At the dinner table, Peter found himself seated between two of the more attractive women. The woman on his left, a blonde, was pretty enough to be an actress, but appeared to be ill at ease, as though this was her first time at such a gathering, and said absolutely nothing. The woman on his right, a brunette, was about forty, dark for a Russian, with black hair, a voluptuous figure and manner to match. "You will be here long?" she asked Peter as they ate their first course.

"I'm not sure," he said.

"You should stay awhile." She smiled ambiguously. "Get to know Russian people."

"Sounds good," Peter said, hoping the conversation would end there.

Jacob had introduced Peter as vaguely as he could, as an associate who would be accompanying him on a trip to Siberia. It was the first Peter had heard about the specific destination of the side trip Jacob had mentioned in Paris; he was far more curious about the trip than the Russians, who seemed satisfied with the explanation. Or perhaps it was the problem of language that kept them from asking questions; while all of them spoke some English, few of them spoke well enough to converse in the language, and so other than his banter with the woman on his right Peter, to his relief, was left pretty much alone. He spent much of the time studying Vassily Krylov, the KGB chairman, who in turn spent his time in discussions with Jacob.

Krylov was short and overweight and such an ugly man by

conventional terms that, like many a character actor, he actually seemed attractive. He compelled attention, despite his frightening aspect. Knowing what he did, Peter guessed that his face had been scarred by fears and memories. If Peter hadn't known that he was sixty, he would have guessed his age as seventy. He did not at all relish the prospect of dealing with such an obviously forbidding man.

The toasts dragged on so long after they had finished eating that Peter began to wonder if his misgivings were irrelevant. Very soon now, the guests would all be leaving. He looked anxiously at Jacob, trying to catch his eye. But Jacob, either deliberately or because he was caught up in the revelry, never looked his way. For the first time in two days he seemed to be in good spirits.

Suddenly, Peter felt a hand on his right thigh. He turned. The dark woman was looking at him unmistakably. "I call you tomorrow," she said. She gave the inside of his thigh a pat and a squeeze, then removed her hand and rose.

When Peter looked around again, his heart sank. Krylov was gone.

"Go into my bedroom," Jacob whispered. "He's waiting for you."

Peter wheeled. Jacob had come up behind him so quietly that he'd been caught unaware.

"I told Krylov that I'd brought you because I was a friend of André's. That's all I told him. Don't give him any theories about me, understand?"

"I understand," Peter said.

"And for God's sake, be careful. This isn't tiddlywinks, pal. That guy's one of the most powerful men in the world."

"I know why you are here," Krylov said in serviceable but heavily accented English the moment Peter stepped into the bedroom. "But I confess I do not understand why you have come. We know nothing of the death of Mr. André Kohl."

There was no time for parrying. "Let's go back to the beginning, Mr. Chairman," Peter said. "In the interest of time, I'll be blunt. I know how André became involved in the story of Camille Laurent. The fact is that you ran him."

"Ran him? I do not know that expression."

245

"You set him up. You wanted him to find the dossier that incriminated Camille Laurent."

"Go on," Krylov said. His voice was cold.

"The plan was conceived by Gennady Gondrachov," Peter said, watching carefully for a reaction. There was none.

"Go on."

"Somehow, in the process of authenticating the dossier in Paris, Gennady Gondrachov got himself killed."

"Supposing you are right. What has all this to do with the death of Mr. Kohl?"

"That's what I'm here to find out. I don't know what it is yet, but I have reason to believe that what happened to Mr. Kohl was related to the death of Gennady Gondrachov."

Krylov stared at him. In the silence, Peter could feel the atmosphere in the room begin to change. The Russian's features softened. "Gennady Gondrachov was like family to me," he said. "What do you know of how he died?"

"Let me first show you something," Peter said. From the wallet pocket of his jacket, he withdrew Gennady's letter to André and handed it to Krylov. The KGB chief read it slowly. When he finished he looked at Peter. "This is the original?" he asked.

"Yes."

"Where did you obtain it?"

"From André Kohl's wife. She found it in his apartment."

"I see. Do you have idea why Gennady believed that it would not—how he said it?—go well for him?"

"The obvious conclusion is that Laurent's people were closing in."

"Is there reason to believe that obvious conclusion is not right conclusion?"

"That's the question I came to ask you."

"I see."

But he didn't, or at least he didn't appear to. Peter could not be sure of what he read in Krylov's eyes, because they were half-hidden beneath a protruding brow and dense, untended eyebrows, but he thought he saw confusion, not clarity. He knew then that he would have to explain it all, step by step. He did: first, the nature of the relationship between Gennady and André; second, the special efforts to kill André; third, the efforts, even now, to make certain that André was dead. The last item was one that, if he had been more prudent, he wouldn't have mentioned, but it issued from him nonetheless because he knew that he had quickly reached the all-or-nothing stage of his investigation. It was like the first round of a tournament: lose and you're out. Without the possibility of Krylov's help, there would be no point in going on, because no matter what his second opportunity provided him, he could not put it to use. Why would Krylov want to help him? The only certain reason would be if there was something in it for him. "So my conclusion, Mr. Chairman, is that whoever went after André Kohl wasn't doing so out of a desire for revenge, but out of fear that he had learned something they didn't want him to know. There were four groups of people involved: Americans, French, Germans and Russians. There was nothing the Americans, French or Germans could have told André that he didn't already know. That leaves the Russians—and his good friend, Gennady. My question, Mr. Chairman, is this: What did Gennady know that, given the danger he found himself in and the nature of their friendship, he might have told André?"

Frowning, Krylov looked away, as though he needed time to assimilate all that Peter had said. For a moment, Peter wondered anxiously if the Russian had fully understood him. But then suddenly Krylov turned to him and said, "Is interesting theory. But is just theory, correct?"

Now or never, Peter thought. "Not just a theory, Mr. Chairman," he said very slowly. The next words were aimed at Krylov as carefully as bullets at a target. "The Arab terrorists sent to kill André were hired by Russians."

He could see the words slam home. For the briefest instant, so brief that if Peter hadn't been looking directly at them he would have missed the reaction, Krylov's eyes widened in astonishment, a response as involuntary as a reflex, and then just as quickly narrowed in an effort to hide his response. But it was too late. Peter had seen it, and the result was as definitive as a tear in a bull's-eye.

"How you know this?" Krylov said at last.

"From impeccable sources."

"Mossad?"

"I let you make your own conclusion."

"Mossad always make us trouble."

Peter shrugged. "Check it out. Make up your own mind. The group is called 'The Popular Front of the Arab World.' The leader is a man called Khalel el Hassan. The assassins traveled on phony Jordanian passports. They started from Damascus. That should give you enough to go on."

For a moment, Krylov regarded Peter in silence. "We must talk again," he said abruptly. "Come to see me when you are back from trip." Abruptly, he walked from the bedroom, found Jacob, said a few words, shook hands, retrieved his hat and overcoat and was gone.

Jacob walked over to Peter, who had watched Krylov's departure from the bedroom door. "Well?" he said. "Did you learn anything?"

"Maybe," Peter said.

Jacob's face darkened. His eyes were icy. "This better not backfire, pal. I've never seen him so disturbed."

In Paris the next morning, as he checked into the Hotel St. Germain following his flight from Washington, Dick Sexton asked the receptionist if she would please ring Peter Burke's room.

"Mr. Burke is away," she said.

"You're kidding. I came here to meet him. When did he check out?"

"He has not checked out, sir. He kept his room."

"Then when did he leave?"

"On Monday morning."

"Did he say when he'd be returning?"

"He said nothing."

"Are you *sure* he said he'd be back?" he'd asked.

"Oh, absolutely," the manager replied. "He paid for a week in advance."

So Peter hadn't been abducted. That news was communicated to Houghton at noon Paris time, 6 A.M. in Washington, along with assurances that the twenty-four-hour a day guard ordered for Meredith's apartment by telephone from Washington the day before was in place, and that she appeared to be well when followed on her morning walk. It remained for Sexton to discover whether whoever had found Peter's trail in England had followed it to Paris.

Houghton had given him Peter's room number. He would have liked to get in straightaway, but it was the worst possible time because the rooms were being cleaned and the staff was all about. He would have to wait until evening.

At 8 P.M., Sexton went to the bar on the corner and ordered an omelet and salad. He was back in twenty minutes. "That was quick," the night clerk said.

"I had a big lunch," Sexton said. He looked into the sitting room. "The hotel's very quiet tonight."

"It's the same every night at this hour. All the guests are out to dinner."

It was as he had hoped. He retrieved his key and took the elevator to the fourth floor, then walked quickly up to the fifth. It took him less than a minute to force the lock on the door to Peter's room. The moment he closed the door and turned on the light, he knew that someone had been there before him. Every piece of clothing Peter had left behind had been unfolded and examined. Papers were scattered around the room. Sexton prayed silently that Peter Burke had left nothing behind that he didn't want unfriendly people to see.

24

They would be leaving for Siberia the following morning, Jacob said when he appeared at breakfast. The excitement of the previous evening had dissipated, and he seemed nervous and distracted once again. But it was obvious that, whatever was bothering him, he was not about to discuss it with Peter. He picked at the blinis his cook had prepared, drank his coffee and left. It was nine o'clock.

The next seven hours were agonizing for Peter. His plan required darkness. Even though darkness fell early in the northern climes in January, that still meant waiting until four o'clock. Under normal circumstances, he would have read or written, but there was nothing normal about these circumstances. At one point he did try to read, but his mind kept drifting away from the pages to the hours he was about to live.

Just before noon the telephone rang. The cook answered it. A moment later, she came into the living room and indicated that the call was for Peter.

"*Gospodin* Jones?" he asked.

"*Nyet.*"

It was that woman, then. He pantomined that he didn't want to take the call. The cook turned without a word and went to the phone. He could hear her making excuses in Russian. In a moment she hung up.

At last, it was four o'clock. Quickly, he put on his overcoat and the fedora he had bought in Paris. He shoved the fur hat he'd bought the previous day beneath his overcoat, at waist level where it would bulge the least and where he could hold onto it through the lining of his pocket. Then he descended to the street.

He took a bus to the center of Moscow, standing in the crowd at the rear. He could see the same man who had followed him the day before standing in the front. At Red Square, he got off and made his way to Gum, the cavernous department store, walking slowly in the gathering darkness. The store was crowded with shoppers trying to make purchases on their way home from work. He mixed among them, stopping every so often at one counter or another. Each time he stopped his tail stopped as well, leaving thirty to forty feet between them.

Over the next fifteen minutes, the customers began moving toward the exits in increasing numbers. Abruptly, Peter was among them, through the doors and into the night. The moment he cleared the store, he whipped the fedora from his head and replaced it with the fur hat from beneath his coat. To anyone even thirty feet behind him he was now just a head in a crowd, one of hundreds of Muscovites, at least half of them men wearing the same or similar hats, heading along the edge of the square and down into the subway.

He had not needed the subway to reach his destination, only to shake his surveillance. Gennady Gondrachov's apartment was less than a mile from Red Square, off Gorky Street, in one of the sturdy buildings that had survived World War II. Compared with the mass-produced apartment buildings that had proliferated in the fifties and sixties, the space was cavernous, with high ceilings and generous room dimensions. Thick walls, another postwar rarity, were an added advantage. André had been to the apartment at least a dozen times, but he had never taken a subway to get there. In the darkness, it took Peter a while to get his bearings once he had ascended to the street, but with the aid of the address written on a slip of paper, which he showed to a pedestrian, he was soon at the right building, and a few moments later in front of the Gondrachovs' door.

As he waited for an answer to his knock, he tried to sort through his emotions. Paramount among them was the anxiety he felt about the coming moments. Would Lusa Gondrachov receive him, or would she turn him away? If she did receive him, could he gain her confidence? To break through her reserve, he was prepared to gamble, but would it pay off? And, finally, would she have anything definitive to tell him?

He also felt a certain mixture of grief and remorse. He had tried hard to distance himself from André's feelings, reminding himself that Peter had never known Gennady and had certainly had nothing to do, even indirectly, with Gennady's death. But now the game had broken down, because there was no control on memory and the sight of that door brought so many memories flooding back—the late nights in this very apartment, the deep discussions with bright and attractive Russians, the epic feasts and heroic bouts of drinking. If the discussions ever turned to arguments, Gennady was always there with just the right irreverent remark to put them all in their place. It was hard to believe that the same man the following morning could be so doctrinaire, but that's the way he was: the quintessential survivor.

No longer. If only André had warned Gennady that he was leaving Paris, Peter thought. Perhaps Gennady too might have left before leaving became impossible.

The door opened. Lusa appeared, almost exactly as he remembered her, a tall, pale, middle-aged woman whose good bones hinted at an earlier beauty that had disappeared along with her illusions. In addition she now seemed tired and worn, as though she had been fighting and losing a battle. Seeing Peter, she frowned.

"My name is Peter Burke," he said in English. "I wish to talk to you about a matter concerning your late husband."

She drew back. "I am sorry. I have nothing to say about my husband." She began to close the door.

"Please!" Peter implored. "I'm not a journalist. I'm an investigator, hired by the United States Broadcasting Corporation to look into the death of André Kohl. Mr. Kohl was a friend of your husband's. I believe their deaths are connected."

She regarded him for several seconds, her expression frozen into a question. "Come in," she said at last. Her voice was pitched low, underscoring her heavy accent.

She led him into the living room, which, though large, seemed crowded with furniture, and indicated a sofa against a wall, above which hung a large abstract expressionist oil that André had tried unsuccessfully for years to buy from Gennady. She sat in a deep stuffed chair next to the sofa and waited for him to speak.

He spoke slowly and carefully, remembering that her English was not nearly as good as Gennady's. "Do you remember Mr. Kohl?"

"Of course," she said flatly. "I did not know he was dead."

"He was killed by Arab terrorists. I have reason to believe that his death was somehow connected to something he supposedly learned from your husband."

Lusa's frown, which had enveloped her face since her first sight of Peter, deepened. "You must explain, please. I do not understand."

He did explain, slowly and patiently, laying out yet again the sequence of events between André and Gennady. The more he spoke, the more the lines in her forehead deepened. Then he showed her Gennady's letter to André. She read it slowly, just as Krylov had. When she had finished she looked up at Peter. "Do you know how my husband died?" she said.

"You don't know?"

"No. I have asked. But they refuse to tell me. Only that he died. I don't know where. I don't know how."

"Who has refused to tell you?"

"His superiors."

"Vassily Krylov?"

"Yes."

"Do you know why they won't tell you?"

"No. I know nothing. Two months ago I write to party chairman, asking for information. I get no reply." She paused, then looked beseechingly at Peter. "Please. If you know, tell me."

He did not know if telling her would hurt or help him. He did not really care. Her appeal, the look in her eyes, transcended calculation. "Your husband was in Paris under an alias. He was posing as a Czech businessman named Milos Novotny. In the French newspapers of May 25 last year, there was a story about a Milos Novotny, along with his passport photo. The story said that his body had been found in the Bois de Boulogne."

Lusa cried out. It was a soft sound, like a scream that had died in her throat. Peter sat there helplessly.

"You are certain the picture was Gennady?" she said at last.

"Yes."

"How you are certain? How you know this?"

The question went through him like an electric shock. How could he have known—he, Peter Burke? André Kohl knew because he had seen the picture in the newspaper. Peter Burke saw the picture in a library months later, but only because André Kohl had known where to look for it. Peter Burke never could have known about Gennady Gondrachov, because André Kohl—the pre-Peter André—had never revealed his source, not to the network, or to Mike Paul, or to Charles Houghton.

Meredith! She'd known about Gennady—André had told her the entire story when he'd thought he'd been hoaxed. She'd even met Gennady during the second effort to authenticate the dossier.

"André Kohl's wife met your husband in Paris. She found the expert to authenticate the dossier. She was with your husband while the work was done. She told me how upset André was after he saw the picture in the newspaper."

Lusa nodded. She seemed satisfied. But Peter wasn't at all. For a moment, he had panicked. Now, the immediate crisis past, he still felt sick with doubt. If he hadn't anticipated that question, what other questions were lurking, half-hidden, along his path of deception? What other mistakes had he made? "This isn't tiddlywinks," Jacob Jones had said. How very right he was. If Lusa could catch Peter like that, what mistakes had he made with Vassily Krylov, one of the most powerful men on earth? Krylov wouldn't accost him directly; he would simply check out his suspicions. Russians *were* the most xenophobic and paranoid people on earth, and here he was among them, a foreigner posing as a man he wasn't. If they found him out, nothing would save him.

"Do you know who killed my husband?" Lusa said.

"I don't *know*. But I believe it was the French secret service."

Lusa closed her eyes. For a minute she sat in silence. Then she rose. "Excuse me," she said, and left the room. He could hear noises in the kitchen. A few minutes later, she returned with a tray laden with a pot of tea, cream and sugar, cups, a plate of cakes, a bottle of vodka and glasses. She poured the tea and served the cakes. "You want vodka?" she said.

"No thank you."

"Maybe later?"

"Perhaps."

She took a sip of tea, then put her cup down and looked openly at Peter. "So. You have helped me. Is better to know than to not know. So, how can I help you?"

"I believe that André Kohl was killed because he supposedly knew something of great importance that others didn't want him to know. I know that the only person from whom he could have gotten this information was your husband, because everyone else is ruled out. So my question is: what did your husband know—something of great importance—that he might have told André?"

She nodded her understanding of the question, but then began to shake her head from side to side. "How could I know that?" she asked. "He did not talk to me that way."

"He never confided in you?"

She shrugged. "He was KGB."

"He didn't tell you that he was going to Paris?"

"He told me nothing. All that you tell me is new to me."

Peter felt lost. His second opportunity was receding from him, and he'd learned absolutely nothing. Desperately, he searched his mind for a new approach. As he did, his eyes fell on the letter he'd shown her. He picked it up and looked at it once again. "Mrs. Gondrachov, was anything troubling your husband before he went away? Did he seem at all different?"

She looked away for a moment, nodding, then shrugging. Then she turned back to Peter. "I explain something to you. My husband and I, how do you say it, we were good friends. When we were younger we were away from each other for very long time. That happens very often in Russia, not so much anymore but very much when we were young. The man has one work, the woman has another work, the work of man is needed here, the work of woman is needed there. So they must be apart for very long time. Good for country, not good for marriage. You understand?"

"I do."

"Gennady's work took him away for long time." She shrugged

again. "He was human being. He met other women. But he was always good to me and the children. He made us beautiful flat in Moscow. Then a dacha in country. The children got best education. Whatever we needed he gave us. And he always came home. Sometimes for week. Sometimes for month." She paused, seeming to reflect on what she had said. "We were good friends," she said again. "But we were not close, like lovers."

"Good friends confide in one another. Did he say anything to you about being troubled, or anything to suggest that something important was going to happen?"

She thought for a long time before responding. *"Da.* Yes," she said at last. "One time."

"When?"

She held up her hands. "Maybe March, maybe April. He was— how you say?—excited."

"Did he say why?"

"He said we would be happy soon."

"You and he?"

"Him. Me. The children. Everybody."

"Russians?"

"Everybody. The world."

"Did he explain?"

"No."

"Did you ask?"

"I never ask. I know better."

"Did he say *anything* after that, anything at all, that gave you any idea of what he meant?"

Once more she fell silent, and looked away. Then suddenly she turned back to Peter. Her face pinched into a frown. "A week later he said something. He said, 'How would you like to visit America?'"

25

"How would you like to visit America?" As they flew east into
Siberia on Jacob's Gulfstream, the question beat in Peter's mind
like a drum roll. Why would Gennady have said that? Had he
intended to defect? Unthinkable. He'd been right when he'd said
that nothing the West could provide him would match the life he
had; the quintessential systems man would never abandon a system he'd learned to play to perfection. Had he expected to be
transferred to Washington? Not in the least likely. Given his special knowledge of all the Western media, a posting abroad, where
he would have been confined to a single country, wasn't in the
cards—even if that country was the United States.

What else could he have meant? That it might soon be possible
to go to America? Anything new and momentous in that? Russians did go to America, but only special Russians. Gennady was a
special Russian. He'd gone to America many times. But Lusa had
never gone, she'd said. If Lusa could go, that meant other Russians could go—which meant that conditions between the countries would have improved.

What else had Gennady told her? That everyone would be
happy soon. Not just Russians. Everyone.

Travel to America. Everyone happy. That suggested only one
thing: a forthcoming deal between the superpowers.

Was *that* it? Was that why Gennady had joked in April, when
André had gone to Moscow, that he might be able to arrange an
interview with the party chairman? Was that the subtext of Gen-

nady's letter to André just before he was killed? Talking to Lusa, Peter had suddenly been pulled back to the letter, as though some hidden meaning underlay its words. What had drawn him to it if not its strangely conciliatory tone? Never, not once, in all their dealings, had Gennady been conciliatory. He'd always been combative—friendly for the most part, rough when required. Until the letter.

The letter, the interview offer, what Lusa had told Peter, were these tiny fragments as insignificant as dead leaves in a wind—or were they advertisements of a fresh wind?

But why, if a fresh wind *was* about to blow, would the KGB want to kill him on the possibility that he knew? That made no sense.

This trip made no sense either. They were traveling three thousand miles, through three time zones, in the dead of winter to one of the coldest regions on earth, for what purpose Peter still didn't know. What he did know was that each mile they traveled took him further and further from the answers he'd come to Russia to find.

They flew for five hours, the last two in darkness, their destination Irkutsk, where Jacob was to have dinner with an old friend who had been transferred there from Moscow, their course monitored by a Russian navigator brought along to make certain they did not stray from their flight plan. But what they might have seen of strategic importance defied the imagination. Staring out the window from time to time, Peter saw nothing but empty land and, after darkness fell, only blackness broken up at long intervals by tiny clusters of lights.

At last, they landed in Irkutsk and stepped into air so cold that it pinched the nostrils together. Peter could feel the skin on his face shriveling.

They spent the night at the Intourist Hotel, unattractive but proper and comfortable like Intourist hotels throughout the Soviet Union. In the morning, they returned to the airport for the one-hour flight to Bratsk. They were going there—Jacob had told him at last—to look over a cellulose plant constructed twenty years before on the Sea of Bratsk, the 350-mile-long lake created ten years earlier when engineers stopped the mighty Angara River by throwing boulders into it and then built the biggest hydroelectric power station in the world.

Peter still didn't understand why he'd been brought along. If Jacob had wanted company he had a strange way of showing it. Throughout the previous day's flight, he'd remained just as remote as he'd been since they'd met at Le Bourget. Worse, his nervousness had escalated to the point that it made Peter edgy; he paced, cracked the bones in his hands and spoke curtly when he spoke at all. To his credit, he knew it. "Sorry, pal," he'd said at one point, catching Peter staring at him. "Too much going on upstairs." With a self-conscious grin, he pointed to his head.

From Irkutsk, it is six hundred kilometers north to Bratsk. They flew at an altitude low enough to provide them with an excellent view. Given the area's repressive reputation, Peter was completely unprepared for the breathtaking panorama that unfolded below him. A mantle of fresh, unmarked snow stretched to the horizon under a cloudless blue sky, broken up by forests of pine and birch trees whose trunks and limbs, encrusted with thick clumps of frozen snow, glistened in the brilliant sunshine. Countless lakes, their contours clearly marked by ice floes, punctuated the landscape, shimmering like windows reflecting the sun. It was impossible to reconcile this pristine vision with the Siberia of legend, the deadly place of frozen wastes, the silent witness to countless horrors.

"Quite a sight," Jacob said. He was sitting in the seat next to Peter's.

"Like Wisconsin with hills."

"Not exactly what you expected?"

"No."

"Not much in this country is." He shifted in his seat, coming a little nearer to Pete. "Let's talk business for a minute."

"Okay."

"I've got a client who's thinking of doing a joint venture with the Russians. Makes paper and paper products. Asked me to take a look at the setup in Bratsk. Since I've explained you as an associate helping me assess the operation, you gotta pretend that you know what you're talking about. Have you had any business experience?"

"Quite a bit."

"For real, or is that your cover?"

"I worked extensively in shipping in San Francisco and the Far East."

Jacob grinned at him. "No shit?"

"Go on," Peter said.

Jacob drew a piece of paper from his coat pocket, unfolded it and placed it in front of Peter. "I'd like you to memorize these questions, and ask them during our inspection. Do you think you can do that?"

Peter looked the questions over. They seemed innocuous enough, the most basic questions one would ask in assessing any enterprise. "No problem," he said, and put the paper in his coat.

"Appreciate it," Jacob said. Then, once again, he fell silent.

André Kohl had thought he knew Jacob Jones well. Peter Burke felt he was seated next to a stranger. André's Jacob had been charming and accessible. The man Peter was dealing with was matter-of-fact and self-absorbed. The contrast set Peter to musing about a familiar, vexing question: how much had André really known about the world in which he lived? Were the important people who had populated his life genuine friends interested in him for his own sake, or were they unable to divorce André the man from what he represented? Was the life they presented to André nothing more than a series of dramas scripted for his benefit? If they were actors, had André ever managed to see through their makeup? Clearly, he hadn't seen through Jacob's. Who was this pint-sized man who had managed to charm his way into such favored status with the Russians that they let him fly his own plane around the Soviet Union and gave him the inside track on deals worth millions in commissions? Peter was quite sure by now that he didn't know—and that André Kohl hadn't known, either.

Whoever Jacob was, and however he had accomplished it, he was clearly a personage in the Soviet Union. Had Peter harbored any lingering doubts, they were dispelled the moment their plane came to a stop and the pilot cut the engines. From an area near the terminal an entourage of eight black cars moved to a point near the plane, and by the time he and Jacob descended the ramp, some two dozen men and women bundled against the cold in fur overcoats and hats and lined boots were waiting at the bottom to greet him. The greetings, translated by a short, round-faced woman with cheeks like red apples and a dimpled smile, were effusive, punctuated by enthusiastic handshakes and an occasional bear hug.

After every member of the reception committee had shaken Jacob's and Peter's hands, they got into the cars for the ride to the cellulose plant. Jacob and Peter sat in the back of the lead car, on either side of the plant director, Leonid Amosoff, who had headed the welcoming delegation. He was in his mid-sixties, a stocky, hardy-looking man who wore a conservative gray suit, white shirt and black tie beneath his dark fur coat. The moment they were settled, Amosoff nodded to the translator. She introduced herself as Rita Nesmelov, and launched immediately into an orientation speech as their car, followed by the others, sped away from the airport. In glowing terms, she portrayed the Bratsk pioneers as heroes, building the dam and then the city under primitive conditions in temperatures as low as minus fifty degrees centigrade.

In minutes, they were driving through one of the settlements, past row after row of colorless rectangular buildings five stories high, laid out in undeviating lines. "Most of the city has been built in the last decade, and almost nothing in it is more than twenty years old," Rita said.

At first glance, the structures appeared to Peter to be the oldest-looking new buildings he had ever seen, their sides cracked or peeling or dirty, their corners chipped. Everywhere he looked it was exactly the same—monotonously, blearingly, paralyzingly dull. It crossed his mind that the city planners could have created anything, and chose to create an encampment.

Had his expression given his thoughts away? "Please," Amosoff said, "don't just see the faults. See the good too. There was nothing here, only an old and dirty settlement. We needed housing, desperately. So we built swiftly, winter and summer, deliberately lowering our standards, pouring concrete and plastering under the worst conditions. We built a flat for everyone, and we dreamed of beautiful houses."

The cellulose plant was by itself in a cove on the edge of the lake. Before they saw the plant, they could see great clouds of steam rising from it from two miles away. And before they could inspect the plant, there was a welcome ceremony in a spacious conference room, which looked surprisingly like the boardroom of an American corporation. A long polished wood table was in the center of the room, surrounded by twenty chairs. On the table was a buffet of ham, sausage and cheese sandwiches, chocolates and other candies, brandy and mineral water. Another party of officials, equal in number to those at the airport, assembled in the boardroom to meet the American guests. The officials at the airport had been from the city, Rita explained. These were officials of the enterprise, and they all came forward, in turn, to shake hands and state their names, the names as indistinguishable as voices in a chorus, the faces as blurred in Peter's mind as moving objects on a piece of film behind a wide-open lens.

But suddenly his mind focused sharply on the image before him, that of a nearly bald, medium-sized man of fifty, so thin as to appear almost cadaverous, a condition that had to make living in Siberia a torture. "How do you do?" he had just said in accented but excellent English. "My name is Fyodor Mishkin." Had he said his name was Andrei Sakharov, Peter could not have been more startled. Standing before him, he was utterly certain, was one of the Soviet Union's most celebrated dissidents, infamous in that country, illustrious everywhere else, a hydrologist whose theories on the occurrence, circulation, distribution and properties of the water of the earth and the earth's atmosphere had bettered the lives of millions. Ten years before, Mishkin, a Jew, had applied for and been refused an emigration visa to Israel, on the ground that he knew too much about Soviet science, and was himself too valuable a part of it. Since that time, he had put his brain on strike, refusing to do further research, a fact that had been remarked and bemoaned by colleagues throughout the world. Two years after announcing his protest, he was abruptly resettled in Siberia, exactly where the Soviets had never said. Not a word had been heard from him since. And now here he was, shaking hands with Peter.

For André Kohl, the sighting alone would have been worth a minute on the evening news. An interview would have been priceless. But was Mishkin free to speak? "It's an honor to meet you, sir," Peter said with a bow.

"Thank you."

"Are you well?"

"I am fine, as fine as can be expected."

"Is Bratsk your home?"

Mishkin smiled. "Bratsk is my universe."

"What is your connection to this enterprise?"

"It is my place of work. The production of paper and paper products requires great quantities of water, first to float the timber to the plant, then to manufacture. There is then the problem of what to do with the waste products produced by the manufacturing process. The temptation is simply to pour them into the water. But that would shortly kill all of the plants and fish, as you Americans learned to your sorrow. So, that is where I come in."

"You are doing no research?"

"No. This work does not require research, merely the application of what is already known."

Peter looked guardedly to left and right. "May I ask you a personal question?"

"Please."

"Would you still emigrate to Israel if you could?"

Mishkin smiled again, this time ruefully. "That part of my life is history," he said. "I must live in the present, not the future."

Just that exchange would have been enough. It would have been flashed around the world, and quoted countless times. As Mishkin walked away, Peter turned to Jacob. "Do you realize who that is?" he whispered.

Jacob looked at Peter. His eyes were twinkling. "No," he said, "I don't have the faintest idea."

For the next hour, as they toured the plant, Peter spent as much time as he could observing Mishkin without giving away his interest. The scientist seemed as unfettered as anyone else in the group, moving freely about, chatting with the others. When the tour moved to his department, he took over, explaining the nature of the pollution and how they were overcoming it. If ever a problem seemed overwhelmed by a man, this one was it; to engage a mind like Mishkin's in a problem so readily solvable made as much sense as using a race car to commute.

But the injustice in their presence did not seem to bother Jacob. He asked multiple questions of Mishkin, and at one point even grabbed his arm and pulled him toward one of his more arcane-looking gauges to ask for an explanation of its function.

At last they returned to the conference room, and there Peter asked the questions Jacob had assigned to him. "What premium must you pay your workers?" he began.

"An initial 40 percent bonus for coming here," Amosoff answered, "eventually up to 150 percent over the same salary in Moscow. In addition, thirty-six working days off a year."

"Are these premiums figured into your costs?"

"Of course."

"What is your profit margin?"

"Ten percent. If our cost per unit is a ruble, we are entitled to charge a ruble ten kopecks."

"What was your basic investment?"

"Three hundred million rubles."

"Any additional capital investment?"

"A hundred million rubles."

"And what is your return on your investment?"

Amosoff smiled. "That depends on the method of accounting you use. You Americans increase the basis of your investment each year by the amount of your earned surplus. In our society, the earned surplus may be diverted to needier areas of the economy. Using your method, we are probably at 6 to 8 percent. Using our method, it is more like 16 to 18 percent."

It surprised Peter that Amosoff was so conversant with American accounting methods that he would speak of such things as earned surplus and return on investment. With only slight modifications, this same conversation could be taking place in Cleveland.

The surprises continued that evening, at a banquet in Jacob's honor to which more than three hundred persons—the ranking government officials, engineers, doctors and teachers—had been invited. The banquet was held in the Angara Culture House, a large building that looked remarkably like the gymnasium of an American high school. Dining room tables had been laid end to end in several rows, at a ninety-degree angle to a long table for the most important officials and the guests of honor. Onto each table had been placed the most extraordinary abundance of food Peter had ever seen: wild cranberries, green mushrooms, sardines, salmon, sausage, pork, everything sprinkled with green onions, as well as several varieties of salads. These plates turned out to be the appetizers; they were followed by roasted chicken, fried fish and ravioli, which Rita Nesmelov, the interpreter, seated next to him, instructed Peter to dip into a sauce of white vinegar, hot mustard and pepper. It was fiery stuff, burning Peter's throat and nose and causing him to cough, to everyone's amusement. Fyodor Mishkin seemed to be having the same problem; his fit of coughing caused him to excuse himself and leave the room for a spell.

On each table were bottles of brandy, vodka and wine, and at each place glasses for all three. The toasts began less than halfway through the meal. First Amosoff, then his deputy director, then several others whose names and functions Peter had learned and forgotten, rose to extol the great American entrepreneur, Jacob Jones, who by his actions had proved the profitability of cooperation between the Soviet Union and the United States.

In between the toasts, Peter, aided by Rita, conversed with the men and women around him. He was particularly taken with the woman on his right, Natasha Georgiyevna, who did not appear to be more than forty but was the government's chief economist for Bratsk, responsible for all planning. It struck him that never before, in all his trips to the Soviet Union, had he been in such a free, give-and-take environment. In Moscow, where most of his work had been done, people were discreet, reserved, often timid; here, three thousand miles from the center of power, they were open and candid. Whatever worries he might have brought with him to Siberia, he put them aside to take advantage of the opportunity. "What about prison camps?" he asked at one point.

"Which do you mean, those of the czars or of Stalin?" Rita asked.

"Stalin."

"Stalin. Our tragedy," Rita sighed.

"It's true," the man next to her said. "They existed. I saw them with my own eyes on my way out here thirty years ago. Then and there, I dedicated myself to the creation of a Siberia that would make people forget the old prison Siberia."

"You know," Natasha said, "before Stalin, in the time of Lenin, we did not have such repression. There was a thriving cultural and intellectual life, with very little censorship. Inside the party, there was open debate. There was even what you Americans call a market economy, with a large private sector that competed with state enterprises. It was Stalin who changed all that—and then the party officials and bureaucrats who perpetuated it. They got used to the power and didn't want to give it up. Our new reforms will change that."

"You hope," Peter said. It was out before he could check it. He knew he should not have said it. But when Rita translated, everyone in earshot laughed.

He felt a hand on his shoulder. It was Jacob. "How you doin', pal?" he asked.

"Fine."

"Some party. Gotta find the little boy's room. Us little guys can't hold it like you big guys." With that he sauntered off alone.

Watching Jacob, Peter frowned. Something wasn't right, but he couldn't think what it was. Then he remembered: At the dinner in Moscow, Jacob had tipped his glass to his lips at the end of each toast, then put it down without drinking. Tonight, apparently, he wasn't being so careful.

The dinner had begun at six o'clock. Now it was well past nine, with no sign of a letup. Peter noticed that the Russians would eat for a while, then rest, then begin again, perhaps with the appetizers. And always, they drank, and toasted, if not en masse then among themselves.

At last, dessert arrived, layer cakes decorated with red, white and blue frosting, one for every table. At the sight of them, the audience began to applaud. The applause increased as Jacob stood to carve the cake brought to the head table. Beaming, he motioned for silence. Then he said, "May this dessert sweeten the feelings between us." Rita stood to translate. As soon as she finished, the applause broke out again, even louder this time, changing after a minute into rhythmic clapping underscored by the stomping of feet. And then a chant began. *"DRUZHBA! DRUZHBA! DRUZHBA! DRUZHBA!"* on and on, "FRIENDSHIP!

266

FRIENDSHIP! FRIENDSHIP! FRIENDSHIP!" Peter sat, engulfed by the sound, his flesh covered with goosebumps.

Jacob was looking his way, and grinning, a wild look in his eyes. "How do you like them apples, pal?" he shouted.

As soon as dessert was finished, a group at one table began to sing. In moments, the singing had spread through the entire room. Peter couldn't understand the words, but it didn't really matter. The voices were full, and filled with emotion. He was as certain as he could be that these people were singing about themselves, much as campers around a bonfire do, and for them, he suddenly realized, this must be like a camp, a year-round camp, close to nature, elemental, pure, evoking feelings of fellowship, acknowledging shared bonds. Moscow was filled with disillusioned cynics; these people were living the dream. And the thought came to Peter in that moment that the most fervent wish Americans should have for Russians was success, because success breeds self-respect, and with enough of that they might stop, at last, suspecting the rest of the world.

There were gifts for the Americans then, sets of lacquered wooden boxes with inlaid designs. Jacob, who had a collection of the same boxes in his apartment in Moscow, nonetheless seemed delighted with these new ones, inspecting them minutely after the banquet had ended while others went for their coats and hats. Then he came over to Peter and handed his boxes to him. "Do me a favor, will you, pal, and hang onto these for me?"

The good-byes were fervent and prolonged, due only partly to the great amount everyone had drunk. There was no doubting the feelings Jacob's visit had produced. At last, their hosts put Jacob and Peter in a car for the drive back to their hotel, the Taiga.

"So. What did you think?" Jacob asked after they had pulled away.

"Very moving."

"You feel any menace? Did you get the sense that these people are killers, bent on ruling the earth?"

"It's not the people. It's their rulers."

"Not the current rulers, pal. Stalinism is history."

They drove the rest of the way in silence.

The next morning Jacob was arrested.

26

Jeremy Croft himself had picked Houghton up at Heathrow Airport on Friday morning, following the CIA director's flight to London from Dulles International. Like Houghton, Croft was in his early sixties; unlike him, he had a totally undistinguished appearance. He was of medium height, slight, clean-shaven, as pale as the average Englishman, and dressed so conventionally—dark suit, white shirt, small-patterned tie, black shoes, dark overcoat, black Homburg—that he blended rather than proclaimed. That, indeed, was his objective; although he had been in charge of MI-6 since his early forties, there were not a dozen people in all of Britain, aside from his colleagues, who would recognize him on the street.

"We showed the hall porter a picture of Richard Hampstead," Croft said when they were in the car. "He was quite certain that it wasn't Hampstead who went up to Fleming's room. Said he would have recognized Hampstead in a second."

"You haven't found Hampstead yet?"

"No. We rather think he's taken himself into hiding somewhere in the U.K. A friend's place, or something like that."

"Too bad. He could have made it easier."

"Can't say that I blame him."

"No."

"What's your plan, Charles?"

Houghton turned to his counterpart. "I've got to ask for your indulgence, Jeremy. I need to do this alone."

"As you wish."

"I promise that as soon as I know what I came to find out, I'll cut you in to the extent that I possibly can."

"Fair enough."

Given the likelihood that someone in British intelligence was sympathetic to the objectives of the American secret network and had even lent a helping hand, both Croft and Houghton had agreed that it wouldn't do to have the hall porter brought in to MI-6 for questioning. The interrogation would take place at the hotel. When they arrived, Croft took Houghton inside to introduce him to the manager, then immediately returned to the car.

"We are most dreadfully sorry about this tragedy," the manager, whose name was Whitely, said. He was stout and middle-aged with a jowly, basset-like face whose sad expression did, indeed, seem a match for his words. "Mr. Fleming was a gentleman, as well as a valued patron. We will, of course, cooperate with you in any way that we can."

Then Whitely summoned the hall porter into his office, introduced them—his name was Ben—and left the two men alone. "I feel terrible about this, sir," Ben began at once. "But all I did was relay the message the gentleman gave me." He, too, seemed genuinely saddened, the skin stretched tight on his bony face. "I been servin' the finest people for forty years, and nothin' like this ever happened before."

"No one blames you," Houghton said. He smiled, hoping to put the man at ease. "From Liverpool, are you?"

Ben's features eased somewhat. "Very good, sir," he said.

"This won't take long at all," Houghton said, drawing an envelope from inside his coat. "I've brought four photographs to show you. I'd like you to tell me if any of those photographs bears a likeness to the man who called on Mr. Fleming, saying his name was Hampstead."

"I'll do me best, sir."

With that, Houghton removed the photographs from the envelope and began to place them one at a time on the desk in front of the hall porter. The first photograph was of Carl Sanders.

"No, sir," Ben said. "Not 'im. Nothin' like 'im. The man I saw was older."

The second photograph was of Philip Loomis. "No, sir. He was younger than that. About between the two, I'd say."

The third photograph was of Ernest McDonald. The hall porter shook his head. "The age is right, but he didn't look at all like that, sir."

The fourth photograph was of Harry Coffee. "That's 'im, sir," Ben shouted instantly. "That's 'im. I'm sure of it. I'd never forget that face."

Houghton looked silently into Ben's eyes, searching for the slightest doubt. Seeing none, he put the photographs back in the envelope. "Thank you," he said. Then he struggled to his feet and swung out of the manager's office.

"Any luck?" Jeremy asked when Houghton had settled back into the car.

"I'm afraid so," Houghton said. He sighed deeply. Then he told him the result, because he could not take the next step without him. "Please, for God's sake, keep it to yourself for the time being. I've got to be absolutely sure."

It took only a minute once they'd returned to Jeremy's office to do a computer check on arrivals in Britain in the last two weeks. Harry Coffee had gone through immigration at Heathrow nine days before. On Tuesday evening, four hours after Fleming was killed, he'd left London on the last Air France flight to Paris.

27

At 7 A.M. on Saturday, the morning after the banquet in Bratsk, Peter was awakened by a pounding on his door. He stumbled to the door and opened it. A man he'd never seen before was standing there. He was in his thirties, solidly built, with a drill sergeant's face. "You will be downstairs with your suitcase in ten minutes," he said.

"Who are you?" Peter demanded.

"Security police." With that he was gone.

Bewildered, with no real choice, Peter did as bidden, cursing at the tepid water with which he had to shave, dressing hurriedly, packing with equal haste. Just before leaving he checked the room to be certain he hadn't forgotten anything. Only then did he see the inlaid boxes he and Jacob had been given the night before; on their return to the hotel, he'd set them on a bureau. He shoved them into his bag and left.

The moment he saw Jacob, he knew that something terrible had happened. Two husky Russians, one of them the man who had awakened him, had Jacob between them. Even normally they would have towered over him, but his condition emphasized the difference even further. Overnight, he seemed to have shriveled. He had the look of a cornered animal. Seeing Peter, his eyes widened briefly in surprise, and the frown on his lined face deepened. For an instant, his eyes darted to Peter's bag, which was slung from his shoulder, and narrowed in perplexity, as though he couldn't understand why Peter was carrying it. He wet his lips and started to speak, but then stopped.

Peter addressed the man who had awakened him. "Do you mind telling me what's going on?"

"You will find out in Moscow," the man declared.

They drove to the airport in silence. A small military jet was waiting, in plain sight of Jacob's Gulfstream. If Peter had any doubts that Jacob had been taken into custody, they vanished now.

The interior of the transport was cold and spartan. Jacob and Peter were ushered to seats on opposite sides of the plane and several rows apart. The plane began to taxi the moment they were settled and turned onto the takeoff runway with motors racing. As soon as they reached cruising altitude, Peter moved from his seat to join Jacob. The Russian who had awakened him stopped him. "Not permitted," he said.

"Oh, come on!" Peter said. "I'm not under arrest."

He attempted to push forward. The Russian grabbed Peter and was in the process of wrestling him back to his seat when the other Russian intervened, saying something to his companion that caused him to relent. With an angry look at the first Russian, Peter took a seat next to Jacob. "What in the hell's going on?"

"Can we talk? Can they hear us? Is the airplane bugged?" The sentences came so fast they seemed without punctuation. As Jacob spoke, his eyes moved wildly about.

Peter looked around. The guards were several seats back, talking to one another. It was conceivable that someone else on the aircraft was monitoring their conversation, but it didn't seem likely. Between the vibration of the aircraft and the noise of its motors, the acoustics were terrible. "Go ahead," Peter said. "But whisper."

Jacob leaned close to him and spoke into his ear. "Did they search you?"

"No. Why?"

"They didn't search your bag?"

"No."

Jacob pulled away. His eyes were wide. "Then I don't get it," he said.

"Don't get what?"

For an answer, Jacob shook his head from side to side. "I don't get it," he said again. He seemed clearly dazed.

Peter drew close. "Listen to me, Jacob. You bloody well better tell me what's going on, because I may be the last American you're going to see for a long time."

"I don't *know* what's going on. They won't tell me. They told me what they told you—that I'd find out in Moscow."

"Do you have *any* idea?"

"I thought I did. Now I don't."

"What did you *think* it was?"

Jacob began to nod his head from side to side again. Peter grabbed him. "Tell me!"

"They didn't search your bag?" he asked once more.

"No."

"You're sure? Where is it?"

"I've got it with me. Why would they search my bag?"

Once more, Jacob looked around. Then, apparently satisfied that the guards weren't listening, he leaned toward Peter and put his mouth to Peter's ear. "Mishkin left some microfilm for me in the men's room during the banquet last night."

"That coughing fit?"

"Yeah. I was afraid he'd overdone it and someone had gotten suspicious. So I hid the film in one of those boxes while everyone was getting their coats."

"And then gave the boxes to me. That's just great."

"I swear if you'd been caught I would have confessed." He wet his lips. "Look, I'll make it up to you. I swear I will. If you'll carry the film to Paris, I'll pay you a hundred thousand dollars."

Peter looked at Jacob, wondering if he was sane. "What's on it?"

Jacob went on as though Peter hadn't spoken. "I mean it," he said. "I'll get word out. You'll be paid."

"What's on the film, Jacob?"

Jacob simply nodded his head from side to side.

"Tell me what's on the film or I'm going to find it and flush it down the toilet."

"Oh, God, don't do that. That film can change the world."

"Then tell me, or it's gone. Do you have any idea what could

273

happen to me if I got caught? They could put me away for life—and you couldn't help me a bit."

Jacob looked at Peter in silence. "Can I trust you?" he said at last.

"What option do you have?"

"Okay." He swallowed. "Mishkin has invented a new desalinization process. He did it on his own. The Russians know nothing about it."

"How'd you hear about it?"

Jacob hesitated. "Mutual friends."

"Who?"

"Can't say. Too dangerous."

The anger that had been building in Peter surged now through his body. "Who's the mutual friend, Jacob?" he said coldly.

Again, Jacob hesitated. "A client."

Peter looked at Jacob so severely that Jacob finally looked away. He knew now why Jacob had brought him to Siberia: to be, if necessary, the unwitting courier of a secret document, and to take the fall if caught. He knew, as well, what Charles Houghton had meant when he'd said that Jacob Jones might not be everything he seemed. Jacob Jones wasn't simply an entrepreneur. He was somebody's spy. There was no paper manufacturing client interested in a joint venture with the Russians; that was a cover story set up to get him to Bratsk so that he could get the plans from Mishkin.

The fury in him was of such intensity he could have strangled Jacob with his hands, precisely what he felt like doing. "Who's your client, Jacob?" he demanded.

"Can't say."

"Who, goddamnit? You tell me who or I'm taking my bag to the can."

"I can't say!" Jacob drew back. "For Christ sake, pal, don't talk like that. If you have any compassion, get that film to Paris. I'll make it two hundred thousand."

Peter stared at Jacob with withering contempt. "Fuck you, Jacob. Fuck your two hundred thousand." Then he rose and, as Jacob watched in horror, fetched his bag and headed for the toilet.

The two Russians eyed him as he walked by, and even eyed the bag, but he kept walking and they didn't stop him.

Why would a man with everything become a secret agent? Peter asked himself as he unzipped the bag in the toilet and removed the wooden boxes. People became agents for money or sex or in response to blackmail or for excitement or out of ideological conviction. Jacob was wealthy beyond imagining and could buy all the sex he wanted. Had he been hiding some horrible secret for all these years? Had he become a spy for kicks?

Peter's hands were trembling so badly from a combination of fear and anger and simple excitement that he had trouble removing the covers. There was nothing in the first three boxes. He wrenched the cover from the fourth box, and there at last it was— a piece of plain cardboard the size of a playing card, with strips of microfilm no more than three-eighths of an inch wide taped to both sides.

If he wasn't so shaken he might have laughed. Amateurs!

The crudeness of the effort changed all his calculations. This wasn't the work of a professional agent, or even an industrial spy. What *was* the game, then? There was only one category left: ideological conviction.

Mishkin was a Zionist as well as a *refusenik*. Soviet authorities had thwarted his life's desire, to emigrate to Israel. What greater gift could he bestow upon the land of his choice than a process that would make the deserts bloom?

"That film could change the world," Jacob had said. If the desalinization system worked, it would be a bounty for Israel almost beyond imagining, doubling, tripling, conceivably quadrupling the country's habitable land. Although he neither hid it nor advertised it, Jacob was a Jew. Did he harbor some unpublicized passion for Israel?

And did he, Peter, hold in his hand the power to alter history? He had been about to flush the card down the toilet. Now, even knowing that the card, if found, was his death sentence, he could not bring himself to release it.

For at least a minute he stood, agonizing, trying to recall those lessons of Jack Fleming's in the Cotswolds to which he'd paid such poor and grudging attention. Fleming had given him a hollow fountain pen for hiding microfilm, but Peter had long since discarded it. The ex-CIA agent had shown him how to slip microfilm under the inner sole of his shoe, but that technique in this moment seemed hopelessly inadequate. Fleming had also shown him how to hide microfilm in a tube of shaving cream of toothpaste. At the time the lesson had seemed useless, even silly; now it struck Peter as his best chance. He placed the card on the washbasin, retrieved his toilet kit from his bag and took out his toothpaste. He wished mightily now that he'd been more attentive; he couldn't remember whether he was supposed to shove the film through the opening at the top, or somehow open the bottom and insert it through there. Either way, it too seemed so inadequate, and even Fleming had said that nothing was really foolproof when hiding microfilm, that professionals would know where to look.

For another moment, he hesitated. You're crazy, he told himself. Then he put the card in his coat pocket.

He returned to the cabin, stowed his bag and walked back to Jacob's seat. Jacob was pressed into a corner of the seat, his head against the bulkhead, his hands over his face. Peter could see his shoulders shaking, and realized that he was crying. It confirmed his conclusion; Jacob Jones might be capable of almost anything, but he would never cry over money. Without a word, Peter sat.

Jacob refused to look at him, and for a minute he didn't speak. "I hope you're satisfied," he said at last. "There's nothing anyone can do to me that's as bad as what you just did."

"I didn't do it, Jacob. I've got it in my pocket."

Jacob turned to him in astonishment, his eyes wide, his mouth open. "Don't kid me, pal. My heart won't take it."

Peter got up from his chair and went through his pockets as though he was searching for something. In the process, he turned his body just enough to be able to see the Russians. Both of them were dozing. When he sat again, he pulled the card from his jacket pocket, showed both sides to Jacob, then put it back. "It's for the Israelis, isn't it?" he said.

Jacob shook his head from side to side for several seconds. Then he stared at Peter. "Okay. I owe you." He took a deep breath. "I made them promise me that if I got it out and it worked, they'd offer it to all the Arab countries." He paused for emphasis. "What happens if they do that? There's arable land for everybody, pal—

Arabs *and* Israelis. That's what I meant when I said it could change the world."

"What happens if the Israelis don't keep their word?"

"I'll have copies made before I turn it over. If the Israelis don't do it, I'll give it to the Arabs myself."

"You're going to *give* it to the Arabs?"

"That's right."

"You're not going to get any money?"

"Everybody who gets it will have to agree that if Mishkin gets out they pay him." Jacob shook his head. "The poor bastard has no use for money in Bratsk."

"But you're not taking a commission or a fee?"

"Nah. You don't do this kind of thing for money, pal."

"Why *do* you do it? Why does a man with everything take a risk like this?"

"Hah?" Jacob said, nodding in recognition of the question as though he had asked it of himself many times. He smiled faintly. "To get something no amount of money can buy."

"What's that?"

"Immortality, pal. What does a man who has everything want? Only one thing. He wants to be well remembered, to create a memorial to himself. In my press clippings, they call me 'The Magician with the Midas Touch.' You know what I really am? A cockamamy deal-maker. How does a deal-maker get remembered? By making deals that change the world. What kinds of deals are those? The kinds where you turn adversaries into allies."

Nothing André Kohl had known about Jacob Jones corresponded to the self-portrait he'd just sketched. He was the author of the statement that the best friendships were those involving equal profit for both parties. And yet, was that statement really inconsistent with the objectives he'd just described? The only international agreements that survived were precisely those with profit to both parties. Had André badly misjudged Jacob? Peter looked deeply into his eyes, trying to see something in them that would tell him if Jacob was speaking the truth. To judge by Jacob's next remark, his look must have been transparent.

"You don't believe me? Let me tell you what else I've been doin'. Let me tell you about the deal that would put me in the

277

history books for sure." He nodded, as though to assure himself that his assessment was correct. "What would be the deal of this or any century? A joint venture by the two most powerful and dangerous adversaries the world has ever known: the United States and Russia. How do you do that, when everything to date has failed?" He leaned close to Peter. "You get them to do something together that doesn't put them head to head and toe to toe, something that involves them, but only indirectly. You don't go for disarmament or test bans. You start with something smaller, a side issue—the theory being that if they have one good experience together they'll be encouraged to try another one, and if that one succeeds, another one, and so on until it becomes a habit. So what is that side issue? The Middle East."

Jacob took a deep breath. "Ever since the early seventies, the Russians have been out of the Middle East. They'd love to get back in, but only on the right terms. Putting them in the picture as a guarantor of the peace along with the United States is the way to do it. It's also the only way to carve a deal between the Arabs and Israelis—by forcing them to the table. So how do you make that happen? You set up an international peace conference on the Middle East, in which both the Americans and the Soviets agree to enforce the agreement that's carved out. Somebody needs to sell it —somebody who's experienced in bringing Americans and Russians together. Me."

"You've been working on that?"

"For the last year I've done damn little else but run messages between the White House and the Kremlin."

"And you feel you've made some progress?"

Jacob snorted. "We're that close." He held up the thumb and index finger of his right hand, separated by a hair. "I was supposed to nail it down on my return to Moscow."

Peter held his hand up. "Just a second. Let me think." Thoughts were caroming off one another in his head. Pieces from different puzzles seemed to be fitting together. For the first time since André Kohl had been shot, a feeling of hope stirred in Peter's chest. For the moment, the feeling emanated from nothing more than a hunch—the wildest, most improbable hunch he had ever had. "Jacob," he said, "how well do you know Krylov?"

Jacob looked at him suspiciously. "What's that got to do with anything?"

"Please. Trust me."

"I've known him for fifteen years."

"How would you describe him?"

"A survivor. And a worrier. He worries about surviving."

"He's done pretty well."

"You betcha."

"What are his politics?"

"Whatever's in fashion."

"So he'd support the present fashion?"

"Absolutely."

"You're sure?"

"Absolutely."

"Okay. I want to go through this step by step because *I've* got to be absolutely sure. In this peace campaign of yours, you've been dealing at what level?"

"The very top."

"The Foreign Minister?"

"Absolutely."

"The Premier, himself?"

"Of course."

"And you've won their support?"

"Absolutely."

"Is it a hundred percent?"

"What do you mean?"

"I mean, is there *any* opposition at all?"

"If there is I'm not aware of it."

"And the entire Politburo knows about it?"

"I would think so."

"You've made no effort, for your part, to keep the proposal a secret?"

"Why should I? I've got the support of the Premier."

For a second, Peter was tempted to answer. But he decided not to. "Okay, getting back to Krylov, would *he* know about the initiative?"

"Absolutely. We've discussed it."

"And he's for it?"

279

"Of course he's for it—because the leadership is for it. What's all this leading to?"

"It's leading to something that could help you."

Exasperation and anxiety in equal measure flew into Jacob's face. "How do you know what can help me if we don't know what my problem is?"

"I have a feeling I know what your problem is."

"What is it?"

"Just a few more questions."

"My heart can't take this."

"Do you consider yourself an intimate of Krylov's?"

"Nobody's on intimate terms with the head of the KGB."

"Do you think he likes you?"

"I don't think that's the question. The question is, 'Am I useful?' "

"Have you been useful to him?"

"Yes, very, if only because I'm the only American he's ever really known. He's never been to the States. He had no idea how we think. I've given him an education into the ways of the West."

"Okay. Do you trust Krylov?"

"Do you trust the director of the CIA?"

"Let me put it another way. When you talk to Krylov is your relationship such that you talk in a free and open manner?"

"You mean confide in him? Are you crazy?"

"I don't mean confide in him. I'm sure you didn't tell him about your real purpose in going to Bratsk. I mean would you be fairly unrestrained in your conversation?"

"For example?"

Peter hesitated just long enough to put the question exactly as he wanted to, uncolored, matter of fact. "For example, might you have ever said anything to Krylov about loaning your plane to André Kohl for his honeymoon?"

Jacob looked sharply at Peter. "What the hell has that got to do with my problem?"

"Conceivably a lot. Please answer the question."

"Is there any reason why I shouldn't have said anything about loaning my plane to André?"

"Are you saying that you did say something?"

"I don't remember. But knowing me, I probably did." There was an instant's pause, hardly measurable. "Wait a minute. Are you saying that *Krylov* had something to do with the hit on André?"

"Not Krylov. "Unless he's a great actor, he was genuinely surprised when I told him that the terrorists had been hired by Russians. But perhaps Krylov told someone what you told him. Or perhaps someone was with Krylov when you told him. Either one would explain how the terrorists found André."

"Oh, God," Jacob said.

"And, Jacob," Peter said softly, "it would also explain what's waiting for you in Moscow."

28

They landed in Moscow at 1 P.M. Two cars drove onto the runway to meet them. Four men came onto the plane. Three of them led Jacob away. The fourth escorted Peter to the other car. "Where are we going?" Peter asked.

"You are to return to the apartment of Mr. Jones and remain there until tomorrow morning, when you will be taken back to the airport for a flight to Paris."

For a moment, Peter was too shocked to respond. Everything he'd planned to do was predicated on his ability to move freely about Moscow. "Are you telling me I'm under arrest?" he said at last.

"No. But because you came with Mr. Jones you are no longer welcome. Your visa has been revoked."

"I insist on going to my embassy."

"Is not possible."

He knew it was useless to argue. He thanked God, instead, for the telephone in Jacob's apartment. He could do it all by phone. "What are the charges against Mr. Jones?" he asked.

"They are very serious."

"But what are they?"

"You will find out in due time."

The Russian let Peter off at the entrance to Kutuzovsky Prospekt 13, and watched as he walked into the compound. Peter forced himself to walk slowly. He did not want to give his escort any hint that he had a program in mind.

At the door to Jacob's apartment, he rang the bell, then knocked. Then, remembering that they hadn't been due back until late that evening, and that the housekeeper must be away for the weekend, he let himself in with the key that Jacob had given him. He dropped his bag, rushed for the telephone and snatched the receiver from its base. The line was dead. "Shit!" he cried, smacking his face in frustration.

There was only one other possibility. If that didn't work, he was finished. Quickly, he moved to the front door, opened it slowly and looked carefully into the hallway. No one was in sight. He crept to the stairway and took the stairs two at a time down to the seventh floor. In moments, he was in front of the apartment of Tony Cook, the USBC correspondent, knocking, praying he was there. In another moment he heard footsteps, and seconds later, there stood Cook, the veteran correspondent André Kohl had recommended for the job, his expression a mixture of surprise and suspicion. He stepped into the hallway and looked up and down. "What can I do for you?" he said.

Peter handed him his passport, and his letter from Mike Paul. As Tony inspected them, Peter studied his face. He'd been forty when hired five years before; now he looked at least fifty. His face was pasty, and his hands shook. He was overdue for a transfer. When he looked at Peter again, his eyes spoke of a wariness burned into them by experience. "I don't know a thing about this."

"Call Mike Paul. He'll vouch for me. And then let me talk to him."

"If this is some kind of trick, I could get kicked out of Moscow."

"It's no trick, and the upside is the story of your life. You'll know in one minute if I'm legit."

For five seconds, Tony stood there, uncertain about what to do. "This better be great," he said. Then, at last, he let Peter into the apartment. "Follow me," he said, and walked down the hallway to his office. As he reached for the telephone, he said, "You realize it's six o'clock in New York."

"I know for a fact that he's a very early riser."

For a second, Tony looked at him, a question in his eyes. "I'm going to have to go through the news desk. They'll patch me through."

"Don't do that," Peter said quickly. "I'll give you his home phone." He rattled it off from memory. Once again, Tony stared at him. Finally, he dialed the overseas operator and placed the call. Peter prayed silently that the light volume on Saturday would enable them to get through. "Just say that there's a man in your office with a letter from him regarding a special investigation. Give him the date of the letter, and tell him I like to remain anonymous."

"I'm not playing games, Burke, if your name is Burke."

"Just tell him that. See what he says."

A minute passed. "It's going through!" Tony said. A minute later, still incredulous, he passed the telephone to Peter. Peter motioned him to get on another line.

"Hello, Mike. I apologize for the mystery, but I promise you it's necessary. I may be close to an answer, and incidentally to a story that your late friend would have called one of the great barn-burners of all time. If you guys will work with me, I'll be more than happy to give you the story, as well as the answer to your question."

"Go ahead."

"Two favors right now. First, I'd like you to call our mutual friend, the one who brought us together, and give him the following message. 'A man who may not be everything he seems has been arrested in Moscow.' Got that?"

"Hang on. I'm writing it down. Okay."

"Then ask him to call me here."

"What if he's not there? Do I leave a message?"

"No. Don't leave a message. But do everything you can to find him."

"Okay. What's the second favor?"

"The cooperation of your correspondent."

"What kind?"

"The use of his telephone. Some interpreting. And maybe the use of his premises to receive some visitors. I wish I could explain why it's necessary. You'll have to take my word that it is."

There was a long silence. "Tony? You there?" Mike said then.

"Yeah."

"What do you think?"

"It's your call, Mike. I never laid eyes on this guy until five minutes ago."

Another silence. Finally, Mike said, "Do it."

When they had hung up, Tony looked at Peter warily. "Okay, what's first?" he said.

"Did you know Gennady Gondrachov?"

"What do you mean, 'did'?"

"He's dead. Killed in Paris last May."

"Damn. I wondered what happened to him."

"Did you know him?"

"He was in this apartment at least half a dozen times."

"That's exactly what I wanted to know. Was his wife with him?"

"Sometimes yes, sometimes no."

"Good enough. I'd like you to call her and ask her to come here as soon as she possibly can. If she balks, tell her it has to do with what she was discussing with a visitor the other day about a visit to America."

Tony made the call. Lusa agreed to come. As he waited impatiently for her arrival, Peter fended off Tony Cook's questions by asking some of his own. "Do you remember that story last spring about the Premier's instability?"

Tony laughed. "How could I forget it? I never worked so hard for so little in my life."

"Tell me."

As he had on several previous occasions during the last hours, Tony regarded Peter quizzically before replying, as though close observation might somehow help him understand Peter's game. "First of all," he began, "the story didn't come out of here. It surfaced simultaneously in Washington and London and Paris. The network called me and asked me to check it out on this end. In Moscow you don't just pick up a phone and call a source at the Foreign Office. Even if you've been fortunate enough to get to know someone well enough to be able to call him, he'd only deny such a story. So I tried every place I could think of—the American embassy, the French embassy, the British embassy, the Yugoslav embassy. I'm cozy with a couple of Czechs, so I even tried them. Then I tried some contacts at Tass, Novosti and *Pravda.* Zip. Nobody'd heard anything. They were all as baffled as I was." Tony hesitated. "Funny you should mention it. I remember thinking that the best source of all would be Gennady Gondrachov—and then being unable to find him."

"That was when?"

"Mid-May."

"He would have just been leaving for Paris." Peter thought for a moment. "So what did the network finally do?"

"A very short piece, half from Washington, half from here, to the effect that rumors about the Premier were circulating in the West, but that there seemed to be no foundation to them. The best information was that he was *not* given to fits of rage. And he hardly drank at all. As to opposition to his program, there was some, but nothing unexpected—and certainly nothing that was about to provoke his ouster."

"Did you develop any ideas about how the rumors got started?"

"None."

I'm beginning to, Peter thought.

An hour later, Lusa was there. "Before I explain anything," Peter said, "I want you to do me a favor." He drew out his wallet, thumbed through it and extracted the piece of notepaper Houghton had given him in Paris. On the paper was the telephone number Virgil Craig, the retired CIA agent with the secret network connections, had called in Moscow. "This is a Moscow telephone number." Peter said. "Do you recognize it?"

Lusa studied it for a moment. "No," she said.

"I want you to dial that number and ask whoever answers to identify himself."

Lusa hesitated, unsure of herself. Then, without a word, she went to the phone and dialed the number. As she did, Peter walked to her side, and stood so close to her that he could hear the telephone ringing.

"Da," a man's voice said.

Lusa's eyelids flew up.

"Da?" the voice said again, impatiently this time. *"Kto éto?"*

"*Kto éto?*" Lusa said.

"*Kto éto?*" the man demanded again.

Without answering, Lusa slowly put down the phone. She turned to Peter, questions in her eyes. "Where did you get that number?"

"I'll have to explain later. Did you recognize the voice?"

"Of course. His name is Valery Yuryev. He is deputy of KGB." She paused, and swallowed. "He *hated* my husband."

Waves of electricity coursed through Peter's body. "Why?"

"He is very reactionary man. Gennady always used to make jokes about him. They had terrible fights all the time. Gennady would say to me, 'What a fool that man is. He still believes Stalin was great man.' "

Peter waited a moment, to calm himself before speaking. "Are you absolutely sure that was his voice?"

"No question. He has very unpleasant voice, very—how you say?—hard."

"Then I'm going to ask another favor. If you were to call Vassily Krylov, would he speak to you?"

"Of course. We are friends."

"Then I'd like you to call him and tell him you must speak to him about a matter of utmost urgency. Ask him to go to your house. When he gets there, bring him here."

"What do I say if he refuses?"

"Tell him I have information about his organization. Tell him there are people in his organization who are conducting operations with Americans that he knows nothing about."

When she had gone, Peter turned to Tony. The correspondent was looking at him incredulously. "Who the hell are you, Burke?" he said.

Five minutes had passed since his private telephone had rung, but Valery Yuryev had yet to move. He had spent all that time trying to figure out the meaning of the phone call. Of the identity of the caller he was absolutely certain. He would know that voice anywhere. But how had Lusa Gondrachov obtained his unlisted number? And why had she called? After another moment, Yuryev conceded to himself that reason alone couldn't help him. He would have to have more facts. He picked up his phone and dialed a number.

One minute later, two KGB agents were on their way to Lusa Gondrachov's apartment building to set up a stakeout.

At last, Mike Paul called back. "No luck," he said. "Our mutual friend's not at home, and the man on duty at his office said he had no idea where he was."

Peter cursed under his breath. "Did he say when he'd be back?"

"Didn't know."

Oh, Christ, Peter thought, what a time to be alone.

29

Charles Houghton, at that moment, was in the air, aboard an Aeroflot flight halfway between East Berlin and Moscow. Had someone told him twenty-four hours earlier that he would be in such a position at this moment, he would have bet the farm against it. But the revelations in that interval had been so unlike anything he had experienced in his forty years in intelligence that this trip seemed, if not normal, at the very least appropriate. He was sorting through those revelations now, his mind a jumble of hunches and circumstantial evidence he was attempting to match up and convert to facts.

He couldn't *prove* that Harry Coffee had killed Jack Fleming. He could only place him in Fleming's hotel room at about the time of the killing—and even then only on the strength of the testimony of one witness. Not enough for a court of law, perhaps, but more than enough for him.

He couldn't prove that Chris Slovotkin hadn't committed suicide but had been murdered instead—almost certainly by Harry Coffee—but that was his suspicion now. The FBI had found nothing to suggest that Slovotkin hadn't killed himself; there were no wounds other than the massive one to Slovotkin's head. That, in itself, wasn't surprising. If Coffee had indeed killed Slovotkin, he was too professional to have left any proof. He could have stepped to Slovotkin's rear, knocked him unconscious with a carefully aimed blow to the right side of the head, then put a gun in his hand and fired a bullet through his brain precisely where the bruise was.

Why might Coffee have wanted to kill Slovotkin? For the same reason he had been willing to nail Carl Sanders, to take suspicion away from himself—suspicion of his involvement in the secret network. A second reason was to keep Slovotkin from disclosing something that would ruin Harry Coffee. Why might Slovotkin have been ready to do that? Again, two possibilities. The first was a crisis of conscience. The second was to take others with him if he felt he was about to be exposed.

Houghton couldn't prove it, but he suspected that whatever incriminating knowledge Slovotkin possessed related to the same knowledge André Kohl was supposed to have possessed. If Harry Coffee had been willing to kill Jack Fleming in his efforts to repress that knowledge, he would have been willing to kill Chris Slovotkin. If he had figured out by now that Peter Burke was André Kohl—as he almost certainly had—surely he would kill Peter Burke, as well, if he could find him, and he seemed to be doing a very good job of just that.

In reconstructing Harry Coffee's moves over the last ten days, Houghton had to deal with suppositions more than facts, but a thread of logic linked them. Once Coffee had learned of the existence of Plymouth Rock, he had gone to England to investigate. With the help of like-minded people in British intelligence, he had learned of the manor house near Broadway, the unofficial capital of the Cotswolds. Questions to neighbors had produced stories of unexplained comings and goings there, and innkeepers had volunteered that, yes, they had had guests from London, some of whom had stayed for weeks, who said nothing about their business in the area but who seemed like professionals, drove nice cars and did set out each day in the direction of the manor. One of the men was an actor whose name they couldn't remember but whose roles in feature films and on the telly they could. That had ultimately given the investigators Richard Hampstead's name, and Hampstead had led them to Kate Berrigan. Either or both had identified the man in transition as "Peter."

Within a very few days, and with only this to go on, Harry Coffee had managed to track Peter Burke to Paris. The pilfering of his hotel room proved that. How had Coffee known to go to Paris? It simply figured that that's where Peter would go if he was, in fact, André Kohl. Paris had been André Kohl's home; sooner or later, most fugitives try to come home. And then there was Meredith's presence in Paris, the most compelling reason imaginable. Coffee would know of that because he was surely the one who had ordered surveillance on her.

How, then, had Coffee found Peter? There were several possibilities. The first was that, with the help of Pierre Gauthier of the French secret service, he had canvased the hotels of Paris for listings of registered guests who were Americans and whose first names were Peter. Tedious, but workable. The second possibility was that Peter had made a mistake. In a telephone conversation with her father the week before, Meredith had told him that she was seeing a man named Peter Burke. Peter, being inexperienced, might have first contacted her by telephone; if the line was tapped, just that would have been enough. If it hadn't been, Meredith's mention of his name would have done it. The third possibility was that someone in Coffee's network had reported the presence of a Peter Burke in Moscow, in the company of Jacob Jones.

That, Houghton now knew, was where Peter was. Desperate to find him in order to warn him of the danger, he'd remembered that Peter had intended to get to Moscow with the help of Jacob Jones. A call to Jones's office had established that he had flown to Moscow on Monday. A man named Peter Burke had flown to Moscow with him. Houghton had tried in vain to reach Peter at Jacob Jones's Moscow apartment; at first there was no answer, and then the telephone was out of order.

Houghton couldn't prove that Harry Coffee was also in Moscow, but he had to proceed on the assumption that he was—particularly since yesterday afternoon at three o'clock, by which time he had figured out just how very good Harry's contacts in Moscow might be. It was then, at last, that Houghton began to believe he might be on the verge of learning the nature of the horrible secret that was claiming lives and producing such desperate efforts to keep it hidden.

Two calls had led him to a tentative answer. Both calls had been made from the American embassy on Grosvenor Square, to which he'd been driven after leaving Jeremy Croft at MI-6. The first call had been to Billy, his assistant. "Get hold of the call sheet of the duty officer on the night Chris Slovotkin died," he'd said. "As soon as you've got it, call me back."

Billy called back in ten minutes. "Okay, I've got it."

"Do you see a call from the District police?"

"Yes, sir. At 2:37 A.M."

"What outgoing calls did the duty officer make after that?"

Billy read off the calls. Harry Coffee's name was not among them.

"Thank you, Billy," Houghton said.

It was Coffee who had reported Slovotkin's suicide to Houghton. He'd said that the police had called the duty officer at the CIA, and that the duty officer had called him. The duty officer's call sheet showed no evidence that such a call had been made. In a court of law, that wouldn't prove that Coffee had murdered Slovotkin—the duty officer, in his excitement, could have forgotten to log the call—but for Houghton, once again, it was enough.

What had Slovotkin known that he was about to reveal, or that Coffee wanted to make certain he would never reveal? Chris Slovotkin was the head of the Soviet desk for the CIA; logically, the information would have had to have been something related to U.S.-Soviet affairs. Acting on a hunch, Houghton had placed a second call, this one to Madeline Martin. "Whatever happened to that inquiry into who paid the Arab terrorists?"

There was a moment's silence. "It's still underway," she said then.

"You haven't gotten anything at all?"

"To the contrary. I do have something, but it's so upsetting that I didn't want to give it to you until I was absolutely sure—and I'm still missing a major piece."

"Madeline, I need to know what you've got right now."

Another pause. "Okay," she said. He could hear the reluctance in her voice. "I'd better tell it to you in context. For a couple of months, I got absolutely nowhere. Finally, I arranged for some local help and got into Alex Eichmann's apartment in Frankfurt while he and his wife were away. Eichmann had a personal computer. I went through his disks. One was a list of names and addresses." She paused once again; when she resumed her voice was shaky. "On that list was the name and unlisted phone number of Chris Slovotkin."

Several seconds passed. "Go ahead," Houghton said.

"I came back to Washington, got a subpoena and went to Slovotkin's old bank. On June 8 of last year, there was a transfer of a dollar amount equivalent to 110,000 Deutschmarks to a bank in Switzerland. The Swiss bank wouldn't cooperate, but we got to Eichmann's account with a little help from our friends. It showed a deposit of 110,000 Deutschmarks on June 15, from the same Swiss bank. Since 100,000 Deutschmarks is what Eichmann paid the Arabs, and he undoubtedly charged something for his services, the connection seems solid. The problem is that it's also circumstantial. It doesn't prove the connection. And it's just so potentially devastating that I wanted to find something more substantial before I reported to you. Also it doesn't tell us where Slovotkin got that kind of money, and I was hoping to get something on that too."

"I understand," Houghton said.

He did, indeed, understand, as unprepared as his mind had been for anything remotely like this. Russians had retained Arab terrorists to kill André Kohl. Americans had paid the Arabs through a German intermediary. There could be only one explanation: the Americans had *asked* the Russians to hire the Arabs in order to disguise their own role.

Why would the Russians be willing to help the Americans in this effort? Because they, too, were afraid of what André might know. Because they, too, believed that Gennady Gondrachov had given information to André that had to be repressed at all costs.

What was this information? Again, there could be only one explanation: that certain American and Russian intelligence agents had discovered a common objective, and were cooperating with one another to achieve it.

What was this common objective? It was time to find out, and there was only one way to do it—a way that coincided fortuitously with his need to protect the man in whose life he had so profoundly intervened. But the way was also so precedential that Houghton took a minute to think it through. Then, his mind made up, he called downstairs to the CIA's Soviet desk and asked for a copy of the unofficial Moscow directory, the one compiled by the Soviet diplomat's British-born wife, which listed both the office and private numbers of almost every key government official and diplomat. In a few moments, he had the number he wanted. He made the call himself, and spoke in Russian to the woman who answered. He had a difficult time convincing her that he was who he said he was, but she finally put him through to Vassily Krylov.

Houghton had wasted no time on formalities with the head of the KGB. "Mr. Krylov, I am calling because I believe that you and I have a matter of urgent mutual interest to discuss. It is a professional matter, concerning destructive actions taken in concert by members of our respective agencies. Is it possible for us to meet on a completely confidential basis, informally and unofficially? If so, I am prepared to fly to Moscow tomorrow morning."

In the instant that followed, Houghton could only wonder what train of thought his call and request had set off in a man who had survived in such a tough league for so long by virtue of extreme caution. On the basis of character alone, he would undoubtedly say no, but this was scarcely an everyday request; he himself would leap at such a request from Krylov, Houghton knew, but their relative positions could hardly be compared. He could not have been more surprised, therefore, by the Russian's prompt and positive response. "I would be pleased to see you, Mr. Houghton, on the basis you have suggested. I believe I have some idea of the matter you wish to discuss, and I must tell you that, because of that matter, I had been contemplating a call to you. To avoid the problem of a visa, I suggest you fly to West Berlin tomorrow morning and cross into East Berlin through Checkpoint Charlie. You will be met there, taken to the airport and flown to Moscow."

It had happened just as Krylov said it would. No one in his own government knew that the director of the CIA was on his way to a rendezvous with the director of the KGB. Houghton could only pray that Krylov would keep his word—and that he would arrive in Moscow in time to do Peter some good.

At last, Krylov appeared at the USBC office, in the company of Lusa Gondrachov. He seemed highly agitated, his face dark with blood. "Excuse us," Peter said to Tony and Lusa. He led Krylov to the kitchen.

"Just a moment," Krylov said. He looked around, spied a radio and turned it on at full volume. The sound of a Rachmaninoff concerto reverberated through the kitchen. The Russian moved close to Peter and spoke in a soft but urgent voice. "I told you to call me on your return to Moscow. There was no need for such mystery."

"I promise you there was," Peter said.

"Then speak quickly," he said. "I have very little time. What do you mean, operations not sanctioned by KGB? How would *you* know what is sanctioned?" There was anger bordering on fury in his voice now, like a man who has just been insulted by a stranger in his home.

"Let me ask you a single question. Do you know where Jacob Jones is at this moment?"

"How should I know that? I am not in charge of his business. He was with you in Siberia. Did he not come back?"

"He was arrested in Bratsk this morning by the security police."

"That's ridiculous."

"I was there with him. I saw it. We came back together in a military aircraft. When we landed, he was put in a car and driven away."

"By whom?" Krylov said. He appeared incredulous.

"I don't know."

"On what charge?"

"The people who arrested him said he would be informed of that in Moscow."

"I must make a call," Krylov said. He turned to leave.

"Please don't. Not yet."

Krylov turned back and regarded him balefully.

"You're familiar with the stories of the secret network within the CIA?" Peter said quickly.

"Yes, of course," Krylov snapped.

"I believe you have such a network within your own organization."

The Russian stared without blinking at Peter. "Go on," he said.

"I believe that the CIA's network and the KGB's network have found a common cause, and are working together."

Peter had expected Krylov to scoff. Instead, he said, "What is your proof?"

"A telephone call on the day of Gennady Gondrachov's death from a former CIA agent to a high official of the KGB."

Krylov edged even closer to Peter. In spite of the music, Peter could hear his deep breathing. "Explain," he said.

"The CIA agent was Virgil Craig, the man who supervised the resettlement of ex-Nazis in Latin America, and then organized them into a paramilitary group. He was the man who interrogated Kurt Hoepner of the Gestapo after the war. He was the man who expunged Camille Laurent's name from Hoepner's statement. He was the man who tried to derail the inquiry into Laurent's past after you people surfaced the incriminating Gestapo report that named him as Hoepner's contact in the French Resistance. Craig had a contact in Laurent's camp, a high-ranking man in French intelligence. On the day that Gennady Gondrachov was taken by the French, Craig made two overseas phone calls within minutes of one another. The second call was to this French agent. The first call was to a number in Moscow. Do you follow me?"

"Yes, yes, go on."

"The calls were so closely spaced that the supposition is they were related. The supposition is that both calls were preceded by a call *to* Craig by the French agent, wanting to know what to do about Gondrachov. Craig then called Moscow to receive instructions. He then called Paris to deliver them."

"Is total supposition."

"I'll let you judge that for yourself."

Peter withdrew his wallet and extracted the same piece of paper he'd given two hours earlier to Lusa. "This is the Moscow number that appeared on Virgil Craig's telephone bill."

Krylov took the piece of paper. As he looked at it, the darkness seeped from his face.

"Two hours ago, Lusa Gondrachov called this number," Peter went on. "She recognized the voice."

Without a word, Krylov ran from the kitchen, found Lusa and pulled her aside. To Peter, he appeared to ask her a single question. She appeared to give a brief answer. Krylov stared at her for an instant, then bolted from the apartment.

For seconds Peter stood motionless, like an actor on a stage who had delivered his last line and was waiting for the curtain to fall. Suddenly, there was nothing further to do. He'd thought of calling the American embassy—the only other option—but then rejected the idea. Seven months earlier, André Kohl had rushed to the American embassy in La Paz for help, only to be turned away by a totally unsympathetic CIA station chief. Who knew what kind of man Peter would find in Moscow, and whose side he'd be on?

Now it was up to Krylov.

As the adrenaline ebbed from his limbs, he felt a desperate need to lie down, if only for ten minutes. He thanked Lusa and Tony, and asked Tony to remain at home, in case he needed him. Then he returned to Jacob's apartment, and collapsed on a living room sofa—much as that actor, his bows taken, might retreat to his dressing room to regain his own identity. In the last days, another metamorphosis had occurred; André Kohl had reentered Peter's brain, preempting the fiction that had been so laboriously and meticulously built since his arrival in the Cotswolds. He had read somewhere that at moments of tension in sports, players abandon newly learned techniques in favor of older, surer habits, even though they are less effective. He'd done exactly that. The man talking to Vassily Krylov may have looked and sounded like Peter Burke, but he thought like André Kohl.

He was what his life had made him, and nothing—no training or cosmetic alterations—could change him. For a while, he had played a role, just as an actor would, but the situation in which he now found himself had stripped away all pretense. He might still be Peter Burke to others, but he could no longer play mind-games with himself. It was the most dangerous of outcomes, and he knew it. Houghton and Fleming had both warned him that if he ever began to think like André Kohl again, he would start functioning like him as well. The last place in the world he wanted to do that was in the Soviet Union. But he couldn't help himself. He'd been stretched to the limit. If he was to save himself, he would have to do it fast, because very soon now he would have nothing more to give.

The key to his salvation—indeed, to his resurrection—was the same it had been since the night of the banquet at the Ritz: to find out who had gone after André Kohl. The key to that discovery was also the same: to find out what it was that he was supposed to know—something that Gennady Gondrachov would have told him.

Come on, André, he exhorted himself, be a reporter. Think! The answer's in front of your face. It's something generic, so simple that it's been overlooked. Ask simple questions:

What did Gennady do?

He was the man who, when the Soviets had something to say, found the best place in which to say it.

Who was his favorite outlet?

André Kohl. But in all their years together, Gennady had never burned André with a bad story. Even the dossier he had given him proving Camille Laurent had been a traitor had turned out to be genuine.

What new story might Gennady have been planning to give André Kohl?

That the opposition to the Russian leader was a fiction. That the stories alleging he was a rummy and an unstable personality, given to wild swings of mood, were groundless rumors.

What is the best way to debunk a rumor?

By debunking those who spread it.

Easy now. A step at a time:

Someone in the Soviet hierarchy had to have been the source of those rumors.

That same person, or persons, had to have planted them with someone in the West.

Gennady must have found out who it was on the Russian side and threatened to expose him—by giving the story of this unholy alliance to André Kohl.

That *had* to be what the network feared he knew. It explained absolutely everything—including what this CIA-KGB cabal was up to.

That must be it, he told himself over and over again, so many times that, mantra-like, it finally lulled him to sleep.

He awakened in darkness, in flight from a nightmare in which someone was driving a stake through his brain. For a moment, he thought he was still dreaming. Then he knew that a man was standing over him, pressing the barrel of a revolver against his head.

30

The room was dark, but not pitch black. A small amount of light was filtering in from the street and the buildings across the way. As his pupils adjusted to the dimness, Peter could make out some of the characteristics of the man standing over him. He was tall and lean, with short hair and appeared to be in his late fifties or early sixties.

"Hello, André Kohl," the man said softly. His voice was utterly calm; his accent suggested an East Coast upbringing and an Ivy League education.

"My name is Peter Burke," Peter answered.

"If you don't drop that pretense I'm going to terminate this interview."

The statement was matter of fact, almost pleasant, but the gun barrel at his forehead told Peter what it really meant. "Who are you?" he said.

"I don't believe I'm going to give you that satisfaction. Now, please, sit up."

Peter sat up. The man sat in an armchair next to the sofa, cradling the gun in his arms, its barrel pointed at Peter. It was a long barrel, Peter could see, probably with a silencer attached.

"I'm going to kill you, Mr. Kohl, because you're too dangerous to me alive. But before I do, I'm going to give you a chance to answer some questions, and an incentive for answering them well. If I'm satisfied with your answers, I won't kill your wife on my return to Paris. If I'm not, I will. Understood?"

"How can I believe you?"

"What choice do you have?"

He had none. He knew at once that he would answer as fully as he could. "Go ahead," he said.

"I want you to tell me exactly what you know about our little group."

"Do you mean the network within the CIA of which Virgil Craig was a member?"

"Exactly."

"I know almost nothing for a fact. It's only what I've surmised."

"Then talk of your surmise."

"I think you should understand something first. If you hadn't come after me, I wouldn't have suspected a thing. It's only because you did that I came to believe you thought I knew something I wasn't supposed to know."

"Interesting," the man said. "Go on."

For the next half-hour, Peter described the evolution of his suspicions as elaborately as he could, knowing that his only ally was time. The man, his features now distinct even in the darkness, listened in silence, nodding occasionally in acknowledgment. At last, and with utmost reluctance, Peter came to the end of his story. "Well," he said, "how close did I come?"

"There are one or two holes, of course, as you admit, and I don't think you quite understand our motives, but on the whole I'd say you did a pretty good job."

"What holes?"

"You made too much of our reason for choosing the Ritz. There were no symbols or gestures involved. It was simply a convenient and practical way of solving two problems at once."

"Meaning myself and Jacob?"

"Exactly."

Peter was sure he knew the answer to his next question, but he wanted to hear it from the source. "What have you got against Jacob?"

"He's an amateur and a fool. Unfortunately, he's also charming and persuasive. He's caused us a great deal of trouble."

"What didn't I understand about your motives?"

"Maybe motives isn't really the word, because we all have the same motives, don't we? We all want to defend our country from its enemies. The real distinction is in the perception of the enemy. Your father-in-law's favorite line is, 'The objective isn't to defeat the Communists, it's to learn to live together in spite of our differences.' Well, you see, that's only possible if both sides agree with the objective. I've seen nothing in my lifetime to suggest that the Russians do. To the contrary, everything I've learned suggests that their every move, even their so-called "openings" and "peace offensives," is part of a comprehensive, exquisitely orchestrated scheme to lull the West into passivity. At the proper moment, when the West no longer has the will or the means with which to fight, the Soviets will strike. And then we'll all be slaves, and I just can't accept that because, you see, Mr. Kohl, I really am one of those people who would rather be dead than Red."

"And to achieve your aims, you're willing to break your country's laws?"

"To save my country? Absolutely. Especially when the laws are inadequate to begin with. There's nothing sacred about the law, Mr. Kohl, when it's nothing more than the projection of lawmakers who don't understand the problem."

"What if it's you who doesn't understand the problem? Have you ever thought of that?"

A moment of silence passed. "You never get anywhere in this world, Mr. Kohl, unless you're willing to act on your convictions."

Another silence. Peter sensed that the conversation had ended, and that he was about to die. Shock waves reverberated through his body, but his mind was surprisingly clear. For six months, he'd lived on the edge, constantly in transition, always wondering how and when this gigantic ruse would end. Now, at least, he knew. "Would you permit me a moment to express a few convictions?" Peter said, desperate to stall for every second he could and, under the circumstances, ridiculously eager not to leave this world with the stranger's statement unchallenged.

"Briefly."

"You can prove anything you want, you know. Just find the evidence that supports your conclusion, and ignore all other evidence to the contrary. *I* could prove that the Russians want to enslave the world. But I could also prove that the Russians think we have the same objective, and that they're as frightened as we are. I could prove that they have maniacs who could provoke a nuclear war. I could prove that we have maniacs who could do the same. The trick, sir, the art, is to assemble all the evidence, and try to balance it out."

"That's fine, Mr. Kohl, if the other side does the same. Unfortunately, that's not the case. I was here after World War II as a young intelligence officer. It was the time of Joseph Stalin. He slaughtered millions. Millions."

"And the fact that the Soviets themselves have denounced and repudiated Stalin means nothing to you?"

The man sighed. "People never change, Mr. Kohl. And these people are evil. That's something you liberals will never understand." He hesitated. "You've been an admirable adversary," he said. Then he raised his gun.

For a moment, Peter looked hypnotically at the barrel. Then a movement behind the stranger caught his eye. The door to Jacob's apartment had been opened so quietly that he had not even heard the lock turn. He could not conceal his astonishment as two men came silently through it. Behind them Peter could see Krylov, and behind him Houghton and Jacob.

"Come now, you don't expect me to fall for that trick, do you?" the stranger said. An instant before he pulled the trigger, the two men seized him from behind. Peter saw the flash and felt the bullet zip by his head.

Grappling with one another, the Russians and the stranger toppled to the floor. One of the Russians grabbed for the gun and missed. A second later, the stranger turned the gun on himself and fired.

"His name was Harry Coffee," Charles Houghton said. "I'll explain more about him as we proceed." Houghton and Vassily Krylov had just taken seats across from one another along the sides of the dining room table, with Peter between them at the head of the table, in the seat normally occupied by Jacob. Jacob, a wreck from his ordeal, was in bed; he had been given a sedative by the same doctor brought in to try to save Harry Coffee, whose second, hasty shot had been poorly aimed. An hour later, Coffee was dead; minutes before, his body had been removed. Now, at last, the meeting between Houghton and Krylov was about to get underway. By mutual consent the two men had agreed to let Peter participate, so that he could fill in elements of the story with which he was more familiar.

"Mr. Krylov," Houghton began, "I don't wish my presence here to be misconstrued. We've come together to solve a problem. Period. I have no illusions about your work, and you should have none about mine. My objective is to learn as much as I possibly can about what your agency and your government are doing. I accept that your objective is identical to mine. Neither of us, however, should have the objective of destroying the possibilities for peace between our countries. Our purpose in meeting is to deal with efforts on the part of a few men in each of our organizations who were trying to destroy those possibilities. That, as far as I'm concerned, is all this meeting signifies. Do you agree?"

"Completely."

First, they established the ground rules: Absolute candor. No holding back. And no reports, ever, to anyone, about this private meeting. How would each know if the other had honored the rules? With regard to candor, the story wouldn't track if either left out any facts. In the case of confidentiality, there were no assurances, but disclosure would create so much trouble for both of them that neither wished the meeting to be made known.

Krylov told his part of the story first. Nine months earlier, he said, in the midst of the sudden flurry of reports about opposition to the Premier and criticism of his personal habits, Gennady Gondrachov had contacted the journalist who had first reported the story, a man with whom he'd had excellent relations for many years, and demanded to know his source. The journalist, Washington correspondent for an English newspaper, initially refused to tell him. But after Gennady accused the reporter of printing unfounded lies, and threatened to cut him off from all further access to Soviet sources, the journalist relented and identified the source as the head of the CIA's Soviet desk, Christopher Slovotkin. When Gennady had demanded to know Slovotkin's source, the reporter said he'd asked the same question of Slovotkin and been told, "Someone in the KGB." With that assurance, the reporter had filed the story.

Gennady held similar conversations with American and French journalists who had used the story, with the same results. Their source had been Slovotkin; Slovotkin's source had been "someone in the KGB." In reporting his findings to Krylov, Gennady accused Valery Yuryev of being the KGB source. "You must understand," Krylov said now, "that between Gondrachov and Yuryev there had been bad feelings for many, many years. They agreed on nothing, and hated one another. It was completely ideological. Yuryev was what you Americans would call a hawk, and Gennady a dove. I confronted Yuryev. He denied the charge, and demanded proof. All Gennady had was the statement from Slovotkin—and secondhand, at that—that his source was a KGB official. Gennady, who was about to take the Hoepner dossier to Paris to be verified by André Kohl, was extremely frustrated. He did not believe Yuryev. He said in Yuryev's presence that two could play that game. *He* would tell a story to the Western press that was sure to get their attention. He insinuated, but did not say, that the story would be about how KGB officials were working with the CIA to discredit their own Premier. The further inference was that he would give this story to André Kohl.

"I must tell you frankly that I did not know what to do. Without proof, I could not act on the matter, and yet because of my great respect for Gennady Gondrachov, I could not dismiss it either. His death, as I told Mr. Burke, was an immense sorrow for me, but I suspected nothing irregular until Mr. Burke told me of the telephone call from Virgil Craig to Yuryev. By that point I had established that someone in our agency *had* hired the Arabs who attacked André Kohl, so I believed not only that whoever it was had something to hide but was, in fact, cooperating with some of your agents. Still I had no proof. The telephone call was the proof. It also identified Yuryev.

"This afternoon, Yuryev was arrested at the airport, as he was boarding a plane for Paris. I interrogated him myself. He has confirmed the essential details of the story. He did not know your

Mr. Slovotkin, incidentally. His contact was your director of operations."

"Harry Coffee," Houghton said. Now it was his turn. "Coffee and Yuryev met in Moscow in the late forties when Coffee was a young political officer at our embassy. They met again in Berlin in the fifties when both were on assignment there, and again in the sixties when Coffee returned to Moscow for a second tour. According to Coffee, the friendship that developed between them was based on admiration not for one another's beliefs but for the conviction with which they were held. I know all this because over the years Coffee talked extensively about Yuryev. He always cited him as the prototype of the kind of man we were confronting.

"The last time I heard Yuryev's name was about a year ago, during a discussion with my deputies about your new Premier and his policies. In that discussion, Harry Coffee expressed his fear that the Premier's peace offensive, together with his charm, could lull our country into a false sense of security. He reminded us yet again of Yuryev, a doctrinaire ideologue, profoundly committed to orthodoxy, who, he maintained, represented the long-term Soviet reality." Houghton sighed. "How and when Coffee realized that his objectives and Yuryev's objectives with regard to the Premier were identical I haven't the vaguest idea. I confess that when the negative stories about the Premier surfaced I made no connection to Coffee. When I inquired about the stories, he said only that he was checking them out. Obviously, he was lying.

"I pass now from fact to conjecture. Once Coffee and Yuryev had discovered their common objective and then successfully cooperated, it was only natural that they would identify other projects. One was the elimination of Gennady Gondrachov, another the elimination of André Kohl . . ."

"Who was your son-in-law, I believe," Krylov said.

"Yes, indeed."

"I am profoundly sorry. I deeply regret whatever role any of my countrymen might have had in that."

Houghton bowed his head in acknowledgment. Then he turned to Peter. "Is there anything you can add?"

Peter had listened in silence, still shaken from his own close call and the sight of yet another death. "I believe so, but I have some

306

questions first." He turned to Krylov. "Was it Yuryev who hired the Arabs to kill André Kohl?"

Krylov nodded. "This is the sequence of that event. As Virgil Craig initially called Yuryev to ask about Gennady Gondrachov, so Yuryev, worried about what Mr. Kohl might have been told, communicated his concern to Coffee. It was Coffee who suggested that Mr. Kohl be eliminated, and who requested Yuryev to arrange it. Yuryev agreed that it would be in both their interests. He maintains that the venture was financed by Coffee."

"That is correct," Houghton said.

"Which brings us to Jacob Jones," Peter said. "My hunch is that they were going to sabotage Jacob's peace conference by discrediting him in some way."

"That, too, is correct," Krylov said. "According to Yuryev, Coffee supplied them with the information that the Soviet-American Trading Company, Jacob's company, was a CIA operation. On Monday, Jacob's arrest as a CIA agent was to be announced. In the meanwhile, he was being held in a safe house just outside of Moscow."

Peter turned to Houghton, unspoken questions in his eyes. *Was Jacob a CIA agent, after all? And if so, how could Krylov release him?* The questions must have been obvious, because Houghton's response indirectly answered them both.

"Without identifying the man, I have acknowledged to Mr. Krylov that one of the two Americans in the Moscow office of SATCO did work for us. Under the extraordinary circumstances we're confronting, he has agreed to let both men leave the country. I have also assured Mr. Krylov that Jacob knew nothing about it."

Was that true? Peter asked himself. Probably. Jacob, the dealmaker, the *macher,* would never traffic in tradecraft, as his clumsy work with the microfilm proved. His work was at the top, as an unofficial go-between for the world's two most powerful men.

There was one more loose end to tie off before Peter said his piece, and it was up to him to do it. It involved a bit of license—for which, under those same extraordinary circumstances, he felt he could be forgiven. It involved, as well, the right response from Houghton. "There's only one more puzzle," he said. "What did Harry Coffee want with me?"

Houghton picked up the cue as though he'd been reading a script. "My guess is he believed that in investigating the death of André you'd gotten too close to the truth."

Peter turned to Krylov. "And Yuryev told him where I was?"

"Exactly."

Had Coffee told Yuryev—or anyone else—about his suspicion that Peter Burke was André Kohl? It was a question that could neither be asked nor answered. Peter would have to live with his doubts. There was, in any case, an infinitely more important question that hadn't been asked—and that one *had* to be answered. Right here, right now.

"Okay," he said, "you've asked me what I can add. Nothing to what's already been said. I believe you've both been comprehensive. I can track the story now. I know who did what to whom. But there's one question neither of you has answered: *why?*

"To each of you, the reason why all this happened may be so self-evident that you felt no need to explain it. And with apologies, Mr. Krylov, you may never have to explain it outside the Politburo. But *you're* going to have to explain it, Mr. Houghton—not just to the President and Congress, but to the media and the people. What are you going to say?"

"He's going to say nothing!" Krylov said angrily. "We agreed that there would be no reports."

"Just a moment. The agreement was that there would be no reports of this meeting between you two," Peter said. "There was no agreement that the episodes themselves wouldn't be reported. Am I correct, Mr. Houghton?"

"That is my understanding."

"Mr. Houghton is still going to have to explain why one of his top deputies killed himself in Moscow. He's going to have to explain how KGB and CIA agents conspired to discredit the Soviet Premier, and to sabotage a peace conference on the Middle East. He's going to have to explain how mortal enemies in the United States and the Soviet Union found common ground."

"He's right, Mr. Krylov," Houghton said.

The two Americans watched in silence as Krylov digested that thought. After ten seconds, he began to nod his head. "All right," he said to Houghton. "Go on. I would like to hear your explanation."

"And I yours," Houghton said.

"I never speculate."

"In that case, it would probably be inappropriate for me to do so."

"No!" Peter blurted. The cry had come from deep within him, as though it had bypassed his brain. "You've *got* to answer that question. You're two of the most powerful men on earth. If you don't understand why all this happened, it could happen again. You can't afford that. The world can't afford that."

Both Krylov and Houghton stared at him in silence. Seconds passed. Neither spoke. He knew then that neither would. If the question was to be addressed at all, he would have to do it. Peter Burke knew he should be silent; André Kohl insisted he speak.

"Shall I take a crack at it?" he said.

"Please," Krylov said.

"By all means," Houghton said.

Peter took a breath. "Okay, let's start with theology, with people so committed throughout their lives to a set of beliefs that any threat to those beliefs is perceived as a threat to their very existence. Those people exist on both sides.

"There are Cold Warriors in America, men with such a big investment in the past that they're uncomfortable with any conceptions other than those that formed them. These men—and sometimes even women—will always believe that the Soviet Union is an evil empire bent on world domination. In their worst incarnation, they'll go beyond the law, where the law impedes their purpose, on the grounds that the ends justify the means, the ends in this case being the protection of the United States against the encroachments of the Soviet Union.

"There are Cold Warriors in the Soviet Union as well—men and women equally uncomfortable with evolving perceptions in conflict with their own. They hold to their own beliefs with as much conviction and fervor as their American counterparts. The basis of their belief is that the United States would destroy the Soviet Union if it thought it could get away with it. Any agreement with the United States is therefore impossible, in their view, and all attempts to achieve agreement are to be resisted."

He looked from one man to the other. Both men returned his gaze, but neither offered a comment.

"How could people so bitterly opposed to one another find reason to cooperate? Let's take the case of the Premier. The Soviet Union's Cold Warriors fear him because he appears to be trying to find a basis for negotiation with the United States. That's exactly what they're against. Therefore, they're against the Premier. They want him out. America's Cold Warriors fear the Premier for exactly the same reasons." Peter looked at Houghton. "What was it Harry Coffee said?"

"That the Premier could lull us into a false sense of security."

"Precisely. So, what do you do when you find a common interest? You combine forces to assist it." Peter looked at Krylov. He nodded but said nothing.

"Next case: a peace treaty on the Middle East, guaranteed jointly by the United States and the Soviet Union. The Cold Warriors would *hate* that idea. America's Cold Warriors would hate it because it would increase the Russians' presence in the Middle East, where they've been shut out for years. Russia's Cold Warriors would hate it because an agreement would solidify the existence of Israel, the boldest, most anti-Soviet state in the world, as well as a force for the preservation of Western interests in the Middle East.

"So far we've been dealing with ideology. Now we come to the gut issue: what's in it for the Cold Warriors."

Peter paused for a moment, to collect his thoughts. He knew that the metamorphosis was complete. He was André again, and although he would surely regret it ten minutes hence, he could not —and would not—protect himself now.

"Can we agree that the overwhelming majority of Americans and Russians would like nothing better than to see their respective countries strike a deal? Bury forever the means of mutual self-destruction? Learn to live together in peace? Okay?"

"Yes."

"*Da.*"

"But what about the people whose lives are totally invested in a conflict between the United States and the Soviet Union, a conflict that gives them identity, importance and employment? Without the conflict, they lose all three. If you asked them whether they'd care, they'd say of course they wouldn't. But do you think that's really true? Maybe it is. But maybe it isn't. Think about what's just happened.

"Whether the reasons are personal or ideological, or a combination of both, the evidence tells the story. And that story, I'm afraid, is that America's Cold Warriors and Russia's Cold Warriors share a common enemy: peace. They've created two impregnable walls of mistrust behind which they're comfortable operating. They're terrified of anything else. They've gotten so caught up in the task that they've forgotten the objective. Willy nilly, our lives are hostage to cloak and dagger bureaucrats—yours, Mr. Krylov, and ours, Mr. Houghton—so in love with their mortal games that they'll do *anything* to keep playing."

The noise of traffic on the Kutuzovsky Prospekt seeped through the windows.

"An interesting theory," Krylov said at last.

"I agree," Houghton said.

Another silence followed. Finally, Peter asked, "What's going to happen to Yuryev?"

Krylov shook his head sadly. "I do not know. He is guilty of a crime for which there is no precedent."

Houghton nodded. "So was Harry Coffee."

31

Peter and Meredith heard the bulletin on the radio while driving to Varengeville-sur-Mer in a rented Peugeot. In a communiqué released simultaneously in Washington and Moscow, the United States and the Soviet Union announced their agreement to cosponsor an international peace conference on the Middle East. All interested nations would be invited to attend. The Israelis had already accepted, as had all of the Arab nations with the exception of Syria and Libya. In a separate but related action, the Soviet Union had agreed to the unrestricted emigration of Jews to Israel, and Israel and the Soviet Union had agreed to establish normal diplomatic relations. Cosponsorship of the peace conference by the Soviets and the Americans, the story went on, had been negotiated over several months with the help of Jacob Jones, an American businessman who had had extensive commercial dealings with the Russians.

"Well, well," Meredith said. "At last!"

"Let's hope it goes well," Peter said.

"At least they're talking. What a week this has been!"

How he would have loved to tell her.

That evening in Moscow, after Vassily Krylov's departure and with Charles Houghton's blessing, Peter had returned to Tony Cook's apartment on the seventh floor and told him as much of the story as he could. It seemed only fitting, Houghton and Peter had agreed, that André Kohl's television network should be the first to broadcast a story whose disclosure hinged on the fate of its late chief European correspondent. A grateful Tony had agreed that his major source would remain forever anonymous. He had further agreed to break the story on Monday, after the source had left Moscow.

The following day, Sunday, Vassily Krylov had personally escorted Houghton, Peter and Jacob to the airport, where Jacob's Gulfstream, summoned from Bratsk, awaited. There were no passport or customs formalities; their car drove them directly onto the tarmac and to the airplane. "You need not worry, Mr. Houghton," Krylov said. "Your presence here will not be reported by me or my people." Then Krylov had turned to Jacob. "I am sorry, my friend. Come back. It will never happen again." The two men had embraced. After Houghton and Jacob had gone aboard the aircraft, the Russian had turned to Peter. "You are an exceptional investigator, Mr. Burke. If you ever need a job, please contact me." They had laughed together, and then Krylov had said, "I think you probably came to know your Mr. André Kohl better than he knew himself." With that he had given Peter a hearty slap on the back and sent him onto the plane.

Did he know, then? Once more, a question that could neither be asked nor answered.

The moment the pilot turned off the seat belt sign, Peter had gone forward to join Jacob. "I've got a present for you," he said. He handed him the card with the microfilm attached.

Jacob turned the card over and over in his hands, saying nothing. When he looked at Peter his eyes were wet. "And I've got a present for you," he said. He reached into his attaché case, withdrew a checkbook and wrote out a check for two hundred thousand dollars.

"That's ridiculous," Peter said.

"Take it, pal. You earned it."

"I can't."

"Come on. With my money, that's one week's interest. Make an old man feel good." He leaned over and slipped the check into Peter's pocket.

On Tuesday, in the wake of USBC's sensational exclusive, the President of the United States and the Premier of the USSR had made it official, issuing a joint announcement to the effect that secret networks in the intelligence services of both countries had been identified and eliminated through the mutual cooperation of both countries. The leader of the American network, Harry Coffee, had committed suicide in Moscow as he was about to be arrested. The leader of the Soviet network, Valery Yuryev, was in custody, pending a trial.

On Wednesday, as the President, acting quickly in response to the public outcry, announced the formation of a special commission to investigate the entire affair, Peter had flown to New York to report to Mike Paul. In carefully chosen words, he had identified to the chief of network news the people who had *set out* to kill André Kohl, and explained the reasons for their actions. He stressed that his information, in which he had the utmost confidence, was nonetheless secondhand, and on that basis, he said, he was withdrawing his claim to the fifty-thousand-dollar bonus for finding André's killers. As before, he'd arrived on the Concorde; as before, he returned to Paris the same evening.

He had spoken briefly to Meredith on his return from Moscow, but had deliberately avoided seeing her in the hope that during his trip to and from New York he could sort through his jumbled emotions and thoughts and reach a calm and sound decision. His promise to Houghton had been that he wouldn't reveal himself to Meredith until he was certain beyond doubt that it wouldn't put her in danger. Could he now be certain beyond doubt that the danger had passed? "I can't answer that question for you," Houghton had said as they flew from Moscow to Paris. "There just isn't an answer. I think you're safe. I'd like to think we got it all. But I can't be certain. We're just never going to know what's still out there."

It was like beating cancer. You want to celebrate. But you never know. Do you kill yourself with worry, or do you say to hell with it and grab hold of life once again? Theoretically, the choice is easy; it's the doing it that's tough. Even doing it would be easy if he were the only one involved.

He made the decision, at last, as his flight from New York came in sight of the French coastline on Thursday morning. He could not bring himself to think about what would happen if he failed.

That morning, he went to the Île St. Louis and walked along the

Quai d'Orléans. The stakeout was gone. For another thirty minutes he surveyed the area until he was satisfied that it was clean. Then he telephoned Meredith, and asked her to have dinner with him that evening. When she accepted, he told her he would pick her up. Then he called the Tour d'Argent and asked to speak to the owner, Claude Terrail, about a matter concerning André Kohl. "My name is Peter Burke," he said when Terrail came on the line. "We have in common a friendship with the late André Kohl. André once offered to intercede in my behalf if I ever wished to dine in your restaurant. I would like to do that tonight because I am having dinner with his widow, who has moved to Paris and is living in André's apartment just across from you on the Île St. Louis. It is an extremely sentimental occasion, so I would like it to be under the best possible auspices. André assured me that there was no better restaurant in the world than the Tour d'Argent."

"It will be my honor, Mr. Burke. At what hour would you like to come?"

Peter reserved the table for eight-thirty that evening. At eight-twenty, he called for Meredith, and they walked across the Pont de la Tournelle to the Left Bank. When he led her to the door of the Tour d'Argent, she stopped and regarded him with surprise. "Good heavens! Have you struck it rich?"

"Exactly."

They took the elevator to the top floor, where the restaurant was located. Their window table gave them a splendid view of the Notre Dame Cathedral and the Seine. They both ordered the restaurant's specialty, *caneton Tour d'Argent,* duck prepared in two styles. The combination of setting, food and service was, quite simply, incomparable.

In their brief post-Moscow telephone conversation, Peter hadn't told Meredith where he'd been. Now, when he did, she'd regarded him in silence, then said, "All the men I like seem to go off to Moscow right after meeting me." He knew exactly what she meant but had to pretend that he didn't. "André suddenly flew off to Moscow the morning after our first night together," she explained.

"Now tell me what you meant by 'all the men I like,' " he said.

Again, that look, straight into his eyes. "I told you what I meant before you left," she said softly. "It hasn't changed." Then, quickly, she asked him if he would accompany her to Varengeville the next morning. The legal tangle had been cleared away and the house was definitely hers; she must decide whether to keep it or sell it. They could drive there for lunch, and return in the afternoon.

Now they were entering the part of France that André had always loved the most, the rich sweeping fields of Normandy, their soft contours made the softer by the gray light of a leaden sky, and the wooded coastal hills dotted with houses built to endure the rain and wind that so marked the region's character. Today the landscape was barren, but a few months from now, Peter knew, it would give birth to a bounty unsurpassed on God's earth. The fields would turn green and the apple orchards white under a sky of pure blue, and the air would fill with perfume.

"It really is so beautiful," Meredith said.

"My thoughts exactly."

And then they were in Varengeville, built on the bluffs above the English Channel, a hamlet of half a dozen shops to service a few hundred homes, most of them with acreage, all surrounded by walls and woods that separated them from one another. Peter drove slowly along the two-lane highway, pretending he didn't know the way.

"There it is," Meredith said excitedly as she spotted the sign, *"Le Pré Ango."* Meredith got out to open the gate. As she reached for the latch, and pushed the gate open to reveal the house and grounds, her body was momentarily in profile. Watching her, Peter felt faint. There, before him, was everything he wanted on this earth: the love of his life, the child she was carrying, this blessed refuge. The small, genuine world for which André Kohl had traded in his old life.

He drove onto the grounds on the gravel driveway. As Meredith closed the gate behind him, he took a moment to regard the house, which he hadn't seen in ten months. It was a stone house, two floors, with a sloping roof, surrounded by a vast expanse of lawn. Suddenly he heard two dogs barking; from the front stoop raced two Bedlington terriers, their teeth bared, outrage in their voices. They streaked across the lawn, directly at Meredith, as she came up the driveway. By the time Peter had struggled from the car, they were at her feet, barking and snarling. "Boys! Boys!" Peter cried. At the sound of his voice they turned, and started to bark at him, but as he approached them their sounds turned to cries of joy and their tails wagged furiously. When he bent to pet them, they rolled onto their backs and wriggled.

"My Lord, you have a way with dogs," Meredith said.

"I do."

Madame Cartet, the caretaker, came out the front door to greet them. Meredith had called to tell her they were coming. She'd insisted on preparing a lunch.

Inside, they went into the living room, where Madame Cartet had laid a fire. It crackled now, its huge flames sending light and warmth through the room. Four sets of French doors ran along the north side of the room. Meredith walked to them and looked out at the tidy rows of apple trees just beyond the lawn. Then she turned back, her eyes sparkling. "Oh God, it's perfect. How could I possibly sell it?" She turned once again, and opened one of the doors and walked onto the lawn. Peter was coming up behind her when he heard her mutter, "Damn you, André. Why'd you have to die?"

With a sentence, two words, he could change it all: "I'm André." He clenched his fists and shut his eyes, willing himself to be silent.

He had a sherry before lunch—Meredith was still not drinking in deference to the baby—and then they went to the dining room. The lunch was epic, Madame Cartet at her best, *moules marinieres,* followed by a pork roast cooked with herbes de Provence and accompanied by sautéed potatoes, followed by a salad and Roquefort cheese and an apple tart for dessert. When it was finished, Meredith patted her stomach. "How'd you like *that,* baby?" she said, then laughed at herself.

After lunch they began a tour of the house. "I hardly remember it," Meredith explained. "We were here so briefly, and we didn't stay the night. There were men from French intelligence watching the place, so we turned out the lights as though we were going to bed and then slipped through the apple orchard to the home of André's gardener. We slept there, and at five the next morning the gardener drove us into Dieppe, where we took the ferry to London."

Neither of them said anything for a moment. Peter's mind flooded with memories, and by the soft look on Meredith's face he judged that the same thing had happened to her. He was close to her now, close enough to touch her. He knew that everything he was feeling was in his eyes. He let her see them, not caring that she knew.

She met his gaze for a moment, and he could see if not love in her eyes, at the very least affection. Then, abruptly, she turned and walked from the room.

He followed her down the stairs and through the living room to the study, where another fire blazed. The room was exactly as it had been nine months before, when he had stood in the doorway as though waiting for permission to approach the piano, its sturdy legs resting on the gleaming oak floor, and begin the year of practice that would lead him, he had hoped, down the road not taken to the life that might have been. It was his favorite room in his favorite house, spacious, with a beamed ceiling supported by high, white walls. Paintings collected in his travels hung from one of the walls in patterns above and below one another. A second wall was covered with books on floor-to-ceiling shelves. French doors ran the length of the north and west walls. He could remember standing that April day exactly where he was standing now, looking through the panes of the doors to the apple trees covered in spring blossoms. It had been a brilliant, cloudless morning, such a rarity for Normandy in the spring that he had construed it as an omen. And then he had walked across the room and sat to play, and then the phone had rung, summoning him to a journey of no return. Now he was back, but as another man. He had nothing now that had been his, not his name or countenance, not his wife or his children, not even the past that he had thought to regain through his practice. The man he was supposed to be did not even appreciate music.

For years thereafter he would wonder what degree of misery had afflicted his face to cause Meredith to approach him. She put a hand on his arm, but when he tried to embrace her she restrained him.

"Don't, Peter. I can't. I know you're supposed to go on living, but he was my guy, and I want to hang onto him for as long as I can. I can't tell you how long that will be. It could be years. That's not fair to you."

Nor to her. He looked deeply into her eyes and he did not see a happy woman. He saw, instead, an affliction, caused by him and curable only by him. Which was better when you became terminally diseased, he asked himself, to die quickly or slowly? He was trembling and his throat was dry. "Tell me," he said, fighting to form the words, "if you'd been given the choice of living another five years with André, or another thirty without him, which would you have chosen?"

She looked at him in pain. "What a terrible question."

"I must know."

"Five years," she said then. "One year. Just long enough to give him his child."

He stood there, unable to move. But his mind was racing. You can't ever know, he told himself, you can't ever be certain. That's the way life is.

He tried to speak but he couldn't. Instead, he shut his eyes tightly and prayed.

He could feel her hand on his arm. "What's the matter?" she said. "Tell me!"

He shook his head. "I can't," he said, his voice faint and dry. "Tell me! Please!"

"I can't," he said once more. The words wouldn't come. In desperation, he turned from her and ran to the piano. As her eyes enlarged with astonishment, and then filled with understanding, he played the "Moonlight Sonata."